Any Kind of Luck

Any Kind of Luck

William Jack Sibley

KENSINGTON BOOKS
http://www.kensingtonbooks.com

For Carlos and Kent, thanks for everything

If a man loses something and goes back and carefully looks for it, he will find it.

—Sitting Bull

CONTENTS

Acknowledgments

Special thanks to my beautiful, redheaded, Leo Mother, Bette Mason, for her many gifts of love, creativity, originality and enthusiasm (and for always standing by her sometimes trying brood through thick and thin). And to my stepfather Dr. David E. Mason as well. Thanks to my late father, Dr. Hobart Q. Sibley, for his powerful gifts of determination, motivation and "grit," and to my stepmother Bobbie Sibley. To Bud Russell and David Sausville for the indispensable Rocky Mountain "Calumet Crest" experience. Profound thanks to my agent Irene Kraas, manager Lisa FitzGerald, and Kensington editor John Scognamiglio. To Autumn Golden for her unswerving psychic acuity, Ronald and Sherra Thomason for their great love and caring, Chris Mann for his undying friendship, Diana Seiffert for her superb grammatical skills, and Miss Julie Brummett for her ever present devotion to all things literary.

1

THERE ARE NO SONGS ABOUT MARCH IN NEW YORK

"They've removed Mother's breast." I sat on the edge of the bed and squinted at the clock. Midnight in Manhattan. My brother Jaston has never fully grasped the significance of time zones. When it's 11 P.M. in Grit, Texas, it's eleven everywhere in the world. The sleeping body next to me disappeared under a gnarl of pillows. My head was empty; all I could manage to impart was, "Which one?"

"I don't know. The one that was causing all the trouble. Clu, you've got to come home."

It was said with an almost delicate apprehension. I felt sorry for Jaston; humility was not his thing. It was a behest I'd both anticipated and dreaded ever since moving to New York eleven years ago. Some unknowable, unavoidable familial disaster that would return me to the scene of the crime. "God, Jas . . . I mean, where's Laine?"

I was stalling. Anything to avoid commitment. It was an old dance.

"Laine's pregnant again. Doctor said she can't travel. 'Sides, Sherrod's still on probation."

Check. Laine, my middle sister, is married to Sherrod—the accountant. Sherrod "borrowed" $50,000 from the Clovis, New Mexico, school district two years ago and forgot to tell anyone. I didn't give it much thought until Laine's explanation of a "piddlin' nothing" affair turned into a court conviction, major fine and two years' probation. Laine had another miscarriage during the trial. To the casual observer it appeared their marriage consisted mostly of court appearances for Sherrod and prodigious couch time for Laine to recover and appliqué baby bibs. "Jaston . . . what's Mom's condition right now?"

"Not good. They say the cancer's all up in her lungs. It's real bad."

"Why hasn't anyone called me?"

"Mother didn't want to alarm anybody."

Mother's way of not alarming anybody was to wait until the national news picked up on it.

An arm wound its way out from underneath the pillow beside me and tugged at the bedspread until all remnants of exposed flesh were covered. "Clu . . . man, she may not have long. You've got to come help out. She's your mother."

It wouldn't have made any difference to remind him we both shared the same parent; his was an entirely different relationship. At six-foot-three, 280 pounds, Jaston was still the "child," Laine "the worrier" and I, "the thoughtful one." Who sets these patterns? Why didn't I get "irresponsible, carefree, must-do-as-he-pleases"? I hadn't seen my mother since Christmas six years ago, and though Jaston lived three blocks from her, it was a moot point. Etched on granite boulders in national parks and announced daily on courthouse squares were the stirring, prophetic words: "Clu Latimore is the Responsible One."

The last time I'd gone home, for the funeral of Grandmother Saunders (Mother's mother), I promised myself no more family assemblages. It was entirely detrimental to one's sanity. All we did was argue, eat, yell and sulk. Then we'd reverse the order and shout and pout while gorging at Red Lobster or Luby's Cafeteria in yet another vociferous clan outing. To what end such virtuous deeds? The world didn't contain enough tragedy to slap the smile off my face already? I required the unrivaled "tribal thrashing" as well? Sure, these familial trysts would start out blameless enough: a constrained observation on world affairs, a generic movie review, someone's favored televison show retelling—light, innocuous, dispassionate. Then the deadly, acerbic aside would be proffered against another's perceived deficiency, and we were off. Showtime! Immediately the wounded would react with shock, followed by agitation, verbal indignation and ultimately protracted moping . . . culminating with the customary indigestion. Couldn't get enough of it.

"Jaston, it's real difficult right now . . ."

"I've got a gun show up in Durango next weekend . . ."

". . . I may be doing a commercial on Friday . . ."

"I don't know who to get. Mother's insurance dudn't cover shit."

"Look, I'd need at least a couple of weeks just to get my life together. . . ."

"She goes to chemo every morning. Somebody's got to watch . . . the dogs."

The dogs. Oh God . . . the dogs. Mother raises Chihuahuas. Prize-winning Chihuahuas. Nationally acclaimed Chihuahuas. Guest appearance on *Good Morning America* Chihuahuas. At any given moment Mother has at least thirty Chihuahuas available for sale, show, advertising, birthday parties and special events. They all have wardrobes; they all have special bowls, diets—needs. (When I was nine I remember driving to the governor's mansion in Austin and watching as Governor Briscoe fed Princess Margaret, Mother's prize-winning bitch, a burrito. I still can't remember why.) Someone had to be with the Chihuahuas. Chihuahuas are not good when left alone.

"So . . . so, what did the doctors say? How long?"

"Maybe six months, six weeks." Jaston let out a long sigh. "Why don't you come back home, Clu? It's been a long time."

Long time? How long is enough? Could I spend a lifetime and never go back? Probably. Would I care if I ever laid eyes on the Grit water tower again? Hardly. Grit, the town that care inundated. Friends in New York were always ragging me with comments like, "Aren't you the guy from Particle, Texas?" Or, "This is my friend Clu, he's from Pebble/Speck/ Sand . . ." or my favorite, Dirt. Cute. And it was funny and unsophisticated and rural. Just like my family. And I've always felt it's truly a shame we can't all be from somewhere fabulous—like Buffalo.

Growing up in Grit was the equivalent of being culturally eviscerated. Art, ballet, music, literature—it all happened somewhere else. Houston perhaps. We heard about field trips to museums and the symphony in Houston. It seemed very exotic and grown-up and refined. In fourth grade our class walked down the street to the fire station for a walk-through. That was our "journey to enlightenment" for the year. For some it was enough. The rest of us consoled ourselves watching *American Bandstand* on Saturday afternoons just to see what the kids were wearing in California.

It's not that people in Grit were any meaner or stupider or more provincial than anywhere else—but there did seem to be a genuine lack of curiosity. A near smugness that they'd seen and learned quite enough, thank you. And it tormented me. How could you go to the movies and see Audrey Hepburn in *Charade* and not want to move to Paris immediately? Or at least start wearing pillbox hats? Or look at Jim Morrison's angelic face and call him Satan 'cause he had long hair. (Satan in bed maybe.) When I saw Andy Warhol's *Brillo Box* for the first time in a *Life Magazine* spread, even though I didn't *get it*, I *got* that there was something to *get*. People in Grit could not surmount the asinine box. It's not about the box, Bubba! And ultimately, they didn't care that they didn't *get* it. Not a rat's ass. They took pride in being uninformed. "What you don't know is a *real* good thing. That way you don't open your mouth and say something foolish and risk being laughed at. So just basically dislike everything you don't understand in life; that's safe, that's smart—that's using your head! Too much corruption and foolishness out there anyway." And so you were held in contempt naturally if you spent any time at all pondering such odd notions as literature, music (other than country) and God forbid, art. Imagination was not much encouraged beyond kindergarten—unless it related somehow to hunting, Cool Whip, football, Christmas wreaths and/or fishing lures.

And the question remained, should I give up my own life as a modestly successful actor/director/hand model—throw it all away, lose the momentum, go home and exchange existences with my dying mother, the Chihuahua Lady? Am I just a selfish, uncaring, yuppie-brat-pig-ungrateful-hideous-bastard child?

"Jaston, I'm going to have to think about it. There are some . . . complications. It's not as easy as just getting on a plane. I have a life here, you know?"

"I know. We saw your Lava soap commercial on the hospital TV last week."

I pulled at a stray quilt thread. Four national commercials, *four*, and all they ever mention is "the Lava commercial." I know they've seen me open the Campbell Soup can; I know they've seen the Timex spot. Tearing open the condom packet, they might have missed; Public Service announcements are always on so late. Still. Do they hate me for making a living with my hands?

"Mother said she saw your rubber commercial a while back. How much they pay you for that one?"

"They didn't. I did it free for an AIDS organization."

"Oh." To Jaston the thought of doing anything free made about as much sense as being a hand model. Jaston made guns and knives in a little shed in back of his trailer. At Christmas he welded Nativity scenes out of fifty five-gallon drums and sold them to the Church of Christ. The irony is that we both have the same hands, his being slightly larger.

"Clu, you're gonna have to make up your mind pretty fast." Jaston ended the sentence abruptly, his voice rising; long dramatic pause—his proven method of zinging the story apex.

"Why?" I asked obediently.

"Mother said she's gonna kill herself next Sunday if she doesn't get to feeling any better." I knew he was telling the truth. She'd tried once before on St. Patrick's Day, several years ago. Mother always chose holidays to make a point.

"Jas . . . I'll call you in the morning."

"Are you coming?"

"I don't know . . . I guess . . . we'll have to see."

"What should I tell Mother?"

"Tell her . . . tell her I'll call her in the morning. Who's with her now?"

"I am."

"Where are you?"

"Mother's house."

"Where's Mother?"

"Here. You want to talk with her?"

"No! Don't wake her up."

"She's not sleeping. She's on the other line. Mother, you still there?"

I must've dropped the phone—or flung it. Two astonished eyes from across the bed were staring out at me from inside a sheet cave. I shook my head, mouthing the words, "I don't believe . . ."

"Mm . . . Mother? Are you there?" Actually, I could believe anything. This is how Mother and Jaston worked. One picks, the other dropkicks.

"I'm . . . here." It was said so weakly it sounded more like a thought.

"Mother, how're you feeling?"

"OK."

"I'm really sorry to hear about all this. It sounds terrible." No response. "Mother, I'd like to come home. I would." My bedmate sat up slowly, turned on a light and stumbled off to the john. "The problem is I've got so much going on right now. I think I may be doing a new play in the spring; we're still renovating the farmhouse upstate with our neighbors, I've got a couple of auditions coming up, I'm volunteering twice a week now at a midtown clinic . . ."

As I spoke I had the terrible feeling God would stretch a hand up out of the receiver and slap me senseless. What was I saying? My mother dying of cancer, and I've got an audition. Yes, I'm guilty, guilty as hell—but why must it always be me? Why am I the caretaker? Of course the immediate answer was, "because there's no one else" which was true, but it didn't mean I had to like it any better. ". . . . so, yes, if I can move some of this around, I'll see, but it won't be easy. Mother?"

Silence. A small clearing of the throat. " I understand." Oh God, is there a sound worse than the quiet acquiescence in a wounded mother's voice? If it weren't so god-awful hard just to say, "yes." But I can't. "Mother, I'll call you back tomorrow. Get some rest now and do whatever the doctor tells you." I start to hang up, then stop. "Mother . . . I'm praying for you."

A few muted clicks, and she was gone. I held the receiver, amazed at my sudden crisis-piety. When anyone in my dyed-in-the-wool Baptist family couldn't think of what to say next, it was automatic. "I'm praying for you." People on the East Coast were always amazed when you tried to explain such cultural aphorisms. The word "prayer" was so rarely a part of anyone's day-to-day discourse in New York. "Hey Clu, you still there?"

The sound of Jaston's voice startled me. "I thought you hung up."

"I was waiting for you to hang up."

"I'm hanging up now."

"Hey, Clu?"

"Yes."

"Could I borrow, like . . . fifty dollars? I'll pay you back in two weeks."

"You haven't paid me back the money you borrowed last year."

"I didn't? I thought I sent you a check."

"No."

"Oh. So can I?"

"No! Not until you pay me back." Silence. Jaston spoke again. "Clu, can I sell your old bike out in the garage?"

"Good night, Jaston."

"What about those weights you never . . ." Click. I lay back in bed and shut my eyes. The thing about family is—there's just not a whole lot of logic behind any of it. Lichen growing on rocks have more coherence about them than most families.

I could hear the flush from the bathroom, followed by several sleepy obscenities. "This cheap-ass, shit-hole . . . cracker-box apartment building is going down the skeptic tank. It's backing up again."

"*Septic* tank. Most of the cynics in New York are still above ground," I replied.

"With the rest of the turds." Chris turned off the hall light and stumbled back to bed. I lay in the darkness, contemplating, temporarily seated at my mother's kitchen table watching her cut and peel figs for her annual preserve-making endeavor—her sole "Betty Crocker" habit still performed before a live audience. I hate fig preserves, but I used to love watching my mother make them. What is it about a mother doing mother-things that's so comforting to men and boys? Those effortless gender-deeds so innate as to be completely unconscious by the renderer and wholly hypnotic to the observer. From smoothing defeated hair to wiping baby bottoms; all the many baffling, staggering graces of the unconscious feminine gesture.

Chris turned in bed and put an arm across my chest. "Clu?"
"Hmm."
"I don't think there are any septic tanks in New York, are there?"
I shook my head. "No."
"No, there aren't any, or no, you don't think so?"
"No, I don't know . . . I don't think so."
Chris nodded, "It's a suburban thing . . . I believe." Pause. Soft
breathing. Chris pulled a pillow up and propped it against the head-
board. "So . . . now, yes . . . the latest from Grit?"

After eight years, Chris was fairly inured to my family's procedure
by now. The 3 A.M. phone calls, the prison sentences, the dog deaths,
the false pregnancies—it had become something dependable—like the
Today Show. "I guess . . . um . . . Mother's dying. Cancer."

We lay there for a time, holding each other. Outside, it was fairly
quiet for a New York evening in March. What a nothing month.
Mostly wet and gray and impossible. I hate March in New York.
Chris suddenly got up, walked to the window of the basement flat
and wrenched open our sole source of oxygen. "Hot as hell in here."

"Yes, but it's a good address," I lied. It was a one-bedroom dump
in a so-so part of town. Best we could afford. I sat up. I presumed
now would ensue our usual practice of diversionary discourse until
the time was right for actual dialogue. You could never get right to
the point with Chris. It took . . . process. I got out of bed to boil
milk. Another vestige from my small-town youth. Plain, boiled milk
tastes like, what—scorched paper? An old ironing board? You drink
boiled milk in the middle of the night. I don't know why. "You want
some milk?"

Chris looked at me as if I'd just casually mentioned seeing Queen
Beatrix of the Netherlands shopping in Gristede's yesterday. "No. Is
there any of that merlot left."

I reached for the bottle of cheap merlot from under the sink.
"All yours." We sat in the kitchen and watched as our retarded
hamster, Mr. Goldstone, chewed on a nickel. "Mr. Goldstone's eating a nickel."

"I know," Chris replied.
"How'd he get it?" I asked.
"Beats me."

"He can't swallow it, can he?"

"Probably not."

"What is he chewing on a nickel for?"

Unable to come up with any feasible explanation for Mr. Goldstone's customary strange behavior, we let it drop. Mr. Goldstone eventually lost interest in the nickel and exchanged it for his favorite toy, a round, empty birth-control dispenser left by a vacationing LA actress. Chris and I spent hours discussing how we could sell the image of Mr. Goldstone and the birth-control ring to Madison Avenue. Problem was, we could never come up with just the right hook.

I live with a Gemini. I learned a long time ago never to push anything on a Gemini. They eventually get it, but they have to get it on their time. I'm a Scorpio. We get everything; too much, all the time. I'm not wild about astrology, but I do love picking up the occasional *New York Post* and perusing the oftentimes helpful suggestions headlined between Ann Landers and Dr. Ruth: *"Scorpio, Today There's No Turning Back."* or *"A Distant Friend Brings Good News To Gemini."* See? Useful.

Chris quaffed the last gulp of red and set the juice glass down. "So Jaston's staying with your mother?"

"Jaston's *eating* with my mother; he stays at his trailer."

"He can't just . . . you know, be with her for the time being?"

I shook my head, "The dogs make him nervous; his guns and knives make her nervous. They don't really like each other."

Chris stood, taking the glass to the sink. "And Laine, she's . . . ?" Chris didn't bother finishing the thought.

"Pregnant. Besides, the last time she went home she had a miscarriage."

Chris rinsed out the glass, placed it in the strainer and turned, arms folded. "What you need is another sibling." The thought, so casually, innocently said, was preposterous. We were suddenly both roaring with laughter. The fantastic notion of yet another wildly dysfunctional, deranged Latimore brother or sister walking the earth was hugely comical. I tried to stand. Chris fell on top of me. Together we knocked over the answering machine. Chris reached for the OUTGOING MESSAGE button and gasped into the microphone,

"Hello . . . this is . . . *Imogene* Latimore . . . sister of Jaston, Laine and Clu . . . I've been away . . ." Huge wails of laughter. "You're probably wondering . . . I was on a mission to the . . . *Chihuahua Convention!*" I put my hand over Chris's mouth. Our eighty-year-old Czech super lived upstairs. Loud laughter made him excitable.

My family was a continual source of wonder and mirth for Chris. I think he looked upon us as some sort of nonsensical *Saturday Night Live* sketch. Which is fascinating—unless you're living it. Chris's family was like some politically correct PBS series where rational, educated adults methodically slather their children with self-esteem, laughter and love, then release them into the world with a fresh MasterCard and their very own used Volvo. They were so hip it was scary. Chris's Dad, George, was a professor of biochemistry at the University of Scranton and his mother, Helen, ran a very profitable real-estate business. They drank good Scotch (lots), played golf and went to Europe every summer to indulge their passion for grand opera. Chris's older sister, Sunny, was already an out lesbian by the time Chris declared his inclinations, so his "news" was received with a certain dry-eyed equanimity. By the time his younger brother, Russell, had fathered the interracial child with his girlfriend Lakeesha, during their second year at alternative high school, George and Helen were seasoned paragons of advanced parenting. They were trauma-proof. Unless, of course, one unwittingly asked for an iced tea during the winter months. This had the peculiar effect of unnerving them to the point of near incomprehension. They stared at you as if you might be hydrophobic or something. (Yankees are so rigid about these things. Tea bag, hot water, ice—got a problem?)

Chris and I spent nearly every Christmas at the Myles's comfortable 1920s fringe-of-suburbia farmhouse. It was a charming and Christmasy place with lots of food and games and good-natured joking. And they were truly decent people to be around. Sister Sunny worked with one of Bobby Kennedy's kids doing something terribly earnest and outdoorsy. I think they rescued trapped beavers, or something. And Russell and Lakeesha, along with baby Equinox, were a constant source of New Age edification. (Was I the last person on the planet to know that sleeping with a rock crystal under your *tatami* mat helped insomnia?)

Try as I might, I could never dig up any really horrific dirt on the Myles family. They reeked of equilibrium and stability. Both parents took matching subscriptions to the *Partisan Review*. The only palpable anomaly (to me) was an unspoken obligation to always appear bright, breezy and well versed. I called it the Terminal Chipper syndrome. The pressure was savage. I, who suffered from spinach-on-the-teeth neurosis, never felt secure enough to just be my usual grumpy, farty-coot old self. I was perpetually "on." We were all "on." It was like the never-ending *Noel Coward from Hell* show. After three days of unbridled "charming," I was ready to sink my teeth into a Girl Scout's leg. And yet, contrasting as our backgrounds were, Chris and I managed to work out a sincere mutual admiration pact that was both profound and lasting. And only God and little green apples could tell you why—but we did, indeed, truly love each other.

Chris took a deep breath and rubbed an eye, drained. "So . . . what's gonna happen?"

"God . . . I guess I'm going home."

"Yipes." Chris rubbed the other eye.

"You don't have to come."

"Of course I have to come. We're married."

"What about your job? Your career?"

"They don't have Latin teachers in Texas?"

My mouth was open. Chris is from Pennsylvania, been to Texas twice. The innocence was heartrending. "Hon, in Grit they don't even have Catholics. What're you gonna do?"

Chris shrugged. "Don't worry about it. I signed on for the long haul. You'll owe me one."

Who was this extraordinary person next to me? To willingly march into hell for the sake of my certifiable family. For me!

"I just have one provision."

The music in my head stopped. "What's that?"

"We don't stay."

"Stay!" It was all I could do not to snicker. "Are you crazy? Stay longer in Grit than absolutely necessary. Am I a torture freak; do I look like a complete victim?"

"I mean it. We leave the day she dies."

I stopped smiling and looked at Chris. It was a strange behest. "Of course, right after she's buried . . ."

Chris interrupted, "The *day* she dies. I've got a 'spontaneous' . . . if you stay beyond that, you'll never leave."

I should explain. Chris is a Gemini; Chris is from Pennsylvania; Chris is the wonderful person I've shared the past eight years of my life with . . . Chris has "psychic feelings." We don't call them psychic feelings because Chris is a good Catholic; any form of the arcane is the work of Satan. We say . . . *spontaneous*. Chris only gets *spontaneous* occasionally, but when it happens it is to be genuinely regarded. There was a *spontaneous* concerning five numbers last fall and it won us $6,000 in the state lotto. Coincidence? A year before *Survivor* hit the air there was a *spontaneous* that some "nude, gay guy" would be the most watched man in America. Like . . . who knew? Six years in a row Chris has correctly predicted the Oscar for Best Sound! "Look . . . I just . . . it would be really weird not to stay for my mother's funeral."

"I'm not trying to be difficult. I said I'll go and live with you in Texas—but we have to leave the day she dies. We have to."

"Why?"

"How the hell should I know? Don't ask stupid questions."

Point taken. What's the use? Maybe another *spontaneous* would come along telling us to (God forbid) stay in Texas; raise llamas; grow ginseng. A *spontaneous* reversal is called a "one-eighty impetus." They happen too. Rarely. "Whatever. You might just change your mind, you know."

Chris frowned. "I doubt it."

I finished the cup of milk, gave Mr. Goldstone a Ritz cracker to gnaw on and got back into bed. The apartment was freezing now, which is of course the bane of all New York apartments. You're only allowed a marginal comfort zone between ice and fire as you constantly adjust, tamper and rectify the environmental extremes wreaking havoc on your bones. Window open, window shut; humidifier off, vaporizer on, fan low; electric blanket, space heater; air cleaners, aromatherapy, white noise; negative ions, flannel sheets, footwarmers; ice packs, ice gel, ice tea, a/c max, misters; incense, candles—Lysol. It was never right; or rather, it was never right for longer than ten minutes. I locked my frozen hands behind my head and stared at the ceiling. Chris scrunched next to me. "What're you thinking?"

Exactly four thoughts were bouncing through my brain at that moment: Does Mr. Slattick, the super, still get erections? I put too much oregano in the lasagna tonight. Who actually does Angie Dickinson's hair? And . . . How am I going to survive . . . Grit? "I'm a little weirded-out about going home."

"It'll be all right. We have each other."

"That's what I mean."

"What?"

"You have no idea how . . . *country* it is."

"We'll wear overalls—make jam, grow a garden. It'll be something new."

"Rednecks are not a new phenomenon. 'They are with you always,' it's in the Bible. Leviticus nine, verse five."

"The world's changed a lot—they get MTV in Honduras now."

"Small towns in Texas never change. They just get more . . . acute."

"Is this some kind of 'fear of your past' thing?"

I managed an apathetic shrug. "I could care less about those ignorant, hypocritical, 'God-fearing' morons."

"Right."

"It's just . . . I'm . . . I'm . . ." Blank. What am I afraid of? I'm an adult. My mother's dying, I have to go home now. Simple. Six weeks, six months—over. Back to the fascinating world of being an actor/director/hand model. Boom. "I'm worried about us."

"Us, why?"

"You're just not prepared. I'm not prepared."

"What do I need, a vaccination? I had a nice time when we visited four years ago."

"Six years ago. One long weekend is not enough to grasp the mendacity of the place."

"Thank you, Amanda, I'll leave my collection of glass animals at home. You're really making a complicated issue over something very simple. Your mother needs you. It's time to go home and be a son. This will happen once in your life—use it." Chris turned off the reading light. I continued staring at the ceiling. An ambulance up on Greenwich Avenue roared past the corner. A drunk stopped to pee under the dead ginkgo tree outside our stoop, making little *rat-a-tat* noises on the dirty ice. Somewhere a woman screamed. A rape? Laughter? Insanity? One heard things at night in New York, cryptic and startling as any echo vibrating through an Amazon jungle.

"Clu?"

"Hmm?"

"I was just wondering . . . I mean, not in Grit per se, but like somewhere in the general vicinity . . ."

"Yes."

"Are there, uh, you know . . . any good gay bookstores? I was thinking I could get a job, maybe do a little coffeehouse type number. What do you think?" My heart was breaking. It was all I could do to not cover my face and howl. Chris was not stupid, or deficient or limited in any way. Quite the contrary. Chris's fatal flaw was a touching, almost ardent faith in humanity. That somehow people, given half a chance, could be just as smart and funny and open as he was. That somehow, anywhere, any day in America a good espresso and a copy of *The Advocate* could be ferreted out with only a smidgen of effort. It was this purity of expectation and trust that attracted me to Chris in the first place. It was occasionally the same reason I sometimes felt tying him to a chair at a VFW hall somewhere in rural Texas might be the most expedient thing I could ever do for him. I slowly cleared my throat and pulled the covers up around my wintry neck.

"Chris, this is going to be brutal—gay men are not a cause for celebrating in South Texas. Gay men are either closeted, married to women, or very, very wealthy—they buy their privacy. Gay couples are nonexistent. Not in small towns."

"You're saying the coffeehouse isn't a good idea?" My mouth was open again. We'd both been in New York too long. Chris interrupted, "Only kidding. So fine, it was just a thought. I'll work at the battered women's shelter, I'll teach underprivileged kids to read . . . I'll tend bar at the Holiday Inn."

"It's a dry county."

"Oh." We lay in the darkness, breathing in perfect synch. How, oh God how, would we ever survive in all that Baptist-bliss? My family was one thing; they're beyond recovery—but the town? Those people? Those tiny-brained, ignorant, dishonest, gossiping, whoring, beer-drinking "Christians" who so enriched and ennobled my precious youth with their breathtaking grasp of denial. How does anyone, much less a gay person, a gay couple, survive such stupendous need? It was a fear that four years in college and eight years of Manhattan had ceased to vanquish—the dread that eventually one day, one would in fact, have to pay the fiddler.

I exhaled deeply. "Home again, home again; jiggity-jig."

"What?" Chris looked at me.

"It's this . . . ditty . . . my grandmother used to sing when we were driving home from the grocery store, or somewhere. Gibberish. She was always singing hymns or something silly."

Chris yawned and stretched his arms under the cover. "It's going to be fine, you'll see. Better than you think . . . stop worrying." Within a minute Chris was out, snoring beside my pillow. I listened to his breathing and slowly began to feel the hot milk do its tryptophan-releasing slumber-number on my dozy head. I was nearly asleep when the car pulled up outside our window and two men began arguing. Almost immediately there were gunshots, squealing tires and the clatter of overturned garbage cans. At last I could sleep.

2

A SHIRLEY JONES WIG

The remarkable thing about leaving Manhattan was that nothing remarkable happened. No street person with grimy squeegee collapsed
in grief at our departure, no tunnel teller blocked our egress; Liz
Smith was clearly mute on the subject. All in all, it was a hushed,
somber parting from the old *manzana* that had so exuberantly wel-
comed my entry, lo those many years ago.

What I learned during my time in Manhattan was: a) I was capable of making a living; b) some of the most provincial people in the
world live in one the world's biggest cities; c) I'll never be a
Broadway star; and d) comparatively, there are as many unhappy
straight people as gay people, so really—what choice does anyone
have? (Like most good gay boys, there was a time in my life when I
felt I needed to be straight. It passed.)

The three novel things about the return trip to Grit were: a)
Dollywood is located in Sevierville, Tennessee; b) Graceland in
Memphis is just down the street from an African-American cafeteria
serving astoundingly good fried chicken; and c) there's nothing to eat
in Arkansas. That Dolly Parton should come from a place pronounced "severe" makes perfect sense. From the women's hair to the
men's expressions, it was all pretty cruel visually. Graceland was
everything we expected (perhaps even more depressing—old kitsch is
really the pits). We concurred wholeheartedly with the pissy decora-

tor from Atlanta who rode in the van with us back to the parking lot, announcing loudly, "This is the first time I've ever been to one of these places I didn't want anything!" The best meal we had in Arkansas was at a Pak-n-Sak in Arkadelphia—two hard-boiled eggs. (How much catfish can a body ingest?)

By the time we reached Texas pulling our distended U-Haul, we were too overcome with sore butts, stiff necks, stinky clothes and carcinogenic road food to care much that Texarkana was the home of Ross Perot, that the world's largest flea market is in Canton and that Dr Pepper was invented in Waco. (All Texans know that stuff anyway. Chris was more or less mute on being apprised of such gripping data.)

There was some thought about stopping in Austin for a day or two, listening to some music and eating real Tex-Mex. The traffic defeated us, however. We watched a dog get run over on Interstate 35, a trailer unhitch with some luckless student's earthly belongings, and a double-semi jackknife virtually parallel to us. Observing all the sundry vehicular calamities transpiring just outside our personal space was eventually overwhelming. Granted, only an idiot drives in New York and our motor skills were less than brilliant, but for the love of God, whatever happened to little old laid-back, pot-smoking, hippie-loving, armadillo-worshipping Austin? It felt more like Pittsburgh with live oaks.

We pulled off at a Wendy's on the south side, and a young woman wearing a clown outfit and a multihued Afro approached us carrying a donation can.

"Hi! Would you like to give to the Sacred Love of Jesus Church for the Homeless?" she asked, all smiles and adorableness.

"No thanks."

"Oh come on, just a little for a good cause?" She was starting to pout. New York had conditioned me so that I could blow off the best conners in the world with deadly proficiency. Maybe it was the wig, or the clown drag, or the whine, or the red-chipped dirty fingernails, or the traffic, or the three-day road hangover. I hated the bitch.

"No really . . . thank you!" OK, I was a little insistent, a little shrill. I suppose I could have blunted it—maybe.

"Wow." Her whine became more determined. She glared at our New York license plates. "You Yankees are all alike. Chill out."

Check. I was pissed off now. Who did Missy Clown Drag think she was dealing with? Rudy Giuliani? "I happen to be from Texas, hon. What exactly is this 'church' about, if I might inquire? Do you have some literature, some credentials, some 501(c)3 tax-exempt status I could peruse? All I see is a Folger's coffee can and a grimy xeroxed label. It just doesn't look real 'official,' know what I mean? And what's with the clown outfit? Is this so I'll think you're some harmless nitwit and double my offering? I don't get your whole approach. In fact I don't even think you're legit. I think you're either a drug addict, a hustler or a prostitute—or all three. Now I told you very politely twice, 'no thank you.' Do you want me to call a cop, or are you going to fuck off?"

And then she did it. Miss Bozo screwed up her little face in a hideous Moonie-Zombie-"David Koresh babe" glare and spit at me, "There's no place in the kingdom of heaven for the *homosexual!*" With that she whirled around and vanished behind a Suburban. I swear I saw a broomstick appear at the finale of her little performance.

"Whoa, the *Bad Seed* Goes *Big Top.*" Chris was leaning against the U-Haul with his arms folded. At least we'd gotten to the truth. Now I almost felt sorry for her. She was just another hapless cult-chick out panning for her "savior." Why couldn't she just say so? I'd at least have bought her a Wendy's. Possession can be famishing. "No place in the kingdom of heaven . . . whew." Chris shook his head. "We're a long way from Christopher Street."

"I told you. Texas is crawling with born-again fervents. The whole state's out to destroy anything that isn't John Wayne or Miss America."

"We're in luck. I packed our tambourines for the talent competition."

"It's not just Texas, the whole country's gone moral values wiggy. What AIDS didn't kill, the bigots will. What is it with these right-wing lunatics and their obsession with men's dicks anyway? They're absolutely tormented by where gay men and presidents stick their 'willies.'" I suddenly yelled at the top of my lungs, "*Leave my prick alone, America!*" It felt awesome. An African-American guy entering Wendy's jerked his head around, and grinned at me, "Don't tell me your shit, friend. I got half the women in Austin trying to get a piece of my Johnson, O-K?"

Chris and I laughed. He shook his head. "So . . . Little Mary Sunshine. How 'bout we go slap around a couple of nuns. Will that cheer you up?"

I tried smiling, "Sorry. I'm exhausted. Clown kid's probably not from Texas anyway. Did you see her face? That zeal, that crystalline Nazi intensity, that . . ."

". . . bad Ronald McDonald hair-day aspect? Forget it. She's nursery school compared to the Lower Broadway corps. Totally amateur." Thank God Chris's ancestors had been calmer than mine. He had a way of putting the proper slant on things.

We left Austin by midafternoon, zipping through San Antonio without incident. It had always bothered me that one was unable to see the Alamo from any of the downtown freeways. From the state that invented drive-thru liquor barns and takeout pharmacies, just a peek at Texas's most famous tourist attraction from a speeding automobile would have seemed almost expected. Chris was disappointed, and I promised him we'd return to "the Shrine of Texas Liberty." I didn't have the heart to tell him how disappointed he'd be upon actually seeing it. Like so many things in life—the movie's better. All air conditioned and garden-clubbed and plunked downtown right across from the post office—it always seemed more like a nice Mexican restaurant than one of America's legendary battle sites.

It was an early spring in Texas and a mild seventies day as we plowed southward on Highway 16. We kept the windows rolled down and sucked in huge gulps of sweet air. I warned Chris, "This is as good as it gets in Texas. By June you'll be barking mad from the heat." It didn't register. It was hard to project beyond the balmy cocoon enveloping us. Fat cattle were grazing under huge mesquite trees, hayfields were lush, flocks of snowy egrets clustered in late-afternoon exhibition—even the roadside Mexican beer joints looked picturesque and benevolent. I had to admit, South Texas looked near arcadian in mid-March.

"Stop!" Chris yelled suddenly.

"What?"

"Stop! You have to."

"What is it?"

"Over there!" Chris pointed to a large meadow between two clusters of live oaks. I guided the van and trailer to a bumpy halt alongside the highway. Chris continued staring out the window. "It's . . . incredible."

"What?"

"Those . . . those, blue things."

And then I saw them. Acre upon acre of bluebonnets, the state flower of Texas. It was indeed . . . incredible. As if a lapis sea had risen up and flooded the harsh brush country. More cobalt, azure and indigo flowers than anyone had a right to properly behold in one notion. A deluge of startling, bewildering creation.

We walked out into the field. Standing in the middle of six trillion perfect sapphires I suddenly remembered a very crucial fact about growing up in Texas—excess is not a sin here. Flamboyance is a virtue; abundance venerated, indulgence advocated. If you got it, by God—*demonstrate!* None of that drab New England puritan bullcorn for this citizenry. Texas millionaires, Texas brags; broads, rednecks, ranches, oil wells, football, cheerleaders, hair, killer bees, heat, murders, roadside trash, executions . . . wildflowers—it's supposed to be larger than life. Halfway is so . . . gutless.

"We have been in New York too long." Chris was kneeling, trying to smell the bluebonnets.

"They don't have much smell. They're just for show."

Chris shook his head. "I smell grass. Do you know how long it's been since I've smelled grass?" Chris began roaming on all fours through the blue jungle, lost in a city-boy hallucination.

"I think I should remind you of something my great-aunt Jean told me once upon a time."

"What?"

"If it don't sting, bite, tear, poke, burn, kick or maim—it ain't from South Texas."

"Meaning what?"

"Meaning if you don't stand up real quick, you're going to be covered in fire ants from head to toe."

"Fire ants? What's that?"

"Heinous little bastards. Sting like hell and leave a pinhead boil everywhere they bite. Lasts about a week."

"Are you serious?"

"Do they serve fried pickles in Arkansas? I think I'd get up." Chris immediately stood and began brushing himself off. "God, what a drag. All this beauty ruined by some low-class insect."

I nodded. "My entire childhood in one sentence." We started back to the van, still marveling at the blue heaven enveloping us.

"Clu?"

"Hmm?"

"I was just wondering . . . how did that chick at Wendy's know we were gay?"

I'd been thinking the same thing earlier. On the "Butch-Scale" from General Schwarzkopf to RuPaul, Chris and I were somewhere in the middle. Average. To the ordinary Joe on the street we looked like two husbands from Hartford. No rings, no tattoos, no hair drama . . . no Chelsea-clone drag. Just plain . . . guys. We had no gay flags or rainbows on the car, no "I Can't Even Think Straight" stickers—*nada*. All I could muster was that somehow Missy Patty Hearst had her own *gaydar*.

"Don't you suppose Clown-girl was 'one of the children'?" I asked.

"A friend of Dorothy?"

"Either that or Jesse Helms's godchild."

Chris shook his head. "Weird. I've been called everything in the book at one time or another, but denied access to the portals of heaven by Rhonda McDonald is a first."

I pulled at a lock of hair behind Chris's ear. "Don't worry 'bout it. Texans are very fair when it comes to hating people—everyone's despised on an equal basis." Chris didn't smile. He was working up his pensive/intellectual/brooding face. One of my favorites. Always made me feel like I'd suddenly married Carl Sagan. Here was clearly an adorable man who wasn't afraid to appear constipated. And I loved him for it. Although he had his own little peculiar vanities (he had a thing about his bangs, and trust me, not since Robert F.

Kennedy had anyone looked so right with bangs) he was relatively "affectation" free. He simply had that effortless, good-looking, good-bones, handsome/boyish thing you find all over America, but particularly ascendant in certain preppy, East Coast families. They can dress like slobs and somehow make it work. "Slobs with good fabric," as my Puerto Rican actor friend Mario used to call Chris and his college pals. Uncombed, unshaven, even unbathed (which was in essence never) Chris looked brilliant. Not that he was model-like or pretty boy, just American wholesome—relaxed, clean, unadorned, smart and virile. When he'd put his little "John Boy" reading glasses on, that was it—imminent damage was unavoidable. I was a chump for that contemplative-stud thing. Made me nuts. He'd be curled up grading some classroom theses on Vergil or Catullus, and I'd catch sight of that torn flannel shirt, threadbare wool socks, old chino and wire-rim glasses action going on, and forget it. Clocks across America stopped. A higher calling was swiftly upon us.

I, who needed quality sleep, gym time, jungle camouflage and charitable lighting to look my best, found his offhand appeal both maddening and powerfully seductive. It certainly kept me steadfast all these years. Sure, there were lots of handsome men to ogle in New York. Scads. Tons. I just didn't particularly want to face any in the morning over my bowl of rice milk and Special K. Chris fit the bill perfectly. I was lucky. We were both lucky, and we knew it. It worked, and it was rare as "tits on a boar hog," as they so aptly had a way of putting it in Grit.

Chris looked at me, squinting. "Do you think I look too . . . gay?"

I laughed. "Don't be ridiculous."

"No, really. Am I going to like . . . stand out?"

I snorted, "Yes, they're going to run from you on Main Street. Mothers will grab their children in terror; old people will make the sign of the cross whenever your name is mentioned."

As we approached the van I did notice from the corner of my eye that Chris was wearing loafers with no socks and *tassels*. When did he get those? Why had I never noticed the tassels before? This was getting dangerously close to the raised-eyebrow zone in South Texas. The potential for setting off silent mini alarms was distinct. Of course, no one would actually say anything; just a glance, a smile, a silent register of association—released until the next provocation. All very neat and precise. You never knew you'd been fucked until the labor pains began.

"Chris."

"Yeah?"

"I've been thinking. Why don't we . . . I really want us both to get some new cowboy boots now that we're back in Texas."

"Me too. *Red ones* . . . with big heels."

We drove silently for the next half hour.

As we approached the fringe of metropolitan Grit I began to feel slightly giddy. We'd done it. We were here. Here was home. God help us.

The old Gulf station at the edge of town was now a . . . hold on to your hats—*delicatessen*. Chris and I cackled over whether or not you could get stuffed grape leaves or a decent celery soda in Grit. Mr. Thompson's dairy barn had been painted blue and yellow and a huge sign hung over the entrance to the milking room, CONNIE'S CRAFTS N' THINGS. I mused out loud that Connie Thompson-Milburn-Hinojosa-Firooz, Mr. Thompson's much-married daughter, must be back home between husbands. The Dairy Queen had added on. There was a new "park-ette" plopped alongside the courthouse. Somebody had torn down the Fashiontique dress shop and put in a Whataburger. Things looked different—in a familiar way.

Chris pointed out the window toward the Chamber of Commerce. "God, look . . . it's a Henry Moore sculpture!"

I shook my head, trying not to snort. "That's Mel Frijole—The World's Largest Pinto Bean. Grit grows more pinto beans than any city in Texas. Mr. Bain, the shop teacher, will be glad to know you appreciate his artistry."

Chris stared pensively ahead. "Oh." He managed a faint smile. "The town's certainly bigger than I remember."

I finally burst out laughing. "Gigantic. Has kind of that 'Chicago energy,' don't you think? Wait till you see our new airport."

Chris put his hand over my mouth. "Try not to speak. You know how long road trips make you light-headed."

At that instant a car pulled up alongside us at the light and honked. I grabbed Chris's hand, glancing across at four pairs of blue eyes locking in, registering and filing the image of two adult males touching one another on Main Street. Do I sound paranoid?

"Clu? Clu Latimore, is that you? I can't believe it, you better get out of that car and give me an' old hug. I can't believe it!"

Chris stared at me blankly. "Is this someone you know?"

I squinted. "I think it's . . . Myla Biggs, my date at the junior prom." I stuck my head out of the window and started to speak. "Let me pull over and get off the street." It was too late. Myla and her three children were suddenly standing in the middle of the road. Myla reached through the window and grabbed my neck while her oldest daughter ran around on Chris's side, opened the van door and kissed him squarely on the mouth. Chris looked as if cardiac arrest were imminent. Cars passed slowly around us, no more alarmed than if we were all leaving a church parking lot on Sunday morning.

"Clu, how are you . . . I just can't believe . . ."

"Myla . . . I hope we're not going to get run over . . ."

"How's your mother?"

"Well, we're on our way. Myla, this is . . . this is . . . Chris."

"Hello, Chris. Very nice to meet you. Clu, do you know my girls?"

"No, I don't think . . ."

"This is Rhonda, she's nine, that's Richelle, eleven—and that's Raelynn, thirteen." Chris and I were suddenly enveloped in pink arms, blond hair and the aroma of bubble gum and Tide. Truly, the most loving children on earth. I caught a glimpse of an elderly man inching past in his pickup, smiling beatifically at this enthusiastic display of Christian warmth. If the mayor had suddenly pulled up lawn chairs and invited half of the downtown to join our "hug-in," it would have seemed the most natural thing in the world.

"How long are you here for?"

"Well . . . um . . . I don't really know . . ."

"Are y'all from New York?" Richelle asked.

"Yes."

"Do you know any movie stars?"

Before I could answer Chris thoughtfully replied, "Lee Roy Reams and I go to the same health club."

All three girls wrinkled their noses in dismay. "Who's that?" The name of Lee Roy Reams, patron saint of all chorus gypsies, was about as meaningful to three pubescent Texas girls as Akim Tamiroff or Toshiro Mifune.

"He's a stage actor and director in New York," I volunteered quickly.

"And movies," interjected Chris.

"What movies?" I asked incredulously.

"He was in *La Cage.*"

"He was in a *touring* production of *La Cage, not* the movie."

"You're wrong."

"I am so-o-o right."

Chris shook his head in disgust. Here we were in town not five minutes and already we were having gay trivia hissies on Main Street. Myla looked at us both curiously, then smiled.

"I think I've heard of him . . . I'm sure I have. Oh, Clu, this is so great—back home in Grit! Who'd've believed it? Lord, I thought we'd never see you again. You were the one out of the whole class we thought would be famous. I guess that honor goes to Johnny Pettus now. Didn't you know? Johnny has the largest car dealership in Houston. Oh yes. He married some old girl from River Oaks or somewheres, and God, he ended up with half of Harris County. Zane and I made a special trip up there when we got the last Suburban. Listen, I got to get Raelynn over to cheerleading practice and Richelle's got band."

"What about Rhonda?" I smiled.

"Oh hell," Myla rumbled. "Rhonda's getting baptized on Sunday. I've got to find something virginal to throw on her wet butt after she climbs out of the church hot tub." Myla hooted and winked at Chris as she took one last drag on her Marlboro Light and pitched it on the curb. "Tell your family 'Hi' and y'all come on out to the place and visit with Zane and me. Zane's as big as a school bus; you wouldn't know him. We'll get the margarita machine whirring and tell a bunch of lies. Bye, y'all!" Myla and girls piled back into the brand-new Suburban and peeled off down Main Street, exactly the way she used to when she'd cruise downtown sipping Dr Pepper and vodka with Debbie Guidry and Sandy Huffaker, *many,* many a summer evening past.

"I have just one question," Chris said after a lengthy pause. "They have their own margarita machine?" I nodded and turned off Main Street, hoping to avoid another run-in with my adolescence. At least until 1820 Newell Drive.

"Myla's father runs the bank. He chartered a plane and flew everyone to Monterrey, Mexico, for her eighteenth birthday. Myla's from money; she married money. People like Myla inherit margarita machines."

Rounding the elementary school I could see Mother's olive green Impala parked in front of the house, under the raggedy salt cedar trees. Nineteen seventy-five was not a great year for Chevrolet. Mother had picked olive green because of the salesman's enigmatic low-maintenance pitch. Who, outside of an army recruiter, drives an olive green anything? For a car that never worked the minute it left the dealer's lot, she might as well have chosen hot pink. Cars were not a Latimore thing. Laine quit driving years ago after running into a pizza van on her way home from the obstetrician. Jaston usually bought a piece of junk every year, drove it into the ground and traded parts for another piece of junk, about as casually as changing socks. I hate driving and usually don't know a Ford from a Ferrari. I *do,* however, thoroughly appreciate the finer points of being chauffeured. The minute I arrived in New York, from taxis to limos—I *got* it. I make a great passenger.

We stopped in front of the leaning chain-link fence, tenuously holding back Mother's front yard. One thousand six hundred and eight miles, three and a half days, enough bad coffee to warrant a kidney transplant—back to where it all started.

I stared at the doleful front porch. I actually remember when people used to sit on front porches. (God, was I getting ancient or was time lashing by at warp speed lately?) My grandparents used to roost on their porch in the late afternoons and watch the cars drive by. As a kid it *seemed* entertaining enough. You never know though; maybe we were just so sugared-out from all the candy and Cokes Grandaddy would bribe us with to help him do "chores," our pleasure might have been entirely coma induced.

There's a picture of all of us, taken when I was about five, wearing our new Easter outfits and holding egg baskets on the porch. We looked scrubbed and wholesome, all grins and innocence. Mother's wearing her latest fashion statement, which I think was some sort of cantaloupe, bell-bottomed, Dacron pantsuit number with huge bangle earrings, a head scarf and aqua eyeshadow. (Fashion was never whim to Mother. "Tactical maneuvering" comes closer to conveying her intent. "Dress to vanquish!" was her silent maxim.) And we *appear* happy enough. When is it that nonspecific unhappiness officially sets in? Parents' divorce? Adolescence? Loss of first love? Inability to find first love? Ultimate realization that (at the time) one's sexual wiring is wholly contradictory to the rest of the planet's? It's all so intermingled.

One thing for sure, I wasn't born sad. I was a bright, borderline chubby, cute, funny kid—"a pill" as Laine used to say. I somehow never mastered the details of "self-conscious." I'd dress up in Mother's clothes and play CanCan dancer for anyone who'd watch. I could imitate every comedian on the *Ed Sullivan Show*. At family reunions I did a drop-dead impersonation of Louis Prima belting out "Old Black Magic" using a garbage can for a drum. I was a continual dervish of "Look at Me!" activity. Where did it come from? Where did it go? One day all the animation ceased, and I became "wary." Constrained as a minister's wife. Somehow, I construed that "they" were not laughing *with* me anymore. And it mortified me. I discovered that cute whizzes to tedious in about the time it takes to consume an average box of Cracker Jacks. It made me sad for a long, long time.

Jaston was always in his own cosmos: building tree forts or playing with his toy trucks, hauling petrified dog turds across the backyard. Laine was "best friend" to about five other Grit girls and didn't have much time for "significant" little-brother moments. I had a few oddball playmates, like Ticho Giles, the mayor's son, who always had a runny nose and ate dirt. And there was Candy Banning who I played doctor with nonstop from first to second grade. She bailed on me after her mother cussed me out for peeing in their zinnia bed. I remained pretty much a small-town loser after that. I just couldn't get a handle on guy things at all. Hated Little League, loathed Cub

Scouts, despised all typical preadolescent male obsessions like playing "tit twister," whacking ears with lethal middle finger snaps and
gobbing loogies on each other. It was hell.

Until high school. God finally answered my prayers and brought
us—*musical theater!* I got the lead as Sky Masterson in *Guys and
Dolls* and I was suddenly a real live human being. I became popular
with girls. I knew how to dance, I was witty, I incorporated Mother's
wardrobe strategy—I was nearly cool for the first time in my life. I
even learned how to fake being a "guy." Watching sports, gruntin',
hangin', talkin' shit, not standing out, being a team player. Puke.
What a boring load of shit gets dumped on teen males. Who made
up these grim rules on How to Be a Man anyway? They should all be
shot.

Chris yawned, stretched and glanced out the window. "No signs
of life. Where are all the dogs?" The thought was barely uttered
when the front door cracked slightly and out flew nine tan-and-
brown rats followed by four mice puppies. Excited Chihuahuas do
this passive/agressive number that oscillates frantically between yelp-
ing hysterically, jumping, baring teeth, trying to rip each other's ears
off, followed by intense shyness, whimpering and curling into tiny
balls of defeated fuzz. The best part is watching the puppies imitate
the adults. You haven't experienced the soul of temerity until you've
been nibbled to death by a twelve-week-old Chihuahua.

"God, they're so . . . cute!" Chris marveled, opening his door.

I nodded halfheartedly. "That's what people say about quintu-
plets. That and, "There but for the grace of God . . ."

I looked up to see Mother standing at the foot of the porch wearing one of her big, bright Texas-lady-jeweled-fringy sweaters. You
know the ones—all flash and sparkle . . . *youth*. How fragile and elderly she'd become! Six years gone by and a parent moves from middle age to ancestor. Still—holding on to the chipped, metal porch
railing, she looked just as pretty and wholesome as the great Texas
beauty she'd always been. Somewhere between Donna Reed and
Ann-Margret—with just a hint of Endora from *Bewitched* for symmetry.

"Hello! I'd about given up on ya." Mother held her hand chest
high, seemingly unable to lift farther.

"Well, we made it finally. I think." I started around the front of the van.

"Don't let those pesky dogs out in the street. We'll be all day getting them back in."

Chris opened the gate quickly and the pack retreated in confusion, unsure of who the invader was. "Hello, Mrs. Latimore. It's good to see you again." Mother sort of held one arm up in front of her and leaned in to let Chris kiss her on the cheek.

"I have to kind of watch my balance or I get dizzy. How are you?"

"Fine, thank you. You're looking well."

"Oh, I wish it were true, but thank you for saying so." Mother turned to squint at me as I trudged up the walk carrying an enormous potted bird-of-paradise we'd hauled from Manhattan. "What is that thing?" she asked warily.

"It's for you. A gift from Chris and me." I set the shrubbery down and started to put my arms around her.

"Don't squeeze too hard. I've got bandages." I hesitated for a second, then sort of patted Mother lightly and we brushed cheeks. Intimacy was not a family distinction. We weren't Italian. Bandages just made it more precise. "That's a beautiful thing. I hope I don't kill it," Mother said cautiously, eyeing the plant as if it might turn on her.

We stood there for several long seconds, each searching for the next pleasantry. Finally, I cleared my throat. "Well, gosh . . . everything looks . . . really green."

"Oh yes. We've had lots of rain. Dr. Conklin told me in church last Sunday they got near four inches down at . . . *Watch your foot there!* You've got some little ones trying to eat your shoes." Chris looked down to see a pair of hamster-dogs gnawing on his tassels. As he started to kneel, one bolted under the house and the other made an attempt to fly straight up. Chris grabbed "spacewalker" in his palm and began rubbing his stomach with a finger. The Peter Lorre look-alike wiggled furiously for a moment, then went completely slack, closed his eyes and stuck his tongue out. Canine rapture.

"That's the baby bitch out of Bessie Smith's last litter," Mother said proudly.

"Bessie Smith is still alive and having babies?" I asked astounded. "She must be at least twelve years old."

"Nine to be exact. I had her spayed just last fall and darn if she didn't fool us all."

"I guess she wasn't through being a mother," Chris said.

"Bessie Smith is one of Mom's top show dogs. She's won about everything," I volunteered. "I'm just amazed she can still have a litter—even with a womb."

At that moment a very decrepit, very feeble male Chihuahua appeared at the front door. Arthritic, spindly legs; scrunched-up, bent spine; filmy eyes; cream-and-gray coat dusted with dander and indentions of missing hair—he gazed up at us slowly and scowled with disgust. He managed to emit a single, listless "woof," then matter-of-factly hiked a hind leg and aimed a stuttering stream of pee onto the front porch.

"*Señor Murphy, shame on you!*" Mother picked up Señor Murphy by the scruff of the neck and set him down in the middle of the canna bushes by the walkway. He glared at us with all the outrage he could muster, tilted his neck back and . . . sneezed. "Dog's got more allergies than a medical encyclopedia. He's on so many pills now his stools look like Rolaids."

I stared in disbelief. "Mother, that's not *the* Señor Murphy."

"The very one."

"He . . . he's as old as I am!"

"Well—he'll be fifteen in June."

"That's impossible. That's . . . a hundred and five in dog years!"

"Mavis Kincaid thinks I ought to take him on the *Letterman Show.* May do it."

I shook my head. "What are you feeding these animals—monkey glands?"

Mother smiled, rubbing her arms. "Idn't it awful. Seems like some of 'em gonna live forever. Maybe we should all be on dog food."

Chris grinned and handed me the sleeping puppy in his hands. "Señor Murphy reminded me of something I meant to do an hour ago. May I use your bathroom?"

"Yes, certainly, down the hall on the right." Chris entered the house while Mother idly fussed with the bird-of-paradise and I stretched my weary body. Long, twisted, arching lunges—anything to wring out the road, stifle the pervasive awkwardness of the "returned-prodigal-phase" we were now entering. We tarried, in the Southern manner. To appear purposeful, to be in a hurry or anxious in any way would have implied—coarseness. Frankly, after New York, unearthing the proper lower latitudes demeanor was unexpectedly exhausting. In New York one simply walks into a store and announces, "I want *this* in *large* and *green* and NOW!" In the South you have to—*visit*. You never get right to the point, right away, ever. "How're yew doin', Miz Clader? How's your husband? He feelin' better? That's good. Yes, they're fine. Uh-huh. No, I didn't plant any peas this year. My old hands has gotten so arthritic I cain't shell 'em like I used to. No, just tomatoes, corn, onions and a little squash. Yes, it's a wonderful garden for someone like me. Uh-huh. Yes, I'd heard they got married. They're such a nice little couple. I wish they didn't have to move. Now what did I come in here for? No, that wadn't it, but those sure are pretty. Oh listen, by the way, do ya'll have something kinda like that in . . . *green?*" Check.

"Chris seems to be a little thinner," Mother announced, examining one of the dogs for ticks.

"He might have lost a little weight since you've seen him. He works out every day."

"I think you've stayed just about the same."

"Pretty much. I kind of move the same five or ten pounds around every year." I sat the puppy down next to who I assumed was the mother. She snapped at the mewling intruder, then rolled over and offered a nipple. Instantly, she was blanketed in hungry mouths. "How're you feeling, Mother?"

"Oh . . . I'm all right. Some days are better'n others. I guess the worst part is losing your hair—and the nausea. Otherwise, I'm just tired a lot."

I stared at Mother's head. It suddenly occurred to me that she was indeed wearing a wig. Red, curly—pert.

"Shirley Jones."

"What?"

"It's a 'Shirley Jones' wig. I tried 'em all, 'Eva Gabor,' 'Joan Collins,' Sears—'Shirley Jones' knows wigs."

"Well, it looks just like your real hair." And it truly did.

"I will not die looking dead. I don't care what you're going through—hair and makeup is God's way of separating the infidels."

I chewed on the inside of my mouth, nonplussed. I finally had to laugh. "Isn't that putting an awful lot of importance on looks?"

"Did I say anything about looks? You can be ugly as a tree stump, God doesn't care! Grooming is what counts. Well-groomed individuals can live and die knowing that they have given it their best shot. Regimen is survival."

One of the things I admired most about my mother was her sense of the unequivocal. It also made me crazy. Truth be told—it made her crazy.

"Well, we might as well go in. I can't see as good as I used to, and I'll sure as the world stand here and wave at somebody driving by I don't want to wave at."

"Why would that be so terrible?"

Mother sighed and placed her right arm around her waist. "Because, son, I don't have enough energy to be nice to everyone anymore. It takes a terrible toll. Twenty minutes of smiling and nodding and I'm out for the rest of the day. Being mean doesn't help either. It's just as tiresome. You really just want to be left alone." I must've looked awkward or something because Mother immediately reached out and touched my hand. "Of course, family's different. They know you when you're not always nice." Mother turned and sort of floated up the porch steps. "I'm gonna just sit down inside for a minute. I'm getting one of my ringing spells."

"Can I help, Mother?"

"No, no. Just . . . make yourselves at home. Jaston'll be by for supper." Mother stopped long enough to snatch up Señor Murphy and disappear into the cool shadows of the front living room. As the screen door shut behind her I heard her say, perhaps to Chris, possibly to no one, "I used to hate cooking when they were little. Now it gives the day a kind of . . . sense."

A new Ford Explorer drove by the house. I turned to look, and immediately the driver and his companion shot back hearty hellos. I didn't recognize them.

3

SEEDS OF CONSTERNATION

"Is this your . . . father?" Chris held up a cheap brass frame. The glass was cracked, the picture dirty and yellow, the corner stamp of the photography studio faded to a dim hieroglyphic penumbra—and yet there, exalted for the ages within four metal junctions of a dime-store shrine stood a smiling likeness as familiar to me as Lincoln on a penny. Herbert Q. Latimore: aka Dad. Stiffly saluting in his Texas A&M cadet uniform, sword in hand, khaki jodhpurs tucked into knee-high leather riding boots that gleamed like burnished cherry wood, he was, as I once overheard Laine coolly apprise a group of fellow high-school girls, "a damn fine-looking hunk."

"Hunk" disappeared from our lives nearly thirty years ago. He and Mother divorced when I was in third grade. Jaston, Laine and I made periodic visits to 'Mammaw and Pappaw' Latimore's farm in East Texas, did the obligatory holiday treks to wherever he was living, once even spending two weeks on the beach in Galveston in some motel he was staying at, until eventually it all sort of petered out: the trips, the phone calls—the Dad. Last we'd heard he'd started an independent oil-drilling outfit up in Wyoming. He was going to send us plane fare just as soon as . . . as soon as what? Who can remember anymore? Whatever it was, maybe it never happened, maybe it did. We lost touch. In a funny way, I don't think any of us ever felt abandoned, including Mother. It just seemed like we were more or less misplaced. Herbert always had a lot on his mind.

"What a babe," Chris whistled. "I don't think I've ever seen this one."

I stared at the picture briefly, then handed it back to Chris. "Mother's probably had it hidden. Where'd you find all this stuff?" Chris was sitting on the floor in Laine's old bedroom (now exclusively referred to as the "company" suite).

"I started putting away clothes and there was this . . . hatbox." Chris reached around to the other side of the bed and held up a burgundy-and-gray-striped, circular box. On top, in fancy scroll, were the words "Lily Basker's Ladies Hats." After a childhood committed to playing "treasure hunt" in every conceivable alcove of our small abode—this was a startling discovery. "It was calling me—'check it out, check it out,'" Chris winked.

I faked reproach. "One of these days you're gonna find something you'll wish you hadn't, and you're gonna rue that siren's call." Ignoring my own counsel I lifted the box lid, half expecting to find an assortment of mother-mementos tucked away for posterity— lockets of hair, grade-school report cards, finger-paint disasters—the usual childhood clichés. Instead, wrapped in a veil of faded rose tissue, were pictures, lots of pictures—of men! Young men. Men I'd never seen before. Good-looking men, average-looking men; short, tall, skinny, stout; some in uniform, some in suits, some in jeans and work shirts; a couple of guys in swimsuits! They all appeared to be snapshots taken around the same time—early to mid 1940s, I guessed. I looked up at Chris with an expression of . . . "huh?"

"Who are these people?" I shook my head.

"You don't know any of them?"

"I've never seen any of these. Where was this?"

Chris motioned to the bottom drawer of the far dresser. "The minute I saw it, I had a *spontaneous.*" Chris touched the hatbox cautiously and intoned in a low murmur, "Seen by all, known by one— something that does not like a certainty."

"Oh, shut up." I grabbed the photograph of my father and stuck it back in the box with the others. "I hate it when Vincent Price overwhelms you. These are, these are . . ." Chris stared at me with the blank expression of a goldfish. "These are . . . *friends* of my parents!"

Chris nodded and calmly began putting shirts on hangers. "An engaging group too. I guess their wives and girlfriends were taking all the pictures."

I placed the box back in the bureau and slid the drawer shut. "What's that supposed to mean?"

"Where are the women?"

I glanced up at Chris, "What are you talking about?"

Chris stopped hanging shirts and looked at me. "Clu, a box full of pictures of men. Think about it. Hairy, ball-scratching, ding-dong swinging *guys*—not a dame in the lot. Wasn't that the era of Betty Grable, Lana Turner? Mickey and Judy? Gay was an adjective then. Every doll had a guy, every fella a . . . etc., etc. Doesn't it seem a tiny bit . . . atypical, your mother keeping a secret stash of World War II beefcake lying around the house?"

I was completely flummoxed. "I think you need to lie down. The drive's made you a tad giddy."

Chris picked up a pile of T-shirts and placed them neatly on a closet shelf. "Uh-huh. When have I ever been wrong about a *spontaneous?*"

"Now! You're making me insane. What? You're saying my mother had affairs with these men? Or, what—Mom was a hooker and these were her tricks? No, no—here it is; my mother's a fag-hag and these were her 'boys'!" I laughed out loud.

Chris smiled serenely, continuing to arrange clothes in the closet. "Beats me. Just odd, that's all. Could be lots of reasons." Chris shut the closet door and belched. "Sorry—Wendy's. Look, they're probably . . . they're probably your father's friends. Yeah, army buddies. That's it."

Chris quietly continued housekeeping. I studied his movements as he proceeded to unpack, straighten, and attempt restoration of Mother's sad guest room (tangerine and toast being the room's primary leitmotif). Sister Parrish would have been defeated. Not Chris. Here he was, looking and acting like he'd just returned from a fortnight at the Golden Door instead of the road-trip-from-hell. An imari bowl here, a Hockney poster there; I shook my head in wonder. Such a guy. Latin scholar, decorator, bon vivant and past master of the Sowing Seeds of Consternation in One's Subconscious School. Where did he learn this fascinating ritual of busy, busy, busy, "I'll-engage-myself-with-my-surroundings/hygiene/music/reading while-you-ruminate-on-what-I-just-unloaded-on-your-clueless-skull" number? I'd experienced it a hundred times. Subtle variations; minor corrections—same results.

I felt myself wanting to be very Zen. I strove for the comportment of a poached pear. Unruffled, still . . . mellow. On the outside anyway. In my head there was warfare. What the hell was this photo trove of forties male ingenues all about? Who were these people? What were they doing in my mother's house? Why had I never seen it before? And where and what, for God's sake, is Lily Basker's Ladies Hats? I was furious. My mother hasn't known that many people, male or female, in her entire life! And nobody, even the most popular kid in junior high school, has that many "buddies." Friends of my father? My father didn't have any friends. That I knew about.

"Y'all sleeping together, or she split ya up?" Jaston had his head in the door, wiping his hands on a pair of dirty jeans. I stared at him. I'd always felt that people's initial reaction to Jaston must pivot somewhere between Lennie from *Of Mice and Men* and "Gee, you know if he'd just stand up straight, comb his hair, shave, put on some clean clothes and smile this guy might even be considered . . . *presentable*, with a slant toward pleasing." And then he'd open his mouth. There was no editing with Jas. His thought processes were a complete shared experience. I got up from my sprawl in front of the bed and extended an arm. "Hey, Jas, how ya doin'?"

"OK. That your Dodge van out there?"

Chris set down the Bose minireceiver he was trying to wire. "It's my uncle's. How are you, Jaston?"

"OK. What ya think he'd take for it?"

Chris smiled. "Well, I don't think he wants to sell it."

"Oh." Jaston shifted his weight. "Y'all sleeping together then?"

I smiled. How exactly did this big bear of lumbering male indelicacy come to reside in *our* family? Mother, Laine and I were as fastidious as nuns on a Lenten fast. We were anal about everything from toothpaste caps to total hair domination. Jaston resembled something blown in on a twister from a panhandle feed lot. The man was sloppy. A *big,* sloppy man. I'd seen children gawk at him at the grocery store as he'd toss bag after bag of frozen chicken wings, Tater Tots and flank steaks into his wire cart. While I could debate for ten minutes over whether or not the single package of Pepperidge Farm cherry turnovers might possibly blow my weekly calorie intake, Jaston would have stashed six one-gallon drums of "mellorine" ice cream (*mellorine!,* not even *real* ice cream) and emptied half the chips and pretzels aisle. Where did this appetite, if that's what you can call it, come from? It was like trying to flood the Great Rift Valley. Short of some Biblical event, it simply wasn't happening. He ate like a maniac in high school, too, but he also played varsity tackle, became captain of the wrestling team and did the shot put. By any logic, he should have surpassed the girth of a small drilling platform today. Oddly, he was large, no question about it, but fat he wasn't. Just . . . profuse.

I looked at Chris, who was managing to swallow a grin. "Uh . . . actually, yes. We are sleeping together, Jas."

"Mom know about it?"

I laughed. "Am I supposed to get approval?"

Jaston shrugged and pulled a wood match and a small knife out of his pocket. He began whittling a toothpick. "I dunno. Y'all didn't sleep together last time you were here."

Actually we did, we just kept separate bedrooms out of my unliberated sense of Baptist decorum. "So. Mom's looking better than I expected. I was afraid she might be in bed or something."

"She don't sleep. I drive by coupla times a night, and she's always got her bedroom light on."

"Don't you come in . . . to see if she's all right?"

Jaston shook his head. "Naw . . . I wouldn't know what to do."

I looked at Jaston calmly. "You say, 'Hello, Mom—everything all right?'" Jaston continued whittling on his match silently. I'd been down this road many times. It was hopeless. Weld cattle pens, build a windmill, mow your lawn, castrate a cat—no problem. Ask Jaston to contemplate any activity orbiting emotional accountability—zip. He became comatose.

"I found this yesterday down at the creek in back of old lady

Byers's." Jaston produced a piece of rock from his pocket. He handed it to Chris, who politely inspected it. "Old lady Byers" was Gladys Byers, an odd, cantankerous old woman who had lived next door to us and died when I was still young. The weird thing was she'd made Mother the executor of her estate, or somehow Mother had ended up paying the taxes on her house and property . . . or something like that. It was all strange, and as things usually went down in our family—deeply vague.

"Wow," was about the best Chris could come up with after much turning and rubbing of the weighty pebble.

"You know what it is?" Jaston asked.

Chris peered from beneath lowered eyebrows, grinning. "I know this is one of those trick questions, but I'll bite—a rock?"

Jaston threw back his head and snorted. A tiny string of snot flew out his nose and was immediately inhaled. It was an interesting laugh—guileless, affable . . . visual. " 'Course it's a rock. Heh-heh. What kind of rock, that's the question?" Chris and I looked at each other. By now we were both enjoying Jaston's little show-and-tell.

I examined the dull-looking stone. "Well, it doesn't look like flint. Maybe it's some kind of . . . carving?"

Jaston cackled even louder. "Y'all been living in Yankee-Land too long. Don't you know what used to be back of Miz Byers's?" I confessed, not a clue. *The oldest gristmill in the county!*" Jaston nearly jumped out of his shoes upon revealing this astonishing piece of news. Chris and I nodded silently, waiting for the denouement. "It was built in 1880 . . . some old German immigrant . . . everybody forgot it was there." Jaston was red-faced and wheezing in gusty snorts. For all his animation you would have thought he was describing the discovery of the *Titanic.* "Guess where I found this rock?"

Chris answered immediately. "In back of old lady Byers's!"

Jaston narrowed his gaze as if enduring a strong odor. "I already told you that, smart-ass. *Where?*"

"Where the gristmill was, for God's sake." Already the anecdote was fumbling its grip. "So what about the rock, Jas?" I groaned.

"Can't ya'll see—it's a piece of the old grinding wheel." Chris held the rock up to the light as if some previously undetected facet might magically appear. "That means the rest of it's probably still buried down there in the mud. Hell, there's no telling what's in that big ole pile of crap."

"Boy, that's great. What a find. I better see if Mom needs help with supper." I started to leave the room.

Jaston put his hand on my shoulder. "It's done—spaghetti. Clu, I need a favor." Check.

I turned, exhausted. "What?"

"Can I borrow a hundred dollars?"

"No."

"I can pay you back in two weeks."

"No."

"I've got to have it by tomorrow, or I can't rent the Caterpillar."

"What? No—I don't want to know. I don't have any money."

"What's a Cater . . . ?" Chris asked innocently. I thought, just for the tiniest second, there might be a window of opportunity where I could leap across the room and stuff a small pillow into Chris's mouth. Wrong.

". . . pillar?" Jaston eagerly answered, turning his gaze on fresh meat. "It's this big tractor with a blade on front, but it dudn't have wheels, it's kinda like an army tank. See, there's this steel band that runs on a track . . ."

Chris interrupted, "I gotcha."

"Right . . . so all I need's a hundred dollars to give Fred Menger and he'll let me have the 'Cat' for twenty-four hours. I don't even have to buy diesel!"

"Sounds reasonable." Chris nodded thoughtfully.

A toothache sounds reasonable. Open-heart surgery—very reasonable. Giving money to Jaston made about as much sense as soaking dollar bills in kerosene and drying them over a roaring campfire. They ain't never comin' back.

"Why does this remind me of the time I loaned you seventy-five dollars to plant jojoba seeds in the backyard? We were going to make millions on jojoba oil, remember?"

Jaston stared at Chris sadly. "It never rained."

"And then there was the time Mother, Laine and I each gave you a hundred dollars on your birthday so you could get a really good suit. You know what he did with the money? He bought six goats and kept them in our basement for a year! *Goats!*"

Jaston bristled. "Hey, I made money on those goats, and you know it."

I was livid. "Jaston! It was bad enough having clothes that smelled like Chihuahua shit all the time—*feta cheese* trumpeting our every arrival was a complete overstatement!"

"Damn, Clu, don't you want to even know what's buried out at Miz Byers's?"

"No! I don't care! I'm not giving you any money, and neither is Chris."

"I'd like to know what's out there." Chris stared back at me defiantly. There's a peculiarly isolating sense of loss that comes from the action of one's older brother and one's gay lover teaming up to "bust your balls." I felt suddenly diminished.

"Fine. Peace and love. Do what you want—I'm out of it." I turned and started to exit, my knees feeling unexpectedly spongy.

Chris cleared his throat. "Clu, if it's not asking too much—I'm gonna need the fifty dollars you borrowed in Knoxville for the motel. I mean, only if you've got it."

Shoot that poison arrow. With a surprising burst of energy I whirled around and began savagely ripping through my wallet. Pacino couldn't have portrayed wounded disgust with greater conviction. I was hoping to see tears of remorse in their eyes. I was hoping to see them choke with shame at their overt harassment of me. I was really hoping I didn't have fifty dollars. Damn. Two twenties and a ten, right there. I folded and refolded the bills into a hot little wad of spite and jammed the burning lump into Chris's pants pocket.

"There. Are we even? Great. Go out and dig up the town; it'll be swell. Fantastic. Can't wait." With that, I turned and attempted to exit one final time. I reached the door, paused long enough to affect momentary contrition, then hissed over my shoulder, *"As a dog returneth to his vomit, so a fool returneth to his folly—Proverbs."* My God! The ability to snatch the right pearl from deep within the recesses of an overtaxed mind—at exactly the right moment. It was a never-ending comfort to me.

Chris didn't miss a beat. *"Consistency is the last refuge of the un-imaginative*—Oscar Wilde.*"* I glared at him with fierce indignation.

"What the shit are y'all talkin' about?" Jaston's upper lip curled in a perfect, sulking snarl. This last feeble attempt at brilliance had completely severed the fan blades from the windmills of his mind.

I shuddered at them both and exited sideways, revulsion secreting from every pore. Let 'em have their fun. Who gives a shit? I'm not going to control this one. Actors/directors/hand models don't need this kind of stress in their lives. I'm a lotus, a jade ring, a glass of chardonnay by the sea. I'm as undisturbed as a Franciscan's lunch. I'm pacifistic, nonpartisan. I'm Switzerland.

I hummed Roberta Flack as I glided down Mother's back hallway, a dream of benevolent assurance. I marveled at my growth. No longer the whiny, angry child who suffered at every family infrac-tion. Let it go! This time it would be different. I would be the adult this interval. They couldn't get to me. I wouldn't let them. I had ma-tured. Really.

I was nearly to the kitchen by the time I realized I was walking in dog vomit. Great, putrid pools of greasy Ken-L Ration. Bessie Smith and her enormous daughter, Delphinium, were staring up at me from a darkened corner, daring me to have a hissy fit. Puke on linoleum is definitely one of the world's great friction eliminators. Remarkable. Like a thrilling new theme-park ride I sailed aloft with the grace and symmetry of a propelled rocket. The beauty of my all-too-brief flight was accentuated by the compelling finale of my six-foot slide to the finish line—a blur of writhing arms and legs pummeling furiously against a sea of Chihauhua lubricant. In spite of my revulsion and horror I remained as cool as lemon pie. Lying there on the floor, in my oasis of detached reflection, I felt around carefully for misplaced bones, in particular fur-covered Chihuahua bones that could be yanked quickly and snapped with satanic bliss.

Mother stuck her head out of the kitchen door and looked at me as if I'd just stepped out of a spaceship. "Clu Lynn, what are you doing?"

I pulled myself up on one elbow, carefully avoiding dragging the last three inches of unsoiled sleeve in the stink. "Well, let's see . . . what am I doing? . . . I read somewhere dog throw up is just the thing for that 'acid wash' jean look. I thought I'd lie down here and see what kind of interesting patterns turn up."

I could have said the word "cocksucker" on national TV and Mother's face wouldn't have looked any more anguished. Gathering herself, she asked calmly, "Is it Delphinium, did she get sick?" I nodded. Mother looked stricken again. "Oh laws. She's about to throw another litter any day now. Poor thing's really suffered this time."

Finally able to stand, I leaned against the wall trying unsuccessfully not to breathe. "Mother—unless Delphinium just ate her brood, the only thing she's 'about to throw' already happened."

Mother turned back toward the kitchen. "I'll get a mop and some Pine-Sol. You step out of your shirt and trousers and I'll throw 'em in the wash." Reluctant to face the grubby infidels occupying the bedroom, I slowly began peeling the wretched garments from my mashed and bruised body. It occurred to me that my life until this very moment had been a series of unsuccessful attempts to avoid confrontation with elimination—animal, human, spiritual. No matter how careful I was to sidestep or soar above the issue, shit was the recurrent underpinning of my existence! A mini nervous breakdown seemed like a golden opportunity all of a sudden.

Shivering in my civvies, I handed the bundle of rankness to Mother, who promptly tossed me a pair of Jaston's old cutoff jeans she was saving in her rag pile. "They'll be a little big, but we're not New York. No one'll care." Stepping into the forty-four waist shorts was a little like balancing a limp hula-hoop. I tied a severed extension cord through the belt loops. Shirtless, shoeless, wholly defeated and swathed in a voluminous denim diaper, the insane likelihood that I might hurl myself at my mother's feet and scream for a Zwieback toast seemed grotesquely looming.

"I ran into Miss Oveta the other day when I was getting gas. She told me to be sure and have you call her. She wants to start a little theater here in Grit." I must've groaned a bit too loudly. Mother turned to look at me with a stern expression.

"Mom, put the mop down. I'll do that." I reached behind her, taking the mop and pail. "You don't need to be doing this kind of thing. That's why I'm here."

Mother sat glumly on a chipped, yellow step stool by the oven. "I'm used to taking care of myself."

I swished around briefly in the piney-puke, then continued scouring the hallway. "Well . . . I realize all that . . . and I know how hard this is . . . for everyone . . . but Chris and I came back to help . . . and that's . . . the game plan." Task completed, I marched toward the sink to pour out the bilge.

Mother stared at me with one of her wide-eyed, semicontentious expressions. "Are you going to call Miss Oveta, or not?"

Staring intently at the swirling barf specks streaking toward obscurity, I answered trancelike, "Now why am I supposed to call Miss Oveta?"

"She's opening a little theater here in Grit. She wants to talk to you."

"Well . . . Mom . . . I don't think I have much to offer Miss Oveta . . ."

"You're an actor in New York, aren't you?"

"Yes, but . . ."

"She needs help. You're here to help, right?"

"Yes, here to help *you.*"

At that, Mother stood holding her right elbow tight against her waist. She walked to the refrigerator, pulled out a head of iceberg lettuce and began chopping. "Clu, I'm not ungrateful, and I am glad you're here . . . 'to help,' but I don't know what you're going to do with yourself all day, every day. I'm not an invalid . . . yet."

"Well, of course you're not an invalid, and you're not going to be one. You just don't have to run yourself ragged doing for everybody. You need to take care of you for a change."

Mother scooped up a pile of lettuce and dropped it in a large, pink plastic bowl. She answered quietly, "What I need to do is exactly what I've been doing—make peace with my savior Jesus Christ and get ready to move on."

It was such a strange declaration that it left me momentarily mute. This was very un-mother speaking. This from the redheaded woman who met me after grade school in bright Mexican ponchos and stretch turquoise capri pants. This from the woman who made me dance the Mashed Potato with her. The only woman in South Texas to subscribe to French *Realities* magazine, who took me to my first play, drank *rosé* and listened to Johnny Mathis when she was feeling sentimental. Of course we went to church like nearly everyone else in Grit, but we were not *Church-people*. *Church-people* were judgmental, unworldly, grim—pharisees. *Church-people* had mothers with weird hair and attitude. Our mother let us play Twister on Sunday nights and served canned potato sticks and leftover roast beef and onion sandwiches. We got to watch Black and Jewish entertainers on Ed Sullivan while all the "saints" in town were strapped into their wooden pews for evening services. (Mother felt three hours of Sunday school and worship services on the seventh day were enough religion for anybody.)

"I didn't know you were planning on leaving us so soon." I tried to make it sound humorous, light. It didn't.

"I'm not going one minute before I'm supposed to, that's for sure. None of us gonna live forever. Who wants to live forever? I'll be ready to go when the time comes, though." Señor Murphy entered the kitchen dragging his afflicted frame, followed by two bitches I hadn't seen before. The females were both wearing tiny pink T-shirts around their middles, one with the word "Chica" embroidered on it, the other "Pistola." Together the three of them sniffed each other's rears in a round robin of information gathering. "Look at Señor," Mother observed. "Old as he is, worn out as he is, still acting like he's got business to do. But that's what it's about—live till you die. And accept Jesus Christ as your personal savior."

Señor Murphy concluded his scent inquiry with a bored yawn and fell exhausted at Mother's feet. The jilted *novias* looked up with worried, wrinkled brows. I had to laugh. "Sorry, girls, looks like your 'personal savior's' having an off-day." Momentarily thwarted, they ran to a corner of the room and proceeded to hump each other instead.

Mother stiffened at the sink, pretending not to hear my last remark. She suddenly turned toward me, beaming. "Why don't you and Chris come with me to the revival next week?"

"Revival?"

"It's the most wonderful thing! Wonderful people, good people. Why don't you come?"

"Oh, Mother . . ."

"I know what you're thinking, 'That's not for me. They're all hypocrites and backsliders,' and some of them are. That's why they're there. To grow! Learn! Transform! And to accept Jesus Christ as their personal savior!" Mother's face was rosy with fervent conviction. She started to say something further, then stopped. Her eyes grew large and motionless as she pressed her fingertips to her throat, seemingly transfixed by some far-off event. She tried to speak again, then suddenly she bent over and began hacking in the most gruesome, choking bark I'd ever heard. Where was this coming from? Who was capable of a sound like that? It scared the bejesus out of me. I helped her into a nearby chair and shakily began rubbing her back as she buried her face in a cup towel, continuing to cough violently. How fragile she was! Her shoulder blades stuck out like tent posts, her arms not big around as juice glasses.

And suddenly, here we were. Me and Mom, in the kitchen, fending off the impending two topics mothers and sons steadfastly avoid discussing like the plague—death and sex. It would get emotional, there was no dodging it. Perhaps the primary reason I hadn't wanted to return home was to avoid this preordained role of mine as the reactive child. I was the feeler, the emotional one, the empathic/tender rube. Jaston was cataleptic and Laine was too hard-nosed. If I wasn't constantly vigilant, I'd catch myself welling up at the sight of first graders holding hands crossing the street. At my age it was downright icky. Insurance commercials, Hallmark cards, news articles on the ebola virus—whatever the pretext, if there was a tear to be wrenched, I could produce one in a New York minute. Twitching nose, wavering voice, sagging mouth, pink eyes—I became an endless Sally Field loop from the funeral scene in *Steel Magnolias*. Loathsome. How many movies had I sat through biting a hole in my tongue to keep from throwing myself on the floor and wailing like a Middle Eastern widow? I was a puddle of spent nerves after viewing *E.T., The Color Purple* and *Schindler's List*. As Chris dryly noted, "You know, you're really the only market research staff Stephen

Spielberg needs." I was the *crème brûlée* of personality orders; crusty, burnt shell outside—massive gooey pudding skulking below.

"Mother . . . do you need your medicine?" She continued to strangle, now panting in little yelps. The bandages on her shoulders heaved and shuddered like useless armor. "It's OK, Mom, it's all right . . . tell me what to do?"

Mother shook her head and gasped, "W . . . wh . . . water."

I ran to the sink, trembling. Don't die! Not here, not on the kitchen floor, not on the day I get home! I handed Mother the glass and she swallowed a few, tiny sips. Why must life be so exasperatingly cyclical! Birth, no teeth, Pampers, steak, intercourse—followed by soup, Pampers, no teeth . . . death. And the lesson is? Surely, one would think, all the time spent in "no teeth/Pampers" befuddlement might be more effectively utilized if we could just proceed directly to "rib eye" somehow. The actual glory of getting old escapes me, except that for a precious few it somehow becomes "illuminating." Everybody else seems to get "harrowing."

Mother set the glass on the table, straightened her back as best she could and took a long, quivering breath. Wasn't this the same woman who only yesterday was bringing me tomato soup and grilled cheese sandwiches when I'd faked some dreaded illness at school? Now I was the attendant on patrol and our routine was wrongly reversed. My duty, it was becoming evident, was somehow to witness her death in slow-motion bursts of rebuking the inevitable. And this, we are told, will make us all better people in the end. And again, the lesson is?

Her eyes were calm now, the dread momentarily vanished. She glanced at me, tears of release sliding down the corners of her nose. "That wasn't so bad, no blood this time." I must've appeared wholly decimated. Mother reached out and patted my hand. "Don't worry 'bout it . . . not near as awful as they were."

I sat, slowly bringing my own heartbeat back to normal. This was the not awful part? What am I going to do when she tears her stitches out from one of these attacks? What if she blacks out? Has a seizure? Jesus—what if her wig falls off? I'm not ready.

"Mother . . . I think maybe . . . you know . . . that was kinda scary for me."

"How do you think I feel?"

"I just . . . I'm not sure I know what to do when this happens . . . maybe you really do need a nurse or . . ."

"Yes," she wiped her mouth with the towel, "a nurse would be wonderful. I'll just send the maid down to the hospital to get us one. Two would be better, they can keep themselves company while I paint." Mother was almost grinning at me now, wiping her eyes. She took a few more sips of water then stood slowly. "I can't afford a nurse, can you? I don't need a nurse. All I want is my children nearby while I complete this—for some reason—extended bow of departure."

"Bow of depart . . . Mother, we're not exactly talking the closing night of *Hello, Dolly* here."

She glared at me. "I'm tired! How long does a person have to go on with their body in constant mutiny?"

"Sorry . . . I realize that, I just want . . ."

Mother threw up her hands, "Stop wanting. Don't . . . want . . . anything."

I looked at her helplessly. Apparently I'd been away so long I had a new mother, or rather a different one. Or rather, someone had emerged that was new and different and beyond my usual expectations. None of this sounded encouraging. Enigmas aren't meant to be consoling.

"I want you to meet Brother Ramirez."

"What?"

"Brother Ramirez. He's the revival pastor, wonderful man. I want you and Chris . . ."

"Ramirez? I don't remember any Ramirez at First Baptist. Is he new?"

"I don't got to First Baptist anymore. They're all a bunch of hypocrites."

"Mother!" I stood up so quickly I hit the table, knocking her glass over. "What do you mean you don't go to First Baptist? We've always gone to the First Baptist Church. Granny and Grandad, Aunt Madge and Uncle Robert, all the cousins, everybody . . ."

"I didn't realize you were such a devoted follower."

"Well, I . . ."

"What was the name of *your* Baptist church in New York?"

"I didn't go to one."

Mother nodded thoughtfully. Faltering, I shot back, "I did listen to the African-Baptist choirs from Harlem on the radio Sunday mornings. Mother, you can't just change church affiliations in a small town like this, people will . . ."

"What—talk? Spread rumors? Shun you?" She smiled serenely, then rose and began slicing salad tomatoes. "You've been away a long time, Clu. Things change." If she'd just announced she was off to India to study with the Dalai Lama, I wouldn't have been more astounded. Nice Christian ladies don't quit the church. Even if they do have problems with it.

"It's not as if I've quit the church or anything," Mother finally said, shaking a jar of Italian dressing. "I've just changed affiliations, that's all."

Mesmerized, I asked calmly, "What's the name of your new . . . church?"

She pronounced each vowel with meticulous care. *"Tim-Plo Oo-knee-verse-owl day Los Hair-monos eee Hair-manas del Amor de Dee-os."* Do you know what it means?"

Mouth open, I forced my head left to right.

"The Universal Temple of the Brothers and Sisters of the Love of God." Just a bunch of ordinary people looking for a little assurance—that's all there is to it."

"Uh-huh."

"Mm-hmm."

"And, wh . . . where's the building?"

"Don't have one yet. Brother Ramirez bought an old circus tent and set it up next to the Lions park on the river. It's nice."

"But . . . your friends? All the ladies from the church?"

"Julia Blalock goes with me. Miss Oveta came once. The rest of 'em can go eat a dirt sandwich."

"Mother!"

"*Two* dirt sandwiches. Let me offer a little motherly advice—if you haven't learned to winnow the wheat from the chaff by my age you're a 'Lost-Lucy.' Will you come?"

I blinked a couple of times. "Mom . . . I don't know what to say. I guess I'm just a little . . . surprised. What happened?"

"Nothing happened! Nothing at all. Nothing in the forty years I went to that church as a newlywed, as a young mother with three children, as a divorced wife, as a senior citizen . . . and you know how I *hate* that phrase . . . never once did *anything happen!* Never did I feel the hand of God, the spirit of redemption, the power of prayer—the true meaning of faith revealed to me in any way, shape or form. As if baking brownies, singing in the choir and making sure there were gladiolus on the altar every Sunday was some form of *enlightenment.*"

Mother stared at me fiercely. The good "Christians" of Grit had made a heathen out of Bettie Jean Latimore. She'd become a born-again—*hermana.* I shook my head. "Mom, I think it's . . . great you've found your . . . assurance. Really. I'm just, you know, I'm just taking it all in here."

"So you and Chris'll come next Monday night?"

"Why do you want Chris to come? He's Catholic."

"Everyone needs to hear Brother Ramirez's message. Everyone."

"What message?"

"Christ died for your sins!"

I stood up, ready to leave. This was way too much information being proffered at one sitting. I was feeling overwhelmingly nonproselytizable. "Yes, ma'am, I heard it all in the church nursery when I was four. Got it."

Mother touched my shoulder as I started to pass. "He died for *all* our sins."

I stopped and squinted at her. "All of them, Mom? Even fudging on taxes and addiction to *The Rikki Lake Show?*"

She appeared stumped for a second, then reached deep into her trunk of stoic expressions and pulled out her "smart-mouthed-child-just-said-something-common-or-rude-and-I'll-radiate-this-mask-of-saintly-comportment-till-he-crumples-into-a-pool-of-stinking-shame-at-his-spiteful-display-of-repellent-behavior" look.

"Sorry."

She smiled. "Seven-thirty, Monday night. The service is on 'Floundering Flocks and the Jesus Emancipation from Worldly Iniquity.'"

I groaned. "Oh, for God's sake."

"What?"

"Mom . . . it sounds like bad *Elmer Gantry*. I don't want to go somewhere they're going to make me feel wretched about being alive."

Mother sucked in her cheeks—the entire weight of the universe was attempting to pull her down, down, down into a black hole of blasphemous, contemptuous, sinning children. "It's all just 'do your own thing' with you kids today . . ."

"Now I'm a kid?"

"'Anything goes,' 'Live for the moment'—not a care in the world about your soul, your spiritual well-being . . ."

"How do you know what the condition of my spiritual well-being is? Did He give an interview when I wasn't around?"

". . . totally disregarding the price of eternal damnation for living a life absorbed in scriptural abomination!"

"Excuse me?" Check. Hello. Cards on the table. Now—*all* our sins were present and accounted for.

"Uh . . . Mom, what are we talking about here?"

Mother snagged a paper towel and blew her nose. "I'm gonna go lie down for a bit. I'm getting one of my ringing spells."

"Fine, I'll go sit with you and we can talk while you're resting."

"Oh, Clu, I'm not ready for this right now . . ."

"Not ready for what? Are we having a 'discussion'? Something to do with me, my eternal salvation?"

Mother, suddenly energized, held up her right hand, thumb jabbing a curled index finger. "I am not a judging person, Clu. You know that. I have 'opinions' like everybody else, but I do not evaluate. That's the work of God. I only know what's right and wrong for me, and I know what the Bible says and I will not tailor my convictions to facilitate this season's prevailing inclinations!"

Whew. Funny how eight years can seem like yesterday when you're having parent "discussions."

"I have a favor to ask—can we just go ahead and say it?"

"Say what?"

"The 'G' word?"

"What are you talking about?"

"'Gay'—as in son, as in son's lover—as in *my* life, *my* salvation—*my* conviction!"

Mother looked grief-stricken. She mustered up her most reliable expression when backed into the defense mode—her "the-child-will-do-and-say-absolutely-anything-to-get-attention" look. "It's always about being gay. Everything's seen through the 'gay-lens' for you. There are other beliefs in the world. Don't ask the world to pull your train, Clu—sometimes it's enough just not to get run over." She pressed the paper towel to her lips and forced back a cough. Eyes watering, she continued in a whisper, "I'm sorry, I didn't want to have this talk right now. I really didn't. I'm very glad you and Chris are here and thankful for all your help. Let's not argue." She then turned and walked unsteadily toward the back bedroom, fingertips lightly brushing the walls as she balanced herself.

I sat at the kitchen table flipping one of her brown Melmac dinner plates with my thumb. Up-down, up-down. *Thump, thump, thump.* The urge to break something was palpable. Of course, Melmac couldn't be nicked with a jackhammer. Mother wasn't the reckless type; with three growing children, stalwart china was mandatory in her day. Covered upholstery, synthetic clothes, dinner in a box—anything to free oneself from the manacles of maintenance, effort or expense. (It was a severely frustrating environment for a burgeoning drama queen to thrive in. Weaned on a steady after-school diet of old Doris Day, Three Stooges and Abbott and Costello movies, I acquired an early, abiding faith in the MGM school of therapy—when anxious, *break something*. If nothing else, it looked commanding.)

Like swallows to Capistrano; like roaches to a departing banana boat—angst swarmed about my head with an appalling intensity. Everywhere I went in life I was a reasonably adult, reasonably happy, reasonably adjusted individual. I was a gay man who was reasonable. Until I went home. Home is the acid test for belief systems. Mothers were put on this planet to make certain we don't trust our illusions too deeply. We can be grateful for that, even thankful, but rarely are we ever pleased by such knowledge. Why was it important for me to have my mother's support, her fealty? (Did I support her newfound religious fervor?) A better question was, why is it important not to have a mother who believes that one's life was scriptural abomination? (Do the parents of adulterers get asked these question? Do the parents of pork eaters get asked these questions?) If one can relate to the idea that the belief system of every gay person is a statement of faith *in lieu of support*—then, at the very least, acceptance by one's family must be one way of God saying—*She believes too!*

So, yes, let's talk about *support*. I "came out" my sophomore year in college—if you can call it that. Why does saying one "came out" always sound like you served cake and ice cream and everyone wore paper hats? There was no "thing" to it at all—no gathering, no presents, no congratulations, no people even—no "thing" at all. It was probably one of the loneliest moments of my life. One simply assessed the reality of the situation—"a life as a lie" or "a life facing one's own distinct actuality." Again, there never was a "choice." And when I realized what had to be done, I quietly said good-bye to *all that*. Good-bye to the imaginary pretty lady I'd grown up thinking would always be beside me at social functions and family events. Good-bye to the adorable children who resembled me in the most interesting ways. Good-bye to teaching a son how to tie a tie, a daughter how to roller-blade. Good-bye to casual social acceptance. Good-bye to particular "friends." Good-bye to organized religion. Good-bye to a very specific, very narrow American Dream. Good-bye to safe. And, oh yes—good-bye to being president. (For now.)

"Coming out" to Bettie Jean, however, was something akin to shoving an ox through a rathole. It had to be done . . . prudently. There were stages and levels, a lot of thrusting and pausing, fuming and cursing. Sometimes, when it appeared the entire beast was finally through the opening, a leg would wind up getting stuck again. It was exhausting work, for both us. And when it was at last accomplished without anyone dying, the "Beast" grouchily declared she didn't care so much for *this* new room either. Tough. You can't put the gravy back in the chicken after it's fried. Mother moped as long as she thought it befitting, then finally gave up the ghost. For her it was like having diabetes. You can live with it, but it's not the way it should've been.

When I told her once during one of our "lively" exchanges that I'd be glad to take a "straight pill" if I could find just one happy heterosexual couple, she gasped and put a hand to her mouth as if I'd suddenly whacked her with a dead tuna. Where are they, I want to know? I've met lots of *assuaged* straight couples, I've even known some *upbeat, assuaged* straight couples. All right, *upbeat, assuaged* and *gratified* even—but *happy*? Truly, deeply down to your corn pads, *joyous*? Umm, no. I can honestly be just as assuaged, upbeat and gratified being a gay man. In fact—it seems to work a little better for me.

Why is it so many people are convinced there's nothing's wrong with the cocoon of convenience they so diligently and obviously weave for themselves? Because everyone thought the world was flat for a jillion years didn't make it any less round. There have, and always will be, those who are bound and determined to convince you there is only one road to Mecca. Terrific, you just stay on your interstate and I'll take the scenic route. And guess what—we'll *all* get to the Holiday Inn eventually.

Laine and Jaston, when apprised of my "leanings" reacted customarily. (And just why is it heterosexuals don't have to declare *their leanings*. How 'bout a little equality here—"Uh yeah, I'm mostly straight, but will wear drag during holidays." "OK, like I'm 100 percent het but I do require a dominatrix to make me hold my poo-poo and eat cigarette butts once a week." Etc., etc.? Maybe we should have National Leanings Day. *Everyone* required to spread their cards on the table once a year. End all the confusion, frustration and misgivings once and for all. Why should only gays be allowed the *fabulous* emancipation of "coming out?") Basically, Laine thought I was just trying to get attention, or so she said. "You just want to be different. You think you're special, and you want everyone to believe you're some kind of *artist* or something. Well you're not. You're just doing this to get back at Mother and me." Check. Jaston just looked at me oddly and asked if I fantasized about Donny Osmond when I masturbated. (Actually, Marie's the one I'm *obsessed* with.)

Jaston suddenly entered the kitchen holding up two twenties and a ten. He grinned. "Ol' Chris is about the only one around here with any sense. He knows a deal when it knocks him upside the head." He smirked and grabbed a lite beer from the fridge, holding up an extra. "Ya'ont one?" I nodded and Jaston sat, opening both cans. He pushed one my way.

"Hey, don't be pissed. I tried to give him his money back."

"It was hard, wasn't it?"

Jaston sniggered. "Nope! But I'd do it if you asked me to."

"I told you I don't care."

"Good. Where's Mom?"

"She went to lie down."

"Y'all fighting already?"

"No . . . we're just talking."

Jaston took a long sip and belched. "She really hates it when you talk about all that homo stuff."

I stared at him, shaking my head. "Hey Jas, you know what . . . fuck you."

"Whoa! Excuse me. All I meant was she dudn't like discussing the 'gay thing.' Pull your drawers outta your crack. Me, I don't care."

"Great, real proud of you, Jas. You're a credit to your species. What do you and Mom 'discuss'?"

"Lots of stuff. Bush, the economy, sports, dog shit—Rush Limbaugh."

"Mom listens to Rush Limbaugh?"

Jaston nodded. "I tell her what he says every morning. She likes him."

"Do you tell her he's a big, fat, xenophobic, misogynist, racist homophobe?" Jaston looked genuinely hurt. "Hey, I'm fat too. Nobody's perfect. Thanks a lot." A grudge was useless against someone as guileless as Jaston. We clinked beer cans. He peered at me over the rim. "She say anything to ya yet?"

"What?"

"Aw come on man! Don't make me spill the beans."

"What are you talking about?"

"Come on, Clu—what'd she say 'bout it?"

"'It?'" Jaston stared at me with his standard Alfred E. Newman grin. I finally shook my head. "So—are you gonna tell me or am I gonna have to torture it out of you with a Cher imitation?"

Jaston slapped his hand to his head. "Oh God, not that shit

again." In truth, Jaston loved it when I did Cher—holding my beer bottle mike and flinging my head and arms about. Biggest laugh of the year for him. But he was required by the cryptic laws of Texas hetero-masculinity to wrinkle his nose at such campy displays of gender-bending. Not "manly behavior." ("Manly behavior"—as in the testosteronic urge to graft oneself onto a La-Z-Boy, rigidly gripping the remote control soldered on ESPN and insert Budweiser feeding tube until coronary ensues.)

"Giiiip-seees, tramps and fleas, youhearitfromthepeopleinthetown, they call us . . ."

"No, no, NOOO!" Jaston covered his ears and bounced his head on the table. "I'll tell you. Stop!" I hadn't even gotten to the part where I faked pulling the strands of hair out of my mouth. Jaston propped his elbows on the scuffed Formica surface between us, resting his head in his palms. He had that insane light in his eyes that clicked on whenever he got an idea about making money—with someone else's money. He stretched another inch or two, squinted, and whispered with a small, knowing smile, "Mom's getting married again!"

4

A NEED FOR DELIGHT

"**O**h, shit, man! I never had nobody play the same six numbers!" The greasy-haired, pimple-faced kicker standing behind Bubba's Convenience Store register looked as if he might cry. "Can y'all do that?"

"Why not?" Chris retorted. He held up his Texas Lotto card with the six sixes smudged in a row. "Is there some rule against it?"

The kid studied the card, furrowing his angry red brow with such intensity the largest of his forehead zits appeared ready to blow. I stood back a step. He finally spoke. "Wul . . . shit y'all, I guess it's awright. You might just be throwing away your money, that's all."

Chris smiled. "You think so?"

"Yep." The kid dropped the card in the computer slot, rang up the sale and tore off Chris's receipt.

"My brother won seven hundred dollars last summer playing four fives in a row," a large Hispanic woman standing behind me volunteered. "He's in jail now for shooting his girlfriend, but he was real happy at the time."

"Who got the seven hundred dollars?" I asked.

The woman rolled her eyes and snorted, "His first wife, big *vaca*. She got a lawyer to claim back alimony. Bitch." She suddenly laughed, stepping up to the counter. "Hell, he owed me five hundred.

He should've paid family first!" She snapped at the clerk, "Gimme a pack of Vantage and some Midol."

Chris stuffed the lotto receipt in his shirt pocket and sang to himself in pig Latin as we headed out the store, "Ere-way, in-aye, the oney-may!"

"You sure about that?"

"When have I ever been wrong about a . . ." He zipped his mouth shut.

"Hope so." We got back into the van and drove north on Hackberry Street. We were headed for Miss Oveta Canfield's once-beautiful home, situated catty-corner from the Methodist church. When I was a child it was the most impressive home in town. Two-storied, white-columned, manicured lawn, circular drive—a southwestern Tara. The last time I was in Grit I'd driven by and was horrified to see its shabby, now ravaged state. It didn't so much resemble a house as a cancerous pile of wood in terminal withdrawal. I shuddered to think of sweet, pretty Miss Oveta—the town's only piano teacher, our sole "cultural beacon" in a vacuum of destitution, Grit's answer to Brooke Astor—locked away in her upstairs bedroom like a latter-day Miss Havisham, drinking bourbon and tea and getting progressively more gaga as Rachmaninoff spun endlessly on her antique Fisher stereo.

"It's hell getting old in these small towns." I sighed.

"It's hell getting old in Beverly Hills. So?"

"Nothing, just talking to myself."

I could feel Chris staring. "Your Mom's not doing so hot, is she?"

I nipped on a piece of flesh on the inside of my mouth. "I'd say that's unusually precise of you, Chris. Breast cancer probably isn't one of the three or four best reasons to spring for Dom Pérignon." And yes—it was a bit snappish of me.

"Thanks. Your sarcasm has a refreshing, almost nurturing quality to it. What a fool I've been."

Crap. Why does it always come out angry, dumb and wounding? I'm sitting there thinking, minding my own business, gliding down the road of life—one question, one comment, one look—I vent. I anoint with my effusive, irrepressible candor. I spume with veracity, whether they want a bath or not. For some, it slides off like melted fat, for others it sticks in their pores like iodine. (Chris wears lots of iodine—I'm not asking him to do this, you understand. At some point one does make a choice whether to pick up the cross or not.) What an asshole I am. Why get riled with someone for not being able to *read* your mind?

"Sorry. I'm sorry. I'm a jerk. It's . . . hard."

Chris turned to stare out the window. He was gone now, slicing me up in his head, realizing what a fool he'd connected with—remembering the words to "The Impossible Dream," wishing he were in Malaysia or someplace—who knew what he was thinking? He was definitely used to my occasional vinegary flare-ups, but clearly not a fan. Chris was a much cooler customer. It took a long time to read his mind and even longer to ascertain his particular *modus operandi.* Frequently you were as wrong as right. He simply didn't come from an environment where people said the first thing that manifested itself. In fact, in Chris's family you were penalized for not formulating your thoughts first. Careful, structured, methodical reflection was the preferred manner of social interaction. It was discerning and interesting and reflective, but animated it wasn't. I think in some ways he was charmed (at first) by my Southern blabbermouth. He found it amusing that I had an instant opinion poll on everything from politics to paprika. But as the years stretched, he was frequently just as happy when I shut up. It was easier . . . on him.

The way I see it, one descends from a family of talkers or one doesn't. It was the great divide between us—a person living a mostly interior thought process and the other verbalizing every notion as if not to be heard was the greatest offense. Our biggest arguments were usually about whether or not Chris had actually said something to me. Time after time, the same scenario:

Chris: "I already told you that."

Clu: "No you didn't."

Chris: "Yes I did, you weren't listening."

Clu: "Chris, you 'think' you've told me that because you've already had the conversation in your head and somehow that translates as a 'discussion' between us."

Chris: "You don't listen."

Clu: "And you don't communicate!"

Chris: "I communicate fine. You're the only one I have this problem with."

Clu: "I'm the only one who tells you that there is a problem! What were you trying to say?"

Chris: "I already told you."

It wasn't particularly fun, this perennial discord over intercommunication, but I'd learned the hard way to semiread his mind, and he'd learned to filter the gab from the substance, and it worked—mostly. When we were on the upward swing of the relationship pendulum, it was rarely an issue. On the downward dip it could get testy. And where were we today? That's the part I couldn't see on the map. Probably dead center—waiting for earth's pull to jump-start the inertia.

I'd sworn to Jaston to keep Mother's matrimonial plans secret until she made the announcement herself. He'd overheard the whole thing from Miz Wynch, the doctor's widow, yelling over the telephone. She sat at her kitchen window and screeched that she needed to keep her voice down. "The Latimore boy's out back cutting tree limbs, and I don't want him to hear none of this. Bettie Jean Latimore's decided to get married again and you'll never in a million years believe to who . . ." and then her voice got all whispery and hoarse and Jaston couldn't make out what she was saying. Which meant everyone in town by this time knew, except for, of course, her own children, which was entirely routine.

"I think I have an idea about all those pictures in the hat box," Chris suddenly volunteered.

"Yeah?"

"They're pen pals! She wrote a bunch of soldiers and G.I.s during the war. They sent her their pictures."

I shrugged. "Maybe."

"What do you mean, maybe? What else could it be?"

"She was like fourteen or fifteen when the war was over. What is she doing writing all these grown men?"

Chris laughed. "Kiddo, that's how they made love in the forties! Didn't you ever see *Mrs. Miniver*? People pined, they sat in windowsills and sang about apple trees and white cliffs. There was never any actual penetration from 1941 to 1945. I shit you not. There are piles and piles of documentation to back this up."

I put my head against the steering wheel and laughed. "You're insaaaane!"

Chris yelled, "Look out!"

I swerved to miss hitting a cottontail rabbit strolling through downtown Grit like it was Big Bend National Park. "God, you nearly killed Thumper. What's a bunny rabbit doing crossing a busy intersection?" Chris was appalled.

"Probably has rabies." Sure enough, we weren't a block away when I saw an old pickup truck stop in the rearview mirror, a rancher get out with his deer rifle, walk straight up to the bewildered cottontail and blow his brains out. Thank God Chris was fixated on looking ahead for more stray varmints. He missed the whole incident. These things were hard to explain to "foreigners." Growing up in rural Texas, I'd seen worse. Lots.

You could've knocked me over with a stick of bubble gum. Oveta Canfield's house was painted . . . pink. Not just pink, but *real* pink. Woolworth's panties pink. As we drove up the driveway I blinked in amazement. Gone was the forlorn air of an abandoned derelict. The place looked downright *groomed*. The yard was mowed, hedges trimmed, a new roof had been put on, and the house was entirely . . . *pink*.

"Wow. Welcome to Jayne Mansfield-Land. Is there a heart-shaped pool in back?" Chris was ogling the rose gazebo recently added to the front yard. "Hell-low—it's Troy Aikman the gardener." A beefy, blond studlet emerged from the back of the latticework structure and wiped his face with a T-shirt that had been stuffed in the back pocket of his cutoff jeans.

"Yikes." I nearly ran over a lawn sprinkler parked ridiculously close to the drive.

Chris intoned dryly, "Easy, Junior, we can't ride all the rides at once."

"What are you talking . . . I didn't see it, OK?"

He smiled. "Hard to see the forest with those big trees in the way."

"Oh, shut up." I parked the van alongside a small abstract statue of what looked like Don Quixote. Or Buddha. It was hard to tell. What was clear was that we'd moved up the food chain in Texas social circles. If you knew it wasn't a flamingo or a concrete deer—it was a safe bet you were somewhere in the vicinity of a real live (hushed tones) *artistic-type*. (Or at least what passed for artistic types in towns with populations under 5,000 in Texas.) "Troy," the gardener, waved cheerfully, then disappeared behind a clump of oleanders.

"Man-oh-man, has this place ever changed." I gaped in amazement. A small fountain tinkled insistently somewhere off to the side of the house. Wind chimes banged along the front portico like manic percussionists in some Munchkin band. I pressed the doorbell, and it rang out the opening stanza of "La Malagüeña." I glanced at Chris, and it was all we could do to keep from both wetting our pants.

Raymond Otis opened the door, Miss Oveta's brother-in-law, a former county judge. Raymond was the kind of short, bald, Everyman endemic to the South: big belly, bland features, tired demeanor, dead eyes—he was just "there." He had about as much zest as a bowl of hominy.

"Hello, Clu."

"How're you, Mr. Otis? It's been a long time." I stuck out my hand.

"Long time."

"This is my friend, Chris Myles, from New York."

"Hello. Come in." They shook hands, and we both stepped inside. Immediately we were practically knocked down by the smell of . . . rotting fruitcake?

"Potpourri."

"Excuse me?" I said, scratching my nose.

"Oveta's discovered potpourri . . . among other things." With that Mr. Otis turned and exited. "She'll be right down. She's finishing her yoga class."

I braced myself against the stair banister and Chris stumbled into a nearby chair. Yoga class? Where was I?

"Whew, this is intense! How long has the florist been dead?"

Chris's eyes were watering so badly he looked as if he'd been Maced. "Clu, I don't think I can take this."

"Sh-h-h, it'll pass. Mother does this every Christmas and after a day or two you don't even notice anymore."

"A day! I'm not gonna survive the next five minutes."

"Shut up, she'll hear."

Chris covered his nose and nodded toward the door of Mr. Otis's departure, "Who's Mr. Personality?"

"He was married to Miss Oveta's sister, Miss Josephine. She died about twenty years ago, and he moved in over here." Chris arched an eyebrow. I shook my head. "Totally platonic, trust me. Everyone in town's dissected their relationship; there aren't even any bones left. Oldest news since the Bible." Chris looked at me doubtfully. "Look, they're both—depressive types, OK?"

Chris nodded. "No shit."

A door slammed upstairs followed by a loud *thump* and *swoosh*. *Thump, swoosh. Thump, swoosh.* It sounded as if someone were dragging a corpse that wouldn't stop banging against the wall. "Clu! Clu, is that you down there!" Miss Oveta's voice was as tinkly and merry as one of her wind chimes. (An *old* wind chime.)

I stood and called out, "How're you doing, Miss Oveta?"

"Wonderful, wonderful! It's good to hear your voice." Miss Oveta rounded the corner of the upstairs hall and stopped at the top of the stairs. I could hear Chris gasp and mutter under his breath, *"Jacta alea est!"*, which if I'm not mistaken is Latin for "Oh, shit, we're in it now!" Oveta Canfield balanced herself tentatively against the railing, smiled regally and blew a kiss—looking for all the world like the hammered and varnished prow of the S.S. *Drag.*

"Cluuuu, you're all grown-up!" To correctly depict Miss Oveta's getup would necessitate some form of metaphor involving a burning Christmas tree. Or a psychedelic bus with all its lights on. To begin with there was the sequined caftan, no, rhinestones—maybe the whole thing was Mylar. It was alive! Mostly red and green, and for some reason, brown. It shimmered, it swayed, it undulated, it breathed, it fluttered—it was positively possessed. The Rose Bowl Parade never had as many things going on at once. Then there was the jewelry. From her gnarled, arthritic fists to her pale alligator neckline—all the earth's major minerals were represented. She could have been a poster child for a college geology class. Something that looked like a concho belt with gold jar lids hung clear to her pubis. "Dramatic" didn't capture the sensation. "Fantastic" was getting warmer. The wig. It had to have been a wig. Sort of a red, Gibson-girl poof. It was matted and thick with what looked like old face powder. Maybe it just needed a bath. The entire concoction was vaguely squashed, as if someone had just snatched it off to dust the dining room table only seconds before. A small green bow sat defeated to one side—an afterthought?

"Well . . . well . . . well, it's been a long time, hasn't it?" It was the best I could manage from a suddenly paralyzed throat. (My voice bounced off about three notes on that first "well.")

"It certainly has. Tooo long!" Miss Oveta warily began descending the stairs, her shiny chrome cane *thump, thump, thump*ing each step as if it were some ripe watermelon undergoing a state fair competition. "I want you to meet Mr. Jeffrey." Mr. Jeffrey? No sooner had the phrase been uttered than the oddest thing happened. A little man magically appeared from behind Miss Oveta's caftan! Had he been there the whole time?

"So nice to meet you." *Swoosh.* "I've been looking forward to meeting you and your friend." *Swoosh.* Mr. Jeffrey dragged his right leg behind Miss Oveta like it was a pesky dog on a leash. *Swoosh, thump, swoosh, thump, swoosh, thump.* I was afraid to look at Chris. One quiver of his nostril, and I would have shit a brick.

"Th . . . th . . . this is Chris." Face forward, I extended a palm hesitantly in Chris's direction.

"Chris. Is it Chris or Christopher?"

"Chris . . . Myles."

"So nice to meet you. I understand you had a long, tiring drive coming to Texas." Miss Oveta held out a gemstone-crusted wrist, and I swear, from the corner of my eye it looked as if Chris actually kissed it.

"It wasn't so bad. West Virginia's kind of pretty."

"Oh I ah-dooore West Virginia." Mr. Jeffrey sidled up behind

Miss Oveta and cooed, "Friendliest folk in the whole country. *Good* people."

Miss Oveta straightened her listing wig a few degrees. "Mr. Jeffrey's been everywhere. Absolutely everywhere. Do you know any other soul on the planet who's been to Ouagadougou?"

I shook my head. "I can't even pronounce it." Mr. Jeffrey and Miss Oveta had a nice jolly over that one.

"Actually, it's in Africa. Upper Volta. I had a business in Upper Volta once." Mr. Jeffrey suddenly grew silent and stared at the floor. What that business might have been or what led him to Upper Volta in the first place apparently would remain a mystery. Mr. Jeffery showed no signs of further disclosure. Miss Oveta patted his little burgundy velour jacket soothingly and pointed toward the living room.

"Shall we?" Miss Oveta led the way. Chris and I followed, exchanging terse looks of horror and elation. *Swoosh, thump. Swoosh, thump.* At the very least, we were finally face-to-face with some real by-God-Texas-gothic weirdness. I'd been promising Chris ever since we left New York we'd be up to our eyebrows in eccentric behavior. And here we were in the presence of masters. "I guess it all appears a little different since the last time, Clu," Miss Oveta queried.

I took a quick breath, "Uh, it seems more, like, it's more like . . ."

"Rosé?" Mr. Jeffrey interrupted with a grin.

I nodded. "Yes, that's it. You've . . . painted."

"Fiesta Blush, Mr. Jeffrey's own creation. Sherwin-Williams developed it especially for us." Miss Oveta smiled.

Chris leaned forward. "Pink is such an interesting color. I was wondering how you came up with—pink?"

"It's the birth color. It symbolizes Oveta's new lease on life. It was the only choice." Mr. Jeffrey clapped his hands. "Who wants a Mai Tai?"

At eleven in the morning? Cripes. As no one else in the room appeared to be terribly anxious about such an obvious lapse in provincial propriety, I nodded mindlessly. When in Rome. (Oh hell, drink, yes, twenty-four hours a day—but never in front of *others—before dark!* Not in small Baptist towns in Texas.) Mr. Jeffrey clinked and gurgled at the makeshift living-room bar while Miss Oveta ex-pounded. "I'll be eighty-two next November. Can you believe it? I don't feel eighty-two; I don't feel sixty-two. I feel forty-seven. That's how old I was when the late Mr. Canfield died of *pernicious catarrh*. I was alone for such a long time, here in this big old house. I truly think I'd have gone round the bend if Raymond hadn't joined me. But you know Raymond's not, well he's not particularly . . ."

"Social." Mr. Jeffrey dropped ice cubes, one at a time, into a Waring blender.

"Thank you. Raymond's a dear, and he's been very sweet, but we don't share the same *esprit de corps.*"

"That's French for *simpatico,*" blurted Mr. Jeffrey, licking the spoon he'd just twirled around an enormous beaker of alcohol.

Miss Oveta leaned in and whispered, "Mr. Jeffrey speaks three languages. French, Spanish and . . . I forget the third one." I caught Chris's face as a huge smile creased the corners of his mouth. Miss Oveta continued expounding. "Anyway, I had my piano lessons and my trips to the symphony in San Antonio. Every year or so I'd make it up to New York to hear some of the great ones, but somehow—I was losing myself. Somewhere between sixty-five and seventy-eight, I just stopped caring—about my looks, about the house, about my music. I was drifting into a kind of premature dotage." Miss Oveta flung a jingling arm. "Oh, I know the whole town talked about 'poor Oveta, she's gone nuttier than a Baby Ruth!' And in a way, I had. I've always been a weird duck. I have! I've never wanted to be like every-one else. Thank God the late Mr. Canfield invested wisely. At least I could *afford* to be an alien. I mean, if you're going to do anything—do it right!" Miss Oveta beamed as she rubbed a green-mascaraed eye. She idly blazed an emerald trail through her brilliantly rouged cheeks, leaving behind a brown streak that didn't detract in the least from her overall perfection.

Mr. Jeffrey set a silver tray down with four brimming martini glasses and made a toast. "*Drink! For you know not whence you came, nor why: Drink! For you know not why you go, nor where—*The *Rubáiyát* of Omar Khayyám."

Miss Oveta applauded and tittered like a schoolgirl. "Mr. Jeffrey read me the entire *Rubáiyát* last year when we were in Corfu. Marvelous!"

"And . . . um . . . how did you two meet?" Chris asked innocently, taking a sip of the foamy liquid.

Miss Oveta knocked back a healthy quantity of greenish concoction and stared at us wide-eyed. "You don't know?"

We looked at each other and shook our heads. Mr. Jeffrey smiled serenely, sucking on a chip of ice.

"Why, Mr. Jeffrey's . . . my son." The room was instantly still. Even the wind chimes were mute. Mr. Jeffrey must've swallowed his ice. I tried to think of something to say, but my conversational file was unexpectedly nil. I thought I heard Chris murmur, "Oops."

Suddenly Mr. Jeffrey began to wheeze, then hack, then flat out bray with laughter. I watched patiently as his Mai Tai stormed in waves around the rim of the glass, threatening to dump mightily into his lap. Miss Oveta joined in the hilarity, covering her mouth with an aquamarine ring the size of a good cherry tomato. The two of them looked like preschoolers on a first trip to the circus.

"A . . . ah . . . actually," Miss Oveta tried calming herself, "Mr. Jeffrey isn't my real son. I have no children. He's my *adopted* son." More laughter, more gasping for air, more wiping of tears.

Chris tried once again. "So. How did you two find each other?"

Miss Oveta glanced at Mr. Jeffrey, then took his hand into hers with a loving pat. "Alaska, seventeen days—he was my hairdresser on a *Song of Norway* cruise. I never even got to see the aurora borealis."

"That was four years ago. We haven't been a day apart since." Mr. Jeffrey impetuously hoisted Miss Oveta's palm and kissed the gold on her fingers. "We're soul mates."

I set my drink down, smiling gamely. "It's none of my business, obviously, but—why not get married?"

Mr. Jeffrey looked surprised. "But I am married."

Miss Oveta picked an imaginary nit from the center of her goblet and flicked it behind the sofa. After a long sigh she spoke with seasoned patience. "Mr. Jeffrey's married to a Pentecostal minister from Shawnee, Oklahoma. She doesn't embrace spiritual transformation in others."

Mr. Jeffrey stood slowly and walked toward the bar. "Laquita was my big mistake. She's a hard, unforgiving woman. We were both so young, so . . . primitive. She doesn't believe in divorce. The only good to come from that union was our son."

The concept of Mr. Jeffrey being someone's actual father was absurdly transfixing. Chris tapped his shoe against mine. I caught his eye staring at the floor beneath me. A small puddle had developed next to my right foot where I'd been dripping Mai Tai onto Miss Oveta's Oriental rug. I slowly moved my sneaker over the offending blotch, concealing it with what I felt was a masterful dexterity.

"Mr. Jeffrey, would you bring a towel with some club soda. I think we've had a drizzle." Miss Oveta winked at me while fluffing her wig with a few nudges of polished nail extensions. "Happens all the time. Mr. Jeffrey doesn't realize the potency of his liquid wizardry."

I wanted to crawl under the coffee table and expire. In no time Mr. Jeffrey had brought me a new, even larger drink, and was on his hands and knees before me blotting up the mishap. He continued to expound in little red-faced bursts of declaration, "After I got out of the navy in '56 I kind of bummed around the world for a few years. Worked in a hotel in Kenya, danced at the Tropicana in Havana—I got stranded in Thailand one winter and ended up an extra in *The Bridge on the River Kwai*. Remember that scene just before they blew the bridge up? The one with Alec Guiness going bloody 'Princess Margaret' on everyone—I'm standing just to the left of the banana tree. Anyway, that's how I bobbed the old gam here." Mr. Jeffrey slapped his apparently artificial calf. "I fell in a canal in Bangkok one night. Got run over by a floating restaurant. Son of a bitch was longer than a Panhandle summer!" Mr. Jeffrey shook his head at the distant memory. He continued sponging, then all of a sudden stared up at me with fierce conviction. "Tending bar and tending hair has been my salvation—if you can do either you'll never go hungry. Would you believe I'll be sixty-five in January?"

Easily. I didn't say it of course, but Mr. Jeffrey had most assuredly earned the face he'd lived. "Where does your son reside?" I inquired.

Mr. Jeffrey stopped blotting again and glanced up between my knees. "Here. With us."

I think I must've nodded. Chris breathed audibly into his glass.

With some effort Miss Oveta yanked her feet up onto the sofa beside her and grunted, "Do you realize, not two years ago I couldn't even reach to take my own shoes off? I tell you, yoga and colonic irrigations have changed my life."

"And Mai Tais!" Mr. Jeffrey gleefully interjected.

"And Mai Tais!" They clinked their glasses. Far be it from me to ascertain the consummate benefits of alcohol and enemas, but the yoga part was somewhat suspect. The image of Miss Oveta in a full-lotus had an unreal quality about it. Like the Queen Mother bungee jumping.

"Did you both meet Preston when you came in?" Miss Oveta asked.

"Preston?"

"Mr. Jeffrey's son."

"Umm . . ."

"He was out front working in the garden," Mr. Jeffrey smiled.

"That's your son?" Chris sounded genuinely alarmed.

Mr. Jeffrey nodded. "Isn't he something? Oveta and I think he's wasting himself here. He could easily be a soap star."

Judging from all the full-time soap actors I'd known in New York, that likelihood seemed entirely possible. Acting ability was viewed as largely problematic anyway; it got in the way of pecs and abs and sullied the work of the hair gods.

"He does a maaarvelous job with the grounds," Miss Oveta declared. "I let things go for so long around here. Raymond doesn't care much about beauty. Or gardening. Or spending money on charm and grace." Miss Oveta's eyes were brimming with remembrance. "Curious . . . the original notion of just wanting to be accommodating plunges so quickly into complete indifference. A day comes when you just . . . surrender. And you don't care, and you don't mind that you don't care. And you don't care for not minding what everyone else thinks either. Oh, it's a vicious, heinous web that seizes our better selves when melancholy ensues."

After hurriedly dabbing a corner of each eye, Miss Oveta drained her glass and slapped it on the coffee table. "But enough of ourselves! You're probably thinking we're just a couple of inflated old

roués—don't have the sense to put jam on a biscuit." Miss Oveta
blew a kiss to Mr. Jeffrey. With great exertion she stood, wobbling,
her silver cane piercing a fallen sofa cushion. Mr. Jeffrey braced his
bum leg against the back of the couch and steadied her. "Change is
in the wind! Can you smell it?" Miss Oveta loudly proclaimed.
Actually, rotting fruitcake was in the wind, but that was a side issue.
"Mr. Jeffrey and I want to bring *change* to this godforsaken, burnt-
up, half acre of hell-in-Texas." It was music to my ears. "Why can't
decent, cultured people seek their interests right here in Grit? Why
must they travel to Houston or Midland for refinement?"

Why indeed? It was a riddle that had plagued me forever. I felt
contrite for suddenly remembering the words "cultured" and "Grit"
were consummate oxymorons.

"Did you know the Grit Tourism Council says that arts-related
businesses and entertainment events bring in over 26 percent of the
city's gross revenue sales tax?"

I nodded, glassy-eyed, reeling from the awesome notion of a
Tourism Council existing somewhere in Grit.

"What this town needs is a *vision*. Someone to imagine; not as
things are, but as they must be!" Mr. Jeffrey had that crimson glow
on his face again. He was fueled with confidence. Or Mai Tais.
"Oveta and I want to bring a sense of inspiration and magic to these
indifferent, unwitting lives that surround us with their great, anesthetized loss. Where is the wonder? The zest for one transcendent
moment; a need for delight?"

Miss Oveta billowed a caftaned sleeve toward us. "We'd like for
both of you to be a part of our little desire. And that's exactly what
it is—one small wish to enthuse and captivate a world gone blind-
ingly inert."

I glanced at Chris. He peered back at me with an expression of,
"If the *Song of Norway* doesn't dock soon, I'm bailing."

I cleared my throat. "I . . . I really think . . . it sounds . . ." I just
nodded.

Mr. Jeffrey took Miss Oveta's hand. "It's providence, providence
that you both came at the right time, isn't it, Oveta?"

Miss Oveta smiled radiantly, then either fell or lunged toward me.

Possibly both. Seizing my wrist and still clutching Mr. Jeffrey, she somehow managed to right herself and gape at us both with an alarming severity. Zip! A sudden call to worship silently convened. We stood, brooding into each other's eyes, clutching each other like startled monkeys. In a calibrating flash the mood shifted again. The overwhelming notion that we might just all run into the yard and play Crack the Whip pulsated from limb to limb; from neuron to dendrite, sock to brow, molar to mole and back again. It was as if we were each feeding from the same telepathic battery. Somehow (don't ask me how) I knew that *they* knew, that *I* knew—*we all knew something was going on!*

Yes! What?

Maybe we'd go do high kicks. Or open another bottle of Tiger piss. Maybe we'd sit on the floor and lick Tostitos off the coffee table, sing Olivia Newton-John songs, read Immanuel Kant through a prism. It was one of *those* times. And whatever it was affecting us, it was penetrating our feeble brain cells like snow through chicken wire. (During one nanosecond of semidetached observation it occurred to me—Miss Oveta's jewels were seriously heavy.)

Finally, Mr. Jeffrey spoke. He turned to Chris, sounding as chipper as Mickey Rooney on speed. "Well, Mr. Myles, what do you say?" Chris stared at us in disbelief. He was practically out the door.

"Uh . . . um . . . uh . . ." Looking at the three of us wrapped around each other like half-cooked bacon, Chris appeared terrified. He freaked once when I held his hand in Macy's during a vacuum-cleaner demonstration. *Never* the touchy-feely stuff. Maybe he saw this as one of those Texas things; like corn bread in milk or the use of "hihow'reyoudoin'" as a completed conversation among Texas males. It was obvious he wanted no part of our newfound intimacy.

Miss Oveta, hands rigidly squeezing ours, began lumbering toward Chris. Flailing in her tow, we tried to both support and avoid collision as best we could. We resembled a couple of tossed cups thrashing in the wake of the Staten Island Ferry. "Chrrrisss-topher!" Chris looked up with dread. Miss Oveta threw her shoulders back and recited loudly, *"I have neither wit, nor worth, action, nor utterance, nor the power of speech—to stir men's blood; I only speak right on."*

Completely thrown, Chris furrowed his brow in astonishment, then suddenly gasped, "Shakespeare, Marcus Antonius—*Julius Caesar.*"

Miss Oveta squealed and bounced our hands off her chest, "Maarrrvelous! I knew you had it. I could tell when you walked in the door you had *quintessence.* Both of you."

"What?"

"Pith! Spirit! *Resource!*"

"How could you tell?"

"I just decided, that's all. I don't need much to go on with men. They're either 'with' or 'without.' Let's not make a *thing* out of this, shall we."

Chris looked at me miserably. "I think . . . we ought to be going." Right. The only problem was, even if I'd wanted to leave, I'd have needed a couple of linebackers to pry me loose from the mortal vise restraining me. And what if . . . what if there were more Mai Tais in the blender!

"Hi, sorry I'm late." We all turned in unison to see "Troy Aikman" enter the room. He appeared freshly showered and neatly dressed. Wearing chinos and a white T-shirt, you could tell where he had nonchalantly run a comb through his wet hair. Stylist nirvana. Herb Ritts and a complete staff from *Vanity Fair* couldn't have pulled off such effortless *élan.* "I'm Preston. Nice to meet you guys." He strode across the room and firmly shook my suddenly free right hand. Preston smiled with all the sincerity and charm of a fifties movie star. Blinding. Scary. This was male beauty at its chilly apex. (The sort of perfection that doesn't radiate a lot of *gemütlichkeit.)*

"You must be Chris," he said, pointing at me.

"That's Chris." I leaned my head in the opposite direction. "I'm Clu."

"Clu! That's such a great name. I've never met a Clu before." I smiled and began to do my usual schtick about being named after the old TV Western star, Clu Gulager, which was of course a lie. My father simply thought the name had the right sort of clubby/old money/ masculine/ buddy-buddy kind of guy bearing to it. Queers liked it, too. Before I could even get the first sentence out though, Preston was over shaking hands with Chris.

"Hi, nice to meet you." Chris flushed and did his little-boy loopy smile thing that was both endearing and only slightly annoying after eight years of *unfailing* consistency.

"Hi . . . Preston."

"So." Preston turned back to the three of us clustered in our little hand-holding vignette. He grinned (looking just a tad disdainful). "Did we reach a decision?"

I felt like an idiot. Slowly, cautiously I disengaged myself from the eleven-and-a-half-limbed monster. The sudden rush from moments before plunged into god-awful mortification. How depressingly icky to get shit-faced at your grade-school piano teacher's house. At eleven in the morning!

"Preston's arrived at just the right moment. All fresh and vital; the picture of youth and enthusiasm," Miss Oveta trilled. At least her buzz was still sparking. Preston pecked her on the cheek. She swooned adorably. Mr. Jeffrey beamed. (Thankfully, we were spared a smooch on "Daddy's" mug.)

"I think we've got the boys just about convinced." Mr. Jeffrey sighed.

"Great. Who's the director?" Preston, all *fresh* and *vital*, looked at us anxiously. I caught just the faintest whiff of excessive rapacity hovering about the room. Could have been the potpourri.

"Excuse me?" Chris barely got the words out before Miss Oveta pounced.

"Preston's about to beat us to the punch." Miss Oveta turned to Preston, wagging a large topaz. "We've been building the boys up. Courting them, bantering, probing. We want to make sure *everybody's* going to be as pleased as we are."

"Pleased about what?" I was starting to sound whiny. Hell—I was drunk.

"Now sit down, the both of you. Preston, you too. Mr. Jeffrey and I have an announcement to make. . . ."

Dear God, my whole life was passing before me now. Why and how did I always get myself into these dilemmas? From chairing the junior prom decoration committee, to emceeing the Cub Scout talent show (I did Maurice Chevalier in drag at nine), to playing Joseph *five years in a row,* freezing my ass off in "The Living Nativity" on the front lawn of the Baptist church—I'd "participated" my young life away in meaningless, crappy events in order to please some parent or adult or so-called friend so I'd be "liked," "popular" . . . "normal." What a crock. They only despised you with a thread more endurance. You were occasionally useful. Once a fruit, always a fruit. No matter how butch you tried to be—the minute they flashed on your number, you were roadkill.

"... and we've discussed it and debated it and run it round and round in our heads till we're both senseless. Our mutual solution is simply to let you both make the decision for us. Whatever your preference is—that's what we'll do. And we'll produce it right here in Grit. In the new, completely refurbished, Espinosa County Livestock Barn . . ."

No. I won't do it. I hate bad theater! It repels me. I've walked out of more theaters than a union usherette. It gives me enormous serenity to rise silently and exit like a cautionary specter from some boring, wretched, egomaniacal, desperate, arch, stilted, banal, manipulative, grueling, cutesy, pedestrian, grotesque, standard, run-of-the-mill, average theatrical experience. Life is short. There is simply too much bad theater for one mortal to endure. That said, I did enjoy *Driving Miss Daisy*. Oh God, please no, they're not going to ask me to direct *Driving Miss Daisy*.

"... and those are our two choices for the season's opener. Well— do either of you have a preference?" I stared at Miss Oveta as if for the first time. She smiled at me with a touching yearning about the eyes. She had a delicate wisp of white hair sticking out from under her wig; a little arm of authenticity waving in defiance. I thought of my two sweet, humble grandmothers. I thought of Mother. I thought of all the shit these women go through just to make peace in the world. (Not that any of them were pushovers, not by a long shot.) Still, as writer Larry McMurty once noted—Texas is hell on horses and women. My grandmother Saunders, although a strict Baptist disciplinarian, stressed education and the Bible in equal doses. Hers was never a conflict between Creationism and Evolution. Apes and dinosaurs were beside the point. Were you *saved* was her sole criterion.

Grandmother Latimore wasn't quite as worldly. Her Baptist faith was literal and grave. There was no wiggle room for discussion. It was strictly her own interpretation of scripture, as handed down through a series of raving radio preachers and local gospel yay-hoos providing the acid test for Christian culpability. The Baptist Church was their sole support system—it hammered continually against backsliding husbands, unruly children and sinful neighbors. These women had a safe place of their own in small, isolated communities. The Church stood behind their constant vigilance against barbarism and lowlife in general. I could feel very clearly, their *need.*

Miss Oveta was suddenly seized by a nervous twitch, and she swung her cane wildly, knocking a floor lamp over onto Mr. Jeffrey's good leg. "Mother MacCreedy!" Mr. Jeffrey grunted in garbled distress, and hobbled off to a nearby ottoman.

"Uh . . . what were the choices again?"

Mr. Jeffrey, cradling his sore limb, cocked his head at a forty-five-degree angle, and snapped, "She said—we can't make up our minds between doing *Agamemnon* or *Butterflies Are Free!*"

The room was starting to spin.

"Well, I definitely have a preference." Chris stood smiling. All eyes turned as he strode before us and flicked a lock of bangs casually aslant. "I'm just assuming, correct me if I'm wrong—you want us to be involved in the production, right?"

"Right!" Mother and "sons" answered earnestly.

Chris casually drained the rest of his Mai Tai and set the glass down, giving me a quick nod. What the hell was he up to? "Now of course Clu and I have yet to discuss this among ourselves, but naturally, he'd be an excellent choice for director. Or perhaps he's more interested in the performance aspects, whatever. I, however, being something of an academician, would be most intrigued in overseeing the design and universal perspective of the play."

"Yes!" Miss Oveta thrust a jangling wrist heavenward in veneration.

I felt a wave of bile burning in my esophagus.

"I totally hear what you're saying." Preston was up on his feet, smoothing the back of his head with an imaginary brush. "There has to be something . . . *unique* about it all. Something completely fresh and original."

Mr. Jeffrey interrupted. "Exactly. We can't just do the tried and true. People have to want to experience the event as a complete happening."

Happening? What year was this? "Ex . . . excuse me."

"Oh . . . damn. We're out of Mile Highs." Miss Oveta was standing at the blender leaning on her cane and looking completely addled. She began to sway in an arthritic hula. "Anybody else want a . . . My-My?" Mr. Jeffrey was immediately at her side murmuring softly into one of her large turquoise earrings. A terse exchange of words followed; heated, curt—and then over before it began. Startled like targeted quarry, they collected their frazzled noblesse and skulked silently back toward the sofa—Miss Oveta assuming the royal hauteur of one having just been apprised the bloody peasants were at the frigging front gates again. Sitting demurely, she cleared her throat and spoke calmly to Mr. Jeffrey, "Tell Raymond to bring us another bottle of . . . *stuff."* Mr. Jeffrey was pensive for a brief moment then stood and *swooshed* out the room.

Chris and Preston stood next to each other, arms crossed, waiting to see if there'd be an additional scene to the unfolding minidrama. Unexpectedly, Miss Oveta blurted a few incoherent words, then let her chin fall slowly to her chest. Soft snoring followed.

Chris smiled, flipped his bangs once again, and asked brightly, "What would be your participation, Preston?"

"They didn't tell you?"

Chris shook his head. "No."

"Well, I'm an . . . actor."

But of course. Even in Grit. Pathetic. I bust my ass in New York for eight years and at the top of my stride I'm doing a two-minute walk-on with Tony Randall in *Charlie's Aunt.* Go fuck yourself, blondie!

"I mean, I'm not a real actor like Clu here. It's just that I've done a few things, you know, college and stuff, and I really want to learn and grow. It's incredible you guys are here in Grit. Y'all are Big Time—New York, Broadway, *Saturday Night Live!* I want to be involved . . . if you want me."

I wasn't moved. Oh sure, he was gorgeous and plausibly twenty-seven or thereabouts, and so full of himself he probably shit little round mirrors every morning. I had my day in the sun, too. I had been everybody's flavor once upon a time—even if it was for only five minutes. I've felt the radiant heat of a captivated following, the concupiscent sheen of focused desire. Big deal. Every competent beautician in America gets the same glory sooner or later.

When I first arrived in New York I was more or less viewed as the bumpkin with the accent and the scruffy cowboy boots. But I was cute and fresh and "aw shucks" enough to get some serious players to take an interest in me. Being the "new boy" got me an agent, it got me auditions and it definitely got me dinner with older producers and grand pashas in the rag trade. What it didn't get me was sex. I just couldn't seem to get with the program (if there ever was one) of sleeping my way to the top. If I didn't love them or at least seriously *like* them, it just wasn't any good. I'd sooner pick the waiter than the Broadway mogul any day. Dumb me. There were maybe two opportunities with casting of shows that if I'd just played nice-nice and worked it a little—but I was still too small town virtuous to be so obviously deceitful. It bothered me, these guys with no social or ethical boundaries. Not that I was a beacon of rectitude, but it was just so painfully obvious when you saw some handsome twentysomething being squired around town by a forty-eight-year-old, fat, balding, neurotic director. Yes, we all know love is blind. Amazing how it can be downright *eyeless* when there's a lead role involved. Anyway, it was all immaterial after meeting Chris. I found what I'd wanted all along, Broadway be damned!

"You'd make an incredible Aegisthus," Chris gushed.

"Who?"

"Clytemnestra's lover."

"Who?"

"In *Agamemnon*. You've read it, right?"

Preston laughed. "Oh, no . . . I keep meaning to. It's just so, you know . . . *wise*. It was J.J.'s idea to do the Greek thing."

"J.J.?"

"You know . . . Dad."

"Right." Chris's zeal was floundering.

I stood slowly, my head dinging from a relentless fight bell that was striking back behind my ears. *Warning! Warning!* "Well, look, Preston—this is all great, yeah . . . but I personally don't see doing

Greek tragedy or tired dinner theater as one of my burning goals right now. Sorry. If you guys want to play 'dress-up' down at the auction barn, super—count me out."

As expected, Chris looked fatally wounded. "Clu, they're *handing* this to you. Whoever did *that* in New York?"

"Exactly. We're in Grit, Texas, Chris—wouldn't you say there's a slight adjustment in standards?"

"God, Mr. It-All-Ends-West-Of-The-Hudson himself."

My eyes were starting to cross from the headache that had now turned into a brain tumor. "You're wasting your time; I'm not going to do it. No way."

"Just think about it."

"There's nothing to think about. I'm not interested. Can we go?"

A small whimper of dismay issued from Preston's lips. "Um. Uh . . . actually, I did read *Butterflies* and I really, really related to Don, the main character. I went into my room, turned off all the lights and practiced walking around in the dark. It's like . . . I totally got what it must be like to be blind."

I looked at him the way an exhausted tuna fisherman stares at the last catch of the day waiting to be bashed in the head. "But Preston . . . could you do it with the *lights on?*"

Raymond Otis entered the living room carrying a large jug. "Jeffrey said y'all needed some more *colonche.*"

"What?" I turned, squinting.

Chris interrupted. "Thank you, but we have to be going."

"Where's J.J.?" Preston asked.

Mr. Otis shrugged. "In bed. Nap time." Miss Oveta, hitting her mark with laudable precision, suddenly let rip a majestic snort and fell sideways on the sofa. Even with her mouth open, head listing and wig smashed, she remained every inch the Southern aristocrat.

"May I see that bottle?" Mr. Otis handed me the liquid and I strained to read the Aztec-looking writing. *Chal-chi-uht-li-cue.* I removed the cap and sniffed. It was smoky and acrid; caustic as paint stripper. Tiny specks of black and God-knows-what-all were floating in the vaporish swill. "What is this stuff?"

Mr. Otis answered with the bored manner of a Lubbock mortician. "I'm not certain. They tell me it's made with Mexican pey-ote."

"But that's . . . that's . . ." Chris stammered.

"Amazing shit, huh? Three or four of those 'Mile Highs' and you can practically see the entire *Star Wars* trilogy reeling on the side of a boiled egg," Preston snickered. "Seer-i-ous brain lubricant."

"We've got to go." I was feeling horribly queasy. The last time I did a "leisure drug" was putting Preparation H under my baggy eyes during the disco years. This couldn't be happening in Grit.

Preston took the bottle from me. "J.J. knows somebody in Piedras Negras that gets this down in the interior. Like he always says, "you can't bake a cake without a little vanilla.""

Chris was livid. (In "Chris-dom" one wasn't allowed to tamper with another's grasp on the *near-actuality* of a circumstance. If Chris said there was tarragon in the fish, and you knew you'd put dill, you were purposely hindering his individual *experience* of the fish; reality being a mostly speculative conjecture at best. Deliberate deception on the other hand was right up there with wife-beating and lying about your IQ. Not done.) Chris aimed for the front door, putting his hand on my neck as he passed. "Thank you all very much. Please give Miss Oveta and J.J. our regards."

"Will you at least think about it?"

"We'll think about it."

"It'd be a great experience for everyone."

"Great."

"We just want to bring a sense of inspiration . . ."

"I know, I know—to all the indifferent, unwitting lives . . . and their anesthesia."

Raymond followed us to the door and stood as we swayed like two Yankees in a nor'easter, aiming for the van. "Are you sure you wouldn't like Preston or me to take you home?"

The blissful notion of lying prone on Mother's living-room couch with a damp towel covering my face seemed to be the most glorious vision on the planet at that moment. They couldn't drive fast enough.

Preston rapped on the glass of the van. I lowered the window.

"I'll read it tonight."

"What?"

"*Aga . . . Aga-mammaw* . . . whatever it's called. Please don't say no yet. Just—think about it."

I nodded and backed the van over the lawn sprinkler I'd managed to miss on the way in. Chris and I—somehow—got home and got to bed. We slept until nine the next morning. We both had dreams about floating restaurants.

5

AND THE ANSWER CAME

"What do you mean she fell?"

"Fell, tripped—whammo! Right over the potty."

"How?"

"She got it in her skull to dye those last four gray hairs the chemo hadn't fried—stuck her head in the sink, got dizzy and tripped over the john."

"Jesus Christ." I set the bag of groceries down on the kitchen table. Chris and I hadn't even been away from the house an hour and a half and Mother had gone and broken her arm. Jaston sat on the kitchen counter eating Cheetos and bean dip from a can.

"Where is she?"

"Mercy Hospital—same shitty room. Four old ladies in a space no bigger'n a good size bass boat."

"Who's with her?"

Jaston shrugged. "I don't know, nurse or something. She'll be all right. Her bones are weak as fallen tree limbs, that's what the doc said."

"God, God, God . . ." I slumped in a chair. Chris walked to the sink to wash his hands. (We'd stopped off to buy St. Augustine grass to patch up the bare spots around the yard. It seemed a springlike thing to do.) Dorita, Max, Señor Murphy and I think Bessie Smith's baby bitch (who for some reason didn't have a name yet) padded around my shoes looking terribly anxious. Where was *mamacita?*

"I'll go down and sit with her if you want me to." Chris turned off the faucet and dried his hands.

"No, it's all right. I'm just going to make something to eat and go."

Jaston shook his head. "She dudn't need anything. They're in there every five minutes—bringing applesauce, foolin' with her pillow—she's never alone."

"Jaston." I sighed. What's the use? "Sometimes you just have to be with a person, you know?" No, he didn't. He stared at me waiting for some factual evidence. "This is our mother . . . she's sick. She's dying."

Jaston swallowed a gob of bean dip, and I could sense he was trying. A chink of mortar fell from his cerebral cortex; he winced. He started to say something, then fell silent.

"What?"

"I was just wondering . . ."

"What?"

"Nah."

"No, what, tell me?"

"Well, I just thought maybe . . . forget it."

"Jaston, for crying out loud, talk to me!"

Jaston stared for a long time into the bean dip can, glanced up at Chris then exhaled. "I was just wondering . . . would y'all like to come see what I dug out behind old lady Byers's?"

Señor Murphy was sleeping next to the oven, soaking up heat from the pilot light like it was "air steak." Chris stood at the counter unwrapping a loaf of bread. I smiled. (Where is it written we all have to share the same awareness?) "Not today, Jas. I'm needed elsewhere."

"I'll go with you," Chris volunteered. He moved from the counter to the kitchen table, setting a peanut butter and jelly sandwich down in front of me. "Here."

"Thanks." I took a bite. *(Blueberry jam,* for cripes sake. That was so Pennsylvania.) Since the incident at Miss Oveta's four days ago, Chris had been strangely quiet. We didn't so much have conversations as mutter grunts. Maybe we were both still exhausted. Maybe *colonche* affected the dialogue zone. Maybe . . .

"Can't wait to see what my investments returned." Chris rammed half a blueberry-nutter in his mouth, mumbling, "Fine . . . an . . . gold . . . et?"

Jaston grinned mysteriously. "No gold yet. I found something though."

"What?"

"You'll see."

Chris downed a glass of milk and wiped the corners of his mouth. "Let's go."

"Right now?"

"Right now."

Jaston crumpled the Cheetos bag and stood. "Let me go put on my work boots. Muddy as hell out there."

Jaston bolted for the back porch and Chris put his plate in the sink, hurriedly swallowing another shot of milk. He was almost out the door when he stopped and turned back toward me. "You OK?"

"Yeah. You?" Chris nodded and stepped off the porch. Dorita stood beside my chair and shivered. I picked her up and did something I never did in the presence of family members. I kissed her. Then Bessie Smith's baby bitch, then Max—they all followed suit, settling in my lap and quivering—huge brown eyes searching for some signs of an emotional echo in my face. I tried. I rubbed, I petted, I scratched. It was lame—my heart's desire was down there on the floor with Señor Murphy. Like some ancient itch for attainment, I craved the canine gift for seizing energy from any probable source.

Mercy Hospital is the Frida Kahlo of institutional buildings. It's got crufixes in its head, a moustache awning framing the front entry, tentacles of dead ivy weaving from its pale, worn exterior and an abiding sense of detachment looming over its dark, despairing core. A good place to end it all. (I would think volunteering as a candy striper at Mercy Hospital somewhat the equivalent of a tour of duty with a religious order in the Congo.)

The Sisters of Mercy have run the hospital since forever. Apparently they've made money—they haven't gone away yet. (Unlike so many other small country hospitals that have abandoned their charges, Mercy goes right on thriving like some ratty old dowager plowing her way through a buffet line. She took what she needed for sustenance—to hell with style.)

The place always seemed amazingly un-Grit. Exotic, veiled; all those nuns and migrant workers stirring about. From the fanciful Canary Island palms lining the drive to the Shrine of Our Lady grotto that the janitor from the Catholic church built from cinder blocks and 8,689 Formica chip samples—to the groups of large families no one had ever seen before (always standing, watching; endlessly enduring)—it was all foreign-film-with-missing-subtitles perplexing. A brick-and-mortar conundrum. Concealed, distant, enigmatic—*Torquemada-ville.*

"Yes?"

"What room is Mrs. Latimore in?"

"I'll check." A very large, elderly woman wearing a name tag that read DOLL HARE (Could that really be her name?) squinted at the computer screen and pointed me down the hall. I walked past the mini gift shop. A teenage girl was watching a TV no bigger than a coffee cup, perched next to the cash register. The three prominent items on display were Junior Mints, hairspray and a stack of Ellery Queen mysteries—all carefully laid out beneath a sign reading EVERY-THING FOR THE PATIENT.

Rounding the corner I passed the grim little cafeteria, which, despairing as it was, was not a McDonald's. (You know you're in Texas when the hospital dietician puts Frito-pie on the menu.) Passing the emergency room, the X-ray lab, the nurses' station, the doctors' lounge—it dawned on me—where were the patients? But for a few spectral nuns slipping about in silent, gray shadows, the hospital appeared empty. Entering a broad corridor of rooms, I peered into the open doors for signs of business. A few "feet posts" staked under sheet tents were all I could see. No faces, no flesh—no patronage was visible. Finally, at the end of the hall an elderly gentleman wheeled out of an entry, very natty in his buttoned-up striped pajamas, chewing on a little cigar and resting his Stetson in his lap.

"How ya doin' this morning, young man?"

"Fine, thank you. How're you?"

"Hadn't got a care in the world—nor a prostate neither. You best keep your legs together round here; they'll get the 'goodies' if you ain't watchin'." He coughed and rolled on down the hall, spitting a little wad of tobacco into somebody's discarded azalea plant.

Mother's room was stashed around the corner: a suite, and it was small, but there was plenty of light and everyone had a TV. Somebody behind a blue synthetic curtain was watching *Guiding Light* (on which I played Alan Spaulding's deranged nephew for one whole week! I stalked him with an electric drill—no lines but lots of air time. What an unbelievably wretched show. Paid well.) The second bed was empty. Finally, I saw Mother, propped up on a throne of pillows, her right arm extending into the air and swathed in white plaster like some statue of an unearthed Greek discus thrower. She was leafing through a *Harper's Bazaar* with her good hand. Someone had wrapped an orange towel around her head and I'm not sure why, but she looked practically chic—old-film-star-at-Betty-Ford chic.

"Hi."

"Hi, yourself." Mother brushed her hand over the fashion spread and grimaced as she tried to straighten herself.

"Let me help."

"Just got a little crick in my neck. There. Much better. Oh—thank the Lord I'm not young anymore." She sighed. "I'd have to go around nude."

I looked at the magazine. "That bad, huh?"

Mother jabbed Claudia Schiffer's blond wonderfulness on the cover with a rigid index finger. "Pretty bad. Well, they're mostly nude anyway—what's the difference."

I sat in a chair by the window. "Mother, do you remember Dovima from the fifties? Richard Avedon's favorite model?"

"She the one with the elephants?"

"Yes."

"Beautiful. A great beauty!"

"Well, she ended up a hostess at a House of Pancakes in Ft. Lauderdale." I pointed to the magazine. "These babes won't even wind up that secure."

Mother looked at me appalled. "The House of . . ." The thought sort of filtered away.

After a moment I asked sympathetically, "How's the arm?"

Startled, Mother stared at me as if I'd just entered the room for the first time. "She was so thin! I wonder if she kept her figure?"

I shook my head. "Have you ever seen a *thin* House of Pancakes employee?"

Mother glared a second longer, then set the magazine on her nightstand. She stared out the window, down the road, way beyond the field of Ed Bascomb's early milo waving in the breeze and out across the Gulf of Mexico. From the expression on her face it seemed obvious her vision was settling somewhere in the vicinity of the Ft. Lauderdale IHOP. Was she making peace with Dovima? Could it be admitted that even if one did end up a hostess, did lose one's looks, didn't marry as fortuitously as expected—could it be conceded that even the pros themselves took a stumble sometimes?

"I've got to wear this for six weeks. I'll die with this thing on."

"We'll have it removed for the funeral. Pretty awful having your arm thrusting out of the coffin during the service." A semblance of a smile crossed Mother's face.

"What were you doing?" I asked.

She moaned, "My hair's starting to come back—it looks like the down of a baby condor. I thought I could bring something of the 'old' me back. The smell of Clairol must've given me vertigo."

"If Clairol gave people vertigo, Mother, all our brains would've spun out of our heads years ago."

"Well finally—the proof we've been waiting for!" Mother tried grumbling a small laugh but gave up when the pain became too acute. She then tried to move a pillow from behind her. I reached for it. "Just move it over . . . there. Thank you." The towel began sliding down around her neck. I twisted it back up haphazardly. I saw that her fingertips poking out of the cast were a shade of light blue. They must have been ice-cold. On top of everything else, Mother had a runny nose. It was hard to imagine a more uncomfortable person on the planet.

"Hello, hello, hello . . . how's everybody in dis room?" I turned around to see a dwarf nun (she was very small) skip into our cramped quarters. "Who you? You da boyfriend? Ha-ha-ha."

"Sister Renata, this is my son—Clu."

"Clu? Das a name? I never hear dis name." Sister Renata was a frenzy of activity. She stuck a thermometer in mother's mouth, turned off the TV and removed Mother's orange towel, all in about five seconds. "You hair look nice! You such a pretty lady. Look like Ingrid Berman in *Joan of Arc.*" Sister Renata giggled insanely.

"Sister Renata's from Brazil," Mother said dryly, her eyes closed. "Sister, why are there no nuns from America anymore?"

"All in Hollywood, makin' movies! Ha-ha-ha!" Sister Renata stopped in front of me and poked my belly. "You handsome man, you in the movies?"

"Uh . . ."

"My son's an actor, in New York. He's very well known."

"Yes, they love me in Greenland."

Sister Renata was astounded. "In Greenland! I never been dere. Someday I'm gonna go. Maybe they got a hospital needs a Brazilian nun. Ha-ha-ha!"

Suddenly the woman behind the blue curtain began sobbing, "Sis-terrr. Sis-terrr! I cain't see the TV no more. I'm going blind."

"You not going blind, Melba. I turn it off." Sister Renata held her hand to her mouth and giggled silently. She poked me in the stomach again.

"Oh . . . is Buddy here yet?"

"No, Buddy not here."

"Will you tell me when he gets here?"

"Sure, sure." Sister Renata rolled her eyes and pulled me down to whisper in my ear, "Buddy her husband. He been dead for ten years. She . . ." Sister Renata rolled her eyes again and stuck her tongue out. Apparently, Melba was missing a few canned goods in the cognitive pantry.

"Dr. Thi Le come to see you this morning?"

"Dr. who?"

"Thi Le, he the new orthopedic surgeon."

"What happened to Dr. Throckmorton?"

Sister Renata smiled. "He go on vacation till end of May. Dr. Thi Le gonna take care you."

Mother stared at me with a look of surrender. "Isn't that dandy? A new doctor to break in. I don't think I can take another doctor. Another stranger to churn out my host of afflictions to. I just can't . . . keep . . ." Mother lowered her head and began to cry softly. Sister Renata held a blue tissue to her already dripping nose. I felt an overwhelming desire to transport myself inside a menthol cigarette ad: somewhere in the Caribbean, floating in a bay, reading about dead royalty. Something vaguely benumbing.

"There, there—you having another bad day, das all. In Brazil we say, 'too many bad days make it rain on Sunday.'"

Mother wadded the blue tissue in her fist and looked at Sister Renata confused. "That doesn't make any sense."

"Sure it do! Rain on Sunday mean good luck all week."

"Well, it'd have to rain a whole year in my case."

"Yeah, we gotta 'nuther saying for that too—something about skinny chickens and old bulls—but you have to be from Belo Horizonte to understand." Sister Renata leaned over and pecked Mother on the cheek. "We gotta lotta sayings in Brazil. I gonna teach you one every day. Now, don't be sad. Jesus love you, Renata love you and Coo love you too."

Coo? Sister Renata passed beneath me, peering up with large, beseeching eyes. She whispered sotto voce, "Coo, give you mama big kiss. Make her feel better." She wrinkled her nose and spun out of the room as fast as she'd arrived. Cathy Rigby couldn't touch her spunkiness. Mother looked at me with alarm, as if I'd suddenly grown donkey ears. No doubt she'd heard Sister Renata's parting entreaty. We were both paralyzed with uncertainty. We were an unabashedly WASP family—no getting around it. It was fearfully hard to be affectionate beyond the obligatory hugs and pats on the back. It just wasn't done. Even Mother and Laine kept a proprietary distance. I think the bottom line was anything too overtly physical was seen as somewhat suspect. Mustn't appear too needy, too "not in control." Chris's family was pretty much the same way, but they were a little more hands-on. Chris and his dad actually kissed one another, which was both cute and totally alien to me. There just seemed to be still too much unsaid, unresolved and unfinished among the Latimores to allow for a whole lot of lively affection. We were undemonstrative in the "pioneer" sense. Breaking horses and palpating a pregnant heifer (sticking one's hand up a cow's rear for the uninitiated, which I'd done on several occasions working cattle with my uncle Pete) didn't present near the obstacles as tendering an innocent peck on the cheek. Too risky, too personal.

In a way, one might assume all this emotional restraint would have presented a formidable obstacle to intimacy between Chris and me. Quite the contrary. It was as if we'd each been saving up all our affection tokens for the *real* ride. When we made love it was a complete no-holds-barred, all-you-can-eat banquet. No one ever left the table unsatisfied.

"How much longer you think they're going to keep you here?" I looked at Mother, worried.

"I don't know, least another couple of days."

"Can I bring you anything from the house: a book, your makeup bag, bathrobe . . . ?" She shook her head. "I'd smuggle in Señor Murphy if you think it'd help?"

She smirked. "Goodness no! He'd leave a trail of body fluids from here to the front desk. You just keep 'em all at the house and follow the feeding instructions on the fridge. Delphenium had her puppies yet?"

"Not yet."

"Odd. She's never been this late before."

I pulled up a chair and sat. "Mother, I've always wanted to understand—what is it with you and these little dogs? What's up with this Chihuahua compulsion?"

She blinked, a semi-amused look on her face. "I love them—that's what's up! Why do you love your kids? You just do."

"But . . . so many? Two or three, I can understand, but . . ."

"Well now, I can't very well just turn out the ones that don't sell. It is a business!"

I shook my head, "Mother, you've put a hundred times more money into raising those dogs than you ever made selling them."

"Museums don't make money either; should we just shut them all down? I run a Chihuahua museum!"

I laughed. She laughed as well.

The momentary tension vanquished, I glanced at her slyly, "So— you'll be thrilled to know I agreed to direct Miss Oveta's *Vanity Follies,* or whatever they're calling it. Make you happy?"

She looked surprised, "Does it make *you* happy? I certainly don't think you should do anything that doesn't 'speak' to you. But you should probably do *something!*"

Of course she was right. I had to do *something* on a daily basis other than scoop Chihuahua shit and make oatmeal cookies for her. Besides, she'd eat two and Jaston would demolish the rest. I for damn sure didn't come home to supply my brother's *illimitable edacity.* But why, God, why community theater in Grit? It's not humiliating enough I've crawled back, the semi-kinda-half-assed "star" from New York who kinda-sorta-didn't really make it? I never met Regis, never was a guest on *Letterman,* hell, I was never even a spear carrier at the Public Theater. And still they raved, "But your hands are so . . . *esthetic!*" And from this a career is launched.

And discarded. I had lain awake half the night debating whether or not to accept Miss Oveta's offer. Pitiful. Just once, it would've been edifying to have life slip you a real stunner and produce some perfect stranger who sees you in a crowd and pronounces, *"You! You're just who I'm looking for. Why yes, you'll be perfect as my new . . . anthropologist assistant!"* No thought, no anxiety, no decision. Just a, "Yes. I can do that."

I called Miss Oveta at 9 A.M. and told her I'd direct her play. She actually wept. So did I.

I looked at Mom. She was perusing the *Bazaar* again. It suddenly seemed the opportune moment. "So, by-the-bye, Chris found a hatbox in the guest room—real old, striped thing. Where'd that come from?"

She barely looked up. "Hmm? Oh that, I picked it up in Gladys Byers's garage one afternoon. I was poking around looking to see if she had any pruning shears, and I thought, 'Well, the rats are just gonna eat this thing,' so I brought it up to the house."

"And all those pictures?

"What pictures?"

"The pictures in the box?"

"What pictures?"

"You didn't look in the box?"

Mother blinked. "No."

I studied her face, it was impossible to tell with Mother when she was playing dumb or deliberately evading a precarious subject. I'd spent a lifetime trying to slip her up. Never worked. But I knew the game as well as she by now. "Oh, I thought you'd seen the photos."

"No."

"*Lots* of photos."

She shook her head. "Nope."

We smiled at each other. I can wait too. She blinked, then slowly, dreamily, she nodded. "Ohhh! You mean the pictures of all those soldier boys?"

I grinned. *"Those."*

Mother shrugged. "Haven't a clue. But let's not talk about Gladys Byers. She wasn't a pleasant person."

"Uh-huh . . . who just happened to leave us her house and her land."

Mother gave me one of her looks. "You don't have to know everything, Clu. Sometimes, what you don't know really won't hurt you." Conversation over. I gnawed on the inside of my mouth for a while. I can wait, too.

"How's Chris doing?"

I looked around, surprised. "Fine. Thanks for asking."

"I like Chris. I do. He seems like a . . . nice person."

I studied Mother's expression. She'd never offered an opinion about Chris one way or the other. "I'll tell him. Where's this coming from?"

She looked offended. "Can't I even say I like your . . . companion?"

I felt a small bump in my throat. *Companion.* Recognition! Feeble, strained, incomplete—but definitely, mindful. "Thank you, Mother."

She fussed with her gown collar and stared out the window. "I just think it's usually better, in most cases, to have a partner. That's all." I looked askance. This coming from the woman who'd spent the majority of my life living alone? She turned back to me, suddenly radiant. "Did I tell you I'm thinking about getting married again?"

I nearly fell out of my chair. All I could do was shake my head, "Unh-unh."

"Yep. Ninety-nine percent certain."

"And . . . who's the lucky man?"

She looked at me, expressionless. "Why Brother Ramirez, pastor at the *Templo*. Didn't I mention something about this?"

"No."

"Oh." Mother continued toying with her collar. "Well, he's extraordinary. I've never met anyone quite like him. He's just . . . an amazing teacher. I'm learning so much through him, Clu. I think he's helping me get beyond my past."

I sat there wide-eyed. Which Bettie Jean was this?

"Buddy? Bud-dy, is that you?" Melba, the next-door neighbor, was calling. "Buddy . . . oh please. Buddy, where are you?" She began to sob.

Mother looked stricken and whispered, "Just peek in there and see if she needs anything."

I frowned. "Mother—I don't know this woman."

"She's harmless. Just see if she's OK."

I exhaled slowly. I hated doing stuff like this. Sticking my nose into perfect strangers' even stranger lives. I cleared my throat loudly, said "Hello," and parted the curtained veil between us. Peering over the covers were two gray eyes glaring back at me behind inch-thick glasses. A knot of white hair was tucked up into an orange knit cap atop her head. The word "howdy" was spelled out in large red sequins across the brim. I smiled politely. "Hi. I'm visiting next door here, and I was just wondering if you needed anything?"

She looked at me puzzled, then instantly burst into tears. "You *bastard*—how could you do this to me!"

I froze. "Uhh . . ."

"You think I enjoy being pregnant with your *whelp*? You haven't come to see me once—why, Buddy, *why*?"

Considering Melba would most likely never see the age of eighty-five again, the paternity threat appeared dubious. "Why don't I . . . I'll just get the nurse."

"Sure! You're two-timing with her, too, aren't you?" She roared at me, "How many women will it take for you to feel like a real man!"

I smiled anxiously, "*Definitely*—wrong Buddy." I backed out of her cubicle and shut the curtains. Turning to Mother, I must've looked a little shaken. With her good arm she scooted the chair beside her bed toward me. "Sit. You look a little pale."

Sister Renata entered on cue. "Oh boy, oh boy—Coo still here causing trouble with my gulls. Bath time. All boys gotta leave. You come back, Mommy gonna be clean and pretty. Maybe you take Bettie and Melba dancing then, yes? Ha-ha-ha-ha!"

Sister shoved me out the door as I quickly waved good-bye to Mother.

Walking down the hall I heard Melba shrieking behind, "*Men!* God help me, I can't *live* without them!"

Check.

6

DAVY CROCKETT'S FALSE TEETH

It was near suppertime when I got home. Naturally the house was empty, no steaming cauldron of soup on the hearth, no roasting chicken—no Rice-A-Roni even. For some reason I'd been left in charge of the kitchen in Mother's absence. This was clearly Chris's venue. Sure I could squeeze out the occasional omelet, a pedestrian casserole, once in a while a fabulous dessert—but cooking had always been Chris's playground. He loved to cook. Only he hadn't so much as opened a can of tuna since we got to Texas. I figured he was still acclimatizing. Soon he'd be back in his culinary groove: filleting *pompano,* dicing *jicama,* kneading *brioche*—just like we were in New York. Very soon.

I sat down to a microwaved bowl of Campbell's broccoli-and-cheese soup. An interesting and visual mélange of Elmer's glue and yard mulch. The screen door slammed behind me, and I turned to see two walking George Segal statues sheathed in grayish muck stumble into the room.

"You ain't gonna fuckin' believe it!" Jaston's eyes were glowing like nuclear rods.

"Clu, it's there. It's really there!" Chris flung open the fridge, retrieving a "Tall Boy" Bud Light for himself and one for Jaston. They both bent their heads back and chugged for a good twenty seconds before resurfacing for oxygen. Jaston belched loud enough to send Bessie Smith and her brood fleeing the room in alarm.

"Guess what we found?" Jaston licked at the foam on his lips.

"I'm done with twenty questions. What?"

"Go on, one guess."

"Nope."

"Come on, Clu, in your wildest dreams—guess what's out there?" Chris grinned at me, looking for all the world like some Bruce Weber model on an ersatz Banana Republic archaeological dig. All sweat, sinewy arms, unbuttoned shirt and mud-speckled smile. He was definitely—hot. (Something about men and mud and jeans unquestionably sparks the old "inner slut" engine. And when, by the way, did we last have sex?)

"OK—you found the Carol Channing wig cemetery?"

"Wrong."

"George Hamilton's first tanning bed?"

"Zip."

Jaston scowled and let out a belch that hit every note on the scale. Impressive. "Shit, are ya'll gonna just do that gay New York trivial crud? I might as well go take a dump."

"I give up, I can't imagine—what did you find?" Chris and Jaston glanced at each other and snickered, followed by great whoops of laughter.

"Come on, we're gonna show you. You won't fuckin' believe it." Jaston grabbed my chair and Chris hoisted me up, spoon still firmly in my grip.

"What about my soup?"

Chris sneered, "That's not soup, that's puke with green sprinkles. Come on. We'll stop at the Sonic on the way back and get jalapeño burgers and 'Ocean Waters.'" I stumbled out the door, escorted by the Mud Men of Lunatic Pueblo. It occurred to me that phrases like "jalapeño burger" and "Ocean Water" had never been uttered by Chris in all my years with him. It was happening. Slowly, resolutely—he was going Lone Star.

The back of "old lady Byers's" place was a Central American jungle of thorns, stinging insects and peanut-butter mud. We trudged through the morass of vines and hateful tree limbs till finally we came to the edge of the creek and what looked like a cluster of collapsed boards and river rocks.

Jaston began wheezing with excitement. "This was the old mill—part of it anyway. See those pinion gears lying over there, all that was part of the main trundle used to grind the wheat. Now I figure the creek came along in a little race about here and somewheres over there was the water wheel." We all stood gazing at the pile of refuse, half expecting it to rise up and congratulate us.

"So . . . this is great. Maybe the County Historical Commission will let you put up a plaque or something. Let's eat." I started to turn, Jaston grabbed my shoulder.

"No, you dick head, this ain't all. Come 'ere." We circled down below the heap till we were almost level with the creek bed. It was apparent Jaston and/or Chris had moved a mountain of rubble and dirt and exposed a small—door.

"What is that?"

"It's a door! Haven't you ever seen a door?"

"I know it's a stupid door. To what?" Again, Chris and Jaston chortled. I was starting to get annoyed. Playing the excluded dupe was not my favorite role.

"Open it up and go on in." I stared at Chris and Jas, who were both beaming like morons. "Go on!" I wavered slightly, convinced this was probably another of the elaborate jokes Jaston loved to concoct out of the vaguest plausibility. What the hell—there was a door before me. It needed opening. I opened.

Stepping inside the dark, windowless and moldy room I squinted to adjust to the gloom. What I saw was a dirt floor, cobwebs, a collapsing plastered ceiling and a crumbling cement wall along back. This was it? I called out, "So what am I supposed to see besides the dead rat and some snake skeletons?" I heard more chuckling.

Chris finally answered, "Follow the back wall with your hands. Here, I'll push the door open wider—you can see a little better." Allowing a fraction more light, I was able to make out a large pile of chipped mortar and cement heaped in the corner. Kneeling closer, I cautiously felt my way in the murk, quietly praying to the rattlesnake/scorpion gods for safe passage. I felt an opening in the wall and reached in warily to touch something cold, metallic. "Hey, there's something here. In the wall." I didn't hear their reaction this time. I was too intent on uncovering my discovery. With both hands I felt along the surface till I grabbed a . . . handle! Then I felt a dial of some sort. "Hey you guys! It's a . . ."

"Safe." I turned to see them both now crouching behind me in the dark.

"Pretty wild, huh?" Jaston was gleaming.

Chris reached over to yank at the handle. "What do you think is in there? Stocks, bonds, cash . . ."

"Flour sacks?"

"Don't piss on this. This could be something big."

"Hey, you had your fun. Snake!" I screamed, and pointed. They both yelled, jumped and whirled exactly on cue. I laughed insanely.

"Asshole."

"Freak. Let's stop fucking around. Jaston thinks we need to pull it out of here, get it up on higher ground."

Jaston growled, "We have another one of these frog-strangling spring floods and this whole room'll be wiped out. Least the door and all that shit blocking it kept some of the water away."

I frowned. "How big is this thing—three by four—we'll need a crane to lift it out."

"Already thought about that. I'll back the Caterpillar up to the door, and we can drag it with a chain."

I shook my head. "Jas, you'll pull the whole building down. Look at this thing; it's ready to keel over."

"Thought about that, too. We reinforce it first, have to anyway. I'm gonna restore the gristmill with the money in that safe!"

Chris interjected, "Wait a minute, bro—the bulk of this dig is being funded by yours truly. I get some say over the booty."

"Fine, we'll split it. I ain't greedy, but we got to get it out of here."

I cleared my throat. "And with my share I'm going to open Grit's first Starbucks." They both looked at me as if I were Satan rising from swamp gas. "Oh come on, it's probably filled with fungus and old whiskey bottles. You don't really think there's anything valuable in there?" Again, they blinked. "So maybe there's a couple hundred dollars—I'll help you and I'll keep my mouth shut. That's worth something."

They glanced at each other, and Jaston finally spoke. "Deal. But if one other asshole in town hears about this, I'm dynamiting the whole thing. This is my discovery, and I don't want nobody else snooping around." We shook hands like a bunch of solemn Cub Scouts vowing to keep girls out of our secret fort.

Backing out of the dank, cramped room, we all gulped fresh air. Snatching at cobwebs draped on my head, I turned to Jaston. "Mom comes home in a few days. She's not doing so well—we gotta try and make her as comfortable as possible."

Jaston scraped mud from his boots. "Yeah."

"No more going to her with every little whine and grievance like when we were kids. She doesn't have the energy to deal with it any-more." Jaston continued stabbing at his boots with a rock. "Besides, she's got other, more important things on her mind."

"Like what?"

"Like . . . her marriage . . . to Brother Ramirez."

Jaston dropped the rock and looked up bewildered. "The little Mexican preacher? Old Short Drawers?" I nodded. *"That's* who she's marrying? She-yut, I knew nothing good'd come from her hang-ing out with that buncha crazy-ass Bible thumpers. What's he see in her anyway?"

I shrugged. For once, Jaston and I were in agreement. Chris pushed his bangs off his forehead, smiling. "Maybe they're in love. Why else would they want to get married? They love each other."

Jaston and I were mystified. Our mother . . . in love? Didn't sound right; some equation was missing. Not that she didn't deserve or even desire to be in love. It's just that we'd never known otherwise. She hadn't even been on a date since Herbert's departure, much less received something as rash as a marriage proposal. It was as if she were determined to wear her divorce as a kind of admonition, "Don't be a fool like me. It isn't worth the frown lines." Mother lived in her own day-to-day ethereal seclusion incorporating dogs, fashion magazines and a personal relationship with God. The aver-age Joe that Grit was able to produce fell far short of the program. There had been the rare, occasional suitor, but they simply couldn't

pass the bar. Mother was too small-town glamorous and unattain-
able for the local gentry. Sadly, all the Aristotle Onassises of her gen-
eration were off building empires and chasing starlets. Mother's
rescue was never even a notion. Grit held her aloft as some distant
beacon of moral character and provincial flair. I suspect, deep down
inside, she was really just a latent beatnik fighting major impulses to
chuck it all and run off to San Miguel Allende.

What she didn't have was much money. That was certain.
Ramirez obviously wasn't a fortune hunter. The facts were—she was
dying of cancer, she was older than he, she'd been a divorcee for
more than half her life . . . and she wasn't Hispanic (if it mattered).
So yes . . . apparently, it had to be love.

Jaston shook his head. "Well, I think it's weird as shit. As usual,
there's something we don't know about. Wait'll Laine hears—she'll
drop another one." Indeed. Mother had said Laine and Sherrod
would be coming to visit next week. Another exciting Latimore reunion in the works. And no question, Laine will definitely experience
"ovary distress" when she gets the news.

Trudging back out of the swamp, Jaston stormed ahead, whacking limbs and bushes with his machete. Chris and I lagged behind,
scrupulously avoiding anthills and yellow jacket nests. Chris unexpectedly yanked at my rear jean pocket to keep from tumbling into
an armadillo hole. "Nice butt, mister."

"Thanks. It's handy."

"The way you move that thing is kind of dangerous."

"Yeah? That's me, old *Walk on the Wild Side*."

Chris stopped. "I wouldn't mind taking a little 'walk' right about
now."

I smiled. "Many are called, dude—few make the cut."

Chris put his arms around my waist and pulled me back, whisper-
ing in my ear, "I'm getting a 'calling'—can I use your phone?"

I glanced ahead at Jaston, who was practically out of sight. Here
we were in the thick of vermin and pestilence hell. It was comical,
bad porno. ("Yeah man—you wanna do it!") I called out to Jaston,
"Chris wants to see the old pecan tree up on the bluff." Or something to that extent. Jaston stomped onward, oblivious. When he
was out of sight, Chris reached around and began unbuttoning my

jeans. No foreplay, no teasing, no "Dance of the Seven Veils." We were heeding a prehistoric summons. Falling against a downed live oak, we crushed against each other like colliding locomotives. It seemed like it had been forever—the gift of carnality. The rough intimacy and cellular licentiousness of spontaneous sex never failed to reduce me to a humping, thumping blob of wantonness. It was primitive, nasty, fast—and damn, did it feel incredible! Come to think of it, it would've made a hell of a porno.

As a rule, the zest of sex between two men is a pretty rudimentary thing. Everyone's basically on the same page. Between Chris and me it was something else as well. Love, devotion and intimacy served up with bountiful libidinous arousal. His obvious desire never failed to jump-start me like an arrhythmia victim on digitalis. *Boom!* "Come on, Sea Biscuit!" Of course, God knows what simple creatures men really are. Women may or may not need all that champagne, music and soft lighting to stoke their passions—from the *correct* suitor all gay men require is a suggestive glance and an unambiguous nudge. Nature expedites the details. Naturally, such impetuosity usually leads to either serious affinity or serious trouble (or both). Chris and I were lucky; we were spared the prevailing "gay-go-round" dilemma of way too much selection. Yes, Virginia, it is a good thing to exit the candy store of boys while you still have your teeth. I like an Almond Joy as much as the next camper—but who wants Hershey when it's flowing Godiva back home?

What Chris had that I'd never experienced with anyone else was the remote control to my pleasure principle. The man was lethal to my *inner virgin*. He knew exactly which switch got which results. It wasn't easy living as a digital love slave. God knows I fought against those unfair advantages he held. For about thirty seconds. Ultimately I resolved to just keep a smile on my face and the hair out of my eyes whenever he reached for that deadly remote. Somehow, it worked. Admirably.

Picking seed ticks out of my crotch later that evening, I contemplated why good, old wholesome, playful, invigorating, red-blooded American sex frequently comes with a little shit note attached. AIDS, herpes, syphilis, crabs, warts—and on and on and on. What was the universe trying to tell us, gay and straight alike? Letting someone else touch your genitals is a guaranteed inferno? Impetuosity equals affliction? Desire causes debacle? Why did something so good, so right, inevitably have a little seed tick of mishap attached to it? Were we not doing it right, often enough, too much, unhygienically, too circumspect, too oblivious, too obsessive—what, what, what?

There was a knock at the bathroom door. I set the tweezers down and swabbed myself with a cotton ball of alcohol. "Ow! Yeah?"

"Is there some calamine lotion in there?" Chris entered, his face mottled in a preposterous red rash.

"Damn, you look like you just fornicated with a giant, poisonous tree frog."

"You took the words right out of my mouth . . . Kermit."

"Here." I reached under the sink and produced a half bottle of the pink liquid. "You're going to look like an amateur drag queen with this all over your face."

"I don't care if I look like Quasimodo on a three-day bender—I need relief." Chris dabbed at his welts and sure enough, the cosmetic results were pretty ludicrous. I tried not to laugh.

"You gonna be all right? Should we see a doctor?"

"I'll be fine. Why is it everything you touch around here causes some kind of blight?"

" 'Cause God doesn't want Texans getting too comfortable. They'd stop voting against alcohol, abortions and homosexuals if it suddenly felt like spring on the Riviera around here. I warned you it'd be harsh."

" 'Harsh' is a bad haircut; 'heinous' is your face half eaten away and swathed in pink goo."

I laughed and put my arms around his waist. "At least your balls aren't being devoured by blood-sucking insects."

"Oh shit! I didn't even check."

"Trust me—you'd know."

There was another knock at the door. Jaston bellowed, "Clu, you gotta phone call."

"Who is it?"

"I don't know. Sounded like Myla Biggs—they all sound alike."

I pulled a bathrobe on and kissed Chris behind the ear. "Sorry about your face, handsome. You were awfully hot down on your hands and knees in those bushes."

"Thanks. You hold that thought as I writhe in agony tonight keeping you awake."

I opened the door and padded down the hall toward the phone. Señor Murphy was slumbering against the baseboard with his feet in the air, making little twitching motions with his paws. "Gotta run faster, *hombre,* if you're gonna catch those *chicas.*" I picked up the phone. "Hello?"

"You rat! You haven't called me once since you got here. I told my girls we used to get it on in high school; they just about split their drawers."

"Myla?"

"No, it's Liz Taylor. Hello? Are you doing designer drugs?"

"Hi. No, no drugs—just a little spacey I guess."

"That's 'cause you haven't had one of my *Herradua Anejo Tres Equis* margaritas yet. It'll knock the fuckin' fur balls outta your head. When ya'll coming out to see us?"

"Gosh, I really want to—it's just been so crazy around here with Mom and everything."

"Bless her heart, I heard she's marrying the Mexican preacher. Good for her. Hell, she's paid her dues."

"How'd you hear about that?"

"Oh honey, it's old as disco. Don't tell me you just found out?"

"No, no—we were just hoping to keep it under wraps awhile longer."

"Liar. Ya'll are the craziest bunch—I mean, *my* family may look like something out of the *House of Wax,* but we do speak to each other. OK—we yell."

"So I guess it's common knowledge."

"Duh. Did Bill Clinton get a blow job? You're still so funny, Clu. I like that. So when are you coming out?"

"Well, whenever. And, by the way—I don't remember us ever getting it on in high school."

"I know, you shit. I wasn't 'cause I didn't try. Oh, you were hateful—I wanted that piece of meat of yours like a starved coyote."

I stared at Señor Murphy, now whimpering as he beat his squatty legs in the air. By now, it was fairly apparent Myla had already had a few fur ball chasers herself. "Um . . . sorry. I was pretty clueless in high school. Besides, if I remember correctly, Zane Biggs took up most of your time."

"Oh God, and did it get old quick! I mean I love him and all—but Jesus, I practically have to give him a Viagra enema just to get a wink and a pinch outta him anymore."

"Well—ya'll were quite the couple senior year. Wasn't he captain of the football team?"

"Yeah, fuckin' yeah . . . and class president and treasurer of Junior Achievement and everything else he could squeeze his big old butt into. What Zane wants, Zane gets. He just doesn't always 'get what he's got.'"

Check. From the mouth of Texas babes. "Maybe we can drive out this weekend. Are ya'll gonna be around?"

"Hell yeah. We don't ever go anywhere less it's Vegas, Cancún or take the girls up to Sea World in San Antone. We're as predictable as dingleberries on a hog. Who's that pretty man you were with? He your boyfriend?"

Silence. Followed by the interior, "Shit!" Two things: a) Does everybody in Grit know I'm gay; and b) How does everybody know I'm gay? (Really three things—Why does this continue to impale me each time it's brought up?)

"Hello?"

"Yeah, hi?"

"You still there?"

"Yeah . . . Myla, I was just wondering . . . why would you ask that question?"

"I don't know. I just figured he was your boyfriend. He's a cutie."

"Yeah."

"Did I say something wrong?"

"No, no."

"Is he?"

"Uh . . ."

"Oh God. Clu, honey, I'm sorr-ee. I'm such a motormouth sometimes. I didn't even think—if you're not 'out,' that's totally cool. It's none of my business."

Now I was pissed and dismayed. "I guess . . . you know what bothers me . . . you just assume I'm gay, right."

"Oh baby, no, no—I don't care what anyone is, really. They can fuck doorknobs if they want. I just figured you're what—thirty-seven, you've never been married, you've hidden away from us all these years, you've kept your looks and your bod, you've led this glamorous life in New York and you're not pushing strollers through the mall. I mean, hey—it was just a wild guess on my part."

Now I felt like a complete turd. Her diagnosis was flawless. If it walks like a duck . . . "Myla, sorry, I didn't mean to snap. I just, you know—it was kinda hard growing up in this town. . . ."

"Bay-bee, sugar lamb—you're not telling Mama anything new! Honey, I'll share something with you—if I'd a been a dyke, I'd gotten my ass outta here on a Trailways faster'n you could say 'Miss Muffy.' "

"Some of us did."

"And I'll tell you something else—it wasn't no day at Neiman's for those of us that stayed behind neither."

"What do you mean? You did the 'right' thing—got jobs, got married, had kids, joined the PTA—you became productive, up-standing, 'normal' citizens."

"I wish you were here right now—I'd throw up all over you! What you call the 'right' thing was the *only* thing we had available. What options did we have—robbing banks and turning tricks? Jesus, maybe I'd have loved to sail to Tahiti and opened a titty bar—but I didn't. I stayed, I played the game—hell, I chose this life. I'm just say-ing, you escaped. And there's no escaping your shit, pumpkin—ever."

Why didn't I have conversations like this in New York? There's something about someone from back home putting it all into per-spective for you. I left Grit, but Grit never left me. I was still hauling around my little high-school "invisible queer" luggage. God, what a bore. "Is he or isn't he?" (I remember once as a preadolescent being convinced that with the proper drag and attitude I could pass for a

Chinese native in Beijing—I was that assured of my ability to control "outward appearances.")

"Clu—oo, hey? Have I said too much? I'm sorry I've got such a big mouth."

"Myla—Chris and I would absolutely love to come for drinks. And yes, he is my . . . lover."

"Grea-a-t! How's Friday night sound?"

"We'll be there."

"Oh terrific. Listen, he is such a hottie; I mean that. After the girls go to bed we'll all get naked in the hot tub."

"Uh . . ."

"You don't mind if I call some of the old gang—they've all been asking about you and your 'friend.' There's Debbie and Jimmy Kinney, and Sandy and Dwayne Langerhorn, and . . ."

"Myla . . ."

"God, who else? I'll think about it. Listen, just show up about six-thirty—we'll have some steaks on the grill. Oh, this is going to be so-o-o fun."

"Maybe you shouldn't invite everyone this time . . ."

"What? In a minute . . . Hon, I gotta go. Rhonda thinks she's got zit on her boobie. Give my love to your mama. See ya'll Friday."

Click. I placed the phone slowly back on the wall mount. "There's no escaping your shit." Amen. Those people—those insane, tired-ass people I feared and wanted so much to be accepted by. What a bizarre reunion. I can just see us all bare-assed in the hot tub talking about cock rings and tit clamps. Who knows—maybe they've changed, too. God knows Myla seems down the road—same randy personality but, I don't know, enlightened somehow? Was it possible?

Shutting the door to our bedroom, I saw Chris curled up in a tight little ball on the edge of the bed. I walked over, sat beside him and started to recount the Myla missive when I noticed long, dangling tears streaking his pink face. "What's the matter?"

"Nothing. I've been thinking."

I rubbed his head. "Baby—you know how that just confuses you."

"Could you be serious for once?"

"Sorry." Chris wiped his cheek, managing to smear even more calamine on the pillowcase. "Talk to me."

"I . . . I don't know what I'm doing here."

"Doing here? You're with me."

"I mean—I don't know what I'm doing. You're with your mom, your family, you're working things out. I'm just sort of . . . weightless. Who am I supposed to be in all this?"

"You're supposed to be Chris, who's with his life partner Clu, being magnanimous and supportive and loving during a bumpy period of adjustment."

Chris stared at me. "I'm not doing so well with the magnanimous part. I'm all confused. It's like I've lost something, and I don't know what it is. Sorry, you don't need this, I know. I just feel . . . alone."

"Alone? I'm here beside you—right here, big boy. Don't you know that? Your worries are my worries, your happiness is mine. What's really going on?" God, he was irresistible. Anytime I got a chance to play angel of comfort I leapt at the prospect. I lived for these moments when I became the wise, elder bird who affectionately coached the wounded chick back into the nest, helped straighten mangled feathers and warbled nonstop hosannas. I was a hell of a cheerleader. I even had the hair for it.

Chris sat up and blew his nose. Lying back against the pillow, he sniffed and dabbed at an eye. Even smudged in pink bubble gum paint, he was adorable. "Preston's asked me to go to the coast with him for a few days next week—you know, see some of Texas. He's moving stuff from Mr. Otis's beach house and needs some help."

Check. "Well, sure—go. I wish I could go, too, but Mama's coming home next week. Go on."

"You don't mind?"

"Of course not. If you think it'll help your head, by all means." I laughed. "Just don't let Preston get any ideas."

Chris stared at me blankly, then half smiled. "Yeah, right, he's really my type. You know I don't go for that gym-clone thing."

I leaned in and kissed him. "But how do I know you're not his type?"

"Look, if you don't want me to go, I don't have to."

"No, no. I'm teasing. I think you should. You can run lines with him on the drive."

"What play are they doing?"

"Who knows? It'll probably end up being '*Cats*—the nonmusical.' Just run some lines with him, he needs the exercise."

"You really don't care?"

"Why should I? You're a free man. After eight years I think we trust each other, right?"

"Right."

"I know this has been hard on you. I just want you to understand one thing—how much I love and appreciate what you're doing for me. I couldn't ask for a better friend or lover. I love you very much, Chris."

"Me too."

We kissed again and I laid my head on Chris's chest, listening to his heart beating. Here I was, back in my old bedroom, holding on to the greatest guy in the world, who loved me resolutely. I cupped my hands around his balls and idly deliberated. If I could just figure out how to hold on to these things 24/7, we'd never have any problems the rest of our lives. There's your answer to world peace! I reached over and turned off the light, and we both fell asleep.

Next morning, practically at sunrise, the phone was ringing like a wound-up fire bell. I stumbled out of bed. Jaston had no doubt gone home, Chris was snoring peacefully. Lurching down the hallway and holding on to the walls in the exact same way as Mother, I sidestepped a Chihuahua turd and dived for the receiver.

" 'Lo."

"Who's this?"

"Clu Latimore—who's this?"

"Only your sister, you big goober!"

"Hey . . . Laine. What time is it?"

"I dunno, it's early. Sherrod's up at the front desk checking out. We spent the night in Sweetwater. We're halfway to Grit."

"I thought Mom said ya'll weren't coming till next week."

"Well yeah, it was 'next week' when I called her last week. How's she doing?"

"OK, I guess. She's getting married."

"WH-a-a-a-t?"

I held the phone at a safe distance. "Yeah—surprise, huh?"

"Are you teasing me? Clu, I swear I'll pinch your head off if you're kidding around."

"Wish I was. She's marrying the preacher at her new church."

"That little Mexican crackpot? Oh my God, what drugs are they giving her? Good thing I'm on my way. We can talk her out of this, just let me steer things."

"Why?"

"Why? Why do you think why? She doesn't need to be marrying anyone at her age and in her condition. Where they gonna go on their honeymoon, the Mayo Clinic?"

I felt a ferocious need to pee. An imperative, morning pee. Cordless phones were still about a decade away in Mother's household. I wiggled over to the sink, nearly pulling the phone out of the wall, and gratefully relieved myself.

"Uh . . . um . . . what did you say?"

"Are you peeing in the sink?"

"No."

"Yes, you are, I can hear it. God, you and Jaston are born white trash."

"Now, Laine—you're on shaky ground if we're talking heredi-tary."

"Shut up. I want that sink scoured 'fore I get there. Is your friend with you?"

"You're talking about Chris? The man I've lived with for the past eight years?"

"Spare me the gay liberation lecture, I'm just asking. Sherrod said you'd probably bring him while our mother's dying."

"Laine, you know what . . ."

"Gotta go. Sherrod's blowing the horn. Now listen, the doctor says I have to be very calm and not get upset. I'm only doing this to be with Mama. I want you to promise me we're all going to be peaceful and cooperative for Mama's sake."

"In other words just agree with everything you say."

"That'd work. What I mean is, can we all just act like adults for once, please?"

"Fine by me."

"I'm coming! Damn—Sherrod's got a sticker burr the size of Dallas up his ass this morning—Now I love you, Clu, you know that; I just don't want any crap outta you and Jaston." *Click.*

I hung up and stared blearily at the eight or so *perros* bunched at my feet. They all looked at me with those crinkled brow expressions of, "Yeah, and like I care—get your ass over to the Ken-L Ration and start pouring, Jack." Another Latimore get-together. Yee-haw.

Laine was my only sister. I loved her. In some ways, I admired her, but I never once bought into her officious sense of entitlement. Growing up, she frequently bore the cranky countenance of one who'd been inexplicably whisked from the Winter Palace nursery in St. Petersburg and dropped from a passing dirigible over South Texas. We lived with our very own Anastasia. (And *not* the cartoon version either.) It isn't that she couldn't be generous, gracious and even downright proletariat when the occasion deemed it. It's just that there were precious few such episodes to recall.

Laine had always felt horribly ensnared by the tricky Latimore Luck, which basically presupposed that shit and fan were a continuum. It wasn't supposed to be like this. She once told me very solemnly, while we were both watching an old movie on TV, that she equated her existence as somewhat akin to being the "love child of Arlene Dahl and 'Errol Flynn meets Chill Wills.' " I never got a handle on the two-fathers thing, but that was Laine. It went beyond B-movie ignominious. It was all just too real for tears. Saddled with the "Queer," the "Crip" and "The Rhonda Fleming of Chihuahua Breeders"—Laine left early, married early and early on began botching her multitudinous pregnancies. It didn't take binoculars to spot a particular talent for loss.

Robotically, I retrieved the fifty-pound bag of pricey lamb and rice amalgamation and began mixing. Mother had precise instructions taped on the refrigerator: "*Dorita* gets straight dry, feed her separately in the laundry room so *Chica* and *Pistola* don't bother her. Bessie Smith needs a little warmish tap water on hers and a squirt of cod liver oil. Not too much, she'll get the runs. Señor Murphy takes ¼ cup prescription Canine Eldercare canned formula, ½ a boiled egg, a tablespoon of Metamucil, one eyedropper of vitamin E and a crushed multimineral stirred well into the mixture . . ." Good Lord, astronauts didn't eat any better than these mutts. It was a full half hour of chopping, stirring, pouring, dicing, blending and dispensing of assorted medications, not counting the innumerable hair-trigger bitch attacks I arbitrated, before I could finally sit with a cup of coffee. No wonder Mother was exhausted. I was ready for a nap at seven A.M.

I stared at my gnawing "Clan of the Cave Chihuahuas" and listened to every burp, slurp, grunt, fart and wheeze with fascination. Does anything on the planet come close to attaining the sheer, transcendent and total absorption of a dog and its meal? I meditated on that and other weighty matters as I scratched and yawned simultaneously. There was a sudden *tap-tap-tap* at the back door. I snapped from my reverie and turned quickly. It was Preston, grinning at me through the café-curtained windows. He spoke through the glass. "Hey! Didn't mean to scare you. You looked like you were off on Planet Yonder, or something."

Now ordinarily I'm not the overly modest type, but here I was in a worn-out pair of ratty briefs with a hole in the crack, my hair looking like something the dogs had slobbered on and my eyes puffed up like terminal kidney failure. Cute.

"Not at all." Liar. I got up and ambled to the door, trying to seem cool and "dude-ish." (We gay boys never give it a rest.) Preston entered looking immaculately butch—a new little goatee, the white "wife-beater" and camouflage clam diggers, way cool Doc Marten leather sandals, the latest Stussy sunglasses, Astros baseball cap with precision rolled bill, tiny gold earring—standard issue, warm weather, gay drag. In addition, he was pumped as hell—veins bulging, muscles shuddering, skin gleaming. What did he do—work out before the sun came up? I didn't need this. He took off his sunglasses and lasered me up and down with a slight smile on his burnished, Aryan face. "Sorry to stop by so early. I had to run out and get the paper, and I saw your lights on. Did you see it?"

"See what?"

"The paper, you're in it."

"What?"

"Miss Oveta and Dad put in an announcement about your directing the play for the little theater."

"Jesus, I just told her I'd do it a few days ago."

"I know, she was really happy to make the paper's deadline."

"But—I don't even know what play I'm doing."

"Oh, they decided. It's *Aga-mammaw.*"

"*Aga-memnon.*"

"That one."

"Nice of them to let me know."

"It's all here in the paper, front page." He handed me the local rag, the *Grit Light*, which it truly was since it never contained more than three or four pages. Someone had dug up a ten-year-old photograph of me wearing a clown suit (!) from when I guest-hosted a kids show in New Jersey one summer. Swell. The clown returns home.

"Did you read the part about the 'innovative and daring' adaptation they want to try?"

I glanced up. "Adaptation?"

"Yeah. It was Dad's idea really. He wants to turn it into a country and western musical!"

Check. Here it was. The shit note. "A what?"

"You know, a Western swing kinda thing. 'Bob Wills Meets Hercules'!"

I handed the paper back to Preston. "Want a cup of coffee?"

"Sure, thanks. You don't seem very . . . enthusiastic."

I stood at the sink, counting to ten. "No, no—I'm enthusiastic. Whoever directs this thing ought to have a ball."

"What do you mean?"

"Whoever directs this—meaning—count me out."

"You don't think it's a good idea?"

"The Edsel was a good idea! This doesn't even register on the plausibility scale." I set Preston's coffee down hastily, spilling a little. Fuming, I squatted under the sink searching for a dish towel to wipe it up.

"Did you know you have a hole in the crack of your shorts?"

I stood slowly, mortified. Attempting indifference, I shrugged. "I like it that way. Keeps my butt cool between orgies."

Preston burst out laughing. "Hey, I'm sorry, man, I'm just playing with ya. How old are you again, thirty-nine?"

"Thirty-seven."

"You're in great shape for your age. No kidding. I can help you with those abs if you really want to get tight."

"Thanks." Again, he started doing the laser thing with those western-sky blue eyes. Preston was a world-class tease, no question. My "gaydar" needle had spun twice around the dial and was now resting on the bottom of the gauge. A serious piece of work, this boy.

"How long you guys been up?" Chris entered the kitchen—showered, shaved and neat as a first-day-of-school haircut.

"'Bout an hour. Preston dropped by to bring me the local gossip sheet."

"Clu's the cover boy."

"Yeah?" Chris poured a cup of coffee and slid the paper off the table.

"I'll spare you the suspense—they want to do *Agamemnon* as a . . . Would you like to sit down? You're holding a hot beverage there."

"I'm fine, shoot."

"They want to turn it into a . . . *country and western musical!*" My eyes sparkled with contempt. Chris sipped his coffee and stared.

"I like it."

"What?"

"It's a little squirrely, but I like it. Set the whole thing in Texas today. It could be a hoot, and I bet a box office hit."

Immediately, and with dagger-thrusting clarity—*I got it!* He was, of course, right. Done correctly, it might be a hell of a hoot. What's wrong with me; where was my usual sense of innovation and risk-taking audacity? Was I slipping or was I just being obstinate in the face of Preston's annoying certitude?

Chris peered at me over the paper. "Why don't you put some clothes on, Studly. I'm sure Preston's quite impressed with your manly physique."

Now that was uncalled for. Chris could be a real little bitch when his mind and tongue got busy. It wasn't exactly as if I was prancing around in my underwear for Preston's sake. Right?

"I told Clu, he's in great shape to be almost forty."

I let it slide. Asshole—thirty-seven is *not* forty. "I was just about to change; thanks, Chris, for your thoughtful reminder. There's English muffins and sausage in the fridge. Chris, if you're making eggs I'll take two sunny-side."

I exited down the hall, hoping my crack hole wasn't being illuminated. I got about halfway and decided to hell with the rude bastards. It's my house, my hallway and my crack! I bent over and leisurely scooped up the Chihuahua turd with a page from the nearby phone book. Reaching the bathroom door I ventured a glance back toward the kitchen. They were both staring, mouths open.

7

THE LACK OF DISTORTION

We somehow managed to get through the first three days of Laine and Sherrod's visit without mortal incident. Laine was her usual three-month-pregnant, persnickety self. Sherrod was his reliable anal-retentive, know-it-all self. Jaston grunted and mumbled through a series of dismal dinners, and Chris took it all in with the perspicuity of a trial lawyer. We were almost a big, happy family again. Mother was due home from the hospital this afternoon, and she had requested that we have a little welcoming dinner party to meet our impending stepfather, Brother Ramirez.

Laine sat in a rocking chair by the sink, shelling peas. She was a younger version of Mom, pretty but not memorably so. She had our father's determined chin and accusing eyes. She still dressed like a small-town princess—little sundresses and cutesy tops for casual—earnest country-lady, "Laura Ashley drag" for the rest of her life. She didn't so much have a look as she gave in to one.

I diligently applied a coat of frosting to a three-layered chocolate cake, which was turning out to be one of my more fabulous creations. Jaston and Chris were down at the gristmill, and Sherrod was napping in the living room.

"If I live to be nine hundred, I'll never get it. Her marrying again makes as much sense as me marrying again."

"You're saying if Sherrod died tomorrow, you'd never get married again?"

"That's different, of course I'd get married. I'd have to. A child needs a father."

I smiled. "Like we had one, right?"

"Like we *needed* one. Maybe if there had been a father figure around, things would've turned out differently. Hand me that knife, please."

I reached for the paring knife on the counter. "Like how, different?"

"For example, Jaston—he might've learned to sit up, look people in the eye, be pleasant, comb his hair and act normal."

I flinched, that word "normal" always made me jumpy. Who in the wide world knows what that actually means? "And me?"

Laine concentrated on her bowl of peas, muttering, "I don't want to get in a fight."

"No, really, tell me."

She shook her head. "It's not worth it. How long has that roast been in the oven?"

"'Bout an hour and a half, timer's on. Let me see if I can guess—if we'd had a father's influence around here Clu probably wouldn't have turned out queer. Am I right?"

Laine looked up from her bowl and rubbed her pooching stomach. "Be an angel and hand me that glass of water."

I passed her the glass and continued calmly frosting. "You know, it's odd. Chris has two loving, God-fearing, upper-class, heterosexual parents, and he turned out gay—what happened?"

Laine snapped her peas with a rhythmic *click-click-click*. "Nothing happened. I'm sure his parents were fine. It's just a decision one makes to go down that road . . ."

"Stop right there." I carefully set the frosting knife down. "You know, I get a little tired of this—when did *you* make a decision to be straight, Laine? I don't recall you breezing into the room one day announcing you were suddenly into dicks."

"Sh-h-h, lower your voice; Sherrod's sleeping." Laine shook her head, sighing. "I knew we'd get into it. Of course I never made a 'decision'—I didn't have to. I never questioned my sexuality."

"And neither did I."

Laine gaped at me wide-eyed. "How can you stand there and say that to me! What about all those girls you dated in high school and college, huh? What was that about?"

"Laine—sister, dear—I come from a long line of heterosexuals. It's all I knew. How was I to know what I was? There were certainly no role models around telling me, 'Gee, Clu, when you put your arm around that girl and you feel all the excitement of a sagging clothesline, you might just want to seriously ask yourself a few questions.' There was no *decision*. There was no *choice*. There was a *determination* to stop living a lie and just be the nonconflicting way God in *His* wisdom made me."

Laine slapped her bowl on the table and rose. "And there it is, the big one. 'The agenda.'—'We want to be treated just like everyone else 'cause that's the way God made us, and it's not fair you're not accepting our lifestyle.' You know what I say—'Baloney!' " She emptied the pea husks into the garbage and poured the remaining contents of the bowl into a pan on the stove. "I accept and love you because you're my brother. I don't have to accept your lifestyle any more than I would a bank robber or a drug pusher."

Amazing. Here it was, the prototypical nobody wins, right-wing fundamentalist vs. gay-accord pissing match that turns every reasonable person into a stone deaf mute in about three seconds. Who needs *Politically Incorrect* on TV when you can live it? But was I going to drop it? Fuck no! "You know, Laine, being compared to a bank robber and a junkie seems a bit excessive, even for you."

"Maybe. I could have gone further. The fact is I don't have to accept anything that's considered an abomination . . ."

"Ohhhh—cut the Holy Roller crap, will you? You only go to church to see what everybody's wearing and get the dish on who's screwing who, and you know it. So don't throw that tired 'abomination' shit at me."

"The Bible says . . ."

"The Bible says mixing cotton with linen is an abomination. The Bible says touching the flesh of a dead pig is an abomination—oops, there goes the NFL. The Bible says . . ."

"Thank you! We can all play that game, Mr. Smart-Ass. I can sit right here with a Bible and match you chapter and verse on any scripture you want to throw at me. I am not God, and neither are you, so don't think you've got all the answers."

"I don't have all the answers, I just know what works for me."

Laine waved her hand in the air. "Hel-lo!"

And here we were, back at intermission. Why do I bother? Why does she bother? Maybe this was sibling love. A love/hate fixation on the other's presumed failings. We each knew how to fix the other—we just didn't have a clue about ourselves. I tried another tack. "So tell me, Laine, how would your life have been different if you'd had a father figure?"

She looked up, momentarily vacant. Gazing toward the living room, she put her hand on her stomach, "Maybe . . . maybe I'd have been less afraid of being a parent myself. Mom did what she could—it just didn't fill me with a lot of confidence, you know?" She turned to the faucet and filled her glass again. "Doctor says I need to drink lots of water. Flushes toxins."

I'd never put it all together. The miscarriages, the false pregnancies, the fertility doctors, the grueling procedures, the expense—here was a woman who really didn't know if she even wanted to be a mother. "Laine, do you want to have a child?"

She turned to me, gasping, "How can you ask me that? After all I've been through?"

"I just thought . . . maybe you're not ready."

"Sweetheart, I'm forty, when do you think I'll be 'ready'?"

I took her hand. "I don't know—maybe never. Not everyone's supposed to have a kid. It's OK, you know."

Laine stared at me, eyes welling. "Sherrod wants a child. What right do I have to deprive him of that experience?"

"You say 'experience' like it's some six-week growth seminar. It's not exactly a once-in-a-lifetime trip to see the pyramids, you know? It's your life, your body, your decision. Yes, I know Sherrod wants a child. Sherrod also wants to be governor of New Mexico one day—it may not happen. And that'll be all right too."

Laine continued staring. She squeezed my hand and spoke softly. "Can I tell you something—just between you and me?" I nodded. "He'd make an awful governor." We both laughed. Laine turned back to the rocker. "Anyway, I'm pretty sure this is my last attempt. If I lose this one, that's the ball game."

"You can always adopt."

Laine smiled ruefully. "He'll never adopt. 'Too many crazy people out there.'" She reached into her shirt pocket and produced a small prescription bottle. "If I lose this one . . . I'll probably lose him, too."

I stared at her, suddenly feeling very sorry for all of us. What weird, binding little stories we'd invented for ourselves. All of us damaged goods, still swinging our crutches and cursing anyone who got in the way of our perceived truths. It was almost a badge of honor, this shared dysfunction. Who were we without our hang-ups?

On cue, Sherrod padded into the kitchen, stretching and scratching. "Man, what time is it? I was really out in there."

"After four—you get a good nap?" They kissed, and Sherrod patted her tummy, nodding. "How's my little mommy? Ya'll solve all the world's problems in here?"

Laine scoffed, "God, if we could just solve our own problems, it would be a better world." Sherrod moved to the stove and picked up the pan lid, sniffing. He'd been a catch in his day. Darkly handsome, in a hillbilly/Sean Connery kind of way, he'd gotten a little soft in his forties. It had all expanded and sort of slumped—but the overall package remained appreciable. High-school athlete, honors student in college, graduate degree in business—he had the ambition of Napoleon . . . and the luck of Mussolini. Job after job, business after business, deal after deal—he's either blown it, overshot his wad, risked all on impulse or flat-out done something illegal. Laine married our father. "I'm starved. What time are we eating?"

"Get out of there. Not till six. Make yourself a bowl of cereal." Cereal—man food, two ingredients—Captain Crunch and milk.

"Well, Clu—you about ready to become an uncle?" Sherrod scanned the pantry.

"There's a box of Life up on that top shelf. Yeah, I'm ready—ready when ya'll are." Laine and I exchanged glances.

Sherrod retrieved the cereal and a bowl and spoon from the strainer. "Oh, we're ready. More than ready. Have you told your brothers about the name?"

Laine looked a little embarrassed, "You tell him."

Sherrod sat and poured milk. "Well . . . if it's a boy, we're gonna call him Sherrod Jaston Clu Miller."

I blinked. My thoughts raced between moved and horrified. "Gosh . . . I'm really honored, but that is about the weirdest name I've ever heard."

Laine nodded. "I told him you'd be ill when you heard it."

"What do you mean, it's a great name—masculine, has substance."

"And if it's a girl?"

"Jane," Laine interrupted quickly and sipped at her water. "Jane . . . Bettie."

I smiled. "Mom'll love that. Who's Jane?"

"Jane Pauley. I want her to go into broadcasting."

"Jane Bettie—it's cute. I hope it's a girl."

Mouth full, Sherrod swallowed. "Hey . . . we'll take anything we get. Long as it's not a Pomeranian." He laughed and nudged Laine. "You ever think about having kids, Clu?"

I actually saw Laine kick Sherrod under the table.

"Maybe one day, who knows? Most states don't allow gay adoptions."

Sherrod held his spoon in suspension. "I thought ya'll were adopting all the AIDS and crack babies of the world." He said it without a hint of scorn.

"Yeah, well—we seem to take anything the world throws at us."

Laine stood and stirred the peas on the stove. "What time does the hospital van drop Mother off again?"

"Between four-thirty and five." I studied Sherrod's face, "Would you ever consider adopting a crack baby, Sherrod?"

Laine stopped stirring and put down the spoon. Sherrod gazed at the box of Life and sighed. "I don't believe I could do that. But I think it's an admirable thing." He continued eating.

Laine broke the silence. "Let's use the good china tonight, what do you think? Hell, we're meeting 'Pa-pa'—I say go for broke." She vanished into the dining room.

I called to her, "I'll give you a hand." Sherrod continued munching. "You think you'll be a good father, Sherrod?"

He looked up, confused. "Sure, what's to it? Hold their hands when crossing the street, teach 'em to throw a ball, kiss their boo-boos—I had a great dad. We were buds. Cinch job." He tilted his bowl and spooned the last bit of milk, then spoke quietly. "Maybe a job I'll even succeed at." Carrying his dish to the sink, he rinsed it out. Laine had trained him well. I watched as he looked out at the backyard. I bet he would make a good dad—the unruffled, slightly absent, here's-my-wallet type. An American dad. He turned to me with a little smile. "How's Chris doing?"

"Good. He's kind of a fish out of water with all these Texans—but he's doing fine."

"He's a teacher, right?"

"Yeah, Latin. Well, he does a lot of things, but that was his last job."

"Yeah." Sherrod nodded, looking puzzled. "You guys been together for a while, haven't you?"

"Eight years."

Sherrod continued nodding. "You know . . . what's that like—two guys living together? I can't see it."

This was a dead-on jolt; he was sincerely inquiring. Big first. "It's like being with anyone you love—'the agony and the ecstasy'—and largely the 'routine.'"

Sherrod nodded. "Do you . . . 'love' each other?"

"Every chance we get."

It took several seconds, but he finally grinned. "Uh-huh." Sherrod scratched his head and folded his arms. "I just want you to know, Clu, I'm not a big homophobe or anything. I think it still kinda pushes Laine's buttons, but I'm cool. Live and let live, I say. I just don't know a whole lot about it. You're maybe the only gay guy I know."

"You think so?"

He nodded. "Yeah—well, you're the only 'out' one I know. I just don't see it in my day-to-day."

"We're there, Sherrod—the grocery store, the car repair shop; the principal, the fireman, the CEO, the Sunday school teacher, the postal clerk—we're there. You just haven't needed to 'see.'"

He looked at me a bit skeptical, then shrugged. "Maybe."

Laine reentered the kitchen. "Would somebody please give me a hand with the serving platter on top of Mother's hutch?"

"Sure, hon." Sherrod walked by and put his hand on my shoulder. "Don't you think Clu looks more and more like that rascal father of yours?"

Laine shuddered. "Oh God, don't give him a big head. Daddy's looks let him get away with murder. Clu's nice-looking—but he's no Herbert Q. Latimore, thank God."

"Please! I thought we were having a party tonight. Keep the name of Ivan the Terrible to yourself." Mother stood in the back door, her arm swathed in a zippy red kerchief sling, looking for all the world like Auntie Mame just back from a cruise. Wearing a navy pantsuit and a jaunty straw hat cocked to the side, she pronounced elatedly, "Oh, it smells like real food again!"

"Mother!" Laine hurried to hug her. "You're early."

"I couldn't bear it a second longer." Mother studied Laine. "Darling, I think you're bigger than you were this last time. Ya'll may just be having twins." Laine flushed and cradled her stomach. Mother stretched her good hand toward me, and stated incredulously, "Melba started calling me Buddy! I had to make my breakout." An African-American driver stood on the porch holding Mom's suitcase. I took it and asked him inside.

"No, thanks. Gotta drop off another one in the van. Sure does smell something good in here."

"Oh please come back and have dinner with us, won't you? This is my family, Latrell helped spring me from the lockup."

"Nice to meet ya'll. Thank you, Miz Latimore, but I got a wife and four kids, and if I ain't home eating her corn bread at suppertime, she gets the law out after me." He waved good-bye and hurried back down the walk.

"I don't remember any Black families in Grit growing up?" I asked.

"Hospital hired him a year or so ago. Nice man. Goes to my church. We're just like the rest of the country now—totally integrated." Mother glanced up. "Sherrod! For heavens sake give me a hug."

Sherrod came from around the table, where he'd been standing. "I didn't want to crowd you. How are you, Mother Latimore?"

"Old as the Parthenon—but still got most of my columns." And suddenly they were upon us. Like a pack of paparazzi chasing a top-less starlet, the entire Chihuahua convention burst into the room. They yelped, twisted, wiggled and snorted till Mother finally sat down and picked each one up, bestowing her undivided attention. "Yes, Señor and Chica—and there's Bessie, how are you, sweet thing? Did you miss me, where your girls at? Come here Leela and Lila. Come on." Two brown rats jumped into her lap and Mother fussed and delighted over them like a pair of Cartier bracelets. (They *were* her Cartier bracelets.)

"Did Delphinium have her litter yet?"

"Not yet, but she looks like she's ready to erupt any second."

"Bless her heart, I don't know what's up with her? Must be un-easy about something."

Laine stood at the sink, rubbing lotion on her hands. "The roast'll be done at five, and we've got baked potatoes and zucchini casserole in the oven. There's salad and peas and dinner rolls and . . ."

"Bless you—no more hospital applesauce! Thank you children for doing this. Where's your brother? Does he know about tonight?"

"He'll be here. He's with Chris, over at the Byers's place."

Mother rose, frowning, clutching the two puppies. "I wish he'd stay away from that wreckage. He's got no business ratting around on other people's property."

"But I thought we owned it?" Laine queried.

"I pay taxes, that's all."

Laine and I looked at each other, confused.

"How do you pay taxes on something you don't own?"

"Oh, honey, I'll explain it one day, I will. Let me just lie down for a bit till my head stops spinning. Everything looks beautiful." Mother drifted through the dining room, toward her bedroom, fol-lowed by the rat pack. "Good, you're using the Lenox. Oh, Laine, see if you can find those Irish cloth napkins you gave me at Christmas. I think they're in a box on this bottom shelf over here. Brother Ramirez is going to be so impressed . . . my handsome, considerate, happy family." Her voice trailed off as we stood blinking at each other.

"Mom's home."

At exactly five past six the front doorbell rang. Jaston was sitting in the living room watching a ball game. Laine and Chris and I were in the kitchen putting together a cheese and cracker plate. I called out to Jaston, "Get the door, will you?" Jaston, who'd shaved, showered and put on a clean shirt that Laine had especially ironed for him, was looking virtually respectable. He lumbered over to the door and swung it wide open. All we could see from the kitchen was his head slowly lowering till it came to rest just above his clavicle. A hand suddenly thrust its way in, and Jaston shook it. He then backed up and then the oddest thing happened—Mickey Rooney entered. Followed by Imelda Marcos.

"Oh, this is a pretty place. Real pretty."

"So nice," the woman nodded. They were indeed a striking pair. She wore a large bouffant and had on a stiff, pink suit and spike heels that I estimated, all combined, put her at just under five-four. He, however, had on the highest-heeled boots I'd ever seen this side of Sunset Boulevard, and if he cracked five-two, I'd have been astounded. Jaston towered over them like a lost redwood. They stood and stared at one another as if awaiting stage instructions.

Dropping the hors d'oeuvres prep, Chris, Laine and I beat a path to the front door.

"Hello, Brother Ramirez. I'm Laine Miller, I'm the middle Latimore sibling; you've met Jaston—he's our big brother, and this is . . ."

I reached out, pumping his hand. "Clu, I'm the youngest—some say the brightest." Forced laughter. "This is my significant other, Chris Myles." If the pronouncement offended any sensibilities, it didn't register in their faces.

"Pleased to meet you."

"Yes, I've got a significant other around here somewhere." Laine turned to look.

Jaston interrupted, "He's out back wiping dog shit off his loafers."

A scintilla of Mother's wounded-martyr guise crossed Laine's face, then the happy headlights clicked on again. "Ha-ha-ha, you probably know all about Mother's little menagerie," Laine trilled.

Brother Ramirez smiled and nodded. "What?"

"Her . . . dogs."

"Oh! Yes, yes . . . the Chihuahuas! I love ugly little *perros*. Forgive me, I'd like you to meet Concepcion—my first wife."

Silence. The famed Latimore vivaciousness fell like a wounded bird to the entry floor. "Uh-huh," we all seemed to nod collectively, unsure of quite what to make of this fascinating bit of news. Sherrod magically appeared from the kitchen and, flashing lots of teeth, stuck his hand out. "Oh, hello, you must be the priest Mother Latimore's marrying." He wound an arm around Laine. "I'm Sherrod Miller, and this is Little Mommy."

There was an odd sense of time suddenly dawdling before us. Like watching an egg slowly revolve to the edge of a table (will it, won't it?) we stood spellbound. Smiling pleasantly, we seemed to anticipate the next gaffe with a demonic tingle. Finally, Jaston, unable to contain himself, let out a little squeal between pursed lips and instantly the jig was up. Everyone burst into goosey laughter.

Laine slapped at Sherrod's chest. "Priests don't get married."

Sherrod's smile never faded. "Did I say priest? I meant *padre* . . . is that acceptable?"

Brother Ramirez wiped his eyes. "Yes, why not?" He put his hand on "first wife's" shoulder. "It must be confusing, Concepcion is my business manager at the church. We have seven children together. We're good friends. Good marriage, good divorce."

Concepcion nodded between giggling jags. "*Good* divorce!"

Mother entered amidst all the silliness wearing a jeweled caftan and embracing what every Leo in their true power serenely radiates: *entitlement*. "Did I miss something? Oh I hate missing a good joke."

Brother Ramirez bowed and pecked Mother's hand, then kissed her full on the lips. (I do believe it was the first time I'd ever seen another man kiss my mother on the lips. If it had ever happened with Herbert Q., I wasn't around.) "You look like a queen, Bettina my dear."

"Thank you, Juanito. That's very sweet of you. Concepcion, how are you? What a pretty blouse, I love that color."

"And you, Bettie! Always a movie star."

"Oh stop! *Silent* movie star maybe. Did everyone meet? Let's sit in the living room, shall we? Would ya'll like some juice or tea, something to drink?"

"Tea sounds wonderful, please."

"I'll bring it." Laine excused herself, and Sherrod followed. The rest of us settled into the living room, which felt odd since it was the one room in the house we never utilized. Now that Jaston had permanently migrated Mother's enormous 1960s TV console in here, it felt even more alien. Like stumbling on a large, walnut coffin in a dentist's waiting room.

"Oh, Bettie, your home is so cozy and cute."

"Thank you, Concepcion; the children have kind of taken over since I've been—indisposed. It's theirs again." (Odd way of putting it, I thought.)

Brother Ramirez held Mother's hand. "And, dear, where are the little *perritos*? Are they sleeping?"

"Sleeping? Goodness no. I've got them in my bedroom, where they'll stay till after dinner."

"Such a wonderful thing, a woman who loves animals. You've always had a big heart for all God's creatures, no?"

Mother fluttered adorably. "I've loved little dogs ever since I was a girl. I don't know why, really. Maybe it's because they're so precise in design. Their personalities are so—absolute. There's a kind of lack of distortion I don't find in humans. It just moves me."

Concepcion interjected, "Like *piñatas*—there are no bad *piñatas*. Each one is its own reward."

"What a wonderful metaphor!"

"Kinda like hunting deer. Dudn't really matter how big the rack is—you always get venison!" Jaston smiled confidently. Mother patted his knee firmly, like she used to do when he was about eight or nine and veering toward rambunctious.

"Are you a hunter, Justin?"

"Jaston."

"Justin."

"No, it's . . ."

Mother swatted Jaston's knee harder. "Oh *Jaston's* quite an outdoorsman. He even mounts his own horns and tans his hides. Quite impressive."

"Yeah, I've got a coon I'm working on right now. He's climbing a tree stump, see, turning around growling, like this . . ." Jaston bared his teeth and snarled. "I could win an award if I get the eyes right. All the new eyes are plastic; glass one's got more life in 'em, you know."

Brother Ramirez and Concepcion both nodded pleasantly. I plunged ahead. "So, I really haven't heard the story yet, Brother Ramirez. How did you and our mother come to . . . connect?"

Brother Ramirez glanced at Concepcion, who beamed. "I did it! I'm the guilty one. I knew how lonely Juanito was since our divorce. He was so sad."

"We'd had many happy years together, Concepcion and me—but we were being called in separate areas of the Lord's Great Tent."

Concepcion nodded. "Yes, we were a team still—but not a match."

"The church was getting bigger all the time. People were coming from all over—and yet, I was not at peace." Juanito's large brown eyes grew melancholy.

"I saw your mother every Sunday, always sitting in the third pew up from the organist," Concepcion continued. "She looked so sweet and pretty and . . . maybe a little lonely herself. After every service I'd try to speak with her but she was very shy."

Mother nodded. "I didn't want to draw attention to myself." Which seemed touchingly ironic coming from the woman wearing the most-jewels-in-an-outfit this side of the Liberace Museum.

"One Sunday, I was watching her from the pulpit—I sit with the other deacons on the rostrum, I think that's what you call it—and suddenly it came to me. This woman was not well."

"Faith healer!" We all turned in alarm to look at Chris. "You're a *faith healer!*" he again proclaimed in a loud voice.

Concepcion blushed. "A *curandera* actually. A Mexican healer—like my mother, and her mother. I apply my spiritual faith with folk wisdom—it's all God's work."

"I knew it. I got a *spontaneous.*"

"A what?"

"Sometimes I get signals. Like the universe sends me telegrams. I knew you were a faith healer when you walked in."

"Chris! I had no idea. How long have you had this ability?" Mother looked truly amazed.

"All my life. Give or take a few wayward years in college."

Concepcion peered at Chris. "Tell me . . . and what other signals are you getting?"

Chris's eyes lit up, he was transfixed. I'd never seen him so "on" before. "For one—I think you're here to help Laine have a baby."

There was loud, sudden clattering of plates in the kitchen. Mother turned with alarm. "Laine! Is everything alright?"

After a pause we heard her stammer between hushed exchanges with Sherrod, "I . . . it's just the Melmac, nothing broke. I . . . I felt the baby kick!"

We again stared at Chris. Concepcion whispered, "What else?"

Chris closed his eyes and shook his head. "I'm not sure, it's weird . . . something like . . . 'bad luck is good luck, when good luck is bad.'"

Jaston stared in shock. "What the hell does that mean?"

"I . . . don't know. But it's clearly meant for all of us." Chris's gaze fell to the floor, unable to impart any further knowledge. We all self-consciously exchanged glances. I half expected to see a Ouija board come sailing out of the closet any minute.

"I've got orange juice and ice tea and fruit punch—who wants what?" Sherrod entered carrying a large tray of drinks, followed by Laine and the "party platter."

"That was the strangest sensation—I was putting the dishes away and I felt the baby . . . but it was like someone else was moving the baby's foot . . . I can't explain it." Laine sat, her face flushed.

Concepcion asked, "What month are you?"

"Third."

"It will be a girl."

Laine stared at Concepcion, dumbstruck, "Why do you say that?"

"Definitely, a girl." Chris nodded.

Laine stared at them both, shaken. "What is this; what are ya'll talking about?"

Concepcion smiled benevolently, "There's nothing to be afraid of, you're going to be a very happy mother."

Laine's eyes began to tear. Sherrod put his arm on her shoulder, and she stood abruptly. "I'm sorry. It's not something I can . . . discuss. Would you excuse me?" Laine exited, and we could hear the hall bathroom door closing as she locked herself inside.

Brother Ramirez glared at Concepcion. "Why do you say these things? Can't you see she's sensitive?"

"But it's good news, is it not?"

Mother restrained a mild coughing bout and rose carefully, imperiously. "She's tried for so long, bless her heart. Don't worry, I'll talk to her. Everything's fine. Clu, tell them about your acting career in New York, I'll just be a minute."

Swell, pass me the stink bomb. I dutifully began to open my mouth when Jaston stood and bolted. "I'm gonna have a beer, anybody else want one?" He didn't wait for a reply.

Again, I tried to speak. Sherrod suddenly leaned forward and interrupted in an urgent monotone, "I don't know anything about Mexican faith healers. I don't know your church, I don't know you—but if you can help my wife, I'm asking, I'm appealing to you—please help her."

Concepcion reached out and took his hand. "It's done. Tomorrow, if your wife will permit me?"

"I'll talk to her. Thank you, thank you." Fervently, Sherrod shook Concepcion's hand and anxiously motioned toward the hallway. He, too, departed.

The remaining four of us stared cheerlessly at the refreshment tableau stranded on the coffee table. "Anyone care for a chutney and jack on a 'butterfly cream cracker'?" I queried halfheartedly.

"Yes, why not?" Brother Ramirez answered.

I passed the tidbits and we crunched away in an odd serenity. Concepcion finally cleared her throat. "And so—how long have you two been a couple?"

"Long time," Chris volunteered. "We started out when cyberspace was still just a theory."

I stared at him. "And now look at us? Ooo-eee! Taking rocket ships to work. What an amazing century it's been, huh, Paw?" I frowned. "You make us sound like we've been around since the birth of fire."

"Sorry." Chris turned back to Concepcion. "We're not newly-weds."

"Oh, I think it's so interesting. We don't see many couples like you in our area."

"And I wonder why that is?" I smirked.

Brother Ramirez finished his cracker, brushing his hands. "I'm not sure, but I would imagine many same-sex couples feel unsafe in unknown surroundings."

"Actually, it's the known environment that tends to dampen the overconfidence factor," I volunteered.

He nodded. "Perhaps. But certainly not at my church. We don't judge the quality of a person's ability to love—just that they love."

"I think Clu feels that nothing will ever change in Grit. The past is resolute, attitudes remain fixed." Chris popped a few grapes in his mouth.

I shook my head, "What I think is . . . progress comes on tiny wheels. There's not a whole lot achieved by me waiting around for Grit to attain enlightenment. I'm not anticipating the new Gay and Lesbian Center opening anytime soon, you know?"

Brother Ramirez smiled. "'If not you, who? If not now, when?' I can never remember who said that, but it's seen me through many a long, discouraging day."

"I can assure you, two Mexican Americans starting a church in a tent in South Texas was nobody's idea of genius," Concepcion interjected. "You go where you're not invited—especially if it means the possibility of replacing fear and misunderstanding with love and hope."

Brother Ramirez's smile grew larger. "God has a funny way of multiplying one's chances when one leads with the heart."

I balanced a carrot stick between index and middle finger. "I hear what you're saying. I just don't see that many opportunities for expansion. Everyone's still so . . . bound in judgment."

"Don't see or haven't looked hard enough?" Brother Ramirez was beaming now. "I usually find half a dozen prospects for transformation before breakfast. I'll even give you the opportunity—come speak before the congregation next Sunday."

"About what?" I rankled.

"About your experiences as a gay man: growing up in a small town, moving off, coming back—the growth, the revelation . . . the ongoing debate?"

I stammered, woefully self-conscious. "I . . . I couldn't possibly. You don't know the trouble it would cause. People just want you to live your 'affliction' in silence."

"I'll do it." Chris stood, brushing crumbs from his lap. "Be happy to. Clu isn't ready to face his past just yet, but I don't have any buried bones here. You're right, 'If not now, when? If not you, who?'"

"Beautiful!" Concepcion clasped Chris's hand. "You're a healer—but of course, you know that. We all have the ability to remedy, but you have an extra gift that God has given you. You must be careful to never undermine that blessing."

Chris nodded solemnly, and I panicked. "You can't do it."

"What?"

"I don't want you to speak at the church."

"Why not?"

"Because you can't. You're an extension of me—this is my hometown, these are my skeletons. You can't hang me out there for target practice like that."

Chris shook his head slowly. "When are you going to let it go? Are you going to live in the past your whole life?"

I recoiled. "You don't get it, none of you do. Look—my family, we're outcasts here to begin with—one more boulder flung on the wagon, and we're all busted. I'm not ready to take on the mantle of gay activist. Sorry, I'm not."

Chris put his hand on my knee. "Nobody's expects you to. Why are you turning this into some call to arms?"

"All God asks is that we live our lives in truth. You being you is all anyone expects." Brother Ramirez said it with such compassion and patience, I felt immediately chastised.

Unexpectedly, Mother reappeared on a slender waft of Estée

Lauder Youth Dew—a little lipstick, some fresh powder—all previous transgressions discarded. "Have ya'll been getting to know each other?"

Brother Ramirez stood. "Bettie, your children are a true testament to your loving nature and magnificent originality."

"Sh-h-h—I've always told them it was my red-hair gene they inherited that made them special. Now they'll know it's just old oddball Mom and her idiosyncrasies that keep them peculiar." Mother laughed and coughed several times. "Shall we eat?"

Brother Ramirez gently held Mother's good arm, and en masse we trooped across the hall. In the dining room I could see Laine busily making last-minute adjustments with bowls and hot pads and salad forks. She looked up, still red-eyed, and smiled at Concepcion. "Please forgive me for acting like such a ninny. My hormones are all over the map lately. I'm sorry for being such a half-wit."

"Not at all! Juanito will tell you—I usually speak first and think later. It's not a helpful trait."

"I think we all share that characteristic, Concepcion. What a dull, predictable old world it'd be if we didn't." Mother shuddered. "Gracious, if we could edit every thought in our heads with a politician's ease, we'd all just be one more cob in the corncrib—nothing special, nothing useful." Mother scanned the table adroitly. "Now let's see . . . Concepcion, if you'll sit over here on this side by me, then Clu and Chris, then Jaston, Laine and Sherrod, and finally Brother Ramirez on my right. Does that work for everyone?"

We took our assigned seats. The table looked beautiful, a true Southern feast. Fresh flowers and good china, real food and Irish linens. When we did manage to get it right, the results were imposing.

Mother took Brother Ramirez's hand and Concepcion touched Mother's cast at the elbow. They bowed their heads, and the rest of us, faltering slightly, followed suit.

Brother Ramirez began praying in a lulling tenor. "Dear God, Infinite Spirit, we are gathered in this wonderful home to share this meal which you have provided with great bounty and joy. Bless us as we partake of your offerings with thankfulness. For my beloved, Bettie Jean, I give thanks that you have brought us together in a great vision of faith. May our time together be filled with abiding love, abounding care and infinite delight. We are so grateful you have led us each to this loving atonement. For Concepcion, may her work continue to heal and help others whose lives she blesses through your fulfilling hand. For Laine and Sherrod, may your unending grace bring them the joy and divine favor they so eagerly anticipate. And may their particular blessing reflect the wonderful physical and spiritual beauty evident in their most deserving and capable souls. For Justin, may his particular needs be especially regarded and realized so that his great talents are fulfilled in ways that both serve and glorify your divine purpose. And for Clu and Chris—a special blessing on their lives as they create a newer vision of your eternal and all-embracing affirmation of love among those who inhabit your ever-expansive earthly consciousness. In your name, we choose and hold these beliefs as absolute and perfect in their wisdom. And so it is, Amen."

Silence. As if waking from a conducted trance we slowly began passing plates and bowls. It'd been a long time since we, the Latimore family, had experienced such a feeling of—what was it—cohesion? *Awareness?* We were the best we had. And it was probably best we honor that in some way. But how? If we'd only had a glimmer of precognition—a sense of consequence—we might have found the courage to begin forgiving one another. That this would be the last time we'd ever all be together, around this table, in this room—never crossed our minds.

8

DROWNED HUMMINGBIRD

"Richelle, baby—bring Mama another Marlboro Light." I sat next to Myla as she stretched indolently on the chaise lounge by the pool. It was close to 7 P.M. and still hot as a "hoosegow in hell." (A hoosegow is what old-time Texans used to call jail—a term my great-uncle Pete frequently referred to from, no doubt, personal experiences.) The bug lights lining the patio were glowing an exotic fluorescent indigo and about every six seconds another enormous Gulf Coast moth would surrender to karma and flutter into the neon inferno, causing a huge pop, hiss and fizzle. The ensuing roasted, meaty vapor only slightly varied from the tang of the burning steaks spattering on the gas grill.

Zane Biggs had probably gained 125 pounds since I saw him last. He'd literally grown another torso. And it all appeared to be wrapped snugly around his middle. With some body paint and an Afro he could have easily passed as a touring Samoan wrestler. He was tall, six-foot-six. Everything about him was big. As he lumbered toward me carrying a fresh pitcher of margaritas, I wondered if perhaps there might be a small man trapped inside and desperate to get out. "Hey, Clu, you oughta come elk hunting with us up in Colorado this fall. Man, you wouldn't believe the old bull I shot last year, had balls on 'im the size of fuckin' coconuts." I abandoned the smallman theory as I accepted my third margarita in forty minutes. (Watch yourself, Clu. Pace it, you big lush.)

"Oh, honey, Clu dudn't care about no elk balls, do you, Clu?"

"Well, uh . . ."

" 'Course he dudn't, Clu's an artist. Zane, sugar, bring me some limes will you? My margarita's not sour enough."

Zane didn't seem to hear. "No shit—sucker had a rack on him like this." Zane gestured with his giant paws. "We just about didn't get his dadgum head in the Suburban."

"You cannot believe the elk shit and blood I had to clean out of that car! I finally said hell with it and drove it down to Mendiola's Texaco. I told 'em, 'Ya'll clean it up and charge Mr. Biggs whatever you want.' Myla turned back to Zane and shook her glass. "Honey—limes?" She then cocked her head back and bellowed in a voice that rattled the pyracantha bushes, "Richelle Tiffany Morgan Biggs! Don't make me ask for a cigarette again!"

Zane reached for Myla's glass and paused before starting back toward the margarita wagon. "Clu, you know anybody can paint? I want somebody to paint a picture of me and that elk. Money's no object—it's just gotta look real."

"Oooh, Zaaane! Not a painting, too. You've got enough pictures of that poor, dead thing to start a museum."

"A painting lives on in posterior . . . postros-ity . . ."

"The word is, '*postudiny.*'" Myla shook her head in disgust.

"Whatever. I want to give it to my grandkids one day."

Myla suddenly sat up and squealed. She waved at a couple exiting from the sliding glass doors of the living room. "Yoo-hoo! Over here, ya'll!" Myla cocked her head to the side and cooed in a soft murmur as they approached, "It's Debbie Guidry—she married Jimmy Kinney. You don't know him, but he's real nice. Too nice, if you know what I mean. Don't say anything about her plastic surgery unless she brings it up. Hey!"

"Hi, ya'll, where is everybody?"

"Oh, hon, I made poor Clu get here an hour before everybody else so I could have him all to myself. You're right on time. Are those pants new?" The two women kissed.

"Oh Lord no. Hi, Zane! I got these in Dallas last year, you've seen them, I know you have." Debbie then turned to face me, full on, hollering almost as loud as Myla, "Clu Latimore! Let me look at you!" Pausing only a millisecond to peruse my countenance, she threw her arms around me and we embraced like it was the final bell on the *Titanic*. "Oh, you look greaaat! And you smell so good, too. Jimmy, smell Clu."

Jimmy obediently stuck his nose in my ear, then backed away, contemptuous.

"I've got some of that."

"Oh, honey, no you don't." Debbie sniffed again, "What is it, Clu—Davidoff, Cool Water? Gio? Havana?"

"You know I . . . don't remember. It was a sample I got for buying a shirt somewhere."

Jimmy eyed me coolly, then stuck out his hand. "Jimmy Kinney. I've got some of that."

"I'm sorry, I didn't even introduce ya'll, this is my husband."

"Pleased to meet you."

"Isn't he just as cute as I told you, Jimmy?" Debbie nodded distractedly as she continued to contemplate my presence with precise scrutiny. She suddenly glanced around, confused, "Where's your 'friend' at, Clu? I want to meet your 'friend.'"

By now Richelle had finally shown up with a cigarette. She lit it and playfully teased Myla, offering it, then quickly yanking it away. "Oh, Debbie, I'm so mad at Clu. He let that cute man drive off to Port Aransas with His Blondness—you know, the big beltbuster living over at Miss Oveta's." Myla finally snatched the cigarette from Richelle and wrapped her arms around her in a tight bear hug. Richelle shrieked in distress.

Debbie appeared breathless. "No! Well, what's going on, Clu?"

"Nothing's going on—he just wanted to see the coast, and Preston's driving."

"We think 'Press-tone' may be one of your 'club members,' Clu." Myla winked and managed to take a drag off her cigarette through tightly wound arms. "Ow! Quit it, Richelle, you're gonna break my nail."

"Well stop slobbering in my ear!" Myla finally released Richelle, who immediately ran to Zane, stood on his size-thirteen feet and took a sip from the margarita he was holding. "Daddy, can I have a frog kiss? Can I?" Zane casually lifted up Richelle, now lying horizontal in his arms like a sofa bolster, and put his mouth on her bare stomach. Inhaling sharply, he blew with such force her pink flesh rippled and shuddered as if prodded by an electrical impulse. It sounded exactly like the loudest, wettest fart in history. Richelle was scarlet from oxygenless laughter. Myla frowned. "Zane, I wish you wouldn't do that. Dr. Zafir thinks it may be giving the girls ideas."

Zane stopped blowing and looked up, his own face crimson. "What kind of ideas?"

"Oh, honey, we talked about it. It may get them too . . . 'stimulated.' " Myla did quotation marks with her fingers.

Zane, at first, didn't appear to comprehend, then slowly he set Richelle down. "Jesus, Myla, we're not exactly Ozark inbreds. Where do you and Zafir come up with this psychological"—Zane repeated Myla's quotation marks with his own bulky digits—"owl shit?"

Myla rolled her eyes and turned back to Debbie. "Come on in and let me get you a Chardonnay. Jimmy, you having a margarita? Zane, I'll pour mine from the blender in the kitchen. Clu, don't tell any good gossip till we get back." The girls padded off to the house. Myla suddenly turned, and barked, "Richelle! Mommy needs you to cut up tomatoes in the kitchen. Move it!"

Richelle stood sipping from somebody else's half-consumed margarita glass. Zane and Jimmy had withdrawn to the adult Slurpee dispenser. "Mr. Latimore, do you think I could be an actress when I grow up?"

Here was an absolutely gorgeous, precocious, "Tuesday Weld" stunner. She could be premier of Russia if she put her mind to it. "Well, probably so, Richelle. Do you want to be an actress?"

She hunched her shoulders and painstakingly fished a lime from the bottom of the tall glass. "I don't know. I'd kind of like to be Oprah, too. She's so neat. I think she's changing the world, don't you?"

I stared, fascinated. Gone were the idols of my youth, Farrah Fawcett and Rick Springfield. When white kids have black role models—the revolution is rendered. Anybody can be anything. "Honey, I wouldn't be surprised if you became Oprah, Sandra Day O'Connor, and Ricky Martin all in one."

Richelle's eyes lit up. "Coooool. Does Sandra Day sing with the Cranberries?" She glanced behind me, a storm cloud crossing her flawless features. Myla was standing at the sliding doors, holding up a carving knife. Richelle yelled, "I'm coming!" She set the glass down, grumbling to herself, "None of my sisters have to do anything. They're too 'busy.' Do you think I'm pretty, or not?"

I nodded. "Yes, I think you're very pretty, Richelle. But I'm more interested in knowing how pretty you are in here." I pointed to my heart. "You can be the best-looking girl in town, but if you're not a good person, what do you have?"

Richelle thought about it for a second. "I don't know. I guess a huge house, a swimming pool, lots of cars and a big old margarita machine. I gotta go." She kissed me quickly on the cheek and ran off to the house, leaving behind a sticky spot on my face and the over-whelmingly nostalgic scent of Tide lingering in the dampish, evening air. Even gay boys are not immune to the paradoxical charms of the female mystery—at any age.

"So, Zane tells me you're going be doing a play at the new Little Theater?" Jimmy stood behind me holding out yet another margarita.

"I gotta pace myself—I'm gonna be plastered before the gua-camole's done."

"Hell, it's Friday. You got big plans tomorrow?"

"No. Just don't want to feel like death when I get up."

Jimmy took a sip from his fishbowl-size glass. It had green saquaro cactuses and sombreros painted on its sides. I wondered if they drink martinis in Mexico from glasses with stock market quotes and Valium prescriptions on them. Zane was doggedly netting downed insects from the pool. I licked salt from my lips, and Jimmy continued to stare at me, searching for what, I couldn't tell. Finally, he spoke.

"I got a brother that's gay."

"Oh really?"

"Nobody talks about it. He lives in Chicago. He's never, like, come out of the closet or anything—but we all know."

"How do you know?"

Jimmy sniffed and kicked back some more margarita. "He's my brother. How does anyone know? You know."

"Is it a problem?"

"Not to me. I don't care. My folks don't take it so well."

"Why not?"

Jimmy looked at me a little incredulous. "Why not? I guess they wanted their son to be straight, how do I know?"

Spurred by tequila, I ventured on. "If you had a son that was gay, would you feel the same?"

Again, Jimmy looked puzzled. "I'd want him to be straight, of course."

"Of course. And a star athlete, class president, marry the girl next door and hold down a six-figure job; got it—but if for some reason the dream didn't pan out? What then?"

Jimmy smiled. "I know where you're going. Look, I'm a straight guy—I want my kids to be like me. What do I know about raising gay boys?"

"Nothing to it, apparently—every gay boy I know was raised by a straight father."

Jimmy peered at me over his glass. "Well, I guess we all play with the cards we're dealt. Just wouldn't be my first choice—having a gay kid, you know?"

I nodded. "Assuming choice is ever a possibility." I plowed on. "But now if you did happen to have this imaginary gay son or daughter, Jimmy—don't you think they'd sooner or later pick up on your disappointment in their not being . . . you?"

He stared into the distance. "I guess. Not something I have to worry about though. I've got two beautiful, very heterosexual daughters. My biggest worry is keeping them unpregnant and out of jail till they graduate high school." He laughed and tipped his glass toward me.

I smiled back. "And do they know about their gay uncle?"

"No-o-o. They don't need to be thinking about that stuff while they're still school kids."

"Right—just birth control and the number of a good lawyer."

Zing. Jimmy lowered his glass, little salt whiskers lining the corners of his mouth. "What's that mean?"

It's usually about now I suppress the alcoholic urge to reach for a two-by-four and simply whale away on whoever the smug, bigoted, annoying-as-hell bastard standing in front of me is. I come from a long line of rednecks—being gay has zilch to do with that ancient-evil, Anglo-male, unspoken-rage conundrum. I've seen Jaston beat a car hood with his bare fists till it dented and buckled from the bloody thrashing. Make any sense? 'Course not. Does bungee jumping and tractor pulling make any sense? (The appeal of which escapes me right now, but I can and do thoroughly appreciate a lurid interest in their existences.)

"Oh, Jimmy—I think we probably shouldn't go any further. I'm happy your girls are doing so well."

His suddenly snarly mouth puffed out in a little blowfish sneer. "Ya'll always pushing yourselves on society—you know, you'd probably get more of people's sympathy if you stopped rubbing it in their faces."

"Uh, Jimmy, bud—I believe you were the one that brought up the fact that your brother is gay."

"Yeah, I was trying to break the ice. Be friendly—let you know we're not all backward hicks around here."

Check. "Well, you know—if you're an example of local progressive thinking, I got news for you, Jimbo—the world is round, shithead!"

That did it. Snarly mouth got all red and started blowing little chunks of salt my way. "You're just like my brother and his fag friends—all got a mouth on 'em. Like a bunch of goddamn women bitching and pissing. Be a man."

Something popped. My hard drive crashed. There was no editing software left anymore. I was spinning on a cracked tequila flywheel—and the shit was flying. "Hey, Jim, hey man—are you under some delusion we're still in junior high school and anything that comes out of your rank little mouth has even the slightest relevance in my life? I don't give an ungodly fuck what you think about me, my life, my personality or my free sample of designer cologne. I'm here to be a friend to Myla and Zane, and you're absolutely meaningless to the context of anything that I can even remotely wrap my brain around at this point. *Comprende?* In short, I think I truly—yes, I re-

ally do—despise your nasty, hypocritical, fucking guts. So why don't
just take your little starched Docker khakis and waddle on over to
the margarita machine and stay-the-fuck-out-of-my-face. Huh? Can
you do that for me—*Jim-bo?*"

Zane suddenly appeared between us holding the dripping net. He
had the look of a child seeing his parents have sex for the first time.
"Uh . . . everything . . . um . . . hey, ya'll ever see a drowned hummingbird?"

The patio sliding doors flew open again. Myla sang out, "Guess
who's here? Sandy Huffaker!"

"Hurrah! Hurroo! There'll be an execution!" (Columbia record-
ing, 1953, "He Had Twins," from *The Boys from Syracuse,* Jack
Cassidy and chorus vocalizing.) The song was blaring in my head as
if I was sitting third row, orchestra, at the Music Box Theater in New
York. Someday, someone will make a lot of money, do all the talk
shows and dine at the White House for scientifically extrapolating
why *certain* show tunes consistently appear in the heads of *certain*
gay men during *certain* categorical situations. Is there a gay man
alive (of a *certain* age) who doesn't immediately think "Don't Rain
on My Parade" every time he sees a tugboat and the Statue of
Liberty? Or get just the tiniest urge to slap a feather boa around his
neck and belt "I'm Still Here" after a grueling, life-sucking day at the
office?

"Clu-u-u-u!" Sandy shimmied across the concrete patio with fre-
netic, itsy-bitsy baby steps, arms extended exactly like a toddler hoping to avoid a spill. She seemed to be wearing a . . . pinafore? (It was
short, anyway.) "Clu, I've watched every episode of *Guiding Light*
since Christmas. When are they bringing your dead-ass back?" Her
arms grabbed me just as she was about to trip over her widdle-bitty
plastic sandals with the big red daisies on the toe.

"Sandy—you haven't aged a day. You just get younger and
younger." And it was true. If she'd pulled a Barbie Doll out of her
big, shiny plastic shoulder bag and started combing her hair, it would
have seemed the most natural thing in the world.

"Oh stop, you big tease. Myla says your 'friend' didn't make it.
Pooh! We wanted to meet Mr. Right." The women giggled in a joint

melodic chorus. The men continued to stare blankly, neither interested or disinterested, just "there."

"You remember Dwayne? Dwayne transferred from Corpus Christi senior year?" Sandy pulled Dwayne around from behind her, a nice-looking, prosaic type.

"Hey, Clu, how are you? Been a long time." Dwayne pumped my hand and it all came tumbling forth like a fly skidding across a bowl of oatmeal—the "Dwayne connection." Dwayne had been best friends with Pat Pickens. Pat was our class Lothario. He was gorgeous in that classic mid-seventies way. A cross between Peter Frampton and (the young) Ryan O'Neal. It was all effortless grace and gracefully precise with Pat. What you saw was everything you ever wanted to get. He knew it, you knew it—neat, reasonable— everyone understood the rules. Pat was destined to break hearts and proceed ever onward in his search for . . . what was it . . . "self-discovery"? He was available (indeed, he seemed to have dated almost every modestly attractive senior girl) but he wasn't "haveable." Those were the rules. At least those were the rules until the night of March 7, 1979, when we shared a room at the Rodeway Inn in San Marcos during the debate club regional finals.

Shared a room. Good Lord, where did *that* particular sense of wonder go? It's all so inextricable now. Must all life-altering events ultimately bestow the same generic imprint as say, moon landings and assassinations? Surely, one's first communal orgasm should occupy a different sensory chamber other than the last TV broadcast of M*A*S*H. I remember Pat, I remember the Rodeway Inn: the room, the smell, the bedspread, the fastened-to-the-wall, wide-eyed, peasant-child painting that we joked about someone actually wanting to steal. That's all undiminished. What's gone is the . . . *awe.* So quickly. Where are those two sixteen-year-old boys and their genuine sense of *discovery?* What did they think, see, envision, dream, fear, hide . . . *know?* Did Pat detect it was my first time? He didn't ask. Was it Pat's first time? I didn't ask. I do recall very clearly the brash, excited enjoyment we took in each other's flesh. That's indelible. And I also recall that after that night—we never spoke about it again. How could we? It was never supposed to happen. We were sinful, vile creatures.

The very idea that we actually might have felt a kind of attraction for each other was a monstrous perversion. Besides, who would we talk to? A friend in school, some adult—our parents? No, it was all to be instantly forgotten. Didn't happen. That's how you got through it. If you can deny seeing your right hand enough times, you eventually don't see what your right hand does anymore. And if you don't see it—must've never happened, right? From there on it's just a short skip to the really dazzling denial stuff—out-of-control sex, drugs, alcohol, relationship catastrophes. Melodramatic, I know. But then again, if you can't see it—must've never happened. Right?

"So . . . how's Pat Pickens?" I asked about as subtle as a turd floating in a punch bowl.

"Oh, you know Pat . . . that's right, I forgot. Weren't ya'll in drama club together?" Dwayne queried.

"Debate team."

"Right." Dwyane stood nodding, trying to pry loose some detail concerning our friendship that was stubbornly evading him.

Sandy interrupted, "Oh, Clu, Pat's third marriage just broke up. He's still trying to find himself. Poor thing's looked harder than anyone I know."

"Ever since he took over his daddy's drilling outfit he's just been kind of foundering," Zane mused.

"*Floundering!* Foundering is what horses do." Myla shook her head.

Zane looked startled. "Excuse me, Miss Webster's, you eat a *flounder*—you *founder* when you're trying to find something to eat."

Myla shrugged. "Thank you, William F. 'fucking-know-it-all' Buckley." She then spun and started back for the house. "Who needs another drink—Clu, Debbie? Jimmy, you look so red, why don't you come sit inside in the air conditioning?"

Jimmy edged around me, carefully shunning my presence. "Beginning to smell funny out here anyway—ya'll must have a polecat hanging around." He flung an arm around Debbie's shoulders and steered her back toward the house, a surprised look on her face.

"Polecat? I shot one down by the tennis courts two weeks ago. We better not have any skunks. I pay the dadgum exterminator a fortune to keep this place vermin-free." Zane distractedly flung the pool net back toward the water. It landed with a splash. I immediately fretted about the sodden hummingbird still encased in the web. Being drowned twice seemed rather extreme.

"Clu, you ought to go by and say hi to Pat; he's become a real recluse. Nobody's seen him since his mother's funeral last year." Sandy spoke softly.

"He's pretty much raising that boy of his on his own. Now there's every parent's dream child." Dwayne accepted a margarita from Zane.

"Oh Brandon's just a little unconventional." Sandy adjusted a bright candy-colored clip pulling her bangs back.

"A little? How many kids in Grit you know have blue hair and a Chinese symbol tattooed on their neck?"

"What's the symbol say?" I had to know.

"I'm a freak!" Dwayne hooted, and Zane joined in giddily.

Sandy shook her head, smiling with the boys. "Ya'll are bad. All Pat can get out of him is something about Free Tibet. Poor kid's kinda lost. Why don't you go see Pat, Clu?"

See Pat? God, why go back there, again? Too many ghosts, too much . . . unsettled territory. I replied unconvincingly, "Maybe." And maybe I would.

After dinner of grilled rib-eyes, porterhouse and brisket, baked potatoes, corn on the cob, pinto beans, Caesar salad, ambrosia, garlic bread, pecan and key lime pie—I was ready to die. I'd lost track of the margaritas. My head was saturated, my stomach distended. All I wanted to do was black out and wake up next year sometime.

"Alright everybody, Zane's got the hot tub steaming. Grab your margaritas and follow me." Myla took off down a brick path behind some crepe myrtle bushes. I stood blinking in astonishment. She's not serious. Here we were, a bunch of middle-aged, porcine children— laden with an extra thirty pounds each of groceries, firewater and intestinal poison—and now she expects us to stew in a kettle of scalding, foul water like some revolting Fourth of July clambake. I'm outta here.

"Here's a beach towel, Clu; it's got the Little Mermaid on it—you don't mind, do you?" Zane chuckled as he flung towels at each of us.

"I think he's got one just like it at home," Debbie grinned as she started unbuttoning her blouse and began to strip beside a chaise lounge.

This is definitely not going to happen. I sat the towel down and held my arm up to wave. "Myla, Zane—ya'll, it's been great. Really. I need to get back home and check on Mother. Thank you so much, it was wonderful."

I turned. Myla stepped from behind an enormous hibiscus plant and looked up genuinely shocked. She was topless, clutching her beach towel around her hips. "You can't go home now! This is the best part. We all smoke a joint and get relaxed and open up to each other."

I felt sick. Not on your life, sister. "You know—let's do it another time. I think I had too much to drink."

Instantly there was a tap on my shoulder and I turned around to see a fully naked Sandy taking a last toke on a marijuana cigarette the size of a baby Tootsie Roll. "Hon . . . it's like this . . . it's kinda spiritual . . . me and Dwayne, we've been going to sweat lodges up in Santa Fe for like, years now . . . you know—skiing, shopping—sweat lodges . . . and we've really gotten into this . . . Native American thing of . . . you know, speaking your truth."

What planet was this? I quickly passed the joint to Debbie, who was now standing beside me, naked as a spoon. I did a double take as Jimmy sidled up beside her, scratching his hairy butt. I was now surrounded by large-paunched, unclothed, smiling people who seemed to have stumbled out of some *Village of the Damned* re-hearsal. "Ya'll . . . I don't think I'm up for this. I mean, it sounds real interesting, but . . ."

Jimmy put his hand on my shoulder. "I think we got off on the wrong foot, man. Really. Debbie thinks I shot my mouth off, and I want to apologize. I didn't mean it the way it sounded. You're cool. We're all cool. Stay man." His glassy, beady eyes and saintly sneer were almost convincing. Now we were suddenly cool—we'd pro-gressed from provincial high schoolers to mellow, college druggies. Jimmy held out the joint. A peace offering. Ordinarily I don't smoke pot; I hate pot. It makes me sleepy and hungry—two of my already more disagreeable traits. I could tell Jimmy was intent on portraying sincerity with reckless abandon. Asshole. What could I do? I took the joint and inhaled.

Myla hooted, "Yah-hoo! Get those drawers off, bubble-butt, and meet us down at the hot tub." They all turned and I watched six naked adults in various stages of bodily evolution traipse across the lawn like vignettes from a Lucien Freud painting.

Frustrated, I started to unbutton my shirt. How do I get myself into these things? And why the hell couldn't I just be more of a "flow" kind of guy. Maybe I am an uptight little priss. Maybe I do judge everybody and every situation with the withering censure of a holy seer. Who made me God? (On the other hand—who made them God? Fuck it, we're all omnipotent nowadays.) I slipped out of my underwear, my head spinning. I knew I was drunk, but I also seemed to be vaguely in some sort of control, or so I thought. This wouldn't get out of hand. I'd make sure of that.

I neatly folded my shirt, put my Omega wristwatch inside my pants pocket and slipped off my gold wedding band. I thought briefly about what Chris must be doing about now and wondering if he were here how he'd react to this particular *divertissement*. Who knows, the way things were going, the way our lives were rapidly becoming uncitified and imminently "Texanized"—he might just find the whole thing a major kick.

"Mr. Latimore, you have a phone call. Do you want to take it on the cellular?"

I spun around so fast I knocked over a small tray table with drinks on it. Grasping madly for my Little Mermaid sheath I hastily covered my bare body. Richelle stood behind me holding out a tiny fluorescent orange phone.

"R . . . Richelle. God, you scared me."

"You're going in the hot tub? You'll like it. We had a family 'truth session' the other night. How much do you weigh?"

"One . . . one sixty—five."

"You're in better shape than the other dads. I'm watching *South Park*—here." Richelle handed me the phone, then turned and skipped back up toward the house. I'd completely forgotten about the girls. Christ, were the others in the bushes snapping Polaroids? What a mess. I stuck the play phone to my ear. "Hel-lo."

"Hello yourself, buckaroo!"

"Chris?"

"No, it's Tab Hunter. Who do you think this is?"

"Where are you? What's all that noise?"

"Oh, baby, I wish you were here. We're at this country and western gay bar in Corpus. What a hoot!"

"Sounds like you're having a good time. How'd you get my number?"

"I called Zane. I just wanted to tell you something . . . I miss you."

"You do? That's nice. Me too."

"Are you having fun? I hope it's not too boring for you there."

The margarita machine loudly shifted gears and I clutched at my towel. "No, no. It's . . . interesting."

"I'll bet. What are you doing now? Watching home movies from the Grand Canyon?"

"Uh . . ."

"Oh, baby—I gotta go. Preston's teaching me to line dance. This is so much fun, we gotta start doing it. Hey . . . I love you."

"I love you, too."

Chris yelled, "I'm coming!" *Click.*

Something didn't feel right. It was obvious he was nearly as drunk as I was. I'm glad he was having a good time, but why the call? To say "I love you"? Or to say, "I love you—and I'm about to be bad." Chris and I had a pretty basic understanding after all these years. "Look all you want—but *no* trying on the merchandise." It had worked so far, and I trusted him. Not that I wasn't fairly jealous in the beginning. I was—insanely so. I simply couldn't buy that a great-looking guy like Chris could actually get all that he wanted from . . . me. It was a revelation. With patience, decency and copious amounts of assurance he made me feel secure for the first time in my life. Even more unexpected, I stopped questioning if I could trust myself. But for a scant few brushes with infidelity (none remotely serious) I took to married life like a "nut-clamped bird dog." Relished it, in fact. I got what I'd always wanted: a loving, conscientious, stable partner . . . who was now drunk and slow dancing with a trashy gym-slut in some redneck-whorehouse-swamp-dive on the Gulf of Mexico. And the adult response would be? Blow it off. Be cool. You're both adults, remember? I smiled and looked down at my hand. I'd just snapped the antenna off the cell phone.

"Clu, you better get down there. The girls are starting to think you chickened out on us. Need another margarita?" Zane lumbered past me, dripping wet and heading for the beverage wagon. His massive body glistened under the bug lights like some shiny new truck. His dick, a good eight inches of prime, floppy manhood, swung from side to side like a broad sailor's rope, hanging from the bow, swaying in the breeze. Never that much of a size queen (I mean, after the initial visual, what does one really do with all that real estate?) still, I'm never not impressed by the supreme confidence abundantly endowed men so effortlessly pull off. What have they got to be shy about? Zane could stroll bare-ass through Buckingham Palace and give it about as much regard as trimming his toenails.

I cinched up my mermaid sarong and approached Mr. Ford Explorer. "So, what exactly happens when ya'll 'tell truths' in the hot tub? Is this going to turn into some kind of orgy?" I thought I was sounding light and waggish.

Zane turned to me with a look of shock. "You think I'm gonna screw Debbie or Sandy with my wife looking on? You nuts? She'd have my balls in a jar of formaldehyde 'fore I could even get Mr. Happy partial to the idea. Hell, we just talk about the meaning of life . . . who the Cowboys are drafting this year . . . shit like that."

Uh-huh. Shit like that. "Zane, don't you worry 'bout your girls?"

"Worry—what?"

"Well, seeing all these naked adults running around?"

Zane smiled and handed me a fresh margarita. (This one in a plastic disposable with confetti and the word "Fiesta!" stamped on it.) "Let me tell you something—my girls have healthy attitudes about the human body. Myla and I have never hid nothing. God knows, we didn't want 'em raised like we were—uptight and ashamed. They've seen us in all our glory since they were babies. They're not impressed."

Compelling argument. It's a theory I could empathize with, I just wasn't too sure about the application. In any event, if they thought every man was as hung as Daddy, they were in for a few surprises.

We turned and shuffled off toward the "lobster pot," each conveying an extra margarita should anyone be suddenly prostrate from thirst. Rounding the little privacy fence of banana trees and oleanders, we entered the "Sodom and Gomorra" pavilion. I guess in my drunken oblivion I was just a tad disappointed there weren't multiple mountings going on. In fact, except for the lack of clothing, it could've been the local canasta club holding a Saturday night smoker.

"There he is! We thought you'd run off and joined the Church of Christ." Myla giggled as she waved a fly off her boob.

"Come on in, Clu, it feels wonderful." Sandy sighed, floating between Dwyane's long legs in a blanket of aerated effervescence. Her breasts rose above the water like two snow cones splashed with a dollop of maple syrup. It was definitely the largest hot tub I'd ever seen. Somewhere between a cistern and a lap pool.

"Lord, ya'll—couldn't you have at least found a bigger kiddie pool so we wouldn't be so crowded?"

Myla giggled again. "Isn't it hysterical. Zane had it 'specially built so he wouldn't feel restricted."

"Just being practical. 'Tween the pool and this thing, we got enough water to survive a six-month drought." Zane slowly edged over the side and sank into the steamy vapors.

My turn. The dreaded unveiling. What am I being so prim about? No shame in being slightly above average. I know, I've seen a few thousand pricks in my day—I know where the standard lies. I've got nothing to hide.

"I won, I won, I won!" Debbie was screeching as I awkwardly plopped into the thirtysomething bouillabaisse.

"Bitch, how do we know you didn't sleep with him in high school?" Myla sneered and lit a Marlboro light.

"I'm sure. Clu, did we ever have sex in high school?" Debbie pouted.

"Uh . . ." I glanced at Jimmy, who had a slightly expectant look on his face. "That would be, 'no.' Did I miss something?"

Dwayne started to cackle and everyone joined in. "You've just been baptized in the Grit Holy Water Social Club. The girls had a bet your pubes weren't the same color as the hair on your head."

"And I won!" Debbie squealed.

"Well, gol-ly. You've always had the most beautiful sandy, copper-colored hair, Clu. How did I know you hadn't been dyeing it all these years?" Myla suddenly looked concerned. "Do you dye your pubes?"

I went with the general giddiness. "After my eyebrows and eyelashes, there's never any time for pubes." That got a laugh. "Besides, Bettie Jean Latimore is the 'original' redhead. I didn't have much say in the matter." We were all "bonded" now. Amazing how plebian a nudist camp could be.

Jimmy suddenly jumped out of the cauldron and sloshed over behind some foliage. "Ya'll excuse me, I gotta pee."

"Stay away from my azalea bushes," Myla barked. "Between you boys and the dogs, they've had a hard year." She then inhaled thoughtfully on her Marlboro. "So tell us . . . how did you and Chris meet, Clu?"

I didn't care anymore. If they wanted to know how many times a week we did it and how many ways we had of sticking it in—I didn't care. The night was balmy, the sputtering bubbles on my back felt good, my head was anesthetized. Who . . . cares.

"We met at a bathhouse in New York."

Silence. Everyone stared, letting that fragment of knowledge ripen on the vine. Finally, Sandy asked quietly, "Didn't you have a place to shower at home?"

It was said with such ingenuousness I had to laugh. I couldn't help it. "A bathhouse is a place where *some* gay men go to have sex. Kind of like a whorehouse—but there's no exchange of money. Just, hopefully—pleasure."

Again, they let that sort of filter in. Jimmy came tiptoeing back. "What happened, somebody let out a fart?"

Debbie answered distantly, as if she were concentrating on a TV moon landing. "It's so interesting. Clu just told us how he and Chris met."

"How?"

"In a . . . bathhouse."

"Isn't that where you guys all go to have sex?" Jimmy dipped back in. I casually observed that he seemed to have the smallest male member present at the gathering. Forceful equation. Tiny dick=tiny brain?

"Now, Jimmy . . . 'pal,' can we stop for a moment? What you're saying is basically the equivalent of, 'Don't all straight people get married and have children? Don't all straight people live in the suburbs, drive a Suburban, have a two-car garage and own a golden retriever?' I don't think it's too realistic to lump all gay people into one mammoth category, do you?"

"That's where you met him, right? A bathhouse?"

"Right. And you and Debbie—where did you meet? A church social? Or is that too convenient a stereotype."

It was Debbie's turn to hoot. She let out a bray that stirred up minitsunamis in the hot tub. "Hippie Hollow! We were both skinny-dipping at Hippie Hollow our sophomore year at U.T. My girlfriends saw this guy and thought he was kinda cute. Hell, I didn't have my glasses on, so I just went along with it." (For the uninitiated, Hippie Hollow, on the shores of Lake Travis outside Austin, is the largest public nudist beach in Texas. Gay and straight—very cruisey.)

I eyed Jimmy coolly. "And were you there studying native plant life, Mr. Jim?" In the dimness, it was obvious Jimmy's face was approaching crimson.

"OK. You made your point."

"How do you know where gay men go to have sex, anyway?" Debbie glared at him.

"Give me a break. We have a satellite dish that brings in over two hundred channels. I get the news."

Debbie sniffed, "You're just watching the porno channel when I'm not home."

"It is not porno, it's soft porn. The don't show 'em sticking it in, for God's sake."

"I knew you were watching that crap. I'm gonna put one of those cable locks on so you can't look at that nasty stuff."

"What's wrong with looking? I'm not hurting anybody."

"You're probably diddling yourself."

Jimbo was incensed. "And am I hurting anybody!"

Now, it was getting interesting. Maybe I could get to like these truth sessions after all. I casually ventured an innocent aside, "Debbie, do you really think Jimmy's causing any harm by just looking?"

Debbie turned to me, scowling. "Yes, I do, he should be doing it with me. Not some silicone-cow throwing her titties around that I'm paying thirty-eight dollars a month for."

Jimmy stood up quickly, his willy bouncing up and down on the water's surface like a discarded Ring-Ding. "Honey—if we had sex as often as I need it and want it, I'd throw the goddamn TV right out the second-floor window." Spontaneous applause from Dwyane and Zane. I think we hit a nerve.

Myla mashed out her cigarette and smiled wryly. "Well . . . before we get back to the original question of how Chris and Clu met—which is what I really am interested in hearing about—I'd just like to say one thing. If you boys made love every time the way we women want it and need it, you'd have so much sex in your life your little peckers would be writing thank-you cards and sending candy." Impromptu applause from the women.

Jimmy was on a roll. "Hey listen, all that foreplay and baby talk is great every once in a while, but sometimes a guy's just gotta get off. There's no time for nicey-nice and ear licking—just stick it in, boom, over. We'll take out the trash, play with the cat, go to your mothers—do whatever you want afterward. Just help us out occasionally! You don't understand the pressure. Isn't that right, Clu?" My new buddy, Jimmy, blinked at me anxiously.

Hmmm. Interesting route this caravan was taking. "Well . . . I had a therapist tell me once, 'Gay men and straight men have more in common with Martians than they do with women.' I think the sex thing is pretty individual, but as a broad *stereotype*—I repeat, *stereotype*—yes, sometimes I think men do just want to stick it in a doorknob and grind away. Get it over with and back to balancing the checkbook."

Zane spoke deliberately, "It's like . . . you're carrying this big salami sandwich rubbing around in your pants all day—you gotta do something about it!"

Myla scrutinized Zane with a look that could melt hair, then purred sweetly, "Well I've got an idea—why don't you just wrap it in wax paper and put it in the fridge to cool off awhile?" She splashed water at him. "Braggart."

"Oh, ya'll, I like a quickie, too, sometimes, but you boys gotta understand, it's no fun for us when you're grinding away just like you're trying to sharpen a pencil or something. We want to feel like we're part of the show, too—not just the prop lady." Sandy inhaled on her joint.

"But we're there with you. We're not doing it with some stranger in a cat house. Man, I don't get it—you get a guy that's faithful, loves you to death, loves your body, loves your mind, grateful as hell every time you give him a little—and it's still not enough." Jimmy, exasperated, submerged himself. (Was he expecting the hot water to have a cooling effect?)

Debbie spoke as he resurfaced. "It's 'enough' . . . A body can live on fish sticks and Tater Tots—it's just that sometimes you want red snapper and a baked potato."

Dwayne finally joined the fray. "I always felt like there's two kinds of sex—great and good, and it's never not at least good when it's with someone you love. Great happens once in a blue moon—anniversaries, birthdays—when your wife loses ten pounds and she's feeling all sex kitten. But who's complaining, it's all good."

"Oh, honey, you're so cute." Sandy and Dwayne mashed lips for a few seconds.

Myla reflected, "Yeah, I always thought there were two kinds of sex too—good and 'What in the world is he thinking?'"

Zane immediately cocked his head in Myla's direction.

"Now don't go getting your eyebrows in a tangle. It's mostly good—hell, it's pretty much always good. It's just that sometimes your head's so far away I need the damn Hubble Telescope just to make contact." Myla dipped her head back in the water to straighten her hair.

Zane was quiet for a moment, then spoke, almost inaudibly. "You know what I'm usually thinking about when that happens—I don't deserve this beautiful woman I'm holding, these beautiful kids, this beautiful home—this incredibly wonderful life. I'm just a fucking, lucky bum, and I don't deserve any of it."

Myla looked at Zane, genuinely bewildered. She then edged over to him, straddled his legs, and put her arms around his neck. "You deserve everything and more, you big peanut. Where would any of us be without you?" They kissed and nuzzled, oblivious to the rest of us.

Finally, Sandy broke the spell. "All right, Jimmy and Debbie, ya'll have to say one thing nice to each other. Come on—we're gonna make you sit here till you're boiled eggs."

Debbie grinned, then turned to Jimmy, pinching his earlobe. "Well, I think he's got the cutest furry buns of anyone here." I could give him that. They were agreeable enough.

Zane whooped, "Stand up and show us that hairy ass of yours, boy. I don't think I've given it a good enough look."

Jimmy smiled and sank lower in the water. "You can go fuck yourself. I'm not giving anybody any ideas." Although he didn't look my way, the inference was obvious.

"I'll try to contain myself," I said in my best George Sanders *All About Eve* imitation. It got a big laugh.

Jimmy now eyed me guardedly as he floated toward Debbie and put his arm around her. "I'm married to the only woman in the world I'd want to share my life with, and even if I'm not perfect . . . I never get tired of wanting to make her happy." Aww. Curtain. Applause. Old "Furry Buns" saves the day.

As Debbie and Jimmy smooched I fished a lime wedge from the bottom of my glass and bit into its tart, acidic pith. I guess it was a full minute later before I flashed on six pairs of hetero-eyes focused on my nose. Now what?

"So this . . . bathhouse . . ." Myla shifted Zane's arm to her other shoulder.

"Oh that. There's not that much to tell. We saw each other, we liked what we saw. We started dating, you know . . . right away."

"You saw each other . . . naked. Then you started dating?"

"Yeah, like Debbie and Jimmy."

Debbie interrupted, "I was wearing a bottom!"

"So, did you have sex at the bathhouse?"

"Yes."

"In the shower?"

"No, in a room."

"In a room next to the shower?"

"Look, forget the shower. It's a bathhouse like McDonald's is a restaurant. You go 'cause it's fast and convenient—not for your health."

"So, they have rooms?"

"Rooms you rent, like . . . cubicles."

"Cubicles."

"For sex."

"For . . . sex."

"It doesn't sound very romantic." Sandy looked alarmed.

"He said it's a whorehouse, Sand—sheesch." Zane shook his head. "Go on."

"So are there other guys in other rooms?" Myla continued.

"Other guys in other rooms on other floors in other beds—all doing the four-legged spider dance."

Silence. "Isn't that . . . unsafe?"

"Do you drink the water in a country you don't know? There are things you do and things you don't . . . period. Life's unsafe—you weigh the risks." Listen to me, Mr. Gay-Fucker-About-Town. They'd shit if they knew I'd only been to a bathhouse twice in my life. Who cares. They were bound to my every breath at this point. Give a ham a stage, and he'll turn himself into *Fettuccini Carbonara* every time.

"So, does everybody have sex with everybody or is it like—you know—date night at the drive-in."

"Date night at the drive-in?" Even Jimmy was flummoxed.

"I mean is everybody on top of everybody else or are there like . . . couples?"

I guiltily suppressed a snort. "I didn't look in every room, Myla. Chris and I were a couple."

Sandy urgently pushed off and floated on her back to the other side of the hot tub, her breasts parting the seas like twin icebergs. She fanned herself as she glided past. "Let's get to the romantic part. There's too many hairy legs knocking around in this segment."

"That's it. We moved in together about a month and a half later. Been together ever since."

Debbie raised her hand. "Now I'm just asking 'cause I don't know—do ya'll see other people or are ya'll like married?"

"We're definitely married."

"No foolin' around?"

"No foolin'. Why?"

Debbie shook her head. "Gosh, I don't know. It just seems like every time you turn on Sally Jessie there's another gay show about everybody sleeping with everybody and it just gets me, like, discouraged."

"Discouraged?"

"Yeah—it doesn't seem like any of ya'll are real happy."

Here comes the button. All gay men are promiscuous, all gay men are miserable—so speaketh the media. "Debbie, that's crackpot, sensationalistic, voyeur TV. If I believed a fraction of the crap on television, I'd be expecting Mr. Ed to come trotting over and sing me his new song about now."

"Careful—you're dating yourself, pumpkin." Myla smiled and hurled the melted residue of her margarita onto the lawn.

Professor Jimmy smirked, "You gotta admit, you guys are pretty well known for the quantity of sex you have with each other."

I smacked a passing swell with my palm. "There you go again, Jimbo. Another one of those vast, overreaching generalizations of yours guaranteed to distort any shred of reality."

"Now come on, Clu, everyone knows gay guys have more sex than straight guys," Zane interjected.

"Hey, I'm a gay guy, I'm telling you—I've had sex with one man for the past eight years. Am I some kind of freak?" And it was true. All right—there was that one time with the Panamanian steward at the health club who got all touchy-feely with me in the steam room. There was no exchange of . . . "reproductive fluids." Not a vow-buster. Anyway, do they have to know everything? "It's hardly just a gay thing having a lively interest in sex, you know. How many of ya'll can say you've been faithful in your marriage?"

Silence. Long silence. Dwayne finally pushed himself up out of the water and sat on the edge of the gurgling reservoir. "Getting a little hot in there. Honey, we better be going if we're gonna pick up the girls at your mother's." He stood and towel dried his wiry body. He was definitely generic nice-looking. Nothing spectacular, nothing coarse. My "gaydar" was telegraphing interesting messages. The gut feeling was Dwayne had been no stranger to gay bars in his day. "And yes—I have."

"Have what?" Jimmy asked.

"Been faithful in my marriage."

"Well I should think so, this is your second marriage each and you haven't been together that long yet," Myla quipped, rising from the pool.

"You don't have to be flip about it, Myla. Sometimes it takes a couple of marriages to find the right one." Sandy stood and tousled her wavy blond hair in the feeble breeze. Dwayne covered her shoulders with a towel.

"Hon, ya'll are still practically newlyweds. Give it to year eight and we'll see how the battle's going."

Eight? Why year eight? I rose from the water and reached for my towel. I started to open my mouth when Zane catapulted out from behind me, causing a tidal wave on the concrete walk and washing away a small caravan of army ants transporting margarita salt back to their fortress. "Hey listen, I'm not preaching infidelity, but the only thing that really matters is—are you willing to hang in there and work at it?" Myla and Zane kissed, the unsaid but obvious declaration being, "Flings come and go—we're here for the long march."

Debbie and Jimmy remained in the tub, watching us warily. Finally, Jimmy cleared his throat and was about to speak when Debbie interrupted. "I was unfaithful—once." We all turned simultaneously. "It nearly destroyed us. I made a terrible mistake, thought I needed something else. What I got was lies, pettiness, boring sex and a yeast infection. Jimmy stood by me through the whole thing. He was, and is . . . my angel. He said it best . . . he never stops trying. And I love him very much, for that." A big tear rolled down Debbie's otherwise placid face and Jimmy gently wiped it with a finger, kissing her cheek. It was such a personal moment it felt rude to watch. I turned to study Myla's beanbag ashtray as if it were an unearthed Grecian urn. I guess you never really know someone until you've shared a truth session in the hot tub. Jimmy was—well, he wasn't what he appeared, how's that?

Shrouded in various permutations of clothing and towels, we trudged back up the lawn toward the tastefully lit exterior of Myla and Zane's football-field-long ranch house. They did have it all—Daddy's money, beautiful children, the house, the cars, a margarita machine—and probably most fundamentally, an understanding of each other's limitations and attributes on some boundless, profound level.

Myla and I brought up the rear. She reached her hand out for mine. "I'm glad you came, Clu. Was it too provincial after New York?"

"Not at all. Absolutely . . . not at all."

"I wanted so much to get a chance to know you better."

"Why?"

Myla shrugged. "Because I like you. I don't know—I feel kinda protective I guess." We walked a bit farther. She squeezed my hand. "I was thinking . . . there's so many things I'll never experience in this life. By having friends like you I get to be a fuller person. Does that make sense?"

I nodded. "Yeah . . . makes a lot of sense." We walked the rest of the way in silence, holding each other's hand like it was first day of kindergarten and we were going to be best friends for the rest of our lives.

9

EATING THE ROCKING CHAIR

By the first of July we were grunting from the heat with every breath. It came at you like lightning from hell—continuous, almighty and inescapable. The added touch of humidity was God's little reminder to Southerners that heaven was even farther than you dared dream. Keep praying.

Mother and Brother Ramirez were busily planning their pending wedding—in August. Outdoors. On a Saturday at noon. Did they hate us? Despite protestations from family, friends and perfect strangers at the Dairy Queen, who when apprised of the situation by the blabbing staff, shook their heads and muttered "must be foreigners." Mother made it perfectly clear—weekend was the only time (Sunday's out), that she couldn't possibly get everything ready before August, Brother Ramirez's tent was the only place that could accommodate everyone, and if you held it at lunch you could get away with just serving punch, sandwiches and cookies. Besides, the heat didn't bother her anymore, so she claimed.

Mother's cast had finally come off, though she still carried her arm around in a festive cloth sling. She never appeared to use her newly freed limb, just wore it like a stole dangling on her chest. I asked her why she wasn't exercising it, and she placated me with, "It's a little sore still, these things take a while." I got the creepy feeling she was methodically letting various body parts go, one member at a time. "Thanks for your cooperation, I won't be needing you anymore. We're shutting down in a little while." She was as frail as ever yet driven by some inner guidance that kept her plowing through most days like a determined salmon bent on reaching "Lake Exoneration." Something gave her strength even in the face of enormous disintegration. I watched her with awe and not a little dread. What was next?

Laine submitted to a "laying of the hands" by Concepcion. Highly unlike her. Concepcion again announced the baby would be a girl, premature but healthy, and "very much like her father," whatever that meant. (Would the kid be a felon?) They both seemed enormously relieved by the procedure. After trying everything else, what was left anyway? Stringing a goat's foot around your middle and burning Pampers on a forest altar? They returned to New Mexico in a state of bliss. I found it intriguing how even middling fundamentalists like Laine and Sherrod could so readily chink a wedge out of their determined thought process and insert a contrary notion as long as it served their intention. Maybe I was the true fundamentalist. Here I persisted in flimsily clinging to all my preconceived notions about everyone and everything as if I held some kind of ethical superiority. How quickly my assumptions were crumbling. Like barn flies in a blast of Raid, the old avowals were dropping to the ground by the hundreds.

Jaston continued to spend the bulk of most days at the gristmill. He and Chris and some guys from the Grit Gators high school football team hauled the safe up into the Byers garage for protection. (It had always chaffed me, incidentally—what Gator had ever established any kind of affiliation with Grit in the first place? We were as ecologically advantageous to alligators as Florida was to penguins. Why not the Grit Ground Squirrels or the Grit Girlfriends with Big Hair?) Jaston had done a yeoman's job of cleaning the site. It was beginning to look like something. What, no one could be sure, but definitely "something."

And Chris remained . . . distantly engaged. Since returning from his weekend at the Coast, he fluctuated from effusive to mute—sometimes in the same hour. He'd be bursting with ideas and humor one moment, then lay on the bed the rest of the afternoon gloomily reading Latin texts of Cicero. The one thing that got him consistently enthused was planning *Agamemnon Ya'll—A Country and Western Musical* with Preston. I seemed to be director as mere formality at this point. Granted, my initial interest had been less than colossal, but I was beginning to see the light. Between the two of them, they'd conceived the whole thing—a modern-day Greek hoedown to be held at the livestock auction barn—complete with beer, a band, animals and chorus of singing ranchers. Why not? After sitting through some of Robert Wilson's (another Texas émigré) impenetrable spectacles at the Brooklyn Academy of Music, I could probably do *Hamlet* at a car wash and make it relevant.

Couple-wise—we were saving our best performances for public consumption only. Alone, we were like two interlopers carefully avoiding some dread suspended above our heads. Chris's sudden distraction with Preston had blossomed into unbridled camaraderie. It was so unlike Chris. He was usually such a cool customer when it came to pretty boys. But now—they wrote songs together, they listened to bands, they researched Bullfinch's *Mythology*, they bartered with merchants for donations—they were quite the team. Naturally my Scorpionic suspicions hammered me with unrelenting, villainous ideas. Were they "doing it"? Was I being superseded by "Presstone"? Was Chris flaunting an affair practically in my hometown living room? With some bleached-blond, muscle-bound, cookie-cutter-handsome sperm dispenser?

Whenever I broached the subject he'd look at me as if I'd just stomped on a portrait of Mother Teresa.

"You're really a mess. Are you that insecure?"

"It seems like you're spending an awful lot of time together . . ."

"For your sake as much as anybody's. Do you want the home-town folks to think your first artistic effort in Grit some amateur screwup?"

"No."

"Why is it you have such a hard time whenever I take on an outside interest?"

"I don't."

"You definitely do. You hate it when you can't control it just your way. It irks the hell out of you that Preston is young, handsome, eager, ambitious and grateful for some like-minded friendship. That he wants to work with you, respects you, even idolizes you to an extent—it drives you bananas."

"H . . . he idolizes me?"

"Yes, Mike Nichols—he wants to be just like you when he grows up. I warned him."

So maybe I was overreacting a tad, misreading the whole thing. Still, I didn't completely trust the sneaky "Eve Harrington." Idolize you one minute—next thing they're wearing your fur to the Tonys.

Against all my wishes, better judgment and infallible sense of deportment, Chris persisted in pursuing the offer of Brother Ramirez to speak at the *Templo*. Nothing could stop him. He was as insistent as Eva Perón with a checkbook. For hours he rehearsed with Preston in our bedroom—demanding that I find something to do with myself as I was making him nervous. Mother was napping, the dogs we're napping—so I sat on the back porch and read back issues of *The New Yorker* till I could practically see a cloud of taxi exhaust rising over Grit.

I suddenly missed the corner Korean fruit vendors. There were very few places on the planet where one could find such implausible combinations for sale in a fifteen-by-twenty-five-foot hutch—the *Daily News*, halvah, panty hose, freeze-dried cabbage soup, ginseng root extract, fresh fruit cups, "blondie" brownies and cigarettes. You never knew when you might need them all at once. I missed Greek coffee shops. Bad coffee and sobbing balalaikas over scrambled eggs and toast. I missed the Carnegie Deli—yeah it was a tourist trap but so was Rockefeller Center, and how could you not go look at the skaters and the Christmas tree at least once a season and pretend you were Holly Golightly in your own New York reverie? Grit had all the charm and mystery of a can of refried beans. Still, the likelihood of stepping in human excrement while waiting for the F train at the Fourteenth Street Station remained negligible. Life was a series of strategic concessions.

The *Templo Universal de Los Hermanos y Hermanas del Amor de Dios* was New Age Barnum and Bailey wrapped around a Tony

Robbins "Unleash the Power" seminar and served up with good old country Christian niceness. Arriving on the day of reckoning I was a complete wreck. I got "howdied" and "how're yew'd" and "bless yer old heart" till I was *ferklempt* with people's appallingly sunny natures. Although Chris had only been allotted a thankful seven-minute platform, you never knew if his inner Tammy Faye would kick in and stretch the whole thing till next Memorial Day. I fervently visualized a hook and a gong as fundamental to my personal reality.

Apparently Brother Ramirez had bought the circus rigging from some traveling Salvadorean carnival people. As part of the deal a fat, disagreeable zebra got passed along to the *Templo*. He stood outside the main entrance eating from a bucket of corn like some corpulent rajah. A sign hung around his neck reading, "Hi, I'm Zaccheus—the Tax Collector—please leave your donation in the basket." I noticed Zaccheus would occasionally take bites from stray articles of clothing if he felt your donation wasn't sufficient. Mother was thrilled with him and thought he was absolutely priceless. After having my sleeve mangled in a tug-of-war over my presumed stinginess, I wanted to brain the loathsome ass with a corncob.

The tent was festive enough, striped in bright red-and-white panels and circled with massive scratchy, old speakers that made everyone sound as if their voices were being percolated through a 1930s Victrola. The effect was pleasing somehow, like having a fireside chat with FDR from the grave. I sat in a folding chair near the rear so I could run like hell when the crowd got wind that sodomites were in their midst. Poor Chris, he'd have to fend for himself. He was as exposed and vulnerable as the young lady who no doubt, once upon a time, hung by her hair in this very hippodrome, high above the center stage. I did notice a floor-length candelabra next to the podium, and if he had his wits about him, he could swing that thing and take out a good row or two. God be with you, my son.

Of course Mother complained about our sitting all the way in back. She was *"Señora Templo"* now and felt it her rightful duty to sit up front in the first few rows with the rest of the holy of holies. I wasn't budging and she reluctantly gave in, thankful, I imagine, that at least one of her sinful boys had made it this far.

The tent filled up in a hurry. It was warm, but not suffocating yet. We each had paper funeral-home fans, which we swung as diligently as a cow's tail swatting flies. I looked around cautiously, but didn't seem to recognize a soul till I caught sight of Miss Oveta, Mr. Jeffrey and Preston, sitting several pews in front. Swell. At least my public humiliation wouldn't go completely unnoticed by at least a few dear friends. I wondered if Preston would stand up to testify, "Yes, I've been chasing Brother Chris's fine ass for quite some time now, and I'm here to tell you, 'Once you've had *schlong,* you'll never go wrong!'"

Mother finally leaned over, and whispered in my ear, "Why don't you take off your jacket. You're perspiring."

To put it mildly. I suddenly looked as if I'd swum my way over. Frankly, I wanted to strip naked and sit in a Coke cooler, but after loosening everything, including my shoes, I felt marginally less humid.

Instantly there was a thunderous bass-guitar riff that squealed around our heads like something from the lost Jimi Hendrix tapes. I twitched involuntarily. Onstage a skinny, pimply-faced teenager with long black hair was getting down with some serious rock-star attitude. He resembled the Latin equivalent of Mick Jagger, whomping away on guitar chords like a seasoned veteran. My mouth hung open. Where was I—the Whiskey Au Go-Go?

Mother leaned in again. "That's your new stepbrother, Manuel. I think he's good." I closed my mouth. A woman began whaling away on a small electric organ next to Manuel. When I say "whaling" I mean, "detonating." She shook the bare earth beneath us. I stared at my feet. Ants were racing to their holes as fast as they could. How in hell could she get that much power out of what looked like some rinky-dink Sears hurdy-gurdy? It had to have been backed up with enough voltage to light Houston.

Mother pulled me in once more, this time yelling, "That's Vicky, your stepsister." I stared in disbelief. Where were the others? Out back warming up with Metallica?

Then, incredibly, there was silence. A moth fell to its death from the chair in front of me. From the back of the tent a loud "Today is the day!" went up, and I froze, convinced the Texas Militia had arrived and drawn guns on us. A tambourine shattered the stillness, and a choir began bellowing "Let There Be Peace On Earth." I managed to turn my head slightly. There was Concepcion, a tambourine in one hand and the other holding a rope around Zaccheus, who shimmied and strutted like James Brown as she led him toward the altar. You could read Zaccheus's face like a post-office wanted poster. "I been in this business a long time, pal—preachers, clowns, crappy dog-acts—just keep the corn coming, you'll get your little show."

Manuel and Vicky started up again in a bout of free-form groovin' onstage. Each one jammed some serious improv licks around what was basically a staid and waxen old hymn. It had the curious effect of hearing something like "America the Beautiful" performed by the Sex Pistols. Odd, but not altogether irredeemable.

Behind Concepcion marched Brother Ramirez, smiling beatifically and seemingly taller somehow in his somber ecclesiastical robes. He appeared to be a nice enough guy. Mother was thrilled by him—why was it so hard for me to like him? Jealous, possessive, judgmental, suspicious? I appeared to sustain all those singular traits in profusion. Was I doomed to being Mama's unhappy little boy for the rest of my life?

Following Brother Ramirez came the chorus—an odd assortment of every age, ethnic, gender and physical type you'd ever want to pile together and throw a bunch of Egyptian-movie caftans over. And Lord help me—there was Chris, wearing one of the Cecil B. DeMille drag ponchos and singing loudly right on the perimeter of the mob. I desperately wanted to follow that last ant into his crater. Focusing solely on the big picture, I knew I would survive this somehow. It might take plastic surgery and the witness protection program, but something would turn up. What had me thoroughly buffaloed was figuring out exactly how I was going to live through the next thirty minutes.

I stared numbly at the program in my hands, smearing the ink with my now dripping palms. Mother was singing along in rapturous delight, and even if I could've remembered the words, my constricted throat wouldn't have allowed so much as an eyedropper of spit. I turned one more time to look at the passing pharaoh glee club,

and my eyes suddenly caught the glance of a male chorister. It was . . .
no, it couldn't be . . . was that . . . *Pat Pickens* from the debate team?
He stared at me with a curious gaze, then quickly resumed marching.
I shook my head, gaping heavenward. "God, are there any more surprises you're saving? Could we just have them all at once? What
about the little girl I played doctor with in second grade? The one I
examined with the spatula? I'm sure she'd like to be here."

Mother was tugging on my sleeve. I honestly hadn't noticed
everyone was sitting. I hunkered down, mortified.

"Good morning, brothers and sisters of the Universal Temple of
the Love of God."

"Good morning!" the congregation rumbled in response.

And we're off. "Isn't it a beautiful Sunday morning? It's such a
feel-good kind of day I think even Zaccheus has something to say
about it." Concepcion then did something with his halter and Fatso
let out a huge, honking "hee-haw" that rattled the canvas. Everyone
burst into uproarious laughter, and Mother started a coughing jag
that didn't end till we'd located her small bottle of water and gotten
most of it down her. Boy, with this crowd I could've done shadow
puppets behind a lit screen and knocked 'em in the aisles.

"We have a full, and I hope momentous service planned for you
today. My sermon will be on 'Faith—Your Best Friend When Friends
Can't Be Bothered.' I hope it will inspire and sustain you in the coming weeks when we hit those walls, as we all do, and we need that
extra push to get us through the doldrums that sometimes stagnate
our spiritual vision. We also have a new song our choir will be performing that one of our very own members, Miss Heidi Pugh, has
written. It's called 'I Am a Diamond On God's Wedding Band.' I did-
n't know God wore a wedding band, but I think you'll agree it's an
interesting idea. The Righteous Ramirez Duo will be accompanying
the singers with their own special arrangement, and I'm sure we'll all
be eager for that. Finally, we have an engaging young man, Mr. Chris
Myles, who it's been my pleasure to get to know recently, and he'll
be speaking to us briefly this morning about 'The Boundaries of Love
and the Limits of Fear,' which I know is going to open each of our
hearts and heal our minds in areas we can all grow and learn from.
But first, I've asked Brother Leo Martindale to report to us on how

the finance committee is progressing with the church building fund, Brother Leo . . ."

How had it all come down to this? This instant, this moment of excruciating . . . exposé? I sat and stared blindly at Brother Leo, not hearing a word coming from his mouth. My greatest fear, the threat of being publicly "outed" before my own hometown of fools and frauds and hooligans was now upon me. In a circus tent . . . in the Lions park . . . on the very frayed fringe of rudimentary civilization in some godforsaken corner of earth's unremitting despair. And the messenger of my personal cataclysm was none other than my own life mate. How? Why? Where did I fuck up, *where?* They could stone me, kick me to hamburger, rip my limbs in a ritual of mob absolution—who cares what assholes did in their mindless bloodlust. But I did care very much about Mother . . . and Jaston. Why should they be subjected to this needless torment because of my life? I know the world is changing, and I know most reasonable people have an over-all live and let live philosophy toward life—but what do you do about the rest of the bastards that plague your existence like buzzards on roadkill? The religious right, the hard-core conservatives, the Moral Majority, fundamentalist, Mormons, the U.S. military, state and federal judges, hate groups, the American Family Association, the Family Research Council, the Traditional Values Coalition, the Christian Coalition, the Center for Reclaiming America, the Eagle Forum, "Doctor" Laura Schlessinger, Jesse Helms, Pat Robertson, Jerry Falwell, Phyllis Schaffly, Pat Buchannan, blah, blah, blah, blah, blah—who gave these godawful unholy freaks the right to predetermine my existence? Why, God? Because of one incredibly mystifying line in the Bible that states "man shall not lie with man"? Is that it? Is that why we kill and maim and hate and ostracize and reproach . . . because of that? Were those the desired effects you were seeking when your word was "rendered by man" into scripture? Forgive the notion, but when you were thinking out loud about all this are you sure the geezer taking dictation didn't sneak in a line item or two of his own? Just a thought. I personally always wondered if what you were really trying to get across in that hoary old verse was something more like, "Hey, listen up—if you're a straight dude I really don't think you want to be lying with no gay bros—and vice versa. Gay man shall not lie with straight man, straight man shall not lie with gay man—anybody confused? You were all created in my image, and I don't screw up. Rarely. Gnats were just an experiment in bird food. There's a reason and a purpose for everything. That's why camels don't hump crocodiles, etc., etc. *Comprende?* So you gay boys and girls be cool with your own flavor, there's plenty of ya'll to go around, and you straight dudes and dudettes concentrate on each other and everybody just chill. There's been gays and lesbians on this planet looooooong time before this Bible was even a first sentence and you know Big Mama don't like it when ya'll go messing around trying to second-guess what she's got planned. And as for you bisexuals—hey, Mama's got a sense of humor, too!"

Just a thought.

I glanced up toward the stage again. Concepcion was discussing the upcoming calendar of events. My eyes wandered over to the choir. There he was . . . It for damn sure was Pat. How peculiar does the world get? If they'd told me Pope John Paul was stopping by for a little sing-along, I wouldn't have been more surprised. Pat . . . here? Why? Mr. Solid-Episcopalian-everybody's-blue-eyed-darling-white-boy-perfection-closet-case. What the hell are you doing in a circus tent on the edge of civilization?

Concepcion sat. Brother Ramirez got up again and walked to the mike. He rearranged his Bible, fiddled with some notes and stared at the lectern beneath him. "I've invited a young man today that I met only recently at the home of my soon-to-be bride, Bettie Jean Latimore. . . ."

Mother squeezed my hand, and it rattled me so I nearly rocketed out of my chair, up through the awning, destined for Mars. I screamed silently, "Please, one more song! Vicky and Manuel, take it away!"

"His name is Christopher Myles and he comes originally from Pennsylvania, but most recently, New York City. He's a Latin scholar—we don't get too many of those around here." The congregation tittered. "I've asked him to speak to us today about something that I feel is an affliction of spirit that affects all of us—and that's lack of love. Lack of love for those we know, lack of love for strangers, lack of love for ourselves. I've asked him to address this in his own words, in his own way—I don't know what he's prepared—but I want us all to keep our hearts and minds open and hear what message this child of God has for *us* today. Chris."

The thumping in my ears was thunderous. My face was on fire. Mother handed me one of her pastel tissues, which I ran quickly across my forehead and wadded into a ball in my fist. Chris walked steadily to the podium, ran his fingers once through his bangs and stared straight out into the congregation like he was born to the post. Cool as peach parfait. Time ceased. I closed my eyes. "OK, God. You've got me. Whatever it is you want me to do about this, show me. Don't make it so difficult that an idiot like me can't get it. And please . . . slow my heart down so I can hear."

"I'd like to thank Brother Ramirez for this opportunity to speak to you today. I want to tell you a little story about when I was a kid growing up outside Scranton, Pennsylvania. We had an old stray dog that lived in our neighborhood, we called him Blackie. Nobody knew his real name or if he even had one—he was just the stray mutt that everyone recognized, and he was solid black. He never let you pet him, but he was always around. Whenever the neighborhood kids were throwing balls, or riding bikes, or went exploring on one of the nearby streams—there was Blackie—not doing much, just watching, hanging out—there but not there. For a while he had this habit of following me home from school. Sure, he knew I'd eventually toss him the rest of my sandwich I didn't eat at lunch, but I also think he just liked being with me. He was the responsible, older-brother type. You just felt better when Blackie was around for some reason. One day Blackie didn't show up after school. Nobody saw him at the playground or with the other kids. A few days went by, still no Blackie. Some of the parents got concerned—he was our mutt—our Blackie. Well, they eventually found him—dead. He was lying in an alley, behind some garbage cans—his head had been bashed in with a rock. Somebody reported to the police that a gang of boys had cornered the dog and stoned him to death. When they asked the leader of the gang why he'd done it he just shrugged his shoulders and said he guessed he didn't like 'nigger dogs.'

"That boy's answer has plagued me my entire life. That kind of unthinking, unloving, unknowing—offhanded hatred never ceases to mystify me in ways that are completely beyond my abilities to reason. By no fault of his own, Blackie was born a 'nigger dog.' And he would eventually die for that. Why? It makes . . . no sense.

"I'm a gay man. I'm also mildly dyslexic, left-handed, of English-German-Polish extraction, a product of a Catholic school education, blue-eyed, flat-footed . . . etc., etc. Being gay is just one aspect of my being—an essential one, I'll grant you—but it doesn't make me special in any way. It's just a fact. Like having green eyes and a heart murmur. So what? And although it may or may not be apparent to you—I was clearly born that way. Just as clearly perhaps as you've always known yourself that you were heterosexual—or at least you've never seriously questioned your basic sexual orientation—that's how I've always seen myself. I assume that you didn't wake up one morning and suddenly shout out, 'I think I'll be straight today'—you just were who you were. A nonissue. Of course, when I was a kid I didn't have the language or complete understanding of what I was because I was raised by heterosexuals in a loving, caring, devout, completely heterosexual environment. It was a straight world—what did I know? My parents did nothing wrong—they did everything right. I simply knew, felt, assimilated, postulated, perceived—call it what you will—that on a deep, deep level something was different. And it was not a comforting 'gee, aren't I wonderful' feeling, I can assure you. No kid wants to feel separate from the rest of the pack. Who chooses to be an outcast at ten?

"Sometimes I think it must still look to many straight people that gays somehow willfully choose to be that way. That somehow we're being difficult or lazy or degenerate because we choose this lifestyle. It seems to me the only real choice a gay person has, at least for every gay person I've ever known, is whether they're going to live their truth or not. *That* is the choice. And it's a hell—there's no other word for it—hell of a dilemma for many, many gay people to have to make that choice.

"Of course, no surprise, gay people get married and have children all the time—but does it make them less gay? Or do they just burrow deeper into a well of camouflage, passing for normal to the shifting throng? I had a Jewish friend who used to go to Mass with me every

Sunday. He didn't suddenly stop being Jewish because of his attendance. He simply liked the music better at our church. No one appeared to question his right to be there—but he knew very well who he was—a Jew in a Catholic church. If you're gay, society for the most part would rather you just shut up and be invisible. Religion wishes you'd shut up, be invisible and disown your genitals. Government wants you to shut up, pay your taxes, die for your country and 'don't ask, don't tell.' Frankly, is anybody, anywhere encouraging gay people to simply 'live their truth?' Is anybody saying, 'It's OK—be the way God made you—in God's infinite wisdom and infallibility you're exactly perfect the way you are.' Perhaps, ultimately, this is the permission one gives oneself.

"I've had straight friends say to me, 'Hey, you know, I could've gone that path if I'd wanted to—sleep with my own sex—but I chose to avoid that sin.' Fair enough—I could've eaten a wooden rocking chair this morning if I'd really set my mind to it—but I would've had to ask myself at some point, is this something I really want to do or am I just making a point? Now if I were a termite, it might seem the most natural thing in the world, but not being a termite, I'd probably pass on that opportunity. If you're truly gay, and not a truly straight person simply theorizing—there is a basic, essential core to your being that you simply cannot pretend doesn't exist. And yes, I think it probably is true—if you strap enough electrodes to a person's genitals and torture them every time they're sexually aroused—yes, you can probably alter their thinking somewhat—but it does not translate that you've suddenly, miraculously turned a gay person straight, or a straight person gay. What you can do, and I'm sure of it, is create a massive psychotic misfit. And we already do an incredible bang-up job of that in this society without the electrodes.

"I'd like to clarify something. I'm certainly not saying that there aren't straight people who don't fool around and gay people who don't fool around with the opposite persuasion. Sexual parameters are infrequently set in concrete. What I'm saying is, as clearly as most people know that they're either male or female—one pretty much has reached a conclusion by the time they're in their twenties which way their gate swings . . . or leans . . . or hangs imperceptibly akimbo. And it's basic and it's fundamental and it's intrinsic. And I can assure you, if you're a gay person—it is not a phase. Now whether one chooses to do anything about that realization—that if indeed they are gay they face the risk of possible societal ostracism—that is clearly a choice one makes. To live openly, or to hide from the world. What would you do?

"And so, this great, troubling rush to judge one another. Clearly the Bible teaches love and tolerance and charity for all. 'Do unto others as you would have them do unto you.' The very basic, crucial tenets of Christianity. And yet we have 'Christians'—and I use the term when applied to these people with a high degree of inexactitude—'Christians' who show up at AIDS funerals with banners reading FAGS MUST DIE and BURN IN HELL, HOMO! Wouldn't Jesus be proud? What possibly can be going on in the minds of those holding the banners and shouting obscenities at grieving loved ones? For me it's exactly the same as stoning an innocent animal to death because he happened to be a 'nigger dog.' It makes . . . no sense.

"And please understand, by my using the story of Blackie as an analogy to unloving, un-Christian behavior, I am not trying to bind injustices against gay people with the African-American struggle or the Hispanic struggle or the Jewish struggle or the People with Disabilities struggle or the . . . pick your struggle. Each striving has its own singular horrors to relate—there's plenty of hatred and ignorance to go around. We don't necessarily have to borrow from each other. And hatred against any human being is basically hatred against ourselves.

"I would ask of each one of you today, as you leave this place of love and peace and brotherhood—think about what value there is in despising any of God's children? Don't I have more important work I can be doing on the planet than worrying about how one group of people expresses their love for each other? Next time your buttons get pushed around this issue I would ask you to stop and think, 'Is this really how God expects me to behave right now? Or can I just look at this with some degree of detachment, and say, 'I don't have to eat that particular rocking chair, today. That's somebody else's calling. I'll just let them do their thing while I go over here and chew on this ironing board for a while.' " Chris smiled. "See, God has a plan for everybody. And your job is to find yours and to be the best *you* you can be. You owe it to God, you owe it to society—you owe it to yourself. Thank you very much."

Chris picked up his notes, turned and quietly sat back down. I was completely wrung. Limp as a phone cord. Mother reached over and patted my knee, her way of showing solidarity. I noticed her wiping her eyes. It suddenly occurred to me, he hadn't even mentioned my name. Not once. I felt, God help me . . . ignored. All this gut-wrenching buildup and not even a passing aside of *our* struggle together.

And then it began, at first gradually, then sporadically and finally, wholly enthusiastically. The entire tent was applauding. A few people stood, then a few more, until finally half the congregation was on their feet. I was completely thunderstruck. I stood next to Mother and clapped till my hands were numb. The emotions coursing through my ragged frame of mind catapulted from intense pride, to shame at my own misgivings, to the fear that somehow, inexplicably, I'd lost Chris. Brother Ramirez walked over and put his arms around Chris. Chris bowed and waved to the audience. He was total, unmistakable class. I felt a huge knob in my throat, my own eyes welling.

As we started to sit someone I couldn't see ahead remained standing and called out in a loud voice, "As a gay man, I just want to say, what Chris Myles has spoken of today not only has opened my eyes and heart to a newer, better vision of myself, but also given me a glimpse of a world that I want to work toward making a reality. A place where each of us is recognized and honored for our gifts and our expressions of love instead of being scorned for our differences." We all stared at Preston in astonishment. He started to sit back down and turned to glance at me, passing the baton, as it were. Several heads followed his, all gazing at my face for some response. Immediate rigor mortis set in. What was I supposed to do? Stand and wave? Launch into my life story? Should I now race down the aisle embracing Preston and Chris in some dramatic gay unity display?

Before I could conceive of any kind of response, Brother Ramirez returned to the podium and thanked Preston for his words of support and regard. He then thanked Chris for his moving and very personal testament of conviction and asked that we each join hands and share a silent prayer asking for God's help in removing blocks and clearing the way for universal love in our hearts. I leaned over to Mother, and whispered, "I'll be right back." Standing, I silently walked out the rear of the tent and didn't stop until I'd reached the river, a good quarter mile away. An old man and a child were fishing on the other side of the bank. I leaned against a hackberry tree and could stand it no longer. I quietly began to sob. I cried like I haven't cried since I was twelve and a solid tangle of quivering hormones. I sat down in the tall grass and covered my face. The tears came in gales of remorse and self-pity. When I'd completely wrung out the last gasp of misery I lay back depleted and stared up at the sky, desperately trying to identify what aspect, if any, of my ridiculously squandered life was worth salvaging at this point. I lay there for a very long time.

10

PENNY IN A SHARK TANK

"I'm certain Miss Oveta said six o'clock."

"Mother, I saw the invitation. It was definitely 7 P.M."

"Well, it doesn't hurt to be a little early. She'll need some help—besides, I think it said six." There were ten of us crammed into Brother Ramirez's Dodge Caravan, en route to Miss Oveta's "surprise" wedding party for the intended couple. Brother Ramirez drove, Mother rode shotgun. Chris, Concepcion and I were in the next row. Behind us sat Jaston, Manuel and Vicky, and behind them, a newly introduced stepsibling, Oscar, and his wife, Lydia. All of us soberly attired in assorted sports coats, ties and dressy dresses—we appeared to be on our way to a funeral. Or a bank opening. Although the air conditioner was blasting at max, a heady brew of perspiration, Jontue, Agua Net and Right Guard coursed around our hermetically sealed environment.

"Bettie, that hairpiece looks so beautiful on you. I don't think you could've found a shade closer to your own." Concepcion smoothed the back of Mother's dramatic page coif. Indeed, the wig was a very youthful affair, lots of red hair, pretty much Mom's usual color, and crowned with a green velvet headband. Very "Jackie Susann" and considerably fashion-forward for Grit.

"Thank you, Concepcion. I know it's a little 'wiggish,' but I suppose when the hair goes it's as good an excuse as any to do something unexpected."

"Is there gonna be anything to eat at this shindig?" Jaston shifted uncomfortably in the rear. He took up nearly as much space as Vicky and Manuel combined.

"She's having a big buffet, and mind your manners, Jas. Don't you be elbowing people." Mother applied pinkish, coral lipstick as she glanced at Jaston in the visor mirror. "Oscar, you and Lydia getting enough air back there?"

Oscar and Lydia were the quiet type. (Most people were the quiet type around our family.) Oscar worked on a nearby ranch; Lydia taught school. "Fine, thanks," Oscar mumbled.

Jaston turned to him. "You the one that shot that old big buck outta season last year?"

Oscar eyed Jaston coolly.

"Damn, how many points that old *viejo* have?"

"Twenty."

"That's gotta be some kinda county record."

Oscar shook his head. "County wasn't impressed. They locked me up for the night."

"Hunting season ended the week before. I think he forgot that fact when the deer showed up in his headlights." Lydia shifted her purse from lap to side.

Manuel, beside Jaston, suddenly turned in his seat and fisted Oscar on the knee. "People that shoot animals should be locked up anyway." Oscar smiled slightly and retaliated with a solid middle finger *thwack* on Manuel's unprotected ear. You could hear the thud resound as Manuel grimaced in pain.

"Mother, they're starting again." Vicky stared out the window with a bored expression.

"You boys quit acting up. Oh, Bettie, isn't it something—all my children grown, and I still have to discipline them?"

Mother turned around, smiling sweetly, "My children are such angels. There's never a cross word between them."

"Ain't we though." Jaston placed his clammy hand on the back of my neck and rattled my head like a coconut, which gave me an instant headache. My immediate impulse was to turn around and

smack him, but I fought the urge mightily. I would not be the insti-
gator of a fifth-grade car-pool brawl.

"Mother, would you ask Jaston to remove his fat hand from my
collar?"

Mother murmured distantly, "Jas-ton . . ." The hand lifted from
my neck.

Chris spoke up, "Manuel, where did you and Vicky study music?"

"Nowhere. We couldn't afford it. Mom taught us a little, but we
just kind of picked it up." Manuel was still cradling his ear.

"We had great record and tape collections. We traded around a
lot," Vicky added.

Brother Ramirez joined in, "All the kids have musical ability. We
had a little family band at one time, *Las Gruas del norte,* The
Northern Sand Cranes. I named us that 'cause we tended to migrate
every season."

"But you learned all that amazing playing just by listening?" I
asked incredulously.

Manuel shrugged. "Even a chicken can be taught to peck out 'Old
MacDonald.' We're just mimics with an ear. The hard part is finding
your own sound."

"I like blues, he likes rock—our sister Sylvia thinks she's Kiri Te
Kanawa. It's all a question of style." Vicky fanned herself as we
turned onto Miss Oveta's street.

I was impressed. The three Latimores couldn't pilot a tune if it
came with wheels and a gas engine. Jaston turned to Oscar. "What
do you play?"

Oscar squinted and gave one of his little sly smiles. "Blackjack."
Jaston hooted, and Lydia elbowed Oscar.

"Oscar has a very nice voice. He used to sing with us in the choir,
but I guess he got bored." Concepcion stared ahead wistfully.

"Not bored, Mama. I got other things going on in my life."

"Oscar's gonna run for sheriff next term." Brother Ramirez
smiled proudly. My God, the thought of having a stepbrother as
county sheriff—who'da thunk it?

"No shit?" As soon as Jaston said it, he looked sheepishly at
Mother. She glanced at him scornfully in the mirror. Cursing in polite
company was one of Mother's chief no-no's. Jaston made a little "o"

with his mouth and turned back to Oscar. "What's your platform gonna be?"

"Moral accountability. No more letting people get away with thieving, fighting, whoring, drinking, cheating—you know, perversion in general."

Jaston snorted. "What are you gonna do, lock up near everybody in town?"

"'Aim high, shoot low'—that's my campaign slogan." I could see Chris's fingers drumming steadily on the door handle. Of course the fact that a sheriff could get elected who broke the law by shooting a deer out of season would make perfect sense to anyone in small-town Texas. We tended not to elect saints—we just expected those we did put in office to make sure everyone else stayed one.

Chris politely changed the subject. "What do the rest of your children do?"

Concepcion brightened. "Sivia's the oldest, she's married to an insurance salesman, they have three kids. She runs a Ladies Fitness Gym up in Wichita. And she really does—has the voice of an angel. Then there's Jaime, second oldest, he's a school principal down in Harlingen. Married to a nurse, and they have two little boys. Then there's Hector, he owns an auto parts store over in East Texas, married to a beautician, and we're still waiting on children there. And then there's Chavela . . ." Concepcion's voice grew soft. "Chavela's a . . . dancer."

"A dancer?

Concepcion nodded.

"She teaches dance?" Chris continued, puzzled.

Concepcion shook her head. "No, she . . . dances." I could tell from Concepcion's evasiveness we were skimming murky water. Chris plowed on.

"What kind of dance? Is she in ballet, folkloric, modern, jazz? Where does she dance?"

After some hesitation Vicky finally dived in, exhaling, "This month it's the Fantasy Playroom, just outside El Paso. Last month she was the headline at Captain Dickie's Love Lounge in Galveston. Vela works all the time. Her stage name is, Frieda Malo—Latin Artist with a Special Talent. And she's gorgeous, too."

We turned into Miss Oveta's drive at exactly the right moment. Chavela's vocational résumé had momentarily put a roadblock in our conversational skills. Mother sang out, "Here we are! Oh look at Oveta's gardens, beautiful as ever."

Concepcion suddenly turned to Chris and held out her hand across my lap. "Vela's the adventuress of the family. Always has been. She can only do things her way. Will you help me send her a positive message right now?"

"Of course." Chris took her hand, and the two of them shut their eyes, immediately beaming love energy toward El Paso. No one said a word. I sat between the two thinking, another ordinary day in Grit. Ten people parked in a Dodge Caravan in someone's driveway praying for an exotic dancer in El Paso. What could be more normal?

Finally, Concepcion let Chris's hand go, then calmly slid open the rear passenger door. As we clambered out Jaston leaned into my ear and whispered, "What was the name of that freakin' club? I think I oughta go check old Sis out." I couldn't help but laugh. Jaston could be pretty witty in his laconic, redneck way. Standing at the front entry, we were once again serenaded by the "Malagueña." The front door opened and a pretty but serious-looking woman, wearing glasses and a rather tight sweater over what appeared to be exceptionally large breasts, greeted us with a smile.

"Hello, I'm Shirley Zavaba, Raymond Otis's niece—the *other* side of the family."

Mother took her hand. "Nice to meet you, Shirley, Bettie Jean Latimore, and this is my fiancé, Brother Ramirez. I told the others I think we may be a tad early. I hope we're not barging in on your preparations?"

"Not at all," Shirley lied graciously, and we began filing in—naturally, the first to arrive. Introductions were made and the last to shake her hand was Jaston. They sized each other up like two accountants inspecting a ledger.

"Nice sweater."

"Thanks. Like your tie. Blue's good on you." Mother and I stood next to each other in awe. Neither of us had ever seen Jaston even grunt at another girl, much less pay her a compliment. The two of them, for the rest of the party, managed to circulate tethered to one another by an invisible cord. It was oddly exhilarating, Mother and I exchanging covert bulletins throughout the evening on their curious little mating dance.

After about a half hour Miss Oveta made her entrance down the grand staircase. This time no cane, just Mr. Jeffrey firmly bolted to her side. Miss Oveta was wearing a striking beaded, aqua dashiki that came at you like a great wave of ocean foam. A pair of green silk cigarette pants, a rope of gold twisted around her neck, drop-earrings the length of ballpoint pens and festively painted toenails peeking out of gold lamé sandals completed her ensemble. No question, the gal knew how to maximize a first impression. "Beh-teeee, you look like a twenty-year-old bride. Wonderful!" Mother and Miss Oveta smooched and cooed and again another round of introductions ensued. We were still the only guests to have arrived, so we prolonged the chitchat by moving to the living room and sitting in a circle around the oriental carpets. Mr. Jeffrey immediately began working the bar, proffering his usual drinks like a time-share broker at a resort condo.

"We're just thrilled about Clu directing the little theater's first offering," Miss Oveta warbled.

"What's it called again?" Brother Ramirez asked, taking a Diet Coke from Mr. Jeffrey garnished with two limes, a cherry and a silver swizzle stick in the shape of an Alaskan totem pole.

"*Agamemnon—a Country and Western Tragedy with Swing Band.* Isn't that divine? I believe it was Preston and Chris that came up with the title, isn't that right?" Miss Oveta smiled at Chris, who nodded.

"That's right. Where is Preston?" Chris inquired.

"He's gone to get more ice and lemons—the ice machine broke down! Of all days. Christopher, you must come here and let me give you a hug. I can't remember when I've been more moved by someone's testimony as your delivery on Sunday. I was completely overwhelmed."

"It's true." Mr. Jeffrey stopped pouring from a wine bottle and reached for Miss Oveta's hand. "We both just came home and wept like babies. It felt like a cleansing breeze had swept through town and whisked away all the offal."

"Offal?" Oscar queried, peering up suspiciously from his Jack and Coke with the jaunty sombrero swizzle branching out.

"Garbage, trash . . . small-town mores." Mr. Jeffrey eyed Oscar somewhat askance. Oscar bit the inside of his mouth and sucked back an inordinately long gulp of Jack Daniels.

Chris hesitantly moved toward Miss Oveta, and she dramatically flung her dolman sleeves around him in a turquoise bear hug. Then it was Mr. Jeffrey's turn. I truly hoped they wouldn't start sobbing again—they both appeared to be getting demonstrative. Chris and I had spoken little about Sunday's event. I was enormously proud, and I told him so, but I was also very much confused. If I was to be "out" in Grit, at least I'd hope to have the assurance of my mate's support. And yet, we were as distant and uncommunicative as we'd ever been. When I'd ask him what was wrong, he'd stare beyond me and say he didn't feel like talking about it right then. When I questioned if he was disappointed I'd not stood up in church like Preston and verbalized my advocacy, he'd shrug and mutter that he "wouldn't have expected it." If I asked how things were going between him and Preston, he'd stare at me piteously, shake his head and quietly leave the room. What was I to do? Turn into a harridan and hurl accusations at him? Guaranteed not to work. Chris would simply vanish, repelled by my jealousy and insecurity. Chris had never been envious of anything or anyone his whole life. He didn't get that kind of neurosis. Completely baffled him. Why be obsessive over something you obviously had no control over? To what aim? Useless endeavor. (He clearly would never comprehend the exquisite and edifying Scorpionic habit of haunting the scene of a crime until some new evidence of betrayal revealed itself. Obsession? I chose to call it categorical atonement. What completely baffled me was the act of betrayal itself. Disloyalty and dishonesty were the two most intolerable words in the Scorpio lexicon. Appallingly nasty traits.)

And then Mr. Youth himself entered the room. Preston was glowing like a polished yellow apple. All sunlight and honey-toned, he was radiant in his white linen shirt and beige silk slacks. A slight sheen of perspiration coated his face, only adding to his luminescence. I marveled silently—could this guy even manage to get a zit once in a while? Would it be completely out of the question?

"Hi, everyone. Had to go to two Stop and Paks, seems to be a run on ice today."

Again, round of introductions, the women devouring him with their eyes, the men sopping up whatever spilled "Preston-glory" sloshed their way. All except for Oscar, who seemed to hug the perimeter of the room as if his bladder was in mortal danger of bursting.

"Oscar, son—have you met Preston? He also testified at church last Sunday." Brother Ramirez motioned Oscar over.

Oscar weaved across the room, managing to pass fleetingly in front of Preston with a barely extended right hand. " 'Lo."

"Hi, Oscar . . . how've you been?"

"Good." With that informative bit of exchange, Oscar sailed back to his moorings in the corner. Did they know each other? What was that brief interplay all about?

Concepcion abruptly stood, a fist clamped to her chest, and let out a sudden "Whoop!" Everyone turned in amazement. Not a tee-totaler like Mother and Brother Ramirez, it was unclear the basis of her sudden action—the white wine she was holding or a passing "walk-in." She spoke in an eerie monotone. "*¡Hijo de Dios!* Before the evening is over there will be new love for some . . . and for some, love anew. What Divine Order brings forth let no one contradict." She then hung her head and rolled her mouth as if exercising a sore jaw.

Vicky, who was standing near me, leaned in and whispered, unimpressed, "She always picks an audience to have these vision-things. I'd be afraid to go with her to the Astrodome."

Mother and Miss Oveta hovered around her, as Concepcion sat back down, suddenly depleted.

Brother Ramirez, looking somewhat askance at his ex-wife's outburst, gamely volunteered a summation. "Well, love in any package is always a welcome present, no?" Before anyone could accord a response, the "Malagüeña" pealed throughout the first floor of the house. Raymond Otis emerged from his hiding spot to open the front door. I glanced around the room. Jaston and Shirley were bunched up on an ottoman having a lively discourse about something. Chris and Preston had moved toward the rear stand-up bar and seemed to be engrossed in their own little dialogue. Mother and Brother Ramirez held hands and beamed like high schoolers. Yes, "love anew" appeared to be our little gathering's prevailing theme, no question.

Raymond somberly appeared at the entrance to the living room, and, mustering all the animation of a stunned horned toad, announced, "Mr. Patrick Pickens and son, Brandon." I looked up from my wine and our eyes met much as they had at *Templo*—two thirtysomething white boys sussing each other out for any evidence of regard. Brandon stood next to him, a virtual replica of Pat in junior high school, same brooding, androgynous glamour, same bored apathy. As well as blue hair, an earring and, for all we knew, a Chinese exit sign stamped on his neck.

Miss Oveta stood carefully and extended a bejeweled palm toward Pat. "So glad you could come, Pat. And this must be Brandon. Oh look, my blouse and your hair! We seem to have both been jumped by the Sapphire Fairy. Isn't it wonderful?" Brandon managed an awkward smile, and Pat stepped forward to greet the partygoers.

"Brother Ramirez, Mrs. Latimore, congratulations to you both."

"Pat, good to see you again. My goodness, it's been a long time since you and Clu were in debate club."

"Yes, ma'am, sure has. This is my son Brandon . . . he's fourteen."

"I'll be fifteen in a month." Brandon extended a manly hand, then quickly averted his eyes in a flirtatious, ambivalent retreat. He was a walking textbook of schoolboy charm and teenage disparity. He could've also been the new poster boy for the latest teen-dream, all-male, singing group. What was this kid doing in Grit?

"So nice to meet you, Brandon, I don't think I've seen you around church?" Mother inquired.

"He spends most weekends with his mom, she's up in Austin. Hello, Concepcion." Pat and Concepcion hugged, apparently pals. Pat then wound his way around the room, chatting it up with Chris and Preston, conferring with Manuel and Vicky, even greeting Lydia and Oscar with lively hellos. It was becoming quite clear, Oscar was a man on a mission—to get wasted as fast as he could. He hoisted his ever-brimming glass in one hand and perpetual lit cigarette in the other and gesticulated animatedly every time someone crossed his path. How long would it take for him to skip from lively raconteur to odious sot was anybody's guess. And it was equally as evident, certainly to me, he was avoiding Preston like a cat at bath time.

A few other guests entered just as Pat was winding down his official round of greetings. It was apparent I was to be the last stop on his itinerary.

He turned to face me, a big grin on his face, "Well, I'd been hearing you'd returned to the scene of the crime."

Funny choice of words. We shook hands genially. "How are ya, Pat? Nearly fell over when I saw you in church last Sunday."

"Yeah. I looked for you afterward. You must've left early. Clu, this is my son, Brandon. He's fourteen." He said "fourteen" as if it would magically explain all that he couldn't.

"Hi, Brandon."

"Hi. Are you the actor from New York?"

"The very one."

"I've seen your condom commercial. Dad told me that was you. Does that pay a lot?"

"That one was free, but some of them pay quite well."

"Oh. I wonder if I could do stuff like that?"

I wanted to grab his little pierced ears and rattle him. "Honey, if Calvin Klein were here, he'd scoop you up in his pocket and whisk you back to New York so fast it'd take a week for that blue hair to find you." Instead I smiled and took a sip of wine. "You ought to see if your dad'll let you get some professional pictures made. You never know."

Pat laughed uncomfortably. "Oh, I think he's a little young for that. 'Sides, school takes up so much of his time nowadays. Wasn't like when we were that age, huh? Remember when a summer seemed to last an eternity?"

Oh, Pat. You're sounding like Fred MacMurray. Let the kid have a dream, huh?

"Son, why don't you go get us something to drink. I'll take a beer—see if they have a Shiner."

Brandon looked down at his long, boy/man feet tucked into a pair of somewhat new Hi-Tops. He then glanced up at me, a little twinkle in his aquamarine eyes. "Nice to meet you, Mr. Latimore. I think it's way cool what you do." He seemed to flush a little, then turn and slip across the room. Peter Pan, Puck, Huck Finn and Enrique Iglesias all rolled into one. I immediately wanted to adopt this kid. Or be his manager. He was completely adorable.

Pat sighed. "You don't know what it's like. Having a child nowadays is wrenching. He's a good boy, but what are you supposed to do about tattoos and piercings and a blue head?"

"Ignore them. Would you rather he ran around in bell bottoms and had hair in his eyes like a sheepdog? We weren't exactly mature at fourteen either."

Pat smiled. "Yeah, but our music was better. Have you heard some of the songs they listen to?"

Now was probably not the best time to reveal I was a major Brittney Spears fan. My turn to smile, "So, the years have been good to you, Pat. Still as suave as ever."

Pat scoffed and produced a cigarette and a lighter from his pocket. This was new. He offered me one, and I shook my head. How could people my age still smoke? Didn't they read the papers? Was it stupidity or apathy or some hybridization of both flaws that led to such a character defect? If he wanted to ruin his looks and kill himself, there was certainly nothing I could do about it. No, I'd just stand here and breathe his secondhand smoke like the nice, polite Southern boy I was brought up to be. I actually couldn't decide which was worse, people smoking or assholes like I'd witnessed in New York who'd hurl themselves across a crowded restaurant screaming and foaming at the first puff of some grandmotherly type enjoying an after-dinner drag. Both reeked of rank déclassé manners.

"Nasty habit. I've tried quitting several times. I'm on the patch now—seems to be working."

"I can tell."

Pat smiled, his eyes all suddenly crinkly and handsome. "Same old sly sense of humor. I miss that. So how've you been? New York treating you well?"

I hunched my shoulders. "Haven't you heard? I'm a Texan again, Pat. I'm here till Mom . . . till Mother does what she's going to do."

Pat pondered his cigarette, "I'm really sorry, Clu. She's a great lady, your mom. At least she's found someone to keep her company. Every time I see them at church, they just sort of look so peaceful and satisfied with each other." Pat took a puff and stared wistfully. "I'd like to have that someday."

"When did you start going to the *Templo*? Haven't your family always been Episcopalian?"

He exhaled, nodding. "Right up to the tips of their golf-shoe tassels. I just looked at the minister one Sunday and I couldn't follow a word he was saying. Same thing the next week, and the week after that. It's like everyone was suddenly speaking Japanese. So I left." Pat smiled again, slyly. "It's my one little rebellion. No one can understand it. Scares the hell out of them, but it makes perfect sense to me. I like the Universal Temple of the Love of God—where all the righteous misfits come to land."

I grinned. "Funny, I never thought of you as a misfit, Pat."

He laughed back at me, "You're kidding, right? No one ever really liked me. I was too odd, too different—I don't know, I just never fit in."

I shook my head. "Now you're kidding. You were the class 'dream,' every girl wanted you, every guy wanted what you had. Give me a break."

Pat looked at me, genuinely surprised. "That tired old joke—me the big 'stud'? Please, why do you think I dated so many girls—they kept dropping me. I was too neurotic, too self-obsessed. I couldn't be alone with myself in the same room, it was just too painful. God, I was a mess. I wouldn't have wished me on anyone."

I looked at him, not sure if he was pulling my leg or what. I felt like I'd just been told Kim Novak was really a male midget with good makeup. No, no, no!

"Anyway, I guess after *three* busted marriages I've finally resigned myself to the fact I'm a confirmed bachelor. Kind of like you." Pat gave a conspiratorial wink.

I hesitated for just a fraction. "Actually, I'm in a marriage." Pat looked confused. I motioned toward Chris and Preston. "Chris is my spouse. We've been together eight years."

Pat stared at me, sincerely confounded. "You mean . . . you and . . . Chris . . . ?"

I nodded. "How did you think he found his way to *Templo* last week? Just wandered into town asking if anyone needed a gay toast-master?"

"I . . . I didn't think about it. Brother Ramirez always has such interesting speakers. Gosh, what's it like for you two in Grit? Have people treated you . . . well?"

I gazed at Pat. What's it been like? "It's been strange. I keep half expecting some unknown disaster to befall us all. Some godawful ruinous thing designed to permanently scar me, my mate and my family. I guess I'm just lucky. It hasn't happened yet."

Pat took a long drag on his cigarette. "Oh, Grit's changed. I mean it's the same—same fools, same foolish behavior—but they won't let you get away with outright illiterate conduct anymore." He sighed. "I guess that's progress."

"How come you stayed, Pat? You always seemed to be searching for something else. You find it in your own backyard?"

Pat grinned. "At first it was family, then it was the business . . . I finally ran out of excuses. Actually, to be honest, I think I've always just been more interested in appearances than in anything of real substance. How's that for four years of therapy? I'm a deeply shallow person, what can I say?"

Pat's smile was so irresistibly engaging, his little-boy-lost façade so good-naturedly tethered to his adult frame—he instantly achieved his desired effect by trumping with the "superficial" card. You immediately wanted to nurture and protect this bright, charming and outwardly lost man/child. It was a powerful enticement. No wonder women threw themselves at him. No wonder they left so quickly.

"Clu, I'd like to ask you a little favor." Pat stubbed out his cigarette in one of Miss Oveta's antique porcelain bowls. He furrowed his brow in a "serious" mien. "I'm glad you told me about you and Chris. I really respect that. It takes some real balls to do what he did last Sunday. I wish you both complete success, I mean that." I nodded. "Brandon's . . . Brandon's been trying to talk to me lately about . . ." Pat stared at me, almost tongue-tied. "I don't know how to put this . . . He says he has a . . . *boyfriend.*" We stared at each other. I hurriedly put my wineglass to my mouth and bit my tongue.

"I was thinking you . . . well, could you maybe talk to him. I don't have a clue about any of that."

I removed the wineglass and crossed my arms. "Clue about what?"

"You know—the whole gay thing. I was thinking of driving him to my therapist in San Antonio, but maybe he just needs to talk with a gay adult. I'm pretty much cool with it all. I mean obviously I think his life would be easier if he were straight, but if that's the way it's meant to . . ."

I set the wineglass down. I could feel the blood surging across my face. "Stop, whoa . . . *alto!* First of all, why would his life be any easier if he was straight? Has your life been a walk in the park just because of your sexuality, Pat? I didn't think so. You see anyone in this room whose life is enhanced simply because they're heterosexual? Me neither. The ability to procreate is shared by humans with fleas, maggots and bacteria. It is not a prerequisite for sainthood. So let's not rush to deposit Brandon in the 'gay-doomed sanatorium' quite so categorically. Secondly, he's fourteen! Do you remember fourteen, Pat? I seriously wanted to have sex with my dog when I was fourteen. At least he's talking to you! His mind is open to lots of things right now. At fourteen you can truthfully say it might very well be a phase he's going through. Leave it alone! And thirdly . . . What the hell do you mean you don't have a clue about 'any of that?' "

Pat looked at me as if I'd just pissed on his loafers. "I . . . I'm sorry, I really didn't expect this kind of reaction. I thought you'd be pleased that I'd trust my son with you for some counseling. . . ."

"That you'd *trust* me? Pat, are you presuming because I'm a gay man that I might somehow be inclined to take advantage of a four-teen-year-old kid? Are you implying such an outlandish assumption? Are you into fourteen-year-old girls, Pat? Those are called pederasts, not homosexuals. Why is this so hard for lazy, straight people to fol-low? Gay men want gay men! Child molesters, who are statistically nearly always heterosexual men, want children. Get it? There's a dif-ference!"

Pat started to back away. I put a hand on his sleeve and leaned in next to his ear. I was just getting cranked. "Pat—old friend—are you conveniently forgetting the night we had sex at the Rodeway Inn in

San Marcos on March 7, 1979, during the debate team regional finals? I lost my virginity to you . . . Dad. Maybe it was just another roll on the springs in your orb, but it left a crater-sized impression in my life. So when you say you're clueless about the gay thing—methinks you're being just a wee bit facetious, no?"

Pat jerked his arm away and stood back. I truly think for a millisecond he thought about hitting me. He quickly gained his composure, and scoffed, "That's some imagination you've got, Clu. We never had debate finals in San Marcos. Ever. It was always Austin or Dallas."

I lit up. "You're absolutely correct—and we spent the night in San Marcos on the way home from Dallas!"

Pat glowered at me, his brain doing an emergency background check. In a way I felt sorry for him. Selective memory must be an unusually traumatic condition. You never knew when some asshole like me would wreak havoc on your reality cocoon. Granted, we did sneak a few beers into the motel room, but he was hardly so drunk that he'd have no recollection. In fact, if memory serves, from the enthusiasm and proficiency of his performance, one would have thought the evening might have made his "Top-Five" roster.

"They only had Budweiser and Heineken." Brandon stood behind his father, holding out a green bottle of Heineken. "I know you don't drink Bud."

Pat took the beer. "Thank you, son." He stared at me a moment longer, undecided whether to put a contract out on me or simply off me himself. Finally, he put his arm around Brandon. "Come on, I want you to meet some other of Dad's friends." Pat nodded coolly, "Clu," and strolled off with Brandon. When they were halfway across the room Brandon turned and flashed me a toothy, kid-grin.

Oh God. What a world! Is this all supposed to appear madly intriguing or desperately farcical? Half full, half empty—which is it? Yes, yes—the beholder establishes the rules, I get it. It's just that I've always had one very important question my whole life that no one's ever been able to remotely address—*what am I supposed to be wearing to this freakin' ball?* Equal footing at the palace doors—that's all I've ever wanted out of life. Is it so preposterous?

I picked up a fistful of olives and started toward Chris and *Press-*

tone. For once I wasn't berating myself for being a big mouth. Fuck stupid, "perfect" Pat and his banal, repressed, ludicrous life. If I'm the only reality test he ever gets, good—I've served a life purpose. So what if his life purpose is to wear blinders? Maybe mine's to rip 'em off. (And who's right, by the way?)

I walked up behind Chris, who was leaning toward Preston, mumbling in his ear. "Hey, guys, practicing a little Greek?" Chris turned to me, and Preston smiled in his usual noncommittal way.

"You and Pat Pickens we're having quite a discussion," Preston opined.

I poured myself a deep glass of Chardonnay. "You noticed."

"High-school friend?" Chris asked, not really interested. It was obvious I was interrupting their woolgathering party.

"I lost my virginity to him in tenth grade. We were just pleasantly reminiscing." They both stared at me.

"Be serious."

"I'm serious as a fire in a shithouse. Sorry, am I interrupting? I know you both have a lot to talk about. Just ask me to leave if I get tedious."

Chris looked at me, resigned. He'd seen this performance on other occasions—"the wounded fuck-up." "How come you've never mentioned him before?"

I shrugged. "It was just one time. There were legions after him. Who remembers their first pizza?"

Chris looked doleful. "What's the matter?"

"Nothing. I feel great. Like a penny in a shark tank—you can't touch me!" I took Chris's hand and twirled him around. Guaranteed to piss him off.

"OK, jerk-wad, you've got everybody at the party staring now. What's your next trick? Gonna kneel and bark for us?" Chris was royally peeved.

"As a matter of fact, I was thinking I'd lean your way, way back and plant a big, wet kiss on your big, pouty lips." They both looked at me with a blend of panic and disgust.

Chris reached out and put his hand on my shoulder. "Come on, let's go over to the buffet table and get something to eat."

I brushed him off. "You don't have to baby-sit me. You guys go on with your little 'intrigue.'" I turned to Preston, smiling. "I think it's real clever of you trying to make time with my spouse. That always makes the director of the show you're about to star in most agreeable."

"'Make time'—what are you ranting about?" Preston looked agitated.

"Am I some complete, utter imbecile to you? You think I can't see how much you want to fuck Chris? Can't you find anybody of your own? I know if you tried just a teensy bit harder, you could come up with someone who isn't already taken."

With that Chris whirled me around and began marching me toward the dining room. I jerked away from his grip. He leaned into my face, speaking calmly but deliberately. "Follow me to the bathroom."

More guests were arriving, and I noticed Concepcion and Mr. Jeffrey looking at us worriedly as we tramped across the room. I didn't care anymore. Ah, the glory of finally hitting the bottom of the barrel. No more having to bolster people's feelings just for decorum's sake.

We entered the ornate, gold-encrusted *"Lou-ee/* Neiman Marcus" powder room tucked under the staircase. Chris shut the door and locked it. He stared at me, grave as a Last Supper waiter. "What are you doing?" I started to speak, and he interrupted, "And don't start with the 'Who me?' bullshit. I want to know exactly what's going on?"

I looked at Chris. I truly hadn't seen him this vexed since the Cuisinart bowl exploded in New York and puked tomato purée all over our apartment. I exhaled. "Odd, the very thought I had in my head to ask you. 'What's going on?' How's this sound—it seems I used to have a mate, a lover, a significant other that I was closer to than anybody in the entire world. And no matter how shitty and hateful the world could get, no matter how obnoxious and ridiculous I could get—this person was there with love and understanding even when he didn't agree, completely understand or feel like showing it. And the trade-off was—that person got it all back in return when the world was busting his own chops. It was their agreement. It wasn't perfect, and it wasn't always commensurate—but it was the bond they made with each other. And it was supposed to be other-guy-proof."

Chris stared at me, emotionless. "And in this pact did it say that if the other partner turns into someone the significant other finds to be a bitter, difficult, alienated and wholly exasperating individual that they're required to give up their own life in order to support the other's accelerating disintegration?"

There we had it. The moment-of-truth wrecking ball guaranteed to lay waste to any illusions carefully nourished through years of blind habit and unswerving obedience to the relationship code. I felt like I'd just been booted in the heart. I wanted very much to sit and catch my breath.

"So . . . I'm a bitter, difficult . . . what was the word, 'exasperating' person." I looked at him, attempting composure. "Why is that?"

Chris leaned against the door and crossed his arms. His sense of moral authority oozed forth with reeking conviction. "Because you've become completely the thing you despise. A sanctimonious, narrow, frightened, small-town Babbitt. All you know how to do is ridicule, reject and disdain. At least in New York your scorn was masked—but here, your own people, your own environment—you annihilate everyone with your contempt. You put down Miss Oveta for still daring to have a dream, Mr. Jeffrey for supporting her foolishness, Jaston for trying to see beyond the obvious, Laine and Sherrod for having differing values, your friends for committing the fatal error of reaching out to you, Preston because he mirrors your insecurity—to tell you the truth, I wonder if you even really like your mother. I think you subconsciously hold her hostage for speeding your conversion into a full-fledged bitter, old queer."

I lunged toward him and tightened my hand around his mouth. "Don't you ever presume to tell me what feelings I may or may not have about my only parent. Is . . . that . . . clear?" I was squeezing his face so tight his lips turned blue. "Goddamn you!" I threw Chris back against the wall in disgust. He immediately hurtled toward me, slamming my head against the vanity mirror and cracking it. It didn't hurt so much as startle me silly. A tiny rivulet of blood sprang forth and drooled down my forehead. Without the slightest sense of shame or propriety, we both began whaling on each other like two giants in a dollhouse. Dainty soap dishes cracked, miniature figurines shattered, mounds of potpourri scattered like mountain snow. The months of pent-up bitterness extricated in one meteoric, blinding eruption.

Neither of us heard the pounding on the door at first. We were both choked in a death grip on the floor beside the commode. "Open this door, right now!" Mother was yelling from outside. "Do you hear me, open the door!" The knocking grew louder. And suddenly, as irrationally as it had started, we both went completely limp. I rolled off of Chris. I saw that his nose was bleeding and his cheek was scratched. Half the buttons on my shirt seemed to be missing. I rose to look in the cracked mirror and saw blood all over my face. For the life of me I couldn't find the cut, but there was an exceptional shiner starting to blossom in full glory on my left eye. What a glorious picture of thirty-seven-year-old manhood in all its dignity and pride. Chris started to puke into the toilet. I turned on the splashing sink faucet out of propriety.

Mother knocked again, "If you don't open this door right now, Mr. Otis is going to have to knock it down." That I was tempted to hold out for. Don Knotts storming the Bastille.

"Just a minute, Mother. We'll be right out." I tossed Chris a wet washcloth and dabbed at my own miserable face. It was useless. I looked like hell. I threw the cloth down and offered a hand to Chris. "I'd like to be able to apologize right now, but somehow it's not forthcoming."

Chris knocked my hand away and stood, coughing. "Go fuck yourself. I'll be moved out in the morning."

I stared at him, amazed. "You really hate me that much?"

"I really hate you." Chris wiped his mouth with a tissue.

I was dumbfounded. "And that's it, eight years and—fuck you. I don't even get a 'Thanks for the memories, Bob'"?

"You get what you deserve, sarcastic bastard." Chris stepped around me and opened the bathroom door. Outside was the entire party gaping at the two aging homosexuals and the sordid residue of their untimely shit fit. I could hear Chris starting to make apologies and discouraging platitudes. Intermittent "Ohhhs" and gasps arose from the outraged rabble and I stared into the mirror. That's it? I felt like Humphrey Bogart moments before he died a miserable, defeated wretch in *The Treasure of the Sierra Madre*. THAT'S IT? And then it happened. Hard to say what it was, really. It just happened. Instantaneous. I started to sing. Full on, Robert Goulet-style, Broadway opening night . . . *SINGING!*:

> "O-o-o-o-o-o-o-o-klahoma, where the wind
>   comes sweepin' down the plain.
> And the wavin' wheat can sure smell sweet
> when the wind comes right behind the rain.
>
> "O-o-o-o-o-o-o-o-klahoma, ev'ry night my
>   honey lamb and I.
> Sit alone and talk, and watch a hawk,
>   makin' lazy circles in the sky.
>
> We know we belong to the land,
> and the land we belong to is grand.
> And when we sa-a-a-a-a-a-ay, YO!
> Ki-yip-eye-yo-eye-yea!
> Were only sayin', you're doin'
> fine Oklahoma, Oklahoma Ok-l-a-h-o-m-a!
> OKLAHOMA, OK."

I found myself weaving and bobbing through the crowd like I was in my very own TV special. I took Concepcion's hand and courtly bowed. I waltzed with Vicky for a few moments. I even put my arms around a catatonic Pat and swayed with him. The look on everyone's face could best be summed up as—apoplectic? All except for Brandon, who seemed to grasp the entire performance on a cellular level. He grinned and chortled like it was a rebroadcast of his favorite Simpsons episode. Pausing at the front door I turned to Miss Oveta and blew her a kiss. "Please don't do a thing, dear lady. I'll return in the morning to repair your bathroom. It'll be totally like new, you'll see. Good night all." With that I twirled and immediately raced down the driveway. I was bursting with endorphins. It felt like I'd stripped off my skin and grown angel wings. *Penny in a shark tank*. I tore off my sports coat and threw it in the air. Just as I was about to enter the street Jaston stepped forth from the gazebo and called. He was holding Shirley's hand. I froze.

"Clu, hey, Clu, come here, man! Guess what old Shirley does? She's with the State Historical Commission up in Austin. She's an archaeologist by trade!"

If I'd ever seen two people in infatuation, this was it. They were as close to each other as peanut butter on bread. I stammered, "That's . . . that's really neat."

"She's gonna be down here for a couple of weeks. She wants to help me at the gristmill. Maybe get us some funding." The smile on Jaston's face almost made me want to cry. I think this was the happiest I'd ever seen him in his entire life. Something inside was undeniably lit.

"I'm really happy for you. Happy for you both."

"Hey, did you know Shirley used to be a champion barrel racer? Idn't that something?"

I nodded. "Wow."

Jaston then scrunched his forehead and squinted. "What'd you do to your eye, man?"

"Oh it's nothing. Pat Pickens tried to kiss me in the butler's pantry. I let him have it. Good night ya'll." Shirley and Jaston stared at me oddly, and I strolled off down the street, whistling.

I think I walked around Grit till about four in the morning. Just walking. Thinking. Walking. Thinking. Jaston finally drove by in his pickup and found me. I was sitting on the swings down at the elementary school. I waved at him, got up and wandered over to his truck.

"Come on, let's go home, brother," was all he said.

I got in and we drove the rest of the way in silence.

11

AIR CONDITIONING, BEER, SOMETHING TO EAT

And I did fix her bathroom. We both did. In silence. And it indeed looked better than before because Miss Oveta decided to let us paint it a neutral satin bone. It was the only sensible thing to do since the blood specks weren't coming out of the gold-flecked wallpaper. The miniatures were salvageable, the potpourri replaced with bags of even smellier mulch called Vermont Wedding—an apple/maple/walnut pie inspiration, and I reglazed the mirror perfectly. Everything like before. Almost—like before.

At first Chris tried to move out. Conveniently Preston had twin beds in his room at Miss Oveta's. Downright wholesome, I thought. But Mother, who was sorely distressed by the entire mess, convinced him to move into the front guest room. Chris agreed to try it for a trial period, not promising anything permanent. It seemed that a lot of people were genuinely upset over our altercation. Myla and Zane called, Brother Ramirez and Concepcion each wrote us letters, Miss Oveta, who had every right to hate our guts for upsetting her party, inquired earnestly if our "disagreement" would upset the rehearsals for *Agamemnon*. Even Jaston, who in his pre–Shirley phase would have treated the whole thing with no more thought than two stray cats fighting in the alley, seemed genuinely concerned.

It was strange—I became some sort of a walking narcoleptic. I alternated between bouts of dazed numbness—virtual sleepwalking—

and intense passages of rage, depression, sadness and stinking self-pity. Of course, I was mortified by my behavior at Miss Oveta's, but what could I do now? The die was cast. If everything that Chris had said was true, then I was indeed a worthless, pathetic case. But somehow the fact that my whole life I'd been a "reporter," that I'd commented, appraised and accentuated on people's foibles since I could remember, didn't appear to be relevant to my case. What Chris saw in my hometown denunciation was me being me. I wasn't condemning anyone to hell for *them* being *them.* Consequently, if the Emperor wore no clothes, who was I to pretend otherwise? Yes, I was a harsh critic. It's one man's opinion. I can't not see what I see, feel what I feel, know what I know! And if I didn't edit for the public's sense of propriety, well, then I'd paid many times over for that right to authenticity.

Chris and I avoided each other like two old-maid pandas in adjoining cages. It worried the dogs silly. Delphinium had finally hatched her brood (in my closet), and she rotated from bedroom to bedroom, usually with a couple of squalling offspring underfoot, trying to figure out what was up. Señor Murphy was so put out with us he'd stake himself in the hallway, legs in the air and tongue hanging out, waiting for someone to notice he was dead and pick him up.

Our one consequential face-to-face occurred one morning outside the hall bathroom. Arriving at the door at the same moment in nothing but our Jockeys, I stood aside and graciously extended a hand. Chris demurred, "You go, I can wait."

"No, it's OK—please."

"You were first."

"I don't mind."

Chris started to turn back for his room. "I'll wait."

I blurted out, "Your cheek looks better. Scratch is nearly gone."

Chris stopped. "I've been putting tea tree oil on it."

"That's good. Is your bed comfortable in there?"

"It's fine . . . how's your eye?"

"Good. No more swelling." Silence. "You left your alarm clock in my room, don't you need it?"

"No. I get up fine. Clu? What happened between us . . ."

I stared at him. "Yes."

"I hope . . . I hope it doesn't change your plans to direct the play."

My heart sank. That stupid play. "Why do you want me still to direct? Everyone hates my guts."

"Because it'll be good for the show. Look, they need the discipline—we all know that. You're the only one with the boldness and vision to pull it together."

"Why don't you direct it?"

Chris stared at the floor. "Because . . . I'm not you. I don't have your tenacity."

I scratched my chin and slowly crossed my arms. "I'll direct it if you'll answer one question." Chris looked up. "Do you still love me?"

Chris stared a long moment, then leaned against the wall and looked up at the ceiling. "I'll always love you, Clu . . . but I don't like you much anymore. I'm sorry this had to happen, here, now—this way. But I can't change the way I feel."

The blood was racing from my head so fast I had to squat down against the wall to balance myself. "So. What . . . do we do now?"

"I hope, genuinely, that we can be friends."

I slammed the wall with my fist. "Fuck friends! I'm sure . . . you and me and Preston . . . we'll all go out to some gay bar and pick up tricks together."

Chris raised his voice. "Leave him out of this. Damn! Why is he always in the middle of our conflict? You want so much for him to be the bad guy—he's not! The only 'bad guys' in this story are you and me. No one else."

"You slept with him, didn't you?"

Chris shook his head, incredulous. "You're so amazingly predictable. You never let me down."

"Didn't you?"

"What do you want me to say Chris?"

"The truth, you shithead!"

Chris threw his razor against the wall. "Yes—I slept with him. There. I did it. Yes! The weekend we went to the Coast. I did. I'm not proud, I'm not happy—it upset me like I've never been upset in my life. Call Preston right now, call him and ask. I got physically—emotionally sick. I threw up, had chills, fever—I cried all night like an insane person. I was a complete mess. And not because I was falling in love with Preston. I don't *love* Preston! You think I'm blown away 'cause he has big muscles and a washboard stomach? He was there! It could've been anybody. It was because I was falling *out* of love with you! And I didn't want to. But I don't love you that way anymore. And I'm sorry for hurting you—but I don't."

We stared at each other. All the years of devotion, all the intimacy and joy, sorrows and shared amity—where does it suddenly go? Till the end of my life I will ask that same question—where *does* love go?

I rubbed my face and stretched a hand out to Chris. He slowly walked over and took it, pulling me up. I put my arms around him and held his soft bare skin and smelled his sweet familiar scent one last time. I kissed his neck and rubbed the back of his head gently. How much joy and utter happiness this singular, much-cherished physical body had given me so many, many times. If I died tomorrow, I could truly say that I had been loved—physically, spiritually, emotionally. For that alone, I would be indebted to Chris forever.

I whispered in his ear, "Thank you for telling me. Believe it or not, it helps. And thanks for loving me as much as you did. You were the perfect one for me."

We held on to each other a moment longer, tears falling abundantly on our arms and backs. Surrounded in the hallway by all the dogs now, they gazed up at us with expressions of true joy. At last, we were together again. How brief would be their satisfaction.

Several days later I spent a long, arduous morning at Miss Oveta's going over plans for the play. Mother had fallen the night before, rambling around the kitchen at two A.M. Nothing had broken, but she hadn't been able to lift herself, and her cries woke Chris and me both. We got her back to bed, but I was too wound up to sleep. Chris sat with me in the kitchen and we drank coffee till about six—discussing the play, writing scenes, doing a minimal lighting diagram. It was almost like being back in New York—as if we'd never left and our lives hadn't changed so irrevocably. Several times I found myself staring at him as he spoke and wanting desperately to hold him, to reach out and make love right there on the kitchen floor. To taste his mouth, feel his warmth, press my ear against his chest and fall asleep to the familiar lulling of his heartbeat—I would have done anything for that overwhelming bliss. Chris, if he felt a thing, suppressed it with the mastery of a cape-twirling David Copperfield. Nothing was revealed.

Miss Oveta and Mr. Jeffrey sat facing me with rapt attention.

"Once again, I just want to reiterate how deeply, deeply sorry I am for the way I behaved at your party . . ."

Miss Oveta held a tinkly, braceleted hand aloft. "Stop! No more. Your penitence is done. It was the highlight of the season. Mr. Jeffrey and I both decided it couldn't have been any more exciting if Gore Vidal and Norman Mailer themselves were laying waste to my powder room. Artists are allowed their occasional rabidity."

If you say so. I laid out my little sketchings and diagrams I'd done with Chris for *Agamemnon, Ya'll*. I'd scratched in a few scenes, doodled with some song lyrics. They both scrutinized my notes with all the solemnity of the Magi viewing the baby Jesus. Mr. Jeffrey nodded in some kind of endorsement, then reached around behind his chair and produced an old, tattered satchel. Opening it, he pulled out a sheaf of rumpled papers the size of a modest city phone book and plopped it on the coffee table. He grinned at me. "Oveta and I have been taking a few notes. We devised a couple of key scenes—now of course this is all attendant on your approval. You're the New York director. We just want to be helpful in any way we can."

I stared at the messy scrapbook before me. It looked like someone's fourth-grade diary, complete with taped flower petals, yarn binding and clippings from *Life* magazine. I smiled. "Boy, this looks like a lot of work here."

Miss Oveta clucked, "Oh, it's been a sheer labor of love. Necessity really. You know we're both frustrated creative types. If we still had your youth and dynamism, we might have undertaken the whole thing ourselves. But you know, the generations are served best when one bequeaths the other the latitude and wherewithal to do what each does best."

In other words, I'll write the check—you take care of the rest. "Well, maybe you'll let me borrow this so I'll have a chance to study it."

"Absolutely! Incorporate as much as you want. None of it's inviolate—just ideas is all." Mr. Jeffrey sniffed, underplaying his obvious pride.

"Now you'll be needing expense money for supplies, copies and an assistant." Miss Oveta reached into her large, baubled handbag and retrieved a checkbook. "I've opened a little account at the bank for contributions and the like to our nonprofit theater group. You'll receive a weekly draft for your salary if that's agreeable."

"Salary?"

"I know we haven't discussed your fee, but it would hardly be professional to ask you to undertake all this gratis."

I shook my head in disbelief. "I wasn't expecting anything."

"Nonsense, as president of the Grit Little Theater you need to be properly compensated."

"President?"

"Yes, the board nominated you last night."

"What board?"

Miss Oveta smiled, peeking over her turquoise bifocals. "Mr. Jeffrey and me, of course. We made Preston an alternate member, in case of a tie vote."

"But I . . . I mean I'm honored; I just . . . I don't know how long I'll be here."

Miss Oveta went back to her checkwriting, unconcerned. "None of us do, dear. Keeps it interesting that way. We came up with a figure of five hundred dollars a week to start out. Of course a raise is scheduled into your contract within a couple of months. Do you think it will be sufficient?"

Miss Oveta finished writing in her checkbook and delicately tore the draft from its ledger. Sufficient? I'd had no income for months now. Damn right it was sufficient.

"Yes. I think that's . . . agreeable."

They both smiled. Mr. Jeffrey cleared his throat. "I do have one suggestion which I hope you'll seriously consider."

"What's that?"

"We both feel strongly that Oveta is the only possible choice to play the role of Queen Clytemnestra. I mean, when you think about it, who else in the community has the stature, grace, bearing and inherent capabilities of Oveta Otis?"

Who indeed? Gotcha! I looked at both of them, keen as the spines on a prickly pear. Miss Oveta's check hovered in midair, idly awaiting delivery. Now where was there room for dissension in this scenario? I hadn't run across sharpies like this since I occasionally dined next to certifiable Mafia members at Umberto's Clam House on Mulberry Street in Little Italy. The two of them could just have easily slipped Broadway in their pockets and absconded without so much as a whimper from the mayor. That's showbiz, kids.

"Terrific idea! Who thought of it first?" They both instantly beamed, and Miss Oveta's check fluttered down into my hand like Noah's dove alighting.

"Actually, we both sort of arrived at it simultaneously. Isn't synchronicity a powerful force?"

I shook my head. "Awesome. And have you considered the role of Agamemnon for yourself, Mr. Jeffrey?"

He looked at me, shocked. "Gracious, no. I'm no Lord Larry, although in my younger days it was said that I held more than a passing resemblance to the young Don Ameche. No, no—my role is to coach and support Oveta in her triumphant return to the boards." They held hands and admired each other.

I stood slowly, folding the check in my hand. "All right then. I'd like to schedule auditions for the chorus and the rest of the cast for next week. Certainly have a lot to do. Thank you both for your faith in me."

Miss Oveta opened her arms for a queenly embrace, followed by Mr. Jeffrey's . . . embrace.

"I'll call the newspaper and the radio station this afternoon to announce auditions. Would the Methodist church basement be all right with you? They're less prone to have a reactionary response toward the arts as other local affiliations."

"Fine."

"Would anyone care for a Mai Tai?" Mr. Jeffrey was already at the bar putting ice in the blender.

I aimed quickly for the entrance. "Not me, thanks. I'll get back with you on your notes. Bye."

I had my hand on the door when Miss Oveta sang out, "Oh, Clu, I forgot one thing. Your assistant!" I turned to look at her. "There's a terribly nice young man from the junior college over in Beeville who's agreed to be your assistant for college credit. He's an English major, seems very savvy. We get to use some of the college lights and props in exchange for our sponsoring him. His name's Tory. Can I tell him to give you a call so you two can meet?"

Sure. Another insufferable, earnest amateur getting in the way and causing mayhem in general. Why not? My new mantra was just say "wonderful" to everything. It's easier. "Wonderful. Can't wait to meet him." But I could.

In a way, directing the play was the best thing that could have happened. I didn't have time to brood exclusively over Chris, which I managed to squeeze in half of every day anyway. We'd actually become courteous to one another—laughing, jesting, conversing. People who didn't know us might think we even liked one another. Now that the threat of my still desiring his body was suppressed (barely) we were free to be pals again. And it ached like a burning prostate. I thought about holding Chris constantly. I even considered scribbling a note and slipping it under his door—"In case you need a quick physical release I'm available, no strings attached." I had no pride. I didn't care. I was a man without a country. Feckless as a teenage hooker.

As for Preston, I found it difficult being even remotely amicable. I was civil, I was correct—but there remained between us an iceberg of spite. I didn't like the beautiful bastard, what can I say? He'd slept with my husband. Yeah, yeah—"two to tango." I didn't doubt for a minute Chris's statement that "it could have been anyone." And I truly believed his disavowal of a love interest in Preston. (How can one love a candy wrapper?) But why did it have to be Troy Donahue? Couldn't he have slept with someone more rustic? Say, a local Walter Brennan type, perhaps? Anyone remotely closer to my comfort level of superiority would have been acceptable.

Chris and I worked furiously trying to pull together some cohesive concept of moving the story of *Agamamnon* from mythological Greece to present-day South Texas. It was roughly the equivalent of turning *Macbeth* into a musical and setting it in tango-era Argentina.

Same roadblocks, same illogic—same zany kick in being able to pull the whole nutball scheme off.

I left the choice of the band up to Chris and Preston, who'd already earnestly commenced carousing the town beer joints perusing possible performers. It was a dirty business, which they both undertook uncomplainingly.

Chris knocked on my door about 10 P.M. one night, pleasantly beered-up and enthusing wildly over some garage band he's seen at the Twin Oaks Lounge over in Floresville. He was so sweet and funny and excitably high I thought for a moment this might be my opportunity to cop a feel or at least stroke his hair. Wrong. He flew off my bed like a startled pigeon the second I casually laid my hand on his back.

"Put your jeans on. They get off in an hour. You won't be disappointed, trust me."

"Tonight? It's late. I'm already in bed."

"It's tonight, or forget it." He threw a T-shirt at me. "Come on, Grandpa. You want the show to be good or not?"

I rolled over on my side and stared at him. Why wasn't I allowed to hold him anymore? Who decrees these things? When did I lose him? When was the exact moment it clicked in his head, I'm outta here. Where was I when the silent sentence was passed? One minute a couple—the next, deferential strangers. I could feel that familiar tightening in my throat and chest—the "longing straightjacket" being adjusted. "I just want everything to be like it was before. Why throw away all the good that was there?"

Chris stood in the doorway, his long, sinewy arms outstretched, grasping the top of the frame. "I would never want to lose you, Clu. But people change—I have to get on with my life."

I bolted upright, slapping my feet on the wooden floor. "I used to be a part of that life, what happened? What happened to us?"

Chris dropped his arms and sighed. His obvious fatigue with my irksome contentiousness pulled his features into an unhappy frown. "I don't feel that way anymore."

"What is it you *do* feel, Chris? Anything? What are you looking for? Tell me, please."

Chris shook his head slowly. He stared at his feet. Chica and Pistola were standing on his shoes, gazing up at him adoringly. He picked them up and put them inside his shirt. They wiggled their bobbing apple heads outside his collar and licked at his face. "I'm not looking—that's the point. I just want to reacquaint myself with me. That's all."

I looked at him, bewildered. I yanked the T-shirt over my head, grumbling, "You're making me crazy, you know that?"

"Good, we're back like it used to be. I'm gonna pee, hurry up." He turned and disappeared. I pulled on my jeans and sneakers and grumpily plodded down the hallway to check on Mother. Her door was slightly ajar, a tiny fissure of yellow light spilling out into the darkened corridor. I tapped on the wall, no answer. Peering inside, I saw that Mother was snoring softly, a library book on Chinese watercolors resting on her stomach. Wads of tissues were scattered about the floor, her pills and medicines neatly stacked in a little circumference on her bedside mirrored vanity tray. She looked almost childlike. So tiny and fragile. Thank God she could sleep. I reached over and grabbed her tea mug and started to shut the door.

"Clu? What time is it?"

"Go back to bed, not quite ten."

"Are you going out?"

"Chris and I are going to check on some band he wants me to hear. We won't be long. I didn't mean to wake you."

"I wasn't sleeping."

"You do a convincing imitation. You need anything?"

Mother yawned and nodded. "I'm fine."

I started to leave, and she called again, "Clu—are you and Chris going to be all right?"

I stood outside her door and stared at the soggy tea bag in the cup. "We're . . . friends, Mother."

"I wish you boys could work it out. You seem like you both do a lot of good for each other."

I wrapped my finger around the string and tugged at the Lipton tag. "Yes, ma'am. Sleep tight." I turned and started to walk off.

Mother called again, this time barely audible, "Clu . . . I love you, son."

I stopped cold, my heart bumping against my chest. When was the last time she'd said those words? As best as I could recall, seldom. We simply weren't loquacious about these things. They were saved for very special, deeply personal and highly precise moments. Like the time I decided to drop out of college and become a waiter in Houston, changed my mind and earned an emotional "I love you" and a hug from Mother. Like the time Jaston and I took her to see the Sally Field movie, *Places in the Heart,* on Mother's Day, and as we were leaving she put a hand on each of our shoulders, and mumbled, "Love you, boys." Jaston and I were so surprised you'd have thought she'd fired a gun at us.

And now. At death's behest, when some deeper form of communication seemed essential, words were entirely lacking. Why couldn't I just turn my childish butt around, walk in, take her hand, and say, "Love you, too, Mom." Was that such an impossibility? Fundamentally, I knew it wouldn't happen until I could absolve the past. Hers, mine—*ours.* All the elapsed transgressions I carried so assiduously in my judicious little heart. Could I forgive her for not being both a mother and father? For not listening when she assumed that meant agreeing? For using love as a tactic? For judging me, once upon a time, as fiercely as I judged her? Good Lord, would I ever be able to forgive this woman for simply not being Jesus Christ herself in a small town in Texas?

I started to speak but couldn't get my voice to cooperate. Finally, I turned and walked slowly back into the room. I sat down beside her and assiduously rubbed a finger on her quilted bedspread.

"Mother . . . I want you to know . . . first—I'm really glad you're my mother." She looked at me puzzled. "And . . . despite all the fights and disagreements we . . ."

"Did we fight so much?"

I stared at her, surprised, "Well . . . yeah." She held a look of curiosity, like I'd just performed an especially wonderful magic trick. It threw me. "Anyway . . . the main thing is, you were a good mom and . . . you know . . . I wouldn't have changed much of anything."

She lifted up a little on her pillow and coughed. "Well, I would've! I'd have sold this house and moved us all to Europe or Kenya or someplace far, far away. Anywhere we could've had a fresh start and a clean horizon before us."

I must've gulped. "Ken . . . ya?"

She waved her hand. "Someplace. What did we all learn by sticking it out in this backwater podunk? For the life of me, I can't figure it out. It certainly couldn't have been any more trying elsewhere."

"Wh . . . why didn't you . . . *we* move?"

Mother narrowed her glance and shrugged, "Why? Because I suspect I'm not any better at doing than dreaming." She pointed toward her jewelry box on the dresser. "Go look in that bottom drawer. I want you to see something."

I rose, feeling lost, and walked toward the antique foot-and-a-half-square wooden chest she stowed all her trinkets and ornaments in. It was mostly costume jewelry, but there was tons of it. As kids, Laine and I would launch secretive raids on Mother's treasure stash, trying on every bauble and ring till we were garnished like Aztec princesses. Jaston would nearly always find us and threaten to tell until Laine cajoled him into playing "Chief" by letting him wear Mother's rhinestone tiara. *Tiara!* (What in God's name was a tiara even doing in Grit?)

Mother coughed again, speaking hoarsely. "Look in the bottom drawer . . . that's it . . . remove that little velvet underside thing. Yep. Bring me the envelope in there."

I felt like Cary Grant in *To Catch a Thief.* There's a false drawer in Mother's jewelry box? Crafty girl. Did she have Van Gogh's *Irises* stashed in a wall panel somewhere? I removed the thick, yellowed envelope that had PERMILLA ROTH TRAVEL, SAN ANTONIO TEXAS stamped on the return address. I Handed the parcel to Mother and she carefully removed four airline tickets. Alitalia. She spread them before her and I gaped dumbly.

"There. I even bought the tickets. Four, one-way to Rome, Italy. A year after your father's stampede from our lives, I made a plan. All I needed was one excuse, one decent pretext to flee, and I'd yank you kids from school so fast your eyes would rattle." She smiled at me, triumphant. I'd never seen Mother quite so . . . *seditious.*

"What happened? Wh . . . why did you stay?"

She continued smiling, eyes glistening with zeal. She touched my hand as if physically embedding her design. "Because . . . it wasn't about going. It was *knowing* that I *could!*" Flushed, she nodded slightly and lay back against the pillow. "All these years"—she proudly tapped the tickets with her fingers—"*here* was the 'escape clause.'"

I stared at her, baffled and thrilled by her covert scheme. What, oh God *what,* would it have taken to actually make her jump? That I might have grown up in Rome or Kenya or anywhere other than Grit—the mind boggled. "Mother—how many times did you actually call the airlines and make an actual reservation?"

She took a sip of water and looked at me blankly, "Never. I told you, it was knowing I had *possibility.* That's the key." She took another sip and nudged the tickets toward me. "They're still good. I know the airline's in business. They weren't cheap then—today you could probably fly four for what I paid for just one. They belong to you kids. Use them."

I studied the thirty-year-old tickets, all neat and unsullied in their little red, green and white envelopes. I felt an immediate jab of anguish. "But . . . didn't *you* ever want to see Rome?"

Mother squinted, a little crinkly smile on her face, "I saw *Three Coins in a Fountain.* It was all grand—just as I imagined."

Gathering the tickets, I put them back in their mail pouch and placed them on her nightstand. "Why don't you hang on to these? A person should always keep an escape clause." I looked at her and without thinking I suddenly leaned forward and kissed her on the forehead. Just did it. No warning, no prep. We looked at each other amazed, then both sort of half smiled, embarrassed. I stood, clearing my throat. "Well . . ."

"Well."

"I better go, Chris is waiting."

"Yes. Should you take a sweater?"

"In July?"

"Yes. I forgot."

"Well . . ."

"Clu . . . I'm glad we had this talk."

"Me too."

"Drive safely."

"I will. Good night, Mother."

"Good night . . . son."

I shut the door behind me and tiptoed down the hall. By the time we reached the bar Chris had inquired twice why I'd been whistling *"Arrivederci Roma"* loudly all the way across Grit. I just laughed.

Larry's Lament was not your average country and western garage band. For starters, Larry was female. Larraine Pilcher, a twentysomething unwed mother who lived with Mariano, a serious-looking Mexican biker with gold teeth, acne scars and a dexterous manner with a bass guitar. The rest of the band was the big surprise Chris couldn't wait to spring on me—Manuel and Vicky. Why it should amaze me that my two impending stepsiblings moonlighted in an alternative country punk grunge band was the only surprising part. I was convinced by now that I was largely startle-proof.

Larraine had an unpolished, plaintive Janis Joplin/Patsy Cline timbre to her voice. Mariano, possibly assisted by some unknown substance, had an intensity and a showman's swagger that was hard to resist. Manuel and Vicky were their accomplished, professional selves, and I had to agree with Chris, nothing average about these guys.

They finished their last set and joined us for a beer at the empty bar. Introductions were made, and I discovered Mariano was Manuel and Vicky's cousin.

"Yeah, Concepcion's *mi tia*. But she thinks I'm a bad influence on her babies. She's probably right." Mariano chugged his beer, and Manuel and Vicky grinned.

"He's the best bass player I know. You asked me where I learned—I grew up watching this outlaw." Manuel put his hand on Mariano's shoulder.

"So you're doing a play or some shit?" Larraine, all businesslike, lit a Winston and rested her boot sideways on her knee. "How much you paying?"

Chris and I looked at each other. I spoke, "How much you making here?"

Larraine smirked and flicked an ash. "We ain't making diddly.

We're just doing this to stay practiced. Ya'll gonna pay us anything, or is this gonna be some Kiwanis charity bullshit?"

Chris cleared his throat. "Well, I think we can come up with a cut of the door, plus your expenses. Look, it's gonna be something entirely new and different. It'll look great on your professional résumé."

Larraine rolled her eyes. "Bite my ass. You go pay my fucking landlord with your résumé bullshit. Shit." Larraine took a deep drag and shook her head.

Mariano spoke softly, "We ain't got another gig, babe. He said he'd pay expenses—you going back to telemarketing?"

Larraine stared at him defiantly. "I'll eat a cow-pie bigger'n John Wayne's ass 'fore I'll do that shit again." Larriane stubbed out her cigarette and scowled. "What's the fuckin' play called?"

"*Agamemnon, Ya'll.*"

"What the fuck does that mean?"

"It's a Greek tragedy set in contemporary Texas. We're doing it at the livestock sale barn."

"You're shittin' me." Larraine looked dubious. We both shook our heads. "Is this some artsy bullshit? I don't do 'art.'"

I shrugged. "Just entertainment. Labels are up to the critics."

Larraine stuck her tongue in her cheek and rolled it around. The "art" suggestion seemed to stick in her craw. Finally, she managed a grin. "Ya'll serving beer and barbecue?"

Before I could speak, Chris interrupted, "Absolutely."

Larraine sighed. "Well hell, you can get anybody in Texas to show up long as there's air conditioning, beer and something to eat. Why the fuck not."

Everyone exhaled appreciably. Chris continued, excited. "I'll get you the songs we've written so far. 'Course, we're totally open to whatever you guys want to contribute."

"Aw Christ!" Larraine beat out her cigarette. "You mean we gotta learn new songs to boot? What's wrong with the shit we already got?"

Chris and I blinked at each other. I delicately persevered. "Nothing. It's perfect. That's why we want you for the show. It's just—we'd like some new material to follow the story line."

Larraine looked miserable; she grabbed her laundry-bag purse and stood. "We'll think about it. I got a kid in first grade and a three-year-old. I don't have all fucking day to learn new shit. Come on, Mari. Later." Larriane waved at the bartender, pecked Manuel and Vicky on the cheek and tromped out of the bar in her snakeskin leggings and drop feather earrings, looking for all the world like the last of the real bad girls.

Mariano tapped my hand with his finger. "She'll do it. She's always like this." He smiled confidently. "She says 'artist' like it's some dirty word. Hell—she's more artist than that fucking Van Gogh dude. Don't sweat it."

Mariano departed with his guitar case and bike helmet. The four of us sat at the bar and stared up at the strangely mesmerizing beer sign above our heads. The Anheuser-Busch Clydesdales revolved round and round in a plastic lit bubble, hauling their beer wagon in never-ending exertion. Finally, Vicky laughed and shook her head. "Well—we're just like those stupid horses, aren't we? Pulling our little wagon hoping somebody'll buy our doodads. Call it art, call it *chingada*—just buy the shit, *please!*"

12

THE SCAMP BULLS

Preston picked us up early the next morning to have a walk-through with Mr. Wheeler, president and CEO of the livestock barn. The only reason we even remotely had a chance of using the barn was Raymond Otis was a part owner. Frankly, after the powder-room incident, Mr. Otis had written us off as contemptible hellions. I suspect, however, he was so overjoyed that Shirley appeared to be having something resembling a romantic dalliance with Jaston, he decided to overlook our detestable backsliding.

We tooled along in Preston's pickup, radio blaring, windows down—three gay bubbas on their way to the butch universe, "Cowboy Central"—the cattle auction ring. I stared glumly out the window as Chris and Preston babbled on about lighting requirements and speakers. Finally, Preston looked in my direction and cheerily declared, "Read some of the new dialogue last night. I really like it. Can't wait for the tryouts. I think we'll have a real good turnout."

"Hope so."

"You heard the ads for the auditions on the radio? Miss Oveta got it right for a change. Pretty doggone slick, if you ask me."

I nodded. "Yep."

Chris turned my way. "You all right?"

I shrugged. "I'm fine. Just worried about Mom. She looks worse.

Brought her in some juice this morning, she could barely lift her head to drink it."

Chris stared ahead. "She fell again yesterday in the living room. I was going in to get the paper, and she just kind of dropped right in front of the fireplace. She wasn't hurt, but I think it scared her. Just seems to happen."

I sighed and studied a herd of fine, white Charolais heifers standing in a knee-deep klein grass pasture off to the side of the road. They looked like Carerra marble sculptures. So robust and sturdy and clean. Cattle don't seem to get old. We eat them.

The sale barn looked deserted. We parked in front and tried to open the double front doors. Locked. Walking around back, we found two billy goats tied to a fig bush keeping the yard mowed. Climbing the stairs to the covered outdoor pens, we surveyed the massive, football-field-sized enclosure. Catwalks crisscrossed the tops of each square corral, enabling early arrival buyers to survey the goods before "running 'em through the ring." It was an efficient, even thrilling sort of operation. Coming out here as a kid with Mother's great-uncle Pete was kind of like being in a Western. Uncle Pete was a professional Texas coot. He had a little old scruffy poor-house of a ranch outside town and loved messing with cattle more than anything. He told us cows were his "golf." They relaxed him. I found the whole mix of whooping cowhands and bawling cattle and cigarette smoke and men with hands that looked like bleeding, mangled baseball gloves pretty heady stuff for an eight-year-old with an eager imagination.

The decades of manure, piss, blood, burnt hide and cowboy sweat left a tang in the sultry morning air as salient as mesquite wood smoke. And to my way of thinking, just as agreeable. The pens were pretty empty but for here and there a cluster of sluggish calves, some sheep, even a Shetland pony—no doubt mean as a wet snake from years of kid abuse and shipped to market to be fobbed off on some other unsuspecting animal lover.

"You boys don't lean on that rail! Son of a bitch is loose. Old bastard fell in a pen of wild Bramha steers here a while back, liked to scared the poor cows plumb silly." Mr. Wheeler was hobbling toward us carrying a cane and little pouch of Bugler rolling tobacco.

He stopped to spit an impressive rivulet of brown saliva squarely on the back of an unsuspecting Hereford bull beneath him. "Which one of you characters wants to put on the 'show-and-tell'?"

We each offered a hand, and Mr. Wheeler held out his old arthritic claw in much the manner of a papal acknowledgment. Chris began, "It's a pleasure to meet you sir. I'm Chris Myles. I'm sort of producing our little play."

Mr. Wheeler turned up his hearing aid and barked. "'Sort of?' Is that like 'kinda takin' a shit?' You're either wiping your butt or you ain't, son—which is it?"

Chris turned red as a strawberry. It was all I could do to keep from busting a gut. My Texas orneriness couldn't help but get tickled whenever a vintage peckerwood like Mr. Wheeler got into a pissing match with a "fer-igner." His type could make coleslaw out of a redwood.

"What kinda Shakespeare is this? You ain't gonna have no nudity, are ya?"

Preston jumped in, "No, sir, it's all costumed."

Mr. Wheeler looked alarmed. "Costumes? You mean like them fan dancers they used to have in the burlesque? Hell, I saw an old gal up in Fort Worth once—naked as a jaybird. She had on some kinda jeweled headgear big as a bale of hay. Damn'd if she didn't get to foolin' around with a bunch of ostrich feathers, and I swear with one hand on the door of the Alamo if she didn't stick one in her old patootie and sing 'The Star Spangled Banner'! Best damn show I ever saw." That broke the dam. We all laughed ourselves senseless. Mr. Wheeler grinned a brown-tobacco smile and with the four teeth he had left, managed to chew a fresh plug of Bugler he'd wadded up and stuck in his mouth. He was the real thing, the last of the old Texas buffalo. After him—posers, blowhards and "folklorists."

We proceeded into the air-conditioned arena, careful to stay to one side of Mr. Wheeler's steady stream of brown rain. "I'll be ninety-one years old come October. You know, I still got an old Polander gal comes to see me 'bout once a month. Hell, I have to pay her but damn if we don't shake the bedsprings good. No, sir, everything works fine—just takes a little longer coming out the well, that's all. You 'member that when you get to be my age. No sense giving up something cheaper than beer and a damn sight more relaxing." He clicked on the overhead fluorescent lights. We gazed around the barnlike interior. Like I remembered, it was a true theater, in actuality my first one to experience. A high auctioneer's booth stood before a small, semicircular dirt-floored enclosure. A towering pipe fence encased the livestock viewing pen, and beyond that rose a classic amphitheater, entirely Greek in execution. Row after row of simple benchlike seating that focused directly on the stage below. From the swaying, hand-painted WHITE WINGS FLOUR MILL sign to the battered tin HERCULES TIRE billboard lining the back wall—it was made to order.

"You sure you ain't got no nudity now. *It's* all right with me, but you get them old Baptist biddies with their tits in a ringer and it's hell to pay."

"No, sir, absolutely no nudity," I reassured him. Mr. Wheeler looked a bit crestfallen.

"Ya'll gonna have singing and dancin'?"

"Yes, sir."

"Pretty gals?"

"Hope to."

Mr. Wheeler grinned. "Well, I sure like to look at pretty gals. Lord, we got the best right here in Texas. Got a little tallow on their bones. Oh Lord—when they're young fillies with that hair a-bouncing and them skirts a-rustling it sure nuf takes an old feller like me back. You boys married?"

We answered simultaneously, "No."

Mr. Wheeler studied us a few seconds then spit, "Buncha old bachelors, huh? Well that's all right. Hell, we can't all be godly, churchgoing family men—who'd run the goddamn beer joints and whorehouses for the self-righteous sons a bitches?"

I smiled, "So we were thinking since your sale is every Tuesday, we could run the show Friday night, Saturday night and Sunday matinee—store everything Sunday night and be outta your way till the following weekend."

Mr. Wheeler spit again, mumbling, "Sure, sure . . ." He eyed us a little aslant. "You boys got girlfriends?"

We each stopped our appraisal of the barn and turned to face him. The silence was immense. Finally, Preston spoke, "No, sir. We stay pretty busy."

Mr. Wheeler leaned on his cane, mulled it over and finally spit his entire wad out. "Well sir, I always say—there's usually a scamp bull in every herd and it dudn't hurt one damn bit. Kinda gentles the cows not having some old reprobate always sniffing their hind ends."

We looked at Mr. Wheeler, each of us I'm sure intellectualizing the "scamp bull" classification. Chris finally smiled and placed his hand on Mr. Wheeler's shoulder. "That's exactly the way I feel about it, Mr. Wheeler. In fact I think we ought to call our production company 'Scamp Bulls, Inc.' What do you think, guys?"

For once Preston and I were in cahoots; we both bellowed together, "MOO-O-O!"

Auditions were set for 7:00 P.M. Monday night at the Methodist "multipurpose cafetorium." I was dreading it and at the same time morbidly curious. Who would show up? Like a public hanging—you went for the horror show, not civic duty.

We sat around the kitchen table hurriedly finishing up Chris's tasty homemade lasagna and Caesar salad. Yes, he was cooking again now that we weren't sleeping together. (I know there's a correlation, but I don't see it.) Shirley and Jaston and Brother Ramirez joined us and Mother sat quietly at the head sipping soup. Shirley in a matter of weeks had become family. She was the perfect foil for Jaston, matching him in every category from bluntness to know-it-all authority to excavating gristmills. They were the two class nerds that actually liked each other. And Jaston was cookie dough in her hands. Every utterance from her lips was followed by Jaston's squinty-eyed grin, which read, "Isn't she just the cutest thing."

Jaston exclaimed rapidly between mouthfuls of garlic bread, "Shirley and I . . . gonna take the door to the safe off next week."

Mother looked at him in alarm. "You shouldn't be messing with another person's property."

Jaston was stumped. "Mother, if it doesn't belong to us, *whose* is it?"

She set her spoon down slowly. "I'm not so sure Gladys Byers wants the contents of that safe known to the world."

"What's that mean?" Jaston wiped the corner of his mouth with his hand.

Mother sipped her water calmly. "I just wouldn't be so all-fired in a hurry to go digging in somebody else's past, that's all."

Shirley interjected quietly, "Mrs. Latimore, I did check the records at the courthouse and had an attorney look at them, and he seems to think since no heirs have shown up and you've paid the taxes on it all these years—it's yours by possession."

Mother wiped her lips delicately and appeared ready to say something when she slowly, uneasily began balling her napkin into a knot in her fist. Her eyes were watering as she put her good hand to her chest. "Would . . . ya'll excuse me? Chris, it was . . . delicious."

Brother Ramirez lightly touched Mother's cheek. "Is it time?"

Mother nodded, unable to speak. She was on injected painkillers now, and they were daily and they were fiercely potent. Helping her up, Brother Ramirez turned back to the table. "Good luck with the play tonight. We're all very proud of you." They shuffled away from us, Brother Ramirez both supporting and exalting Mother with his extraordinary tenderness. Where do you find someone like that? In a thousand years I couldn't have dreamed of such a coupling. And yet, here he was. This angel that appeared with all the premeditation of a blooming dandelion. How? I never thought of myself as particularly spiritual, but the entire unfolding of Mother's "departure" moved me in ways I couldn't express or fully comprehend. What awesome timing God has.

No one said a word until we heard the bedroom door shut at the end of the hall. Finally, Shirley sighed. "Maybe we shouldn't be doing this. It upsets your mom pretty much."

Jaston drained his ice tea and hiccuped. "Listen, there's always been some kind of bad blood between Mama and old lady Byers. It happened a long time ago, whatever it was. It ain't gonna change now."

"How's the site coming?" I asked impassively.

Jaston scrunched his eyes and chuckled. "Tell him, Shirley."

"Well, I was able to get a little seed money from the Texas

Historical Foundation. It's not much, but it gives us legitimacy. We formed a nonprofit organization, The La Parita Creek Gristmill Society. We're going to have a quarterly bulletin, sell memberships, and hold a couple of fund-raisers. Eventually we'd like to open it up as a museum and full-scale living history site." Shirley was as buoyant as Jaston.

I marveled again at the probability of it all. How? A month ago Jaston was a virtual bag man, skulking around town like Grit's own Boo Radley. Today he had a bright, chesty, graduate-school girlfriend who for all intents and purposes had abandoned her former life to come dig in a ruin on a rattlesnake-infested creek with a six-foot-three madman. The unceasing wonder of life.

"We better go. I told the church janitor we'd arrange all the tables and chairs the way we wanted them." Chris stood and carried his plate to the sink.

Shirley followed suit. "Excellent lasagna, Chris. Where'd you learn to be such a good cook?"

"I don't know. My mom would usually rather eat out than open a jar of peanut butter. I guess I just fell into it. 'Follow your bliss' thing." Chris laughed as he rinsed his plate. Jaston scooped up the rest of the dinnerware and sneaked up behind Shirley, kissing her on the neck. They smooched affectionately, Chris whistled a tune as he washed. We were some new kind of lively, doleful, "overextended" American family. People dropped in and out like flies at a picnic. I stared at my plate and blinked as one sloppy, burning tear fell on my knife and skidded down the blade. What was it all—profoundly synchronistic or just convenient hallucination?

"I did *Dames at Sea Annie Get Your Gun The Mousetrap* and Sartre's *No Exit* in summer repertory at Texas Christian University last year and I was briefly in the chorus of the summer pageant up at Palo Duro Canyon but my uterus dropped during rehearsals and I had to quit." I looked into the face of a classic, willowy blond Texas beauty who talked and chewed gum so fast and effortlessly it seemed that her tongue might actually have been a speech impediment.

"What part were you thinking about?"

"Well I heard some of the leads have already been cast which seems kinda unfair but hey it's ya'll's production I just wanted a shot at it but hey I'm willing to read for anything except the chorus 'cause really that's mostly what I did at T.C.U. and I'd you know like to grow as an actress and try new things but hey I'm willing to read for anything what do you think I'd be especially good for?"

I shoved a page toward her. "Iphigeneia."

"Great! Is she like a lead?"

"She gets murdered in the first act. But it's a real scene-stealer."

She looked at me like she couldn't tell if I was serious or not. "Oooo-kaay, is there like anything else I should know?"

"She's the daughter of the king, who in our version is a county judge—Judge Aggie."

She nodded slowly, the chewing momentarily stopped. "So this is like what a comedy musical thing?"

"Yes, in that vein."

"Is there a love scene?"

"Not really, it's mostly about a woman who murders her husband—but funny."

She stared down at the script. "Is this the best part for someone like me?"

I nodded. "Since you're not interested in the chorus, which incidentally is going to be a lot of fun since they get to interact with the band and lobby the audience in the sale barn for political advantage during the play."

"Sale barn?"

"Yeah, the livestock commission on the edge of town."

"That's where you're doing the play?"

"Uh-huh."

The chewing started again. Her face grew very somber, and her eyelids fluttered in dismay. "I don't think I could do a play in a . . . *cow barn* thank you very much." She flipped the sheet of paper back at me and turned briskly for the door. Just before exiting she called back over her shoulder, "You know it's an insult to real actors like myself to have to put up with people like you in this business. I was in *Hedda Gabler* for God's sake." She slammed the door.

Chris muttered under his breath, "Thank you very much, Dame Judi Dench. Call us when your series gets picked up. Who's next?"

We looked around the room, there were exactly four people—two mothers with children. I stared at Chris. "Maybe you better go stop Dame Judi. I could write her a big song-and-dance number where the audience gets to throw chewing gum at her."

We all snickered, and finally Preston motioned to a pleasant-looking Hispanic woman and her lively seven-year-old son. They approached.

"Hi, what's you name?"

"Augie."

"Augie, have you ever been in a play?"

"No."

"Would you like to be in a play."

"Yeah."

"You're hired. I want you to play 'Augie, the Chorus Boy.'" I handed him a few pages, and he practically levitated.

Augie's Mom was near tears. "Oh thank you so much. You don't know what this means to him. Since my husband ran off last year and I lost my job at the grocery store it's been real hard on us. He's such a good little actor. Go on, *mihijo,* show 'em how you do Jay Leno."

Augie stretched his chin out, put his hands on his hips and did a knockout impersonation of a seven-year-old Jay Leno.

"That's amazing. You're really talented. You go over those lines with your mom and we'll see you back here on Thursday night." Augie beamed. If I'd just handed him a Tony award it wouldn't have thrilled him more. They left in a bluster of giggles and chatter. The other woman and her child stared at us warily. I was about to call them forward when she suddenly stood, grabbed her kid and bolted from the room, knocking over a folding chair.

I blinked. "Well . . . that seems to be the last of them." I glanced at my legal pad. "Four people auditioned and we cast . . . one." I stared out at the rows of empty seats and called, "Anyone hiding under the tables?" Silence.

Chris cleared his throat. "We've only been here a little over an hour. There's still time." I nodded, convinced once more I'd taken the perennial wrong road in life again. It's a sad day when even the town hams don't even show up for a part that would be virtually handed to them with a wet kiss and a back rub. I stood and stretched. Thank God I'd persuaded Miss Oveta and Mr. Jeffrey not to come. If they'd been hovering around in their usual state of feverish rabidity, there'd have been bloodshed for sure. A person can only take so much unbridled enthusiasm.

Preston sighed and took off his perfectly starched white Ralph Lauren shirt and hung it on the back of the chair. His little skimpy undershirt did nothing to conceal his rippled and bulging torso. He proceeded to do push-ups with his feet up on the chair. I despise show-offs. I pretended to be reading the script, while Chris followed Preston's every exertion with rapt concentration.

I finally nudged Chris. "In this scene between Clytemnestra and Aegisthus, before he seduces her, I was thinking of putting all this up in the auctioneer's booth. Works better from the audience perspective, don't you think?"

"What?"

"I said . . ." It was hopeless. The steroid master was performing. He had his undershirt off, doing one-arm push-ups. I could have lit a flaming baton, stood on my head and done splits to no avail.

"What do you call this muscle right here?" Chris pointed to someplace under Preston's arm that I doubt very few people on the planet ever knew existed.

Preston stood, red-faced and dewy. He gulped. "That's the *serratus anterior,* very difficult area to properly define. There's a couple of free-weight exercises you can do. It's like the *adductor longus* down here on the inner thigh." Preston unzipped his khakis and pulled his briefs to one side to show us some odd bump parallel to his manhood. It was reassuring to discover he wasn't a natural blonde.

"EW-w-w-w-w! I knew we came to right spot. I wanna play your mama so I can breast feed you, honey!" Myla Biggs was standing in the doors at the back of the room with a grin on her face big as Dallas. Preston frantically zipped up his pants and threw his shirt back on. "Oh damn, show over? Baby, anytime you want to pick up a little cash working a 'bachelorette party,' you let me know." Myla floated into the room hoisting a cigarette and a huge beverage tumbler, followed by Zane, Sandy, Debbie and Jimmy. Dwayne, in

Bermuda shorts and flip-flops, brought up the rear, holding the hands of his two little girls.

"Myla, what in the world are ya'll doing here?" I smiled, happy to see them.

"Well, the radio said ya'll wanted all 'lesbians' in the county to show up, so here we are!" Myla put her arms around Debbie and Sandy and they groped each other in mock passion.

"I think it said 'thespians' but welcome anyway." We all air kissed and Zane grabbed me in an enthusiastic bear hug, which I found odd but sweet. Even Jimmy and I were cordial, shaking hands just like we were both running for the position of Rotary Club treasurer. "I don't think ya'll have all met Chris and Preston."

"Cu-u-u-u-te. Uh-huh." Myla nodded as she appraised Chris like some shiny new Weber grill. "I didn't get a good look at you when ya'll drove into town. Yes, ma'am, 'Everything's up to date in Kansas City.'" Myla put her arms around Chris and squeezed him. "Oh and you smell so good, too. What is that? Sandy, Debbie—come here and smell this cute man."

Chris was enveloped in female noses. "Is that Per Lui, Drakkar Noir?" Debbie had her hand on Chris's shoulder, sniffing the air around him like a beagle.

Sandy shook her head, unconvinced. "Givenchy, Obsession?"

Chris smiled shyly, not entirely sure how this game was played. Oh, Texas girls and their flirting! Hell, Texas boys and their flirting. I found the whole thing anthropologically fascinating. It was all designed to throw you off-balance and get your bodily fluids activated so you'd focus solely on the flirter until the next "flirtee" was spotted, then you were casually dismissed until it was your turn to be fussed over again at a later date. And they'd been doing it in the Lone Star State since Cabeza de Vaca washed ashore on Matagorda Island.

Chris finally stammered, "Actually, it's . . . shampoo."

"Shampoo!" the three of them trilled jointly. It was as if he'd suddenly announced the cure for dengue fever.

"Isn't he adorable!" Sandy nodded as she ran her hand up and down his biceps.

"And this one." As expected, Myla turned her attention to Preston. "Where do you hide yourself, handsome? It's not fair you don't let us get to look at you more often." Myla snaked her arm under Preston's shirt and squeezed that area on everyone else called a love handle. On Preston it was a room divider.

Preston knew the ropes. He smiled brashly. "I'm around. You're just not looking hard enough, darlin'."

Zane's cue to make his entrance. "Zane Biggs, I don't believe we've met." Zane looked down on Preston, his massive bear paw pumping Preston's grip like a tire jack.

"Preston Hayden, how are ya." You could see Zane sizing up the known town "poof" with a beady eye of discernment. It didn't help that Preston was handsome, butch and somewhat aloof. It was that much harder to squeeze him into any known category. Since he was an outsider to boot, he was simply not entirely trustworthy.

"Where is everybody, Clu? I was expecting lines clear down to the Minute Market?" Debbie asked in a concerned voice.

"You just missed our last wave of talent. Some high-strung Miss Cotton Growers' Association, and a seven-year-old comedian. I think we're ready to open," I joshed only half in jest.

"Well that's why we're here, sugar. We wanna be in your play. Whatever you need, we'll do it." Myla blew a cloud of smoke and chugged from her mystery beverage.

"You're serious?"

"As a canker sore on a nun's lip."

I could've scooped her up in my arms and squeezed her till her eyes popped. "Gosh . . . ya'll are too much. Well this is . . . *this* is great!" I turned to look at them all, completely moved. Finally, Dwayne approached, still holding on to his daughters' hands. I shook my head, smiling. "Now come on, Dwayne, you don't really want to be in this play. Sandy holding a gun to your head?"

Dwayne shrugged and smiled. "No, no—you wouldn't want me to do anything approaching acting anyway, but I figure, hell, I can hang lights, build sets . . . all that stuff. These are our two girls, Brittany and Kimberly. Is there anything for them to do in the show?"

I kneeled down to look at the girls. They were about three and five and cute as cottontails. And no, I couldn't think of a damn thing they could do in the play. I looked at Dwayne. "Sure, we'll find something. Which one of ya'll is Brittany?" They both raised their hands. The oldest turned to the youngest and yanked her arm down.

"She does everything I do. *I'm* Brittany."

We shook hands, solemnly. "Brittany, you and Kimberly are going to play fairy princesses. You're going to fly through the air and sprinkle magic dust on everyone that comes to the show. How's that sound?"

Their eyes were big as doughnuts. They both leapt in the air and shouted with glee. Everyone began talking at once, and I started passing out scripts. As I passed the last one out I suddenly glanced up toward the double entry doors. There stood Brandon. All fidgety movements and rigid arms rammed in baggy jeans, it seemed as if he might just fly away at the slightest provocation. I waved to him cheerily. He stopped twitching, and I began walking toward him.

"Brandon, nice to see you. Glad you could make it. How've you been?" I shook his hand, which was tentative as a child's.

"Good."

"Have you come to try out for the show?"

"I was thinking about it."

"Great. We can really use you. How's your dad?"

Brandon shrugged. "We kinda had a fight. He didn't want me to come."

I looked at him. "Sorry to hear that."

"He told me I should do what I felt like. So . . . here I am."

I nodded. "I think your dad made a wise decision. Ultimately, it's your life, isn't it?"

He smiled sheepishly. "Yeah."

"Well, come on in and meet the others." I started to walk off, but Brandon stayed anchored. He stood there with his hands screwed into his pockets.

"Mr. Latimore, I was wondering—that big fight at Miss Oveta's? I was wondering—what was that about?"

I looked at his young face, his eyes intense with inquiry. "What did your dad say?"

"He didn't."

I hesitated for a brief moment. "Well, Brandon . . . it's kind of personal, but since you were there I'll tell you. The man I was fighting with is my lover. We've been together for over eight years. And now . . . now things have changed between us. I guess I'm not very happy about that . . . so we fought."

He smiled. "You must really love him. You tore the bathroom up pretty good."

I frowned. "I'm not proud of that. I apologize for my rude behavior, Brandon. Come on." I put my hand on his shoulder and started back again.

Brandon quickly blurted out, "I'm just like you, too." I stopped. "I'm gay."

"Why do you say that?"

"I know. 'Cause I like men. I have a boyfriend—sort of."

"Brandon . . . you're still a young guy. You're feeling lots of things. You don't have to make any big declaration about the way . . ."

His eyes widened, a look of desperation clouded his features. "Why won't anyone *listen* to me? I know what I am. Didn't you? Why should I pretend to be something I'm not? I've read, I've re-searched on-line, I've talked to other guys on the Internet—I'm not stupid. Why does everybody want to act like this . . . *basic* part of me doesn't exist?"

I looked at his goofy blue hair, his earring and tattoo and remem-bered how brutally frustrating being fourteen was. This was com-pletely foreign territory to me—how do gay men mentor gay boys? Especially, how does one steer clear of the sex land mines? No, I did-n't "desire" him in any way, but did I trust myself completely around his potential desire . . . for me? God, what a nightmare. Just be his friend, Clu—be his friend.

"I believe you, Brandon. And yes, I did know when I was your age. We didn't even have any decent books at the library that I could read. I was pretty ignorant. I can see that you know what you're talking about. So—let's start over." I stuck my hand out. "Friends?"

Brandon smiled. "Friends."

"Here's the deal—I'll be honest with you and you be honest with me. And when your dad's ready to listen—we'll both tell him."

"Deal." We shook and started toward the others. Putting my hand on Brandon's neck I felt the strangest sensation. I'd never experienced anything quite like it. I was both deeply touched and surprisingly nervous. Here I was, at thirty-seven—a "gay father."

13

THE GORDON MACRAE ENDOWMENT

Mother was back in the hospital again. She started coughing up blood and running a high fever. Her marriage was three weeks away, and tomorrow was the first day of full cast rehearsals. It was as if time were speeding up to force some kind of showdown. But what? I didn't allow myself to think beyond the play opening and the wedding. The concept of losing Chris and Mom simultaneously was too devastating to contemplate. Even now Jaston and Shirley were talking about moving in together. Everybody . . . gone. Where do I go? Who am I this time?

The banging at the back door had apparently been going on for so long it was fused into my dream. I was on some island somewhere, under a coconut palm, banging away on the safe from the gristmill. For some reason I knew I could open it with a machete. And I was just about to break the dial off when . . . Shit! I looked over at the alarm clock: 7:00 A.M. Who the hell is knocking at seven o'clock? I stumbled out of bed, completely not in my body. I was definitely on that island—about to crack the safe that contained the answers to all life's unsolved riddles. I lurched past Chris's room—bed made, no one there. He'd been with Preston hanging mikes at the sale barn when I left him last night to go to the hospital to see Mom. I guess he and Preston—got "tied up." I felt a knot in my stomach. My Chris with that vacuous "Li'l Abner" of intellectual black holes. It didn't make sense. *Knock, knock, knock.*

"I'm coming!" I hollered. I was unhappy and pissed, and of course I stubbed my toe rounding the table. It hurt like hell. I winced in agony and fell toward the doorknob.

"Yeah."

"I . . . I'm sorry, are you Clu Latimore?"

"Yeah. What's up?"

"I'm Tory Roberts. I'm your assistant—on the play?" I dropped my foot and squinted at a rather nice-looking young man in shorts and a baseball cap carrying a backpack. He spoke again. "I believe you have a rehearsal at eight o'clock."

Shit! It had completely slipped my mind. Miss Oveta had a doctor's appointment and had asked if we could meet early to go over lines. "Damn, I'm sorry. Come on in." I backed up, hopping toward the sink. "I hit my big toe. What's your name again? Have a seat."

"Tory, Tory Roberts. I want to apologize for not making the auditions the other day. We had finals this week and that night was my only chance to schedule practice time with my tutor."

"Tutor?"

"I'm an English and music major. I'm hoping to play the piano professionally someday."

"Wow—how old are you?"

"Twenty-two. I should be with a symphony already—but I have patience. It'll happen."

"And confidence." I looked at Tory. Slender body, nice physique, great legs. He removed his baseball cap and he had a thick head of brown, wavy hair. Hazel eyes, masculine nose, big hands . . . Oh, stop it! For God's sake, you're old enough to be his baby-sitter. "Listen, would you do me a big favor. There's a can of coffee in the fridge—would you mind making us a pot?" I pointed to the Mr. Coffee on the counter.

"Not at all. You take anything with it?"

"Just black. Tory, I'm gonna go put some clothes on. You just make yourself at home. Did you eat breakfast?"

"Sure did. Can I make you some?"

I looked at him again. Every time I saw this kid from a different angle there was something further to notice. Nice teeth, nice skin . . . nice . . . "That's very *nice,* but I'll just have an apple or something."

He smiled. "OK."

I turned and headed back down the hall. I remembered something and turned around. Tory was staring at my back, a big smile on his face. "What?" He shook his head, still grinning. "Tory, there's bottled water next to the pantry. I use Grit water for scrubbing and flushing only."

He nodded. "No problem."

Poor kid, I probably looked like Jed Clampett to him—all baggy and unshaven. It's a wonder he didn't bolt and run. I stepped into the bathroom, shut the door and yanked off my underwear, turning on the shower. I glanced at my drawers lying on the floor. Picking them up I noticed there was hole in the crack you could stick your hand through. What is it with me and the strategic-hole underwear? Am I the official test site for butt blowouts in the nation? Disgusted, I wadded them up and threw them in the wastebasket. Now, at least, we had an explanation for Tory's 'happy face.' I shook my head as I stepped into the shower. "Keep it professional, Clu. Scrupulous standards of decorum and behavior at all times." Soaping up, I pondered briefly if buying new underwear might not be considered part of an assistant's job duties.

The rehearsals, as expected, were a debacle. It was like trying to herd parakeets. Hopeless. From the first hour it was complete chaos traversing utter absurdity. If anything went right, it was an aberration. And still, one could sense that a mustard seed's worth of imagination was trying to crack the surface. Something was there—nobody could be sure exactly what though.

The good news *was* Tory had managed to persuade a whole gaggle of college kids to be in the play, so at least the cast was set. Chris and I had taken the hoary old narrative of *Agamemnon*—the saga of Queen Clytemnestra butchering her husband (King Agamemnon) in the bath to avenge his sacrificing of their daughter, Iphigeneia, who was bumped off to appease the god Artemis—and on and on—and turned it into a *Dallas/Dynasty* meets *Hud* meets *Zorba the Greek* kind of thing. Why not? This was theater in a cow barn. If you didn't apply a little inventiveness, why bother?

We followed the plot like birds use road maps. Negligible. Here was the basic premise—set in a small Texas town called Greeceville, there are some deep, deep evildoings going on in Mycenae County. Local honcho and county judge, 'Ag' Memon, a good-old-boy politico, is married to the shrewish Clementine, sister of the beautiful and fair Helen, who lives over in Troytown. Helen has caused a scene and run off with some guy from Paris. Ag's half brother, Manny Laws, also a county judge, is married to Helen! It's a hell of a mess—two brothers married to two sisters. Ag and Manny go out to their deer lease to plot revenge and get stinkin' drunk. Ag's daughter Iffy comes looking for them and Ag, hearing strange voices, thinks it's an intruder out to harm him. He accidentally shoots Iffy. Dead. Only he doesn't realize it and the next morning, when the weather clears up, he and Manny head off to Dallas to find Helen and straighten things out. Well naturally, Clementine's fit to be tied when she gets the news about Iffy. To top it all off, Ag's first cousin, the studly, up-to-no-good E.G. Festus turns up in Greeceville and starts two-timing with Clementine. Not that he's so crazy about Clemmy, but he's secretly there to redress the nightmare that occurred when Ag's old daddy, Atty, got bent out of shape with his brother T. Estes (E.G. Festus's father) and ended up going bonkers and making sausage out of T. Estes's kids and serving them up to him in a pancake breakfast! Whew! Ag hightails it back from Dallas, worn to the bone, and Clemmy surprises him by telling him she's remodeled his office and recarpeted it with a new blood-red shag. Ag hits the fan. Clemmy tells him everyone in town is waiting for him to come inaugurate the new headquarters. Against his better judgment, Ag parades across the flaming carpet and it doesn't sit well with the local populace. He heads home to take a hot shower and get some shut-eye when Clemmy, driven to a tizzy by the loss of Iffy, and E.G. Festus constantly scheming in her ear, pulls a *Psycho* number and stabs old Ag in the bath. End of story. Sort of.

Incorporating an abundance of country swing tunes, ballads and cotton-eyed Joe dance numbers, a chorus keeping track of the story line and old man Zeus up in the auctioneer's booth running commentary—it was calculated to be a lively, visual and uncommon crowd-pleaser. Thoroughly utilizing the premises, we had guys on horseback, herds of longhorn steers, three-wheel all-terrain scooters pulling sets, guns firing, and, of course—beer, barbecue and air conditioning. Andrew Lloyd Weber had nothing on us.

A kid from the college asked me at one point what the moral of the story was. I said I didn't have a clue. We both seemed satisfied with that answer until my conscience got to bothering me. I assembled the cast and crew and judiciously announced that the moral of *Agamemnon, Ya'll!* was something along the lines of crime begets crime, murder begets murder—and without some form of law and order in the land, chaos reigns. In a state that leads the nation in public executions and where it's perfectly legal to carry a concealed weapon with you to church, law and order (of a specific ilk) was sacrosanct. It seemed to suffice.

Larraine was dragging her feet on learning the new songs. Chris and Preston had written most of them, and while not Kander and Ebb, they weren't particularly bad either. Larraine, Mariano, Manuel and Vicky would get about a quarter of the way into each lifeless rendition and inevitably, it would all turn into something sounding like "Faded Love." Finally, in exasperation I threw my notes down and yelled, "You know, the idea is to hear more than just one song during the course of the evening."

Larraine slouched and lit a cigarette. "Sorry. Your songs suck."

I responded immediately, "Then *you* write some, Carole King! Quit bitching and dragging the rest of the show down. Either be a professional—which I know you are because I've seen you at your best—and play the music, or bring me something better."

Everyone stood rigid, waiting for the two divas to start slinging shit. Larraine narrowed her mouth into a tight little cleft, and hissed, "I told you . . . I've got two kids to raise and I don't have *time* to write you a goddamn Broadway musical."

I stood calmly and stepped around Tory into the aisleway. I faced Larraine and singed her eyebrows with a look. "And I have a mother dying of cancer in the hospital that I go over and sit with half the night after every rehearsal. I'm not real amenable to hearing anyone's whining right now—especially from the only performers in the show actually getting paid!"

That did it. Larraine whirled around, grabbed her guitar and stomped out of the barn, blaspheming my name all the way. Mariano looked at everyone, sighed wearily and removed his guitar. "She'll be back." He then departed as well. Manuel and Vicky stayed behind out of some filial loyalty, I suppose.

We struggled on with half the band. It was clumsy, tedious and mostly detrimental. I finally threw my hands up in desperation. The moment had arrived when every decent director must stand and have, as my great-aunt Jean used to say, "a walleyed shit fit." And these prescribed eruptions always began with the same all-encompassing word . . .

"*People!* I don't think that I have to remind you that this show opens in three weeks. That's three weeks to get our sorry, slothful, half-baked acts together. Now I know you're tired, I know you have other lives, I know you have pressures—we all do. You didn't decide to be a part of this play because you thought you'd make me happy, or your mom happy, or your boyfriend or whomever—no, you did it to prove something to yourselves. That you're just as good and capable and worthy as any cap-toothed, hair-dyed, face-lifted actor in Hollywood or New York. You're each and every one of you uniquely and eminently suited for your individual roles. Each of you has the potential to be a *star*. I see it, I feel it and I *know* it. I've worked with some of the best in this business and none of you, *none* of you, have anything to hang your heads about. But I can't do it for you. I'm asking as your director—give me your absolute best from now until opening night. I want to be able to walk out of this temple of art— and that's exactly what it is, we've turned a cow barn into a cultural mecca through sheer 'Grit' determination—I want to be able to say to myself each evening as I head over to that hospital to sit with my mother . . . "*God—they're good!*" I let my neck quiver just slightly, Kate Hepburn-like, as I scanned the room making eye contact with each of them. Then I slowly sat and picked up my script. The applause began almost immediately.

"Three cheers for Mr. Latimore!" "We won't let you down." "We're proud of you!"

Taking my cue, I stood, looked around in self-effacing awe and bowed slightly. The applause, whistles and stomping grew louder. I turned to Tory, and murmured through smiling teeth, "Never fails." Tory grinned back at me, clapping enthusiastically.

Jaston had insisted we be there. Me, Chris and Shirley. If Mother could have been sprung from the hospital, her presence would have been mandatory as well. He'd rented an arc welder, and the opening of the gristmill safe was now upon us. Seated in folding chairs in Gladys Byers's dilapidated old garage, we watched entranced as Jaston blazed an aperture in the iron receptacle. Shirley had rigged up a video camera in a corner of the room and the event had all the tingle of a Geraldo Special. Would there be jewels, bonds, dollars, secret maps, illicit paraphernalia . . . or just roach dust?

Jaston was bent over the vault, his face shielded behind a tinted visor. We squinted and averted our eyes from the blinding glare of the oxyacetylene incandescence. Suddenly Jaston flicked off the blazing rod and stood. He raised the helmet and wiped his forehead with a sleeve. "This is it, ya'll." We stared at each other, speechless.

Finally, I called out, "OK, Indiana, let's see what's in King Tut's tomb."

Jaston squatted before the dismembered door and gave it an enormous tug. He fell back on his rear as the portal snapped and detached in his hands. We all stared into the obscured opening, half-expecting green smoke and a genie to emerge. There seemed to be a lot of . . . papers. Jaston at first cautiously removed document after document as if sacred texts of pharaonic canon were suddenly laid bare. "Ownership deeds, patent applications, warranty vouchers, titles . . ." Nothing remotely approaching buried treasure seemed to be revealing itself. Jaston looked anxious. I silently prayed for an Indian arrowhead, a Civil War button, a St. Louis World's Fair fountain pen . . . something to appease Jaston.

"What's that?" Shirley pointed to a small ledger on the top shelf.

"Some record book. It idn't worth anything." Jaston sighed.

"Let me see it." Jaston tossed her the book and returned to ravaging the now exposed scraps of business correspondence and prosaic legal documents.

"Man, I just don't get it. Not even a little old money box. They needed a safe 'bout like I need hair plugs on my ass." Jaston sat on the floor scratching his head.

"Don't feel bad, man. You've got enough documentation here to restore the mill with complete integrity." Chris patted Jaston's shoulder. "Besides, if you did find something really valuable, the government would just take half anyway. You've still got your grant money coming."

"Yeah, Jas, it was a long shot, you knew that. Hey listen, the safe alone will make a cool exhibit." I tried to sound encouraging.

"Who's . . . Herbert Q. Latimore?" Shirley looked up from the ledger. We turned to her. "Is that some relative?"

After a few seconds I answered, "Uh . . . that would most likely be . . . our father. Why?"

Shirley blinked at us, then slowly held up the ledger. It had been turned into a photo album filled with pictures of . . . *Herbert Q. Latimore.* We stared at our very young father in various poses. There he was wearing his World War II uniform, here he was dressed in a natty suit and hat. In swim trunks that covered his navel, playing cards with army buddies, standing before a new Ford roadster, riding horseback somewhere out West, and . . . apparently, an entire series taken on his wedding day. A wedding that appeared to be to someone other than . . . our mother.

"Who's that woman?" Jaston snapped as if suddenly aroused from a nap. Elegantly dressed, she looked to be considerably older than our father.

Although I remembered her only hazily as a testy old broad I ventured a guess. "I would say that—is Gladys Byers."

"Naaaaah." Jaston shook his head in complete disbelief. "Married to our father? You got to be kidding?"

I shrugged. "Alright, I'm kidding. Who is she?"

Jaston just stared, dumbstruck. "Jesus Christ in Arkansas—what we don't know about our fucking family you could fill a library with." He looked up at me, innocently, "You think we ought to tell Mama?"

I sighed, shook my head and stared down the lawn toward the creek bottom. "What I'd like to know is—*when* is Mother going to tell us?"

Mercy Hospital was silent as a bank on Sunday. I plodded slowly down the gleaming waxed hallways, thinking how very much alike clinics and morgues must be. Both resolutely disguising their true ambitions behind a veneer of Pine-Sol and calculated tranquillity. Way stations for the newly refitted pilgrim. Could there be any other viable option for leave-taking other than a sterile, fluorescent cubicle flawlessly rendered to sever heart and humanity entirely from the departure process? Must we end up dying in brilliantly lit waiting rooms?

I entered Mother's antiseptic box to find Brother Ramirez smartly dressed in a dark suit and another gentleman, equally as dapper, standing near them. Mother was wearing some kind of silk bed jacket with a little bunch of flowers pinned to it. Sister Renata was fluffing her pillow, and although Mother looked physically exhausted, she smiled blithely as I approached.

"Oh, Clu, you just missed it."

"Missed what?"

Mother, holding Brother Ramirez's hand, displayed her ring finger. On it was a very small diamond ring. "We did it. We're married!"

I opened my mouth. Nothing audible was forthcoming.

"I know this is a surprise. But we just decided not to wait any longer." Mother appeared to be genuinely elated. Brother Ramirez kissed her hand.

I stammered, "But, but . . . what . . . about the wedding? Your plans, the church . . ."

Mother shrugged. "It would've been such a production. Why spend all that money? Clu, this is Brother's friend, Pastor Whitlock from San Antonio. He performed the service for us. Sister Renata here was our witness."

Sister Renata turned to glance at me. Gone was the animated

Brazilian live wire. She looked as if she'd been crying. Wiping her nose with a tissue, she picked up a tray with medicine on it. "Es-cuse please, I gotta do rounds. *O que os olhos não vêem o coracão não sente.*" She darted from the room like a disturbed quail.

I shook my head. "What about . . . the families?" That uncomfortable feeling of forever being a stranger to my own actuality was resurfacing. Why did Mother continue to treat her children like out-of-work actors assuming bit roles in her life? "This is all you've talked about. I don't . . . understand."

"We'll have a little private something. Soon as I get out. Honestly, Clu, I thought you most of all would be pleased to be spared the whole ordeal?"

I looked at her, at Brother Ramirez, and finally at Pastor Whitlock. They each shared looks of vague unease. I sat in a little chair by the door and slowly began to grasp the emerging obvious.

"H . . . how long do you have, Mother?"

Mother looked at Brother Ramirez and squeezed his hand. He lowered his head to hers and kissed her on the lips. He then turned to Pastor Whitlock and extended an arm toward the door. "Why don't we go have a coffee?" He suddenly beamed. "It's my wedding day! We'll have some *pan dulce,* too." As the two men started to leave I stood.

"What . . . what would you like me to call you from now on?"

Brother Ramirez grinned and put his hand on my shoulder, "Some of my closest friends call me, Mano. It's abbreviated Spanish for *hermano*—brother."

I nodded. "Mano."

He looked at me a moment longer. "And may I call you, 'son'?"

I nodded, surprised. He put his arms around me and we embraced. Although he was more than a foot shorter than I was, I felt like one of the biggest men I'd ever known was standing before me. His complete, passionate and robust embrace of life's extraordinary predicaments was both alien and simultaneously reassuring. When they left the room it felt as if whatever confidence I might be able to muster was largely a poser's ruse. I looked at Mother and took a deep breath. "What do the doctors say?"

She didn't flinch. "A couple of weeks. Maybe."

I nodded. "Are you in pain, Mother?"

"No, just tired. Tired all the time."

"Do you want to go home?"

"Yes. I really do."

I nodded again. "I'll see about getting you out."

Mother shook her head. "Brother's already spoken to the doctors. I can go home in the morning."

I sat there, staring at an ugly ivy plant with ridiculous plastic ducks stuck in it. No doubt someone's idea of a cheery gift. Why do we insist on cheering the dying? Why not just offer up Häagen-Dazs and reruns of *All My Children*? Skip the denial crap and deal with *want*. I was completely at a loss for words. I finally said the first thing that came into my head. "Jaston opened the safe at Ms. Byers's. There were no jewels inside, just lots of pictures . . . of our father."

She stared at me, far, far away. "Oh. I'd like to see them."

I remained impassive. "I guess what I'm trying to say is—why is he in a photo album—in *her* safe?"

She cocked her head, as if trying to hear better. "Well . . . they were married. Gladys was your father's first wife." She said it as if it were the plainest, most apparent of facts.

I nodded. "Actually—I didn't know that."

"Of course you didn't. It was over and done years ago. She was a sick old lady by the time you were born."

"But . . . let me get this straight. We lived next door to our father's first wife . . . because why?"

Mother stared at me as if I'd gone berserk. "She gave us our home! It was a wedding present. I never cared for Gladys, but she could be generous when she felt like it."

"Um . . ." As usual, I was completely buffaloed.

Mother suddenly lifted her head, made a horrible face and stammered, "Oh . . . I . . . I think you better call for the nurse. I'm feeling . . ." And then she spit up some blood. I leapt for a nearby towel. Putting my hand on her shoulder, I was again amazed at how little more than hide and bones she was. Although I knew she was heavily narcotized, the pain must have been fearful.

"I'm right here, Mom. I'll get the nurse . . . I just don't want to leave you alone."

She looked at me with tears in her red eyes and nodded slightly. I continued on, shaking. "Shall I get the nurse? Will you be all right? Mother . . . are you OK now?"

She lay back slowly on her pillow. "I'm . . . OK."

I pulled the chair next to her bed and held the diminutive, bony forearm of her still-bandaged right limb. My insides were flipped around like lottery balls. Like a fist to the brain I completely grasped that I would not have this arm to touch, this face to see for very much longer. This familiar, comforting, annoying, strange person, who was so much like me and so foreign at the same time, would be gone forever. I wanted to say so many things, and yet I didn't have a clue what actually needed to be expressed. There was absolutely no need for her to hear me blather on at this point. I continued patting her arm softly, finding some odd comfort in the ritual. Maybe just sitting there was the entire need expressed. Like rocking a restless baby, proximity was integral. I stared at the dwarfish repository of sinew and white hair before me and marveled. How would anyone know that this was once a bright, alive, juicy, vibrant, gorgeous, knockout dream of a human being? You can recall that person so well, and yet the incarnation is distant memory, too. And so you sit with the uncomfortable present—and you remember the remarkable life that was.

Mother spoke in a soft whisper, her eyes closed. "Clu . . . I want you to be nice to Brother Ramirez. He's such a good man. He's truly made the end of my life a . . . beginning." She took a sip of water. "He insisted we get married now. He wanted to be able to tell everyone he was my . . . husband." She smiled. "Some mystery life—huh?"

I stopped patting and just held her arm.

"You explain to Jaston and Laine not to worry—everything I have goes to you kids. Not that there's much; the house, a car . . . a lot of dog food." We both smiled. "We just married . . ." Mother frowned, trying to dislodge the words. Her face relaxed. "Because we *did* . . . that's all. I'm not dying alone . . . and I'm not afraid."

I straightened the rumpled collar of her nightgown. "You would never die alone, Mother. We're here, aren't we?"

She touched my hand with a cold fingertip. "I know I've been hard on you in the past, son. It was difficult for me to support what I didn't understand. Even when I thought I didn't approve—I never stopped loving. Ever."

It was hard to speak. "I just wish—we had more time, Mother. I feel like I've never really known you as a person. You've always been so distinctly—*you,* and I still don't know really who that is. I know I'm a reflection of your hopes and desires, but I'm not sure what to do with that. And I'd really like to know."

Mother opened her eyes and turned to me, determined. "What I'd like . . . is for you to find another good person and love them with all your heart. You are a lovable man. Don't shut it away like I did for so long. Somebody out there very much wants you to love them back."

I could barely see, my eyes were so blurry. I glanced down at Mother's bony hand, and it suddenly seemed worthy of a da Vinci etching. Every line, every blue vein, dark spot and bruise—explicit and detailed as an Arab mosaic. And equally as baffling. I, who got paid for having flawless hands had none of Mother's character or earned distinction. My hands looked amazingly weak by comparison. I'd always wanted to preserve them like I sought to preserve my life. Never-changing, immaculate, lifeless—perfect.

Mother, her eyes closed, mumbled, "One more thing . . . sell the dogs when I'm gone. Just try to find them good homes, will you?"

I was appalled. "Mother I couldn't sell your children. Neuter them, maybe."

"Oh . . . I know they bother you all underfoot. Just find them nice homes."

"That's not true, I do like them. Some—maybe more than others."

Mother smiled and shook her head slightly. "You won't stay in Grit. You never cared for it, though when you really think about it—people are just people anywhere you go."

I looked at her. Her eyes were shut and her mouth partially open, as if she were taking a short nap. I hadn't thought much about what I'd do after her death. Returning to New York seemed largely "retro" at this point. Not enough time had passed to be truly nostalgic for more abuse. Where exactly was the next best thing? The eternal question. Was it here? Right in your own backyard, Dorothy? I shuddered. Did I really dare to have that question answered?

We were both silent for a minute longer, then I spoke again. "Mother . . . did I ever tell you . . . I always thought you were the prettiest mom of any of the mothers I knew? I was so happy when you'd come to school for one of our class parties. All the other kids would say, *'That's* your mother? She's *pretty.'* And you were. You just never looked like the other moms. You were . . . unique. And I was always proud to say, 'Yeah, that's my mom. She's *special.'"*

Mother still had her eyes closed. One long, wandering tear slid down the side of her cheek and dampened the pillow. She cleared her throat. "Thank you. That's a very sweet thing to say. I never did anything to earn what I was born with, but I did try to make it more *interesting.* Don't forget—the king of England gave up his throne for a very plain woman who simply knew how to sell *possibility.* Anything's possible if you believe."

I nodded slowly. The obvious becomes crystalline in a sigh. Here was all the proof I'd ever need that one doesn't have to run off to Paris and dance on tabletops in your underwear just to be *special.* You can stake out a non-herd life, even in a town as prosaic and underdeveloped as Grit, by just being authentically yourself. In fact— it's *mandatory.* Why had I never fully grasped that? From Mother to Miss Oveta to Mr. Wheeler to Brother Ramirez to Myla, and on and on—they'd each created a distinctive and inventive life within the stretchable parameters of small-town conformity. Was I so blind to my own fear of being the perpetual pariah that I couldn't fathom the notion we're *all* outcasts equally in our own fashion. Even if I could be more fully "me" in New York (whoever *that* was), did it inexorably negate any other likelihood for self-fulfillment?

Mother squeezed my hand. "Sing that song why don't you?"

"What song?"

"The one where you and Chris destroyed Miss Oveta's bathroom. I never realized how much you sound like Gordon MacRae before. Would you?"

I do believe it was one of the nicest compliments Mother ever paid me. I looked at her, amazed, "Right now?"

She nodded dreamily. I cleared my throat and a tinny croak came out. I started again, this time gently crooning:

> "O-o-o-o-o-o-o-o-klahoma, where the wind
> comes sweepin' down the plain.
> And the wavin' wheat can sure smell sweet
> when the wind comes right behind the rain.
>
> We know we belong to the land,
> and the land we belong to is grand.
> And when we sa-a-a-a-a-ay,
> Ki-yip-eye-yo-eye-yea, OH!
> Were only sayin', you're doin'
> fine Oklahoma, Oklahoma . . ."

Mother, almost asleep, mouthed the last words silently. "O-K."

14

THE HUMAN RESPONSE

The dress rehearsal before opening night was horrendous. It was the miserable, the bad, and the Nightmare on Cow Barn Lane. And yet, in spite of nearly everyone's steadfast efforts to render the whole thing contemptible—something mysterious appeared to be happening. Notwithstanding the myriad of missed cues, dropped lines, faulty props, antiquated lights and obstinate animals—damned if the whole thing wasn't veering toward something approaching an honest-to-God theatrical experience. As with celebrity funerals and mass executions, the public had their demands. Cattle Auction Drama appeared as if it might be on the periphery of some Texas cutting-edge cultural attainment. As Myla told me during one of her innumerable cigarette and Miller Lite breaks, "Hon, this thing is a hoot!" The Hoot Factor could not be dismissed offhand. A deficit of hootable spectacle was looming throughout the land. Our task was hugely providential.

Larraine, after sulking for two days, finally reappeared hauling a Wal Mart bag full of songs she'd handwritten. And they were good. Better than good, they were entirely right. She'd captured the entire funky, illusory and melodramatic essence of the show and bound it all up in some truly rousing numbers. She even penned a first-act butt shaker called "Beer, Barbecue and Air conditioning" that was guaranteed to blow the pigeons out of the rafters. Chris and Preston didn't seem to mind much that their own musical efforts had been abandoned. At that point, everyone was hell-bent on just getting the show opened.

Preston, I was pleased to observe, had actually prevailed in his role as E.G. Festus. All his irritating preening and posturing had crystallized into a workable blueprint for the role's mostly conniving aspects. He played a good schmuck. Brilliantly.

Stepbrother Oscar Ramirez had been hanging around for several weeks after showing up one afternoon unexpectedly with a truckload of much-needed scrap lumber. He didn't seem to be particularly interested in the show, but he didn't seem to be much interested in being anywhere else for that matter, so he just sort of hung and watched, occasionally offering a hand. I did notice that he seemed to be around every time Preston was onstage. Watching.

Tory had attached himself to me in the most nonintrusive of ways. He was always there without being sticky about it. Bright, funny, good-natured, helpful—he was a delight to be around. I counted on him for endless trivial chores and boring responsibilities, but mostly I relied on him for his positive, easygoing disposition. I hadn't been around anyone in a long, long time who made me feel so . . . assured. Tory gave me back a huge chunk of self-confidence. I was "accomplished" in his eyes. Poor kid, it seemed heartless to disillusion him. Sure there was the older-guy-adulation thing going on, but it was largely discreet. And, let's be honest, it was flattering as hell. Although we'd never discussed our private lives (I didn't even know for certain if he was gay, or just another "sensitive" straight boy) it was obvious we weren't averse to each other's company. I was greatly appreciative of his friendship.

During a ten-minute break, we were both poking around in the huge enclosed storage area under the wooden bleachers, searching for spare lightbulbs. Unable to locate any, we decided to search in the next storage compartment under the adjoining seating section. I shut the door and Tory walked across the aisle, pushing open the already ajar wooden door. I made a mental note to find out who'd forgotten to lock the storage cubbyholes as we'd been repeatedly warned by Mr. Wheeler he wouldn't allow "no thieving or chicanery" with his possessions. Stepping into the darkness behind Tory, I noticed that he had stopped a few paces ahead. Approaching behind, I started to speak when I glanced over his shoulder. About fifteen feet in front of us, through a maze of file cabinets, boxes, crates and stacked chairs was the eerily highlighted image of Preston standing under the sole lit bulb—his pants and underwear crumpled into a loose heap around his feet. Squatting before him, fastidiously venerating Preston's pink, bald-headed, one-eyed monster—was Oscar Ramirez! We both stood for a few seconds blinking in awe at this impromptu performance (specifically the "offbeat" casting) until finally I put my hand on Tory's shoulder and motioned I was exiting.

I stepped into the hallway and Tory followed behind, quietly shutting the door. We looked at each other a bit uncertain, then finally burst out laughing.

"I . . . I'm sorry. I just wasn't ready for that one," I snickered.

"Wow . . . isn't that guy running for sheriff or something?" Tory seemed genuinely alarmed.

I nodded. "It's a dirty business—you never know when you might be called to perform your duty."

He shook his head. "I guess that explains Preston's giddiness for the past week. Hey—it's none of my concern, but I thought Preston was kind of seeing your friend Chris?" Tory looked at me, slightly apprehensive.

I looked back. "I don't know, Tory. Chris and I aren't sharing our 'personal life' details anymore."

"Oh. So like—were you guys—together once?"

"Eight years like."

Tory nodded. "And . . . are you seeing anyone now?"

I shook my head. Tory looked at me sheepishly then began fumbling with a notepad he was carrying. I wavered between wanting to ravish him right there and sitting him on a stool and teaching him the alphabet. The fifteen-year gap seemed daunting. What do I know about Gen X anything? Good Lord, he was two when I graduated high school.

Miss Oveta approached in full theatrical regalia. She looked like she was wearing about nine pages of the Neiman Marcus Christmas catalog. She'd decided the wife of a county judge should dress always with great abundance. At the time we didn't know that meant wearing a chandelier with a red wig wrapped around it. But whatever, it was her money. She could wear cigarette butts glued to a bikini if she felt like it.

"Clu, I think I saw some extra folding chairs in the storage room there. I need one to prop my foot up. Touch of the gout, you know."

I snapped to. "Here, we'll bring you one. Is it for backstage?"

"Not a problem, I can get it." Miss Oveta placed her hand on the door. I stood in her way.

"Actually . . . the better chairs are over here." I pointed across the hall.

"Better?" She looked confused.

Tory interrupted. "Newer . . . softer seats."

She smiled and removed her hand from the door. "Lovely."

I shifted to the opposite door, calling, "Tory, can you give me a hand moving these tables?" Tory obliged, and Miss Oveta stood watching us as we rearranged Mr. Wheeler's carefully constructed disarray.

We were just about to reach the folding chairs lying atop a storage shelf when Miss Oveta announced, "Oh I forgot, Mr. Jeffrey wants a trash can for the men's dressing room. I saw one next door." She disappeared before we could react.

Tory and I looked at each other. I carefully retrieved the chair and stepped back down. "Well . . . this will no doubt be one of those highly instructive moments one longs for in the broad overview of life experiences." We both positioned ourselves outside the Iniquity Room and waited for Miss Oveta to reappear. And we waited.

Finally, the door swung open briskly and Miss Oveta emerged smiling and carrying a yellow plastic garbage can. "Here it is. Just as I remembered. Oh that's a perfect chair. I'll just take it with me. Clu, I want you to know—you've infused us all with great imagination and magic. It's going to be a marvelous success!" With that she took the chair from my hands and breezed off toward the front of the arena. As she approached the first rows she suddenly turned and announced in crisp, regal tones, "Oh—would you tell Preston when Mr. Ramirez is through blowing him to please bring me my makeup kit." She then proceeded to her dressing room. Myla, Debbie, Sandy and Zane, who'd been sitting up in the bleachers, stuck their heads over the railing and blinked down at us. I slowly waved back.

Late one afternoon, four days before the opening, I got to the barn earlier than expected and found Larraine, Myla and Vicky sitting in the bleachers laughing, gossiping, and judging from olfactory indicators, having just knocked off the remnants of a killer joint. Since none of them were scheduled for rehearsal that day I must've looked a bit surprised. "Well . . . all I can say is . . . you're lucky Mr. Wheeler hasn't walked in and gotten a whiff of your little festivities. He'd have *all* our butts in a sling."

Myla, at first, stared at me perplexed, then immediately doubled over in hysterical, nasal snickering. Larraine and Vicky followed suit. After much effort, Myla lifted her head and whined between gasps for air, "Nowww . . . don't go getting . . . all school principal on us. Old man Wheeler . . . left about twenty minutes ago. Said he was going home to meet some"—Myla glanced at the others—"*Polish gal!*" Instant giggle jag.

I grinned. Good for Mr. Wheeler. "Live till you die!" I looked up at the wayward trio and tried feigning maturity, "So, what are ya'll doing here anyway? You're not scheduled today."

They furtively glanced at one another and immediately began cackling again. Fun. Nothing I like better than three stoned women hell-bent on giddiness.

Larraine finally flipped up her cowboy hat, took a deep breath and beamed. "We got something for ya."

I nodded blankly. "O-K?" Again, more tittering and snorting, but it was starting to wind down.

Vicky reached into her shoulder bag and produced a brown paper sack. "This is for you." She handed me the mysterious parcel, and I stared at it dumbly. "Go on, open it up!"

I stuck my hand into the bag and retrieved a—trophy! A tall brass trophy of a . . . goat? "My very own . . . *goat trophy*. Thanks."

Myla snorted, shook her head and lit a cigarette. "It's not about the goat, you *goober*. That's just some 4H Club reject they had left over down at the Hobby Shop. Read the plaque!" I glanced at the inscription.

"Read it *aloud*," Larraine growled.

I cleared my throat. "For Clu Laine Latimore—our new Favorite Guy! In appreciation for your hard work, dedication, creativity and all-around expertise. By unanimous vote: If we were gay men you'd be our first choice for a date! PS: We like your butt, too. 'The Greek Sisters.' Vicky, Larraine and Myla."

I was silent. "Um . . . thanks, ya'll."

There followed an awkward hush. I really couldn't think of a snappy retort. I was truly surprised. Finally, Larraine spoke up. "We got this for you, too." She instantly produced a beribboned fifth of Jack Daniel's from her purse and handed it to me. "You'll need it when you're done putting up with all our bullshit."

Vicky leaned forward. "We just wanted you to know we appreciate all your hard work and commitment. It's been a lot of fun. You're a really interesting guy, and we wanted to say thanks. That's all."

I could feel that familiar bump in my throat, predictable as a prom pimple. I began stammering. "Wow . . . I don't know really what to say. It's been a lot of . . . I'm not sure 'fun's' the word— '*growth*' maybe. Ya'll have really taught me a lot about friendship and decency; caring and talent, determination . . . so many things. Things I'd kind of ignored till recently. So . . . thanks. Ya'll mean a lot to me, too." I could feel my face burning. I'm sure I was blushing like a junior-high virgin.

"Hip, hip and rooty-toot-toot!" Myla tossed her cigarette and applauded vigorously. "I think it's only proper we inaugurate that bottle with a little ceremonial consecration." The women cheered in unison. Who was I to buck a trend?

Larraine produced four paper cups and after pouring us all a sizable jigger, she stood to toast. "Here's to the craziest-ass show in Texas. I hope I get a fucking great-paying gig out of it." She then knocked back her drink. We all followed suit.

Vicky immediately thrust her paper goblet forward. "I need to make a toast! One more." Larraine dutifully obliged, and we stood once again at attention with our replenished mugs. "Here's to finally getting a boyfriend this year. I want a boyfriend! Is that too much to ask? He doesn't have to be *macho* or beautiful or rich—he just has to worship my ass!" Vociferous huzzahs. We sucked back more brew.

Myla's turn. By now we were all appreciating the firewater warm and fuzzy bubble, and Myla, in particular, was experiencing no evident distress. She grabbed the bottle of Jack from Larraine and stood up on the bleacher seat, swaying. "I just wanna say . . . right now . . . ya'll are the best group of broads . . . I've ever had the tendency . . . of being intermingled with." Myla thrust the bottle aloft. "And that includes Clu! Especially Clu. I hereby dub thee *'honorary broad.'*" Myla dribbled some bourbon on her fingers and flicked me with droplets. She then chugged a sizable swig and passed the bottle back to Vicky. "I gotta go pick up Raelynn . . . at band practice."

"Hang on girl, you're in no position to *dive* . . . drive." Larraine reached for Myla's keys, mumbling to herself.

"What the fuck are you ranting about?" Myla protested.

"I'll *dribe* us home. I can smell you've had too much to think."

Myla clutched her keys tightly, "You ain't *dribing* me nowhere, Peppermint Patty. I wouldn't trust you to operate a hair dryer right now."

Vicky, who seemed marginally less tight than the rest, held up her own car keys. "*I'm* taking everyone in the church van. Nobody's gonna stop a bunch of 'born-agains' on their way to prayer meeting. 'Sides, it can't go faster than fifty." With that edict the women turned and stomped out of the sale barn, noisily disputing the others' sobriety.

Myla spun around as she exited. "Clu, hey I nearly forgot, Brandon Pickens and his friend were looking for you. I think they're out in the cow pens. Love yew."

I nodded and stared at my trophy. My own goat trophy. Apt somehow. I guess it's a certifiable compliment when three straight women confess they'd jump your bones if they were only gay men. Bizarre . . . but heartfelt. But that's never been the problem, has it, Clu? Women have always liked you. You're the perfect date: looks, wit, charm, focus, clothes—everything but the passion. But in the end, who needs passion when all we *really* want is someone just to hold us in the dark? Perhaps that will be the ironic denouement to this lumpy *sturm und drang* you call your life; Clu ends up with a woman. Or becomes one. I can't decide.

I picked up my script, boom box and bag of paper bluebonnets

and assorted *tstochkes* for the Greek chorus and headed for the auctioneer's booth. Glancing at my watch, I gauged I had a good thirty
minutes to go over music and lighting cues, uninterrupted. Climbing
the stairs, I glanced out the tiny window overlooking the back cor-
rals. About 150 feet away I could see Brandon and some taller
Hispanic boy leaning against the railing, staring absentmindedly
down into the sheep pens. Now what? I cracked open the grimy window, and called, "Brandon, did you need me for something?" They
both jumped, looking startled. Brandon waved, conferred with his
friend, then began walking toward me. I set my load down and
reached for a Tic Tac sitting on the desk in the booth. Why, you ask,
bother masking whiskey breath when Myla has already baptized
your clothes? Because I was a paragon of parochial habits, that's
why. One at least had to make an effort to hide the truth from innocent bystanders. That was code. Let them observe what they will—
you're not required to provide the slide show.

"Hey, Mr. Latimore. This is my friend Danny Gutierrez."

"Hey." I shook Brandon's hand and reached toward Danny. He
warily offered me his paw like it was broken in nine places. What's
with kids nowadays? Nobody shakes hands anymore? And why is it
always like you're holding a beaten diaper? "Hi, Danny, nice to meet
you." He twitched and stared off somewhere to the right of my
shoulder. A nice-looking kid: thin, intense, solemn. Kind of a baby
Anthony Quinn. He also had shaved most of his head, wore a nose
stud, and sported a series of crudely elaborate tattoos transversing
both arms. A guaranteed "Mom pleaser."

"So, what's up with you guys? Brandon, are you scheduled this
afternoon? I thought it was just the male chorus?"

"Yeah, no. We're just hangin'." Silence. "My friend wanted to . . .
meet you."

I looked at Danny, smiling. "Me?"

Brandon twisted his fists in his jean pockets and rocked on his
heels nervously, "Yeah, you know. It's nothing."

I looked at Brandon, trying to ascertain what exactly we were
communicating here. Somehow, it wasn't plugging in. "So . . .
Danny. You and Brandon in school together?"

"No."

"Oh, you go to another school?"

"I dropped out."

"Uh-huh. How old are you?"

"Sixteen."

"So . . . you and Brandon are like 'best buds'?" Silence. I looked at Brandon, who was now staring at a crack in the wall. "Well, guys, I'd really like to visit awhile but I've got some tech work on the show to do before the rest of them get here. Umm . . . Danny, would you like to help out?" Suddenly, it was if Aphrodite had risen from the ocean floor and hurled rainbows on us all. Danny flashed a smile that could melt glaciers. I hadn't seen a transformation quite like it since Ivana Trump became a single mom.

"Yeah, that'd be cool."

"Uh, all right. Why don't you guys go through those bags there. I need to separate everything into piles—the chorus gets one of everything." They both sat on the floor like preschoolers and cheerfully tore into my old grocery bags. I watched, marveling. What a capricious age, dashing from childhood to adult—oftentimes concurrently. Thank God it's not a highly reflective time of life. One could get a brain tumor from following the progression.

"What's this?" Brandon held up my goat trophy.

"Oh, just some gag from a few cast members." Brandon read the inscription silently. I watched his face. He handed the trophy to Danny.

"So, are you like—*in* to women too?"

I leaned back in the antique office chair and stretched. "It's a goof award they gave me, that's all. I like women fine. I'm a hell of a lot closer to them than a lot of guys I know. How 'bout you two?" I was being mischievous. They looked at me puzzled.

"Yeah, girls are cool. Some of them. Danny's got a girlfriend," Brandon shrugged.

"Oh yeah?"

"She's not a girlfriend. We just have a kid together." Danny said it as nonchalantly as announcing the time.

"You've got a kid?"

"Cody. He's ten months. We're not married or anything."

"H . . . how old is . . . the mother?"

"I don't know—fifteen, I think."

My brain was stumbling. "Boy—that's young."

"My dad got married at seventeen. Anyway, I'm never getting married."

"Why not?"

Brandon and Danny stared at each other. After a pause, Brandon spoke softly. "Danny's my boyfriend." They looked at each other again and grinned shyly.

Check. I did a little readjusting in my seat. That this scenario might have even been *dreamed* of in Grit when I was their age extirpates the mind.

"Oh."

"I'm dropping out of school as soon as I get my Learner's Permit." Brandon was stacking paper bluebonnets into a neat, precise pile. I couldn't help but think that if Pat were here right now, he'd have shit a nuclear rod through his drawers.

"So. I don't get it, why drop out of school?"

Brandon frowned. "This place sucks. We want to go to California or Amsterdam." Sounded reasonable.

"People are too judgmental around here. They want you to be like some cookie-cutter shit. Buncha ignorant rednecks—Mexican and Anglo both." Danny, disgusted, scratched his illustrated, sinewy arm.

I studied them while pondering life's strange, cyclic orbits. Wasn't that just *me* five minutes ago—planning my getaway from "Hell Town" Grit? Here we are, back so soon. And what's changed other than nose rings and expanded hair drama?

"So, Brandon, I'm curious—what do you think your father's going to say when he hears about your plans?"

"You're not going to tell him?" Brandon looked at me apprehensively. I shook my head. He rubbed his Chinese tattoo thoughtfully. "He'll have a cow. He doesn't like anything I do. It won't make any difference."

Danny suddenly interrupted. "Can I ask you a question?" I nodded once more. "Are you like . . . a 'top' or a 'bottom'?"

"Excuse me?"

"You know—do you 'give it' or 'get it' when you have sex?"

"Um . . . I gotta know. Why on earth you would possibly need that information?"

"'Cause like—we don't know any gay adults. Me and Brandon have done it both ways, but we don't want to get any AIDS or nothing."

"What do they teach you in school?"

They looked at each other and laughed, answering simultaneously, *"Just Say No!"*

"What else do they say?"

"Some shit about a girl's time of the month, having wet dreams, don't play with yourself too much. It's all bullshit. They don't tell gay guys anything 'cause we don't exist, you know?" Danny frowned and shook his head.

I sat there, bewildered. When exactly were things supposed to get any better? These babies were nearly as dumb as I was at their age. Thankfully you couldn't die from illiterate experimentation back then. This is nuts! Must we keep living season to season in wholesale denial simply because a few religious conservatives desperately need their comfort zone honored? My comfort zone got dismembered forever when I buried my nineteenth friend from HIV infection.

"Listen, guys . . . I'm gonna level with you. Both of you are considered legal minors. You now what that means? You *don't* exist under the law. But since you're already having sex—and Danny's having babies, no less—you *cannot* walk around here being complete, stupid nitwits. *Lives* are at stake! Now I'm going to say it, and you're not going to like it—you're both *really young.* And it is definitely not an adult's place to interfere with anyone's budding sexual development, but when it comes to teenage pregnancy, disease, unsafe practices, ignorance and flat-out denial of the *rudimentary* facts of life—that's when the blinders come off and the school door opens. I'm gonna make a deal with you both." They stared at me like I'd gone slightly bananas. I had. "You say you want to leave and go to California. I'm telling you, you guys would last thirty minutes on the streets of LA. Trust me, the West Coast doesn't need another diseased, boy-hooker hauling his lame butt around Hollywood. I'll make you a better offer. Brandon, you stay in school, and Danny, you start studying for your GED, and I'll take you both up to Gay

Pride Weekend in Dallas. You can see real live gay people! Living their lives! Nobody hassling them. Holding hands in public and wearing bronzer! What do you think about that?" They glanced at each other. "And you tell the rest of your gay friends in school— we're gonna have a weekly social hang-time at my house. You can ask questions, get the news, be yourselves—and I don't give a god-damn what the *community* thinks about it. What do you guys say about that?"

You could hear a mouse fart. I couldn't tell if they were going to run from the room or kiss my ring. Finally, Danny nodded his head slowly. "Awesome."

Brandon smiled broadly. "Are you like . . . serious?"

"Do flies like stink? Hell yes, I'm serious."

They both laughed, and we all shook hands. My God, I was turn-ing into a radical old poof. What the hell, *'If not you, who? If not now, when?'* Somebody had to stand up and offer the human re-sponse. What good are we if we can't occasionally surpass our nar-cissistic impulses and simply reach out to our younger siblings in earnest.

For the next half hour I was bombarded with questions that would have ignited a nun's habit. But the best part was . . . I even knew some of the answers!

15

GOD'S LARK

Opening night was a pretty heady mix of exhilaration interspersed with horror and melancholy rearing their nasty heads simultaneously. (Utter glee would have been unthinkable, but couldn't a slight case of extended euphoria been feasible, just this once?) We sold out, much to everyone's amazement. The Grit glitterati were in full attendance, owing in no small part to Miss Oveta and Raymond Otis's countywide directive to show up or suffer the social repercussions. Even Grit had its patrician hierarchy, for what it was worth. The Ford dealer had more clout than the Dodge dealer—who knew, understood, or even cared why?

Sandy and Dwayne's two little girls greeted the arriving audience members as Greek nymphs who'd been sent to Texas to spread classical and cultural enlightenment. They were hoisted above the spectators in special straps and pulleys, where they strummed lyres and sprinkled Lucky Charms cereal as they flew above the patrons' heads. Then the lights dimmed and Mr. Wheeler in Stetson and bolo tie rode out into the spotlighted arena on his old sorrel mare, Georgia Brown, followed by an honor guard from the high school carrying the American flag, the flag of Texas and a banner displaying the Acropolis in Athens. After everyone stood and sang the state song, "Texas Our Texas," Manuel started strumming a traditional balalaika as Mr. Jeffrey, wearing a flowing Greek robe, a crown of mesquite leaves and cowboy boots, narrated the crux of our tangled Greco/Texan epic speaking into the old radio microphone on Mt. Zeus—the auctioneer's booth. Larraine picked up the beat as Larry's Lament opened the chute doors with their first song, "Frat Scat—The Greek Chorus Hymn." The chorus, in contemporary Texas attire (but for garlands of bluebonnets on their heads) entered in a series of dirt bikes, all-terrain vehicles and a lone go-cart. They tromped around the dirt pit, climbed the pipe fence separating the audience and warned of dire doings ahead. By the time Zane (Ag Memon) and Dwayne (Manny Laws) rode in on horseback herding a couple of longhorn steers—we had the audience by the eyeballs.

By the very last scene, when Miss Oveta in a climactic frenzy, stabbed Zane in his horse-trough-on-wheels bathtub to vindicate their daughter's death—the audience was as engrossed as a nail-biting last inning at the Cotton Bowl. Oveta and lover Preston hightailed it on their specially built "chariot" pulled by two Shetland ponies. The haunting strains of "The Dead Husband Blues" commenced as they hurriedly skedaddled into the painted sunset beyond the livestock stalls. When the lights finally came back up the audience was instantly on their feet stomping, whistling and cheering like we were handing out free Stuckey's Pecan Logs. For such acclaim one would have gladly severed a small finger in New York. I think the cast and crew took a total of eight or nine curtain calls. (Curtain being the cattle chute doors, which were opened and closed by our Greek Gods in Training, Brandon and Danny. Dressed in cowboy hats, sandals, sunglasses and single strap minitogas, they performed their duties with the drop-dead aplomb of touring rock stars.)

By the time Chris and I were brought out to take a bow we were "riding the gravy train on biscuit wheels," as Uncle Pete used to say. It was a heady moment standing under those fresnel spots before my hometown. Chris and I stared at each other. To fully assimilate the peculiar journey our lives had been up to this moment was largely preposterous. Why here, why now? And then, as always . . . why not? I put my arms around him and we embraced before God, Jesus and the elementary-school principal. Nobody produced a lynching rope and that, we could definitely say, was progress.

Afterward there was a celebratory bash, and I met and shook hands with more people from my past than I'm positive I could have ever possibly known. Everyone was an instant acquaintance. "Remember the time you . . ." "Oh you know me, I used to . . ." "Sure you do, we were in auto mechanic club together . . ." Nope, nope and *hell* nope. Still, everyone was overwhelmingly complimentary, and it felt, well, completely wonderful.

The only downside to the evening was Mother's absence. She was at home with a round-the-clock attendant now. Mano had put a little rollaway in her bedroom and even with him there Mother had to be lifted, carried, cleaned, fed and nursed constantly. The attendant, a large farm woman, Mrs. Kubish, was as engaging as a pit bull. The Medicare coverage had finally kicked in a death aide. Although Bettie Jean Latimore had never fought in a war, run for public office, found a cure, led a movement, climbed the highest, run the fastest or painted anything that hung in a national museum—the government now deemed she could die with a complete stranger beside her—as long as she didn't dawdle about it.

Mother drifted in and out of consciousness as serenely as a napping child. The bother of life had slipped entirely from her face. What particle that remained of her physical essence was some form of extended bliss. The drugs, the purifying act of completion, the newfound refuge of her marriage—whatever it was that gave her this final rapture was mesmerizing to behold. Death was not the adversary we'd expected. Death was simply a big, fast car that sped one quite sensibly out of harm's way.

Jaston and Shirley had by now moved in with each other. Work was progressing on the gristmill in a completely organized, un-Jaston-like fashion. A crew of local historical fanatics had been assembled through Shirley's resourcefulness, and they were as fervently devoted as groupies at a Star Trek convention. With Shirley's commanding sense of order and Jaston's steam-engine endurance, no obsolescent junkyard, outhouse or pig barn in Texas could be considered safe from total rejuvenation. What a team they were! The phenomenon of life in pairing up just the exact two right loners. That it ever happens and that it seems to happen so effortlessly? It was beyond reasonable discernment. Another of God's larks.

The phone call from New Mexico came at six in the morning on a Sunday. Laine had delivered a premature, five-pound, eight-ounce baby girl. Mother and daughter were doing fine. Sherrod was so emotional I thought I'd have to call someone at the Clovis hospital to administer a sedative. I hung up the phone, smiling. Good for them, at long, long—long last. They named her Jane Bettie Clu-Jas Miller. "Clu-Jas" sounded like some infection a dog might get, but I was moved enough to sit down and write Jane Bettie a "welcome to the world" letter. She'd just inherited a long distinguished line of eccentrics, and we fully expected her to live up to her illustrious heritage. Me, an uncle—who knew? Now what little girl on the planet wouldn't want a doting gay uncle to fuss over her and buy her her first matching Beatrix Potter tea set? Some babies are just born lucky.

Mano and I tried telling Mother that she was a grandmother, but it was hard to know if it registered. She seemed to smile at the news, but her face was mostly a placid glinting anyway as she floated through her final hours in a benign mist.

And at the end she was not alone. Mano, me, Chris, Jaston, Shirley and Concepcion were all in the room. And every last one of the dogs. At one point we put all twenty-four of her pooches on the bed with her. I thought Mrs. Kubish would blow an artery. They licked and nuzzled and curled up beside her, and Mother's face absolutely beamed in contentment. Shirley suggested we take a picture. If I were only able to retain one single memory of what my mother embodied in her life, that final picture of her said it all. In her little red-silk bed jacket, her head wrapped in an exotic turban, nails immaculately painted pinkish plum and surrounded by twenty-four of the best-fed and well-loved hounds in America—Bettie Jean Latimore Ramirez was her own profoundly atypical creation. And she wore it very, very well.

There was no dramatic last gasp of clarity, no final words, no flickering of the eyes in signaling farewell. Her heart simply stopped. She'd made precise stipulations that no special resuscitation efforts be administered, and she was adamant that we honor her desires. Thankfully no torturous last-minute struggle ensued. Just a final weary breath and then . . . rest. Mrs. Kubish took her pulse and turned back to us, nodding. "If ya'll want to be alone with her, I suggest you wait outside and take turns coming in." Dazed, we turned as Mano knelt beside the bed holding her hand, softly crying.

The rest of us stood in the kitchen, each finding a private vista to concentrate on. The act of looking into each other's eyes seemed unbearably personal for the present. Finally, I heard Jaston choking behind me, and I started to crumble. I'd never heard my brother cry in my entire life, and it sounded like a great, injured animal. Thank God he had Shirley. She held him in her arms like a collapsed bear. I put my hand on his back and to my surprise Jaston turned and put his arms around me, shaking uncontrollably. His big, warm tears rolled down my neck as we hugged. I was bawling now just as hard as he was.

"W . . . we've lost our mother. We've lost her, Clu." Jaston could barely get the words out.

I rubbed his back. "We'll be all right, brother. We'll be OK." And then I said something it had never occurred to me to say before. "I . . . love you, Jaston."

Jaston sucked in a gulp of air and stammered, "Me too." I think we both knew that would probably be the last time we'd ever say those words to each other, and even though we assuredly did love each other, it was simply too hard for certain grown brothers to say such things. Jaston squeezed my neck, and we patted each other's shoulder one last time. Then Concepcion abruptly gasped and Chris murmured aloud, "She's with us." And as sure as I could see my own hand—Mother was standing there beside us, smiling. Not a ghost, not a vision—actually there! And she looked incredible. Her old pizzazz and strength back, she emanated a kind of elation—a golden glint that seemed to be expanding from inside her. She clearly expressed the words "I love you," yet made no utterance. Jas and I still had our arms around each other, and I immediately felt his body clench. We were both experiencing it together. And then a sudden shift and Mother's face vanished—gone in a cat's breath. We stood apart, and Jaston stared at me, mouth open. He suddenly declared, "She's gonna be all right."

I nodded. "Absolutely." Chris stepped forward and handed me a paper napkin. My face was wet with tears. I turned to him. "Did you see her?"

Chris shook his head. "No. But I truly felt her here."

Concepcion nodded, tears in her eyes. "Your mother's a child on a swing now—it's all limitless."

I put an arm around Chris, and we held each other. He had indeed kept his word—he'd stayed till the end.

Mother's funeral turned out to be an impressively large event. Brother Ramirez held a Saturday afternoon service in the circus tent and apparently near everyone in Grit was in attendance. And why not? She'd lived her whole life there. She didn't have any enemies that I was aware of. She paid her taxes and kept her yard mowed. Overlooking a few erratic breaches of conduct (marrying Brother Ramirez on her deathbed was seen by many as peculiar), the bourgeoisie liked to pay tribute to their own. Bettie Jean had earned their regard whether she wanted it or not.

Laine and Sherrod drove all night to make it to Grit with Jane Bettie. Meeting my niece for the first time was an unqualified act of infatuation. Unfortunately, Laine kept her swaddled up tighter than an Eskimo baby, terrorized some germ or chill might find its way to her most cherished treasure. Undoubtedly there would be large therapists' bills ahead, but for now, we had an esteemed and beautiful tourist in the family. Of all the strange and entirely fitting times to make her debut.

Mano gave a very moving eulogy praising Mother's strength and courage and also her great physical and inner beauty. He told the gathering that he and Bettie Jean had married because they'd each discovered in the other a fulfilling sense of belonging. If that meant a day or a hundred years together, it was irrelevant; they'd found each other at last. Laine spoke of our mother's courage and grace, and Jaston told a funny story about one of the dogs getting stuck behind the refrigerator and after freeing the frightened pooch he realized how much our mother truly loved him when all the puppies in the next litter had Jaston for middle names. When it was my turn to speak I was momentarily inarticulate. Finally, I mumbled something about the greatest gift my mother bestowed on me was her character. It had enabled me to survive, and at times, even excel in my own life. For that legacy of sturdy mettle alone, I would forever be grateful.

Afterward there was a meal served by the ladies' auxiliary of the church and as we stood pushing bites of King Ranch casserole around a plate I stared at this mass of milling people. If I died in New York, who would come? Everyone was so damn busy, it would be grossly inconvenient and entirely thoughtless on my part. Who did I know anyway? A bunch of hazy acquaintances. Good-time miscreants. "In for the party, out for the swan song." It was depressing to think no one in New York would give a damn, and equally distressing to realize everyone in Grit would care too much. I pondered the expediency of truly moving to Italy.

At one point Myla Biggs ushered her grandmother, Miss Arnetta, over. Another Grit matriarch, Miss Arnetta was a feisty old dowager who'd seen it all and wisely kept her mouth shut when silence rendered the most opportune indemnity. She'd secured her rank among the local philistines long, long ago.

"Clu, you remember Gram Gram don't you?" Myla held out her grandmother's wrist. She was evidently pretty much blind now.

I took her hand. "How're you doing, Miss Arnetta. Thank you so much for coming today."

She stared away from me, across the room. "Bettie was a sweet gal. I know it hadn't been easy for ya'll."

I nodded. "No, ma'am."

Miss Arnetta cocked her head toward me and blurted out, "What come over her to up and marry that little Mexican fellow, you reckon?"

Myla rolled her eyes. I smiled. "I think they were both real partial to Chihuahuas, Miss Arnetta."

She frowned at my answer and shook her head. "It's too bad Gladys Byers couldn't be here."

I looked at Miss Arnetta, puzzled. "Why's that?"

"Well, they were cousins, of course—Gladys and Bettie Jean. Oh Gladys thought the world of your mother. Back during the war Gladys ran the U.S.O. club up in San Antone. She loved hanging with the fellas. She knew every good-looking boy in Texas." Miss Arnetta smiled at some private recollection. I blinked in amazement. Thus . . . the hat box.

"Bettie Jean used to help Gladys out when she was just a kid. Come to think of it, I believe that's how she met your daddy up at the U.S.O. Herbert thought Gladys hung the moon! She was older, more sophisticated. Her family had money. They say Gladys was even married herself once, but by the time she moved back here and built that little house for your mama and daddy, she was finished with the whole matrimonial load. She was always more a pal to the boys anyway. 'Tween you and me—I always thought she was probably an old lesbo."

Check. Myla stared at Miss Arnetta in bewilderment. "Uh . . . Gram Gram, honey, I think I see Zane waving at us across the room. Come on. Clu, shug, I'll give you a call in a day or two."

I stood there trying to assimilate the "Arnetta epiphanies." The Rosetta stone of Latimore concealment had been partially decoded. It was starting to make a modest amount of sense. Older cousin (Gladys) has attachment to younger cousin (Bettie Jean), younger cousin has attachment to older cousin's spouse (Herbert), spouse remains attached to older cousin, even after brief marriage, but marries younger cousin anyway—and they all live next door to each other. No wonder she didn't want to talk about it. Gladys loved Mother, Mother loved Daddy, Daddy loved Gladys—what a mess. And Jaston restores the gristmill! God has a smoke and a laugh—curtain.

It had been a long, fatiguing day. By the time we got home from the funeral and the prolonged visiting with the multitude it was well after dark. Jaston and Shirley were drinking a beer in the kitchen, Laine and Sherrod were fussing over a crying Jane Bettie in the guest room, and I had instantly ripped out of my suit and put on a pair of shorts and a T-shirt. I began walking toward the kitchen when I looked into Chris's bedroom and saw that he was . . . packing. I stopped, confused.

"Going somewhere?"

He looked up at me calmly, "Yeah. It's time for me to go."

I felt my legs slowly being anesthetized, and I slumped against the wall for support. "Now? You're leaving . . . *now?*"

Chris continued packing. "I told you back in New York we'd have to leave the day she died. Obviously, I don't expect you to go anywhere—but I have to."

I shook my head, bewildered. "But . . . why?"

Chris looked at me and pointed to his head, the *spontaneous* thing. He continued packing in earnest. "This is your home, your family, your friends. It's truly been one of the most amazing opportunities for growth in my entire life, and I wouldn't have missed it for the world. And now . . . I have to go."

I put my hand on his suitcase, distraught. "Wait . . . wait! Opportunities for growth?" What are you talking about? I can't just let you leave like this. You're a huge chunk of my life. I've lost my mother and now you? Chris, I'm almost thirty-eight. We were supposed to grow old together. We talked about it all the time— two old 'poofters' holding hands in the park, remember?" He stared at me sadly, then picked up the suitcase. I held on to it. "Look, I don't care—you can see anybody you want to. You can sleep with Preston, it's OK. You can sleep with anybody—just *stay,* please."

Chris stared at the floor, mortified. "Don't do this. You know it's not about Preston, and it never has been. One thing I've always, always admired about you, Clu, is your sense of self-respect."

"Fuck self-respect!" I raged at him. "I love you, you bastard. Why can't you love me back?"

Chris yanked the suitcase away. "Not like this, Clu. I'm asking you please, let's not end it like this."

Tears were rolling down my face now. "God, just stay till morning—give me some time to get used to this."

"I can't." He picked up the suitcase and hurried down the hall.

I stopped him in the living room and grabbed the suitcase like a madman. "*Where* are you going? Why do you have to leave now? Why? Why are you doing this?"

Chris, trembling, finally dropped the suitcase and grabbed my shirt. He roared in my face, "Because I can't breathe anymore! I can't! Because I don't want to live in Grit, Texas, the rest of my life. Because I can't stand another minute of remembering how much I used to love the person that's gone forever. Because I'm tired of wanting people to change. Because it's finished . . . and I have nothing more to give." Chris let go of the shirt, picked up the suitcase, and bounded out the front door. He turned as he reached his van, and called back, "I'll phone you from the road." And then he drove away.

Laine, Sherrod, Jaston and Shirley were all standing behind me in the living room, no doubt in as much shock as I was. I couldn't bear to face them. I held up my hand and walked slowly toward the front door.

"It's OK . . . it's all OK . . . I just need a little . . . air." I walked outside barefoot and made my way over to Gladys Byers's abandoned front porch, where I sat in the darkness and cried till I, too, had nothing more to give.

Chris called a few days later from Sapello, New Mexico. He said he thought he was making his way to Los Angeles, but he didn't know for sure. He was just going where the road led him. He said he'd call next week and hung up. Something inside me had permanently died or shifted or been slit open—I had no idea what was going on. I had no response. I didn't know what to feel, so I felt nothing. The past few days had been a blackout. I got up, I ate, I went back to bed, I watched TV, I ate, I went back to bed. I sat for hours staring at my bedroom wall. Laine would sit with me rocking the baby, and we'd take turns not speaking. It was oddly reassuring not having to feel anymore. I knew I could completely master this new sensation with just the tiniest effort. I wanted to be good at something again, and I felt I'd found my objective.

And Jane Bettie kept me preoccupied. We held long, contemplative deep-breathing and eye-blinking sessions. We practiced yawning procedure. We vocalized at regular intervals, finding new notes that were startling to both of us. We studied each other's faces and hands with complete mindfulness, discovering new and interesting details every time. We were basically thoroughly satisfied with each other's presence. Maybe the rest of the world didn't get us—but we knew we were fabulous.

The play went on without me. People would call, and Laine would tell them I had the flu. I didn't care. I didn't give a shit about anything. I'd just wanted to sit in the house (it was now a third mine) and eat crap and watch TV till I died. Jane Bettie and I would have a wonderful life together coloring and cutting out paper dolls. It was completely perfect. Then Laine announced she was returning to Clovis. With Jane Bettie. I begged her just to stay awhile longer. At least let me keep Jane Bettie for a few weeks . . . or a year. Laine had a look of deep anguish on her face. I could tell I was freaking her out, so I just shut up. Fine. At least I'll have the dogs. It had finally come to this. I was now completely my mother. In a few months I'd be wearing her clothes. Sometimes these things happened. To an outsider it might look unfortunate, but there were many inexplicable folds in life's wretched cloak. One should never demand too much sanity. A great many opportunities were lost to such inflexibility.

The day before Laine and Sherrod's departure, Jane Bettie and I were sitting in the kitchen synchronizing our mood swings. Laine was taking a nap, and Sherrod was with Jaston, snooping around the Byers estate. Jane Bettie's bottle was ready, and I had my light beer positioned, both of us primed to get mellow. There was a knock at the back door. I turned to see Tory standing there. Tory? I was unexpectedly thrown. It was like a visitation from another planet. I suddenly realized I hadn't shaved or bathed in several days; I must look scary as hell. And then I thought, who gives a shit? Jane Bettie didn't, that's for sure. We were free to wallow in our urine as long as we felt like. I waved for him to come in.

"Hey."

"Hey."

"How are you feeling?"

"I'm fine. Have you met my niece? This is Jane Bettie Clu-Jas. Isn't that a kick-in-the-ass name?"

Tory smiled and held her little hand. "It's different all right. She's a real cutie."

"Oh yeah. She's the neatest little package in the whole wide world. Got to go back to bad old Clovis, New Mexico, tomorrow and leave her poor uncle behind." I looked up at Tory, petulant. "I'm thinking of kidnapping her." I then grinned. "Sorry, would you like a beer?"

He smiled uncomfortably. "No, thanks. We've really missed you down at the show. Everybody's been asking about you. You know we've been sold out every night."

I continued feeding Jane Bettie.

"Everyone's hoping you'll be there this Thursday. Larraine redid the lyrics on the death-scene ballad; she really wants you to hear it."

I wiped Jane Bettie's chin.

"Miss Oveta wants to start planning the next show. She'd like you to pick something you'd like to do yourself this time. We've got tons of plays over at the college; if you want me to bring some by I can . . ."

I interrupted, "No." Tory stared at me. "I'm not interested. Why don't you direct the next show? You're better with the actors anyway."

Tory looked surprised. "Me? You're the director. We need someone like you, who's not afraid to knock a few heads together. You've got all the ideas, your instincts are the best."

I smiled. "No, thanks."

He looked at me dolefully. "What are you going to do?"

I sighed and shrugged. "I don't know. Become even more weird. That's what small Texas towns are for, aren't they?"

Tory placed a hand on the table and smoothed the place mat. "I heard about Chris leaving. I'm sorry."

I smiled apathetically. "These things happen."

Tory tapped his fingers on the table, cleared his throat, and then stood quickly. "Well, I just wanted to see how you were doing. Everyone would really like to see you again."

"Tell 'em I said hi."

Tory paused for a moment, then headed for the door. He suddenly stopped and turned back around. "Clu . . . I was wondering . . . if you'd go out with me on Friday night, after the show?"

I watched Jane Bettie sucking contentedly on her bottle. I slowly glanced toward Tory, not following. "Go out?"

"Yeah."

"You mean like . . . like what?"

"Like . . . you know, just go out . . . together."

It still wasn't registering. I slowly began stitching his frayed request in my addled head. I think what I heard was twenty-two-year-old Tory ask me out—on a *date*. I stared at him, mute. Tory stammered, "I'm sorry. It was just an idea, forget it. I know you've got a lot of stuff . . ."

I shook my head. "No, no, Tory—I just . . . I'm . . ."

He shrugged nervously, "It's OK. I just thought . . . you know I don't know too many gay guys. Even fewer ones I'd like to get to know better. You've been a real . . . I don't know, inspiration I guess. Look, I know you think I'm young and everything, and I am a little naive about some things, but I also know quality when I see it. And . . . I think you're a neat guy. We don't have to do anything, just go to the Sonic and get something to eat. It's not like a real date. Maybe you could think about it and give me a call if . . ."

"OK."

"OK . . . you'll call?"

"OK, I'd . . . like to go—out with you."

"You're serious?"

I nodded. "Yeah."

Tory smiled. "Wow. OK. Wow. Well, OK, I'll . . . I'll . . ."

"Why don't I meet you at the sale barn after the show."

He nodded, "Great. Fantastic. OK."

"OK."

He grinned and rocked in his sneakers. He was priceless. He then walked slowly to where I was sitting and stopped beside my chair. I figured he wanted to say good-bye to Jane Bettie so I sort of shifted a little and he suddenly leaned down and kissed me softly on the cheek. In one millisecond a zillion frazzled neurons commingled with Tory's smell, touch, heat, lips, breath and mouth. Sleeping Beauty awoke.

"See ya Friday."

"F . . . Friday."

Tory shut the back door and I heard him jump down the steps and race toward the street. I looked at Jane Bettie, astounded. What just happened? I swear, she was wearing the biggest toothless smile in

America. I shook my head. "What are you grinning at? It's just a date, not even a 'real date.' Look, he's a kid—yes, a cute kid."

We stared at each other, both shaking our heads. She was on to her old uncle. I'd never be able to get one by this sharpie. I put her on my shoulder and started patting her back. I took a sip from my beer, and we both burped simultaneously. I laughed and whispered in her ear, "Jane Bettie—you think we might just make it in this big, cruel world after all?"

I kissed her fine head and held her close. I could feel little puffs of breath on my neck as her head wobbled to the side, and in a second she was out for the count, snoring like old Señor Murphy who was curled up in the corner. I kissed her again. "Yeah, angel baby—any kind of luck—we'll be just fine."